HEARTS ON FIRE

"I never knew," Jackson said quietly. "Is it just today, or have you always been beautiful? Look at you. Your skin is soft and smooth. Your mouth would tempt a man into hell. Your eyes make promises that drive a man wild."

"I don't need your pretty words," Regan blurted out.

"Of course you do, but that's not why I'm saying them. I'm saying them because they're true and six years ago I was a damn fool."

Her breath caught in her throat. She desperately wanted to believe him. *How could she?* a voice in her head screamed. How could she not?

This time he didn't have to tell her to shut her eyes. Her lids fluttered closed and his lips pressed softly against her skin.

He pulled back. "Relax."

"I can't," she said. "I'm scared."

"About what?"

She inched back, then winced when he grinned at her. "It's not funny."

"Yes, it is. You'd rather face an armed gunslinger than risk being this close to a man."

✄ S U S A N   M A C I A S ✄

HarperPaperbacks
A Division of HarperCollins*Publishers*

This is a work of fiction. The characters, incidents, and dialogues are products of the author's imagination and are not to be construed as real. Any resemblance to actual events or persons, living or dead, is entirely coincidental.

HarperPaperbacks *A Division of* HarperCollins*Publishers*
10 East 53rd Street, New York, N.Y. 10022

Cover illustration by Aleta Jenks

First printing: August 1995

Printed in the United States of America

HarperPaperbacks, HarperMonogram, and colophon are trademarks of HarperCollins*Publishers*

❖ 10 9 8 7 6 5 4 3 2 1

To Tony, with love

Fire in the Dark

1

Texas—1874

They caught him with his pants down.

Jackson Tyler bit back a curse as the cold water in the stream rushed over his calves and knees. He could feel his skin pucker. It was mid-March and only a damned fool would stop to take a bath, even if the sun was shining bright in the clear blue Texas sky. But he'd been called a damned fool enough times to suspect it might be true. A man had to die sometime, he reminded himself, even as he groaned softly at the thought of his embarrassing end.

Shot in the back. Caught standing buck naked with his Winchester two feet out of reach.

An involuntary shiver rippled through him. He wanted to turn around and step onto the bank but he didn't move. He could feel the guns aimed at him from behind, could hear the breathing of three, maybe four, men. They must have crept through the bushes alongside the flowing water. His splashing accompanied by his loud rendition of his favorite song had given them all the cover they needed. He shook his head slightly. Couldn't blame anyone but himself.

"Raise your hands and turn around."

"Raise my hands?" he said, addressing the tree in front of him. "Where the hell would I be hiding a gun?"

He didn't turn around. Bad enough to be caught naked, but the whole situation was made even worse by the slight nip in the air and definite chill of the water that combined to make his pecker shrivel up.

Coming here had been a bad idea, Jackson thought grimly. As a rule he liked Texas. His rule had just changed. If he got out of this alive, he was riding straight for the nearest border. He should have known better than to come looking for what was his. Better to have left it all alone. Six years was a long time. Knowing Elizabeth—which he hadn't at all, unless finding comfort between her warm, willing thighs counted as knowing a person—the whole thing might be made up. Damn his pride for making him want to find out in the first place.

"Turn around slow," the voice behind him ordered. "I'd rather not shoot you in the back, but I will if you don't do as you're told."

Jackson sighed. He'd always been too lucky. It was bound to end sometime. But why like this? He drew in a deep breath. Thank the Lord, at least he was wearing his hat.

He raised his hands until they were shoulder level, then turned slowly. As he'd suspected, there were four men, all with rifles pointing at his chest. He took a step toward them.

"Stop right there," the man on the left ordered. He was tall, with a hat pulled low on his forehead. The men were dressed similarly, buckskin shotgun chaps over wool trousers, shirts, vests, and hats. He couldn't see their eyes, but the set of their heads and jaws, not to mention the rifles, told him they meant business.

"Shoot me if you have to," Jackson said as another shiver rippled through his body. "But I aim to get out of this stream."

No one moved. He took a step, then a second, until he reached the bank. There he paused, and waited.

Even the birds were silent as the men considered him. The slight breeze that had been pleasant before his dip in the stream made him wish he'd just stayed dirty. Small rocks dug into his bare feet.

The silence made him uneasy. Jackson decided he had nothing to lose by trying to talk himself out of the situation.

"You know, gentlemen," he said, glancing at his horse and wondering if he had a prayer of reaching him before they opened fire. He figured he didn't. "I expected to die because of a woman, or whiskey. Maybe even over cards, although I've never been one to play much. But I sure as hell never expected to die because I had a hankering for a bath."

He reached up and drew off his hat. After fingering the brim and wiping off a smudge of dirt from the beaver felt crown, he looked up and smiled. "You can shoot me if you have a mind to, but I'm going to get dressed."

Nobody said a word. They didn't glance at each

other, they just stood there, rifles still pointed at his chest. He could feel the afternoon sun drying his skin, but it wasn't doing anything about warming him. Come summer he would remember this day and long to be shivering, but for now, the thought of living to sweat again seemed mighty fine.

He took a step toward his horse.

"Stop right there," the man on the left said. "You wouldn't be the first man I've killed."

Jackson slapped his hat against his thigh. "You mind telling me what it is you think I've done? I know some people take exception to bathing, but last I heard it wasn't a shooting offense."

His attempt at humor was met with silent stares. He'd definitely lost his touch. Before he could decide what to do next, he heard the sound of hoofbeats. Squinting against the sun, he could just make out the silhouette of a rider coming through the brush. The man on the left lowered his gun.

"Over here," he called. "We got 'im."

"Is he one of Daniel's hired guns?" a voice asked.

Jackson closed his eyes and groaned. He told himself it was his imagination, but he knew it wasn't. Yup, his luck had run out all at once. No trickling away of good fortune for him. That voice belonged to a woman. Bad enough to be caught naked in front of a bunch of men. But in front of a *woman*?

"Ah, you better warn your lady friend there," he said, motioning to his midsection.

Two of the men grinned at his discomfort.

The one on the left didn't crack a smile. "I don't know who he's with. We caught him in the stream. He's naked."

The rustling of the bushes told Jackson the woman was moving closer. She didn't bother slowing at the man's warning.

"At least we know he's not hiding any weapons," she said.

Jackson couldn't believe it. She sounded as if she was laughing.

"What the hell is going on here?" he asked, his voice low and angry. "All I've done is wash off a little trail dust. There's a woman about to come out and see me as bare as the day I was born. I don't know who you are or who you think I am, but there's been a mistake."

She broke through the bushes. The men stepped aside, two moving left, two right, leaving her a place in the middle. She was of medium height, not very threatening at all. Jackson glared at her. He'd been right. She *was* smiling.

"Men sure look a lot less dangerous without their clothes," she said, glancing at his chest, then dipping her gaze lower.

Jackson tightened his jaw. He'd been plenty dangerous, naked or not, in his time, and this damned female wasn't going to stand there and make fun of him. He thought about holding his hat in front of himself, but it seemed like too little too late. She was already moving her gaze higher, having looked her fill.

"Who is he?" she asked, then she glanced at his face.

Her smile faded so suddenly, and she gave him such a look of horror that he glanced over his shoulder, half expecting to see a bunch of Indians come riding over the hill. There was nothing but a few bushes, a black willow tree, and some bird watching the entire proceedings with great interest. Jackson turned back to face the group.

"What are you doing back here?" the woman asked. "How dare you show yourself like this."

Jackson raised his eyebrows. "Show myself? Lady, I've been trying to cover up, but your boys here don't want me to put on my trousers. Seems to me—"

"That's not what I meant and you know it." Her voice shook with emotion. "You lying, cheating bastard."

"Me?" Jackson stared at her, then at her cowboys. They looked as confused as he felt. "Would someone please tell me what the hell is going on here?"

"You know him, Regan?" the man on the left asked.

Regan? Regan? Jackson felt his mouth drop open. Holy mother of— He'd nearly forgotten all about her.

"I know more than enough about Mr. Tyler. I'm sorry you didn't shoot him when you had the chance."

"Shoot me? What have I done?" Jackson was afraid he sounded like a wet-behind-the-ears brat, but this whole situation was out of control. "None of this makes sense. You've made a mistake."

Regan continued to stare at him. A wide-brimmed hat covered her hair and shaded her face. He wished she'd remove it so he could see her eyes. He wished more that they would let him put some clothes on.

Like her men, she was dressed for work. A long-sleeved light blue blouse had been tucked into a full skirt. He thought about the rider he'd seen and was sure that person had been astride the horse. Regan? He'd seen females riding that way once or twice before, but it wasn't common. Her boots were scuffed brown leather, good quality, but well used. A pistol hung on her right hip, the butt facing forward, just like the rangers wore theirs. She cradled a rifle in her arms, holding it with the ease of someone accustomed to using it.

She didn't look big enough or strong enough to lift it, but he wasn't taking any chances. Six years ago she'd been hell-bent on learning how to run the O'Neil ranch and do her daddy proud. If nothing else, she'd been a determined little cuss. The way his luck was running, she was probably a crack shot.

"Daniel hired you," she said flatly, accusing him of God knows what.

"Daniel?" Is that what this was all about? "Is he giving you trouble again?"

"Don't pretend you don't know. You're here because you work for him."

"I'd rather burn in hell than work for your cousin, Regan. You should remember what happened last time he and I had words." He glanced longingly toward his clothes. "I came to get something that belongs to me."

If he'd hoped to ease the situation with his words, he was proved wrong. She stiffened and handed her rifle to the man on her right. That should have made him feel better, except then she placed her hand on the butt of her pistol. "Liar. You're a hired gun. That's your profession. I say Daniel O'Neil paid you to work for him. You're here to make trouble."

"I'm here because I have a letter from Elizabeth," he said.

Once again her reaction surprised him. She glared at him as if he'd blasphemed her sister simply by speaking her name. Cold sweat broke out on his back. Even her cowboys had straightened at his claim of a letter.

This wasn't funny anymore.

Jackson placed his hat back on his head and folded his arms over his bare chest. The breeze kicked up, raising chill bumps on his skin. He tried not to think about how small his pecker must be now.

"What do you want?" she asked. "Elizabeth?"

Something tickled at the back of his mind. Some memory about her and Elizabeth. Something that happened one night while he was drunk. He generally didn't indulge while he was working, but the two O'Neil girls had tried his patience and his self-control. He'd been willing to put his needs aside until Elizabeth forced his hand. He grinned at the memory. It hadn't been his hand, and he hadn't needed much forcing.

"Bastard," Regan said, her voice low and angry.

Jackson's grin faded. "I'm not here for your sister. I want my son."

After the way the four men had threatened him, the last thing he expected was for them to lower their rifles to the ground. They looked at each other and shrugged. Even Regan relaxed slightly and removed her hat. It dangled down her back, exposing her face and bright red hair. He recognized the color, a little darker than it had been six years before. He recognized the tight curls dancing defiantly on her forehead. The straight nose was the same, as were the tanned skin and freckles. Even the stubborn lift of her chin was exactly as he recalled. He wondered how he could have forgotten she might still be here, then reminded himself that she was a pale imitation of her beautiful sister. Of course he would have forgotten.

The man on the left leaned over toward Regan. "What's he talking about?"

Regan shook her head. "I don't know. What are you talking about, Jackson?"

Why were they pretending they didn't know what he was asking? He lowered his hands to his sides. "Elizabeth sent me a letter last October. She said we had a child together and asked me to come and get him."

Regan's expression of faint amusement hardened into hatred. "My sister, who never had any children, has been dead over a year."

"But I have a letter." He pointed toward his clothes. "And I want my son."

"You have no son. At least not here. I can't say what results of your whoring might live elsewhere."

"Listen, Regan. I'm sure you know Elizabeth and I—" He paused, wondering how to say this delicately. He eyed the gun at her waist and the rage in her eyes. Yup, delicacy was required. "We had an understanding of sorts. Apparently I left her in the family way."

Regan practically shook with rage. "Shut up! Shut your damn mouth. I don't want to hear your lies. You've soiled my sister's reputation with your filth. I never want to see you again."

He noticed her eyes were a dark shade of blue, much darker than her sister's. They were beautiful eyes, even when the hatred spilling from them made him worry for his life. Hell of a time to notice a woman's eyes.

"Look, I'm not saying she was easy or anything,

but what happened, happened. Not speaking the truth isn't going to change it."

"No!" Regan screamed. "She wasn't like that. I won't listen to you. How dare you? Elizabeth was good and pure and you're just some bastard who wants to sully her reputation."

"You're as crazy as—"

He didn't get to finish his sentence. Before he knew what was happening, she'd pulled out her pistol and was looking down the sights.

The gun fired.

Jackson felt something hot and hard hit his arm, as if he'd been punched by an iron fist. He stood there stupidly, not believing she'd really winged him. She'd actually winged him.

"Son of a bitch."

"Shut up." She took aim again. He hadn't been wrong. She *was* crazy. Damn it all to hell, he didn't want to die like this.

The muzzle pointed directly at his chest. From this range, she couldn't miss. He saw her finger tighten on the trigger. Everything suddenly stopped moving normal like, and went very slowly.

"Regan, no!" The man who'd done all the talking reached for her arm and pushed it down.

It wasn't enough. The fire didn't explode in his chest as he'd expected, but in his leg. Hot liquid that could only be blood poured down, dripping onto his foot. He drew in a sharp breath, waiting for the pain. There wasn't any. Nothing except a rushing in his ears.

Only then did he realize he couldn't move his left arm at all, and that his shot leg was buckling beneath him. He tried to brace himself, but nothing was working the way it should. He fell hard.

As his head hit a rock poking out of the ground he knew he was going to have a hell of a headache come morning. If he lived that long. As the blackness descended he wondered why he had to die naked—and shot by a woman.

Regan stared down at the silent, bleeding man. She'd shot him. She'd actually shot him. Her mouth grew dry and her stomach heaved. Dear Lord, she'd never shot anyone before in her life.

Her hands shook so badly she could barely hold on to her pistol. The trembling made it difficult to slide the still-warm barrel into her holster. She forced herself to be calm, not to cry out in shock.

The cowboys stood frozen in place, staring at her as if they'd never seen her before. She read disbelief in their eyes. She'd shot a man in cold blood. He wasn't armed. He wasn't even threatening her. Oh, Lord, what had happened to her?

She swallowed. She couldn't show weakness in front of the men. Not now. She had to be strong. She was in charge.

Pete moved close to her. "You all right?"

She glanced at her friend. "Fine," she lied.

Pete nodded. He'd obviously seen past the lie but he wouldn't say anything until they were alone. Her gaze was drawn back to the fallen man. Blood seeped out of the wounds on his arm and leg. It pooled in the dirt. Already flies were buzzing around him.

"Is he dead?"

Pete jerked his head toward the body. One of the men crouched down beside him and turned him over. "He's breathing."

"Good." She sent a silent prayer of thanks. "Have them bind his wounds. Use his clothes if you have to. They'll need to take him back to the ranch." She folded her arms over her chest to hold the pain inside. She'd shot a man. No, it couldn't be true. She didn't even like shooting game birds for supper when they were camping out.

Her body felt hot and cold at the same time. She shivered. One of the men straightened Jackson's legs. He groaned, but didn't awaken. She turned and started walking toward her horse.

Pete followed her through the brush. When she reached the bay gelding, she leaned against his warm side and inhaled the familiar scent of horse and leather.

"Who is that man?" Pete asked quietly, coming to a stop beside her. "How'd you know him?"

Why'd you shoot him? The question hung in the air between them. But Pete was too much of a friend to ask that right off. He would wait until she calmed down. If she ever did. She could still feel her heart pounding in her chest.

"His name is Jackson Tyler. He's a hired gun."

"You hired him?"

She tried to smile. Her face felt numb. "No. Six years ago he worked for my father, helping him when there was that trouble with Daniel." She risked glancing at Pete. "You were gone with Fayre, I think."

"Yeah, in Kansas." He shook his head in disgust. "Your pa shouldn't have sent me away that summer."

His hazel eyes darkened as he looked at her. "Everything was different when I came back in the fall."

Regan closed her eyes and rested her forehead against the gelding's shoulder. She knew what he was talking about. Before Pete left, they'd had an understanding of sorts. When he came back, everything was different between them. It wasn't Pete. He'd never been the problem. She was—and Jackson Tyler.

She pushed those memories away.

"Dad didn't want me to know much about what was going on with Daniel," she said. "He was so upset that kin was making trouble. All I know is that he hired Jackson to take care of things. There wasn't to be any killing either."

"But that's not what upset you when you saw him?"

She shook her head. "He . . ." She swallowed hard, hating the bitter taste in her mouth. The shock still lingered, as did the shame, for what she'd done. But the bitterness also came from the past. "He used her. Jackson Tyler seduced my sister. He lied to her, then rode away without ever looking back."

"I'm sorry."

She felt Pete's hand on her shoulder. The familiar gesture comforted her. "Thanks." She raised her head and looked at him. "I shot him. When he said those things about Elizabeth, I got so angry. I didn't plan it, but then the gun was in my hand and I . . ." Her voice trailed off. "What are the men going to think? Will they still want to work for me?" She had enough trouble being female and running a ranch. She was young and it was coming hard to her, but she was learning. Still, this wasn't going to make the men trust her any.

"I'll make it right. I'll explain," Pete promised. "Besides if they think you might shoot them for no reason, they're gonna do their best to obey orders." He smiled.

Her lips curved up slightly as she stared at his familiar face, the dusty hat and tired lines by his eyes. They'd all been working so hard since her father died. Putting in extra hours to keep the ranch going, not to mention the time they'd spent defending the place since Daniel had started making trouble again. Her good humor faded. They didn't need this.

"You'll see to him?" she asked.

"Tyler?"

She nodded.

"I'll make sure they've bound up his wounds, then we'll get him back to the ranch."

"Not the bunkhouse," she said. "It'll be too loud."

"I'll find something. I'll have one of the cowboys look after him."

"Thanks." She grabbed hold of the reins and swung into the saddle and adjusted her custom-made split skirt. She settled her hat on her head and prepared to return home.

"You gonna be all right?" Pete asked.

Regan thought about lying, but Pete had known her since she was seven. She shook her head. "No, but don't tell the cowboys. They'll probably forgive me for shooting a man but not for being weak. See you back at the house."

She turned her horse north and rode away. The familiar vistas of low rolling hills, cattle grazing, and trees blossoming in the near-spring air should have brought her a measure of comfort. For as far as the eye could see, she controlled the land. Everything her father had worked for was her responsibility. She could make it all right. She had to. If only Daniel would stop tormenting her and sabotaging the ranch.

Nothing had been right since her father died two months before. She drew in a deep breath and stared out toward the horizon. If only Jackson Tyler hadn't come back looking for what was his.

She hadn't meant to shoot him. Not really. But when he smiled like that while thinking about her sister, something in her head had gone a little crazy. She'd recognized his slow, teasing smile.

The worst part of it was six years ago she would have sold her share of the O'Neil ranch for Jackson to toss just one grin her way. But he hadn't. Instead he'd seduced her sister, leaving Elizabeth broken and sullied. Regan knew she should be happy Jackson had dismissed her that summer long ago. She told herself she *was* glad, even as she recognized the lie. Knowing he would have left her as he'd left Elizabeth didn't make her feel any better, but then she'd always suspected her heart was a foolish and contrary organ.

She urged her horse to a trot, ignoring the budding beauty around her. The air tasted clean and sweet from a recent rain. She drew in a deep breath that somehow turned into a choking sob. Her eyes burned with unshed tears.

Control, she told herself. She had to get control. She wasn't allowed to give in to emotions as other women did. She'd never been allowed. The rule wasn't her father's or even the result of the cowboys' teasing. It was her own code that made her stiffen her spine and blink back the weakness. This time, though, it didn't work.

The horror of what she'd done swept over her. In cold blood—worse, in anger—she'd shot an unarmed man. Not once, but twice. She didn't have to close her eyes to see the blood pouring from his wounds and the look of shock on his face just before he fell to the ground.

Regan glanced around at the familiar trail, then turned her horse east and gave the animal his head. As the sure-footed gelding raced across the land, she bent low and clung to the saddle. The tears in her eyes were from the wind, she told herself. The pain in her chest the result of the cool air.

As the miles between her and the creek increased, the memories grew more vivid. She could hear the sound of the pistol firing, feel the recoil, smell the powder and her shame. Again and again Jackson Tyler fell to the ground, blood gushing from his two wounds.

At last, when her horse was winded, she dismounted and walked the animal to cool him. They paused under a tree. Her stomach lurched from the images in her mind and she retched sharply, throwing up her breakfast and the coffee she'd had at ten.

Trembling, she clung to the furrowed bark of the cedar elm and closed her eyes. Her father had always warned her about the responsibility that came with knowing how to use a gun. He'd made sure she was a fine shot and then made sure she never had cause to use the weapon. But Sean O'Neil was gone. There was no one to stand between her and what had to be done.

And what she had to do was get back to the ranch. There were chores to do, books to be kept. The men would need instructions, and someone had to watch

over the hired guns. She'd hated the need to employ
dangerous strangers for protection, but her cousin had
left her no choice. Daniel's last attack—ambushing,
then beating up three of her cowboys—had only been
the latest in a long line of trouble. He wouldn't rest
until he ruled the O'Neil ranch as well as his own.

Regan swung into the saddle and headed for home.
Once again the images from that morning came to
her, but she ignored them. She had to. There was
more at stake than the man. As soon as he was able,
Jackson Tyler could be on his way. She was sorry
she'd shot him, but she couldn't deny a small part of
her wished she'd finished the job. Pray God he didn't
plan to stay long enough to make trouble.

"You okay?" Pete asked as she rode up. It was late
afternoon.

She tossed him the reins and slid off her horse.
"I'm fine. Everything get done?"

Pete called for one of the stableboys, then moved
into step with her. Years ago she'd grown accustomed to keeping up with long-legged men so he
didn't have to adjust his stride to hers.

The yard between the barn and house was filled
with its usual cacophony of cowboys, horses, and
dogs. The two-story house her father had lovingly
built in memory of her mother rose in front of them, a
small version of a plantation mansion. Peaked roofs
stretched high toward the heavens, while sparkling
glass windows reflected the activities in the yard.

"Tyler's holding on, though he hasn't woke up yet."
Regan stared at her friend. Dust coated his face

and chest. There was a dark stain on his sleeve that could only be blood. "Where is he?"

Pete pointed to a small building behind the house. It had been used for storage until last summer, when a larger cellar had been dug close to the kitchen. "He's in there. Jimmy's going to see to him."

"And his horse?"

"In the barn. I went through Tyler's saddlebags. He's traveling with a lot of cash and this." He handed her a folded piece of paper.

Regan took it. She didn't have to open it to know what it said. She didn't need to see the writing to know who'd written it. Jackson Tyler might be the worst kind of bastard, but he wasn't a liar. Elizabeth *had* sent him a letter.

But why did he think he was coming to claim a son?

"Is he going to live?" Regan asked.

"I don't know. You winged him pretty bad and he's lost a lot of blood." Pete placed his hand on her shoulder. "We all saw what happened. I've talked to the men. They understand. There's not going to be any trouble, Regan. He said those things about your sister and then he made a threatening move toward you."

"What are you—" She clamped her mouth shut. He was telling her the men would lie in case there were questions from the sheriff. She'd shot an unarmed man. Even out here, the law didn't much care for that.

Regan placed the letter into her skirt pocket and turned toward the house. The back door banged open and a brown-haired young girl in a calico print dress came flying down the steps toward her.

"Mama, Mama, Fayre and I made an apple pie!"

Regan crouched down and held open her arms. The five-year-old barreled into her, then hugged her tight.

"I tasted it and it's 'licious." Amy grinned. "You want some?"

Regan smiled at her daughter, then brushed her too-long bangs from her face. It seemed no matter how many times she trimmed them, they were always falling in Amy's eyes. "Yes, very much. I'm sure Uncle Pete wants some, too."

"Do ya?" Amy asked.

"You bet."

Pete bent down and scooped the child into his arms. She clung to him with the familiarity of someone who still believed in absolute trust. Pete tickled her until she was screeching with laughter, then he lifted her high onto his shoulders. Amy settled herself and kicked his chest with her heels.

"Go fast this time, Uncle Pete. Real fast. I'm not scared."

Regan started toward the back porch. At the top of the stairs she turned back and watched her daughter ride on Pete's shoulders. With her brown hair and hazel eyes, Amy looked more like the ranch hand than either of her parents.

As they galloped around the yard, Regan's gaze strayed to the small storehouse standing alone in the sun. She reached in her pocket and clutched the folded letter. Why? Why had Elizabeth written to him?

And why, after all this time, had he returned?

2

It was nearly eight when Regan slammed
the thick covered journal closed and glared at her
housekeeper across the kitchen table.

"I know what you're thinking," she told Fayre.

The gray-haired woman glanced up from her
sewing and smiled. "That's a powerful gift from
God," she murmured, then turned back to her darning. Amy was as hard on her dresses as Regan had
been. Her frequent adventures usually resulted in
torn skirts and worn elbows.

"What's a powerful gift from God?" Regan asked.

"Being able to know what others are thinking.
How long have you been blessed?"

Regan glared at the older woman. "You know what
I mean. You think I should go out and help Jackson."

"It's not for me to say."

"I don't wish him ill." Regan ignored Fayre's sniff. "I don't. Jimmy's taking care of him."

Fayre dropped her darning into a basket beside the kitchen table. "Jimmy doesn't have the sense God gave a potato. But if you think he's doing a good enough job of lookin' after that man, then that's just fine with me."

"Fayre!"

"No. You're the boss. I just work here."

Regan grimaced. "I wish that were true," she muttered.

The sun had long since set, and the only light in the room came from several lanterns hanging from the crossbeams as well as from the larger one hissing on the table. Shadows danced in the corners of the rooms. Regan was used to their distorted shapes, welcoming them each night as quiet guests. Until tonight when in their erratic movements she saw Jackson's form as he fell again and again to the ground.

Fayre didn't say another word about their uninvited guest. She didn't have to. She'd come to the ranch when Regan was Amy's age and was as much a part of her life as the land itself. Regan knew the older woman's moods and thoughts on most issues. She insisted on cleanliness, on not swearing in the house, and on being punctual for meals. She also believed that it was everyone's Christian duty to help out the less fortunate, which is why she and her husband had adopted Pete. All of which meant she didn't take kindly to Regan leaving a wounded man in the care of a cowboy.

Although Fayre had put down her mending, she didn't start another task. Instead she sat there, staring, not saying a word. Regan opened the ledger in front of her and tried to concentrate. Normally she could get lost in the numbers, dreaming about how much the steers would bring up north in Kansas, planning her breeding program. Tonight the numbers couldn't hold her interest. They danced in front of her eyes, not slowing enough for her to focus. The loud ticking of the grandfather clock in the corner counted off the time until bed. Fayre's eyes bore a hole in the top of her head. She felt like she was ten again and about to get in trouble for boiling sumac berries and pouring the cooling liquid on the family goat. She'd wanted to know if the dye worked on the animal as well as it had on her new dress. Fayre had paddled her bottom but good.

Regan shifted in her seat, remembering the tenderness that had lasted for days. She slammed the ledger shut and rose to her feet.

"I'll go check on him," she said. "Then will you leave me in peace?"

Fayre smiled. "I've got a basket of supplies all ready for you. It's right by the back door. You're probably going to have to sit up with him all night. You want me to come spell you?"

"No," Regan said, her teeth clenched. "I can do it myself. It's my fault he's shot, isn't it?"

She whirled toward the door and took a step. Fayre's hand on her arm stopped her. "I know you didn't mean it, Regan. You don't lose your temper very often, so he must have vexed you something fierce for you to shoot him. I was gone that summer six years ago, so I don't know Mr. Tyler. I wish him well, but you're the one I'm worried about. This trouble with Daniel, on the heels of losing your daddy and Elizabeth, has been a big burden—maybe too big. You've always had a sweetness about you. I miss the Regan you used to be."

Regan stared at her friend's familiar face. Deep lines fanned out from her warm pale blue eyes. Fayre had given up fighting the sun years ago and her skin was permanently tanned. Weathered hands, creased and spotted, still worked a needle skillfully and could coax a tenderness out of the toughest cut of beef. She was the only mother Regan had ever known. Now Reagan trusted her child to that same raising. But Fayre's critical words, however well meant, hurt her.

"I'm not that different," Regan said. She placed her hand on top of the other woman's and squeezed. "I'm trying hard. Sometimes I don't think I can go another day worrying about the cattle and land. Wondering what Daniel's going to do next. I know finding those hired guns was the right thing to do, but I worry that I can't keep them under control."

"They are a wild bunch, aren't they?" Fayre gave her a faint smile. "You're a strong woman, Regan. You'll be fine. Just don't forget you *are* a woman. I know it pains you at times. But complaining and acting different aren't going to make you a man."

"I don't want to be a man," she protested. "I just want . . ." She paused. She didn't have time to think about what she wanted. She glanced down at her practical but unflattering blouse and split skirt. She didn't have time to fuss with her hair or use potions to keep her skin white and smooth. She didn't have time to be a lady. She had her ranch and her responsibilities. And Amy. They were enough.

Regan gave Fayre a quick smile, then moved toward the door. "Can you stay here tonight, in case Amy wakes up?"

Fayre nodded. "I've already made up the guest

room for myself. Hank's riding around picking out the fence lines you asked for. He won't be back for a couple more days, so I'm pleased to take care of Amy. If you need any help with Mr. Tyler, you come get me."

Regan picked up the basket and opened the door. "I'll be fine." She stepped out into the night air.

It was cool and damp outside, but not as cold as it had been just weeks before. The threat of a freeze was gone. Soon it would be time for the spring roundup. She looked past the barn toward the open ranch and knew Daniel could easily destroy years of work if he set his mind to it. The only thing that had kept him from riding in with his men and setting fire to her whole place was that he wanted it for himself. He wanted the land, the house, the horses, all of it. He even wanted her.

Regan shuddered at the thought. Even if she'd cared for Daniel O'Neil, she could never have married him. He'd become her cousin when her uncle Michael took him in and gave him the O'Neil name, and her brother-in-law when he married her sister, Elizabeth. He'd killed her sister as surely as she'd shot Jackson Tyler. Regan had sworn she would prove it eventually.

Her gaze swept over the barn and quiet corrals. Several horses stood bunched together, dozing in the darkness. In the distance, she could see the fire from the camp of the men she'd hired to protect herself and her land. The faint sound of their laughter made her stomach clench. She'd been around men her entire life, she ran one of the largest spreads in all of Texas, but those men frightened her. With their cold eyes and their slick ways. They killed for a living. She paid them well, and so far they'd done as she asked.

But for how long? If they turned on her and her family, how would she stop them?

Regan let go of her worries. She couldn't do anything tonight. The situation would look better in the morning. It always did.

When she reached the shed, she pulled open the door and stepped into the darkness. She felt along the wall for the lantern Pete had told her about. She struck a match and set it to the wick. After adjusting the flame so it burned brightly, she turned slowly to look at her patient.

The men had followed her orders. Jackson's stretched-out form had been covered with a blanket. Fresh bandages had been wrapped around his arm and thigh, but blood had continued to ooze out, staining the cotton. A washbowl filled with bloody water sat on the dirt floor next to an empty stool. Jimmy had apparently left his patient for the night.

Regan moved closer. There was a gash on Jackson's head where he'd struck a rock when he hit the ground. She could see the blackened flesh on his leg from the powder burn.

Revulsion filled her. She'd done this to him. She had no one to blame but herself. He'd defiled her sister's name, she reminded herself, searching for the anger that had spurred her to shoot him in the first place.

She stared at his swollen face. Yes, he'd defiled her sister's name, stolen her innocence, but it hadn't been rape. Elizabeth had whispered of his seduction, of pleasure found in Jackson's bed. Never once had she hinted that he forced her. Oh, dear Lord, Regan thought, horrified again at what she'd done. She'd shot an innocent, unarmed man.

The basket slipped from Regan's hands and landed on the dirt with a thump. At the sound, Jackson stirred, moaning in pain. Her eyes widened as she watched the slow rise and fall of his chest. Bending at the waist she reached her fingers out and touched his shoulder.

The heat of his skin burned her. She jumped back and hurried from the shed.

To the left of the foreman's single-story house was a smaller structure containing three rooms. Despite the early hour, the windows were dark. Regan remembered that Pete had been up the previous night with a sick mare. She hated to disturb him but it couldn't be helped. She ran to the back door and pounded twice, then let herself in.

"Pete," she called out. "Pete, it's me. I need you."

Pete stumbled into the kitchen. He wore trousers and nothing else. Strands of his sandy hair were sticking up in all directions. He rubbed his hand over his face and peered at her in the darkness.

"Regan? What's wrong? Is it Daniel?"

"No. It's not that. I need you to help me get Jackson inside."

"Huh?" He shook his head and stared at her. "I thought Jimmy was taking care of him."

"He's not doing a good-enough job. Jackson's burning up with fever. I need to get him to the house so Fayre and I can tend to him." She started for the door. "Hurry!"

Regan ran to the house and called for Fayre to prepare a bed downstairs. By the time she returned to the shed, Pete was already standing in the small room, staring at the man.

"He looks bad," he said. "All flushed. Probably from infection."

"Probably," Regan agreed curtly. "Help me carry him inside."

Pete glanced at her. He'd pulled on a shirt but hadn't taken the time to button it. "He's naked under that blanket, Regan. I don't think you should be here."

She rolled her eyes. "I saw him naked before and that didn't bother you."

"That was different. Now with him sick like, it doesn't seem right."

"I'm not going to stand here arguing with you." She bent down and grabbed Jackson's bare ankles. "You get his shoulders."

Pete did as she asked, all the while muttering about how it wasn't right. Now that he'd mentioned Jackson's nakedness, Regan became aware of the expanse of bare male skin. She could feel the heat of his body where her hands held on to him. The light dusting of hairs on his legs tickled her fingers.

Pete hefted him and started backing up toward the open shed door. Regan followed, straining against the heavy weight. She was strong and could wrestle a steer with the skill of a cowboy almost twice her size. But wrestling steers was a lot more about smarts and leverage than sheer strength, and Jackson's dead weight dragged at her. The dark path to the back of the house had never seemed so long. Up ahead, the windows in the kitchen glowed from lamplight. Jackson's blanket slipped off, but she was working too hard to worry about looking at the forbidden.

When they reached the porch her breath was coming out in short puffs and her arms felt as if they were being pulled off from her shoulders. Pete started up the two stairs.

"I can't go any farther," Regan wheezed.

"We'll rest." He set Jackson down on the top step and supported him. Regan couldn't be as gentle. Her fingers slipped as she lost her hold on his ankles. His legs flopped down and hit the stairs. Jackson groaned softly but didn't wake. She bent over at her waist and rested her hands on her knees.

"He's heavy," she said, relaxing her aching muscles.

"He's also bleeding again."

Regan glanced up at Jackson and saw blood seeping from the bandage on his leg. "Okay, I'm ready." She got a firm hold on him and lifted.

Before they reached the back door, Fayre had it open and was giving them instructions.

"Don't bump his head, there. Pete, you be careful. Regan, you have his feet all right? It's through here. In the main bedroom."

Regan raised her head and stared at the older woman. "That's my father's room."

"Sean wouldn't have minded. If we take him upstairs, he'll be harder to take care of. All those stairs between him and the kitchen, not to mention the necessary."

And Amy, Regan thought. She needed to keep Jackson as far from her daughter as possible.

"You're right."

Pete backed through the kitchen and hallway into the large downstairs bedroom. Fayre had already lit several lamps and pulled back the covers on the oversized bed. Regan glanced from the clean linen sheets to Jackson's dusty body, then figured it couldn't be helped.

Pete set him on the bed, then motioned for Regan to swing around his legs. "That should do it," he said. She let go.

"You get back to bed," Fayre said, brushing Pete aside and stepping close to her patient. "You won't be any use to anyone if you don't get some sleep. Regan can stay up with me and Mr. Tyler." She didn't say anything else, but her accusation hung in the air. It was Regan's fault Jackson was in this mess to begin with. It was only right that she be the one most inconvenienced by his condition.

Pete hesitated. Regan moved over to stand next to him. "She's right, you know. You'd just get in the way. We'll be fine."

His hazel eyes met hers, then he reached up and laid a hand against her cheek. "Are you fine?"

The tender gesture made her chest tighten. Pete had been a part of her life since they were both kids. Sometimes, like now, she wished it had been different between them, that she could have accepted his sweetly worded proposal. He'd wanted to marry her because he felt obligated to take care of her. Not because he had any manly feelings toward her. Thoughts of her didn't keep him from his work. She knew—he'd never once tried to kiss her.

She covered his fingers with her own and smiled. "Go to sleep, cowboy, or I'll have to fire your sorry hide come morning."

"Yes, boss." He grinned, tipped an imaginary hat and left the room.

Fayre finished adjusting Jackson on the clean sheet. She reached over and picked up a basin from the nightstand. "Don't just stand there taking up room. Fill this with warm water and bring some clean rags."

By the time Regan was back with the requested

supplies, Fayre had cut off the bandages and was staring at the open wounds. "You winged him good."

Regan studied his upper arm. The wound there was clean, still bleeding, but not too bad. However, the skin on his upper thigh was puffy and an angry red. Blood trickled out, pulsing slightly in time with his heartbeat. The swelling stretched from his knee to his—

Regan turned away from the apex of his thighs. "I meant to shoot him in the chest. Pete stopped me."

Fayre sat on the bed and dipped a clean cloth in the warm water. She pressed the wet pad against his leg. Jackson stirred slightly, his hands fluttering above the sheet before falling heavily to the bed.

"Wash him," Fayre ordered, tossing her a clean rag. "And thank the good Lord that Elizabeth was the one foolish enough to be sweet on him."

Regan sat on Jackson's other side. She dampened the cloth, then leaned over and brushed it gently against his shoulder. "What do you mean?"

Fayre brushed a loose gray strand of hair off her face. "You shot him, child. First you saw him as naked as the day he was born, then you shot him. A man don't take kindly to that kind of humiliation. I don't guess he'd ever be likely to forgive or forget."

"You're right," she said softly. "No man would forget what happened." Certainly not one like Jackson. He'd always had his pride. She remembered so many things about him, and that most of all. He'd been good at what he did, and he didn't mind who knew it.

"Well, looky here. You can see where the infection's starting to take hold. The pus is just ready to ooze out." Fayre stood up. "I'm going to have to get some powders and see what I can do. I don't suppose

Mr. Tyler would be happy if we saved his life, only to have him lose his leg."

Regan looked up at her. "He's not going to lose his leg, is he? Not that?"

Fayre shrugged. Her once-blue calico dress had faded to a soft gray from many washings. Regan often told her to order in some fabric, but the older woman was stubborn about wearing out what she had before bothering with something new. She stood beside the bed unbuttoning her cuffs and rolling up her sleeves.

"I can't rightly say. I'll do the best I can." She jerked her head toward his chest. "You're doing more talking than cleaning. Wash him up. When I come back we'll roll him over and you can do the other side."

Her shoes clicked on the wooden floor as she left the room. Regan dipped her cloth in the basin and then brushed it against his uninjured arm. She tried to keep her gaze on what she was doing and not look at anything else, but again and again she was drawn to study his face.

Six years had changed them all, she thought, giving up and staring at his features. She'd filled out some, although she never did catch up with Elizabeth's abundant curves. Jackson had gotten a little broader in the shoulders and leaner in the face. Before, despite his worldly hardness, she'd been able to see traces of the boy he must have been. Now he was only a man.

Stubble shadowed his cheeks and outlined his firm mouth. A scar cut across his chin. She remembered it from his last visit, although the scar by his left temple was new. Gold-blond hair tumbled over his forehead. She brushed back the strands, stopping to linger when she felt their silky softness. She loved the color of his hair. Hers was a wretched shade of red. Too bright, too curly, too everything. She wore a hat as often as she could. Elizabeth's hair had been auburn, a deep brown touched by the radiance of a sunset. That's how an admirer had described it once. Regan still remembered the words. She used to hope someone would find something nice to say about her hair. She didn't anymore.

She touched the well-shaped eyebrows, then the prickly stubble. The fever still raged; he was overly warm.

"You broke my heart, Jackson Tyler. I hated you as much as I wanted to love you. I suppose that's one of the reasons I shot you. Which makes my behavior worse than yours. I've never done anything like that. You've had your revenge. I hope you're happy."

He didn't answer of course. If he'd been awake she never would have said the words. She would rather burn in the fires of hell than admit how she'd once felt about Jackson. Memories from the past threatened, but she ignored them. She couldn't think on them tonight. It would hurt too much.

After dipping the cloth back in the water, she went to work on his chest. Under the thin layer of dust, his skin was clean. No wonder. After all, Pete said they'd caught him washing in the stream.

A faint smile tugged at her lips. She'd gone as fast as she could when one of the cowboys told her they'd caught a stranger on their land. With the trouble she was having with Daniel, she'd assumed it was one of his men looking to start a fight. She hadn't expected the stranger to be naked. It had almost been worth it just to see Jackson Tyler trying to bluster through while his privates flapped in the breeze. She'd seen what he was thinking. Bad enough to get caught unawares, worse to be seen that way by a woman.

Fayre was right. He would never forgive her for that. Or for smiling.

"I don't need your forgiveness," she said curtly, scrubbing his shoulder harder than was necessary.

She shifted her weight onto the hip that was pressing against him, then slipped her hand over his midsection to brace herself. Her palm brushed against his hot skin and the cool crinkling of hair that arrowed down from his chest.

She'd seen naked men lots of times. At twelve she was fascinated by the differences between the cowboys and her own rapidly changing body. She spent much of that summer curled up in the bushes alongside the stream where Jackson had been caught. She watched as the cowboys had come to cool themselves in the rushing water.

She let her fingers rest on the warmth of Jackson's skin. She'd seen plenty of men naked, but had never touched one intimately. Not the way Elizabeth had whispered about touching Jackson.

A yearning filled her, frightening in its intensity. Regan steeled herself against it and quickly continued her ministrations. The water was cooling and she wanted to be finished before Fayre returned.

She washed his legs, staying away from his wound and the very tops of his thighs. When she was done she stood at the foot of the bed and studied him. Except for the occasional grunts of pain, he was silent. She admired the lean length of his legs, the muscles in his chest and arms, the handsome planes of his face. He was, in every sense of the word, beautiful.

"I don't need your forgiveness," she whispered into the silence. "But I'm sorry."

She gripped the iron footboard and squeezed tightly. In the distance she heard Fayre's shoes on the wooden floor as the older woman returned from collecting her medicines.

"You all done?" she asked, bustling into the room, a tray held out in front of her.

Regan nodded.

"We're going to make a poultice," her housekeeper said. "Give me that bowl there."

Three hours passed before Regan was able to make her escape. The temperature had dropped enough to make her shiver despite her woolen shawl. She had a thick coat she usually wore in the winter, but in her hurry to escape the sickroom, she'd left it behind.

She sat on the top step of the porch and breathed in the clean air. She could smell the horses and the hay, the scents of the budding trees. She closed her eyes and tried to forget the odor of infected flesh and Fayre's herbs.

The wound in Jackson's leg was worse than she'd first thought. If the infection got out of control— She shook her head. She couldn't think about that now.

How had this all happened? Why had she let her temper get the better of her? She'd shot a man. Regan pulled her knees to her chest and wrapped her arms around her shins. What would her father think?

Shame filled her at the thought of Sean O'Neil's

disappointment. He'd always expected more of her than he had of Elizabeth. He'd spent more time with her, had taught her about the ranch. He'd known from the beginning that she would be the one to inherit. They'd spent hours together discussing how to work with the hired hands. He'd explained about working with men and what that would mean to her as a woman. He'd taught her to think before she acted. She hadn't thought today. She'd only felt and reacted.

Pete understood, and even if he didn't, he wouldn't hold it against her. What was going to happen when the other men found out what she'd done? She didn't need any more trouble. Daniel was creating enough, but here she was making it worse. In the morning she was going to have to—

By the side of the house a match flared. She stood up and reached for the pistol she'd started carrying ever since the first threat against the ranch. At the same moment her fingers grasped nothing but the cotton of her dress; she'd left the gun in the kitchen when she went to get Fayre fresh hot water.

"Who's there?" she called, then realized she should have slipped back into the house without alerting the man to her presence. Too late now.

"McLane, ma'am," a low voice drawled. "I'm on patrol."

McLane. Gage McLane. One of the hired guns. They were all frightening men with their fast guns and cold stares, but McLane was the worst. He had a way of looking through her that made her feel as if he could kill her before breakfast without spoiling his appetite for steak and eggs. He also had a reputation

for being one of the best shots around and not easily
bought off, which was why she'd hired him.

"Are you alone?" she asked.

He stepped away from the house and into the light
spilling out from the kitchen window. Except for the
glowing cigarette tip, he was all in black. He stared at
her for several seconds, then removed his hat. She
supposed it was a kind gesture, designed to put her at
ease, but it failed. She didn't like his dark penetrating
stare or the cynical twist of his mouth. Gage McLane
had seen too much of life to believe it still held any
value. If he turned against her or if Daniel convinced
him the battle would be better waged from the other
side, McLane would be a merciless enemy. She
prayed his reputation for loyalty was factual.

"It's late, ma'am," he said politely. Each word skittered down her spine, making her shiver as if she'd
seen a snake cross her path. "You shouldn't be out
here by yourself."

She tossed her head, sending tight frizzy curls
bouncing across her forehead. By noon most of her
hair had escaped from the braid; by nightfall, the
morning's hairstyle was simply a memory. She
brushed the wayward strands over her shoulder. "I've
hired you to keep this property safe from my cousin,
sir. As long as you're about, I shouldn't have to worry
about him."

"Maybe he's not the one you should be afraid of."
Black eyes, the color of night, the color of death, held
hers.

She could taste the fear. Had the hired guns
decided to try something? What about Amy? Could
she protect her child?

"What do you mean?" she asked, carefully controlling her voice so it wouldn't shake. "If there is talk of going over to Daniel's side, I can pay—"

He cut her off with a wave of his hand. Behind him the tree branches swayed in the slight breeze. He should have been dwarfed by their size, but instead he was the one who made them look insignificant. He took a step closer.

"I can't decide if you're foolish or just innocent."

"What?" She didn't dare back up even though every part of her was screaming to.

"Those men you've hired, the ones you're afraid of."

She bristled at the insult, but he went on as if he hadn't noticed.

"They've been out here a long time. You're a woman. You tempt them."

Regan blinked several times. The hired guns wanted a woman? McLane thought they wanted her? She stared at him, wondering if she'd understood him correctly. The relief was so complete, she burst out laughing.

In the faint moonlight she saw his mouth twist in displeasure. Instantly she sobered. "Mr. McLane, I assure you I am not likely to be a temptation to the men. However, if you're advising me that they need time off to visit town, I'll be happy to arrange it in the morning." She pulled her shawl closer and folded her arms over her chest.

"That'd help, but you need to watch yourself all the same."

"Me?" She shook her head. "Hardly."

He took the cigarette from his mouth and tossed it into the dirt. "You don't act foolish, so you must be innocent."

That line of thought was dangerous. "I have a five-year-old daughter, Mr. McLane. I might not be a married woman, but I'm hardly—" she hesitated, not sure what to say, then realized what she *had* said, "—that is to say, I'm not—"

He raised his dark eyebrows. "Yes?"

A virgin, she thought, then knew she could never say that aloud. "Men don't find me attractive." She motioned to her hair, then to her worn dress. "Obviously."

McLane looked at her. Starting at her shoes, he slowly worked his way up to her face. By the time he got there, her cheeks were burning. The darkness hid her blush. If she hadn't been unarmed, she would have ordered him off the ranch.

"Innocent *and* foolish. I'll say this, Miss O'Neil, you do a damn fine job for a woman. But you are just a woman. Advice is worth what you pay for it, but I'll give you mine just the same. Watch yourself with the hired guns. They don't like taking orders from somebody in skirts."

He turned and started to walk away into the night. Regan stepped down from the porch and moved after him. He was right. Everything he said made perfect sense. She'd been wrestling with it for weeks, ever since the first gunslinger arrived on the ranch. Hiring them was trouble, but she didn't know what else to do. Her cowboys were good with cattle but no match for Daniel's professionals.

"Mr. McLane? What about you? Would they take orders from you?"

He stopped in his tracks and slowly turned to face her. "What are you asking?"

Her father had taught her to trust her feelings, and the voice in her head said to take a chance. "If you'll take charge of the hired guns. They take orders from you, you take orders from me."

He stared down at her, the moonlight glinting off his black hair and the pistols strapped on both hips. "No," he said curtly. "I'm not interested."

"Why?"

"It's not how I do things."

"But—"

He silenced her with an angry shake of his head. "Haven't you figured out I'm the most dangerous one of all?"

With that he turned and disappeared into the night. She stared after him wondering what was going to happen to all of them. "Oh, Daddy," she murmured. "Sometimes I feel as if you left out some important parts of my training. Just when I think I know all I need to, something happens that shows me I'll never understand."

She turned back toward the house. It was past midnight but she wasn't sleepy. She was afraid of what would happen when she lay down and closed her eyes. Jackson Tyler rested under her roof. How would she keep the memories out of her mind? It had been hard enough with him gone these six years, but now that he was back . . .

She sat again on the porch and drew her knees to her chest. She wondered if she was ever going to forget. Gage McLane thought she was a fool. He was right. Only a fool would hang on to such unhappy recollections.

She sighed, feeling the weariness stealing over her,

knowing she wouldn't be able to escape the past. It had been inevitable from the moment she saw Jackson standing beside the stream. She'd looked at his face and known the past had returned to destroy her.

She braced her elbows on her knees and supported her chin. The silhouette of the tree in front of her blurred until she saw the inside of the barn all those years ago. It had been hot. A sweltering Texas night when arguments escalated to brawls and the weak-minded went quietly mad. She'd been so young. Eighteen, but still a girl. No matter how she tried, she'd never learned Elizabeth's womanly serenity or her instinctive knowledge about how to attract a man.

Never had Regan wanted it as much as she had the summer Jackson Tyler came to help her father. Jackson had been her ideal. Handsome, strong, intelligent. He had a grin that could melt ice. Lord knew she'd felt peculiar every time he was near by. He'd treated her with casual indifference, never spending time with her alone, never starting a conversation with her. But she hadn't minded. She kept her eye on him all that summer, trying to make sure her chores took her near him. Until that night in the barn.

Regan fought against the memories, but they were too strong. Despite the cold night air, she could feel the heat of that summer, taste the salty sweat that had coated her upper lip and feel the heavy longing in her thighs.

By choice Jackson had bunked down in the barn. She'd gone out on some pretext of taking him a message from her father, but he'd known it was a lie. The half-empty whiskey bottle had given her pause, but her newfound courage had been too hard won to waste. Besides, time was short. Not only was Jackson to leave as soon as the trouble was over, but Elizabeth had mentioned she thought he was attractive. If her sister decided to claim Jackson as another of her beaux, Regan knew she wouldn't have a chance. That night was her only hope.

The memories came faster now, one on top of the other, half-formed pictures, flashes of conversation. He'd talked to her that night, had told her about his plans for the future. His shirt was undone, and again and again her gaze strayed to his bare chest. She wondered about Jackson's body and her own, and about the things her father had told her men and women did together.

It was then she realized he'd stopped talking and that the barn was filled with an uneasy silence. She prayed for him to kiss her. He would have been the first. Elizabeth was the one the men all wanted. Except for Jackson. He hadn't noticed her sister at all. Just one kiss. She wanted to know what it was like, but more than that she wanted to know what it was like with him.

She'd held his gaze, thinking her request so loudly he finally heard.

He stared at her, at her lips, then at her uninspiring breasts. He'd picked up the whiskey bottle and swallowed hard, then he set it down and wiped his hand across his mouth.

"Go back to the house, Regan," he said. "I'm not that drunk, and I'm not likely to be."

3

He didn't think anyone would be humming in hell. Jackson stirred slightly, trying to escape the noise. His movements sent shafts of angry pain through his left leg. He groaned. This couldn't be heaven because he felt like horseshit that had been run over by a stagecoach, so he might still be alive.

The off-key humming, punctuated by an odd word every few bars, was just loud enough to keep him from drifting away. He thought about moving, but the echo of incredible pain kept him still. Instead he risked opening his eyes.

Big mistake, he thought as he blinked in the bright sunlight. Instantly his eyes began to water and he shut them again. He didn't recognize the room or the woman. That was never good.

"I saw that," the woman said, moving close to the

bed. "Don't you go playing dead on me again, Mr. Tyler. You've done enough of that already. I'm too old and too set in my ways to have much patience with a young man such as yourself. Besides if you wake up, I just might let you put on some trousers."

Trousers? Did that mean— He reached under the sheet and touched his bare belly. His eyes snapped open.

"Who are you?" he demanded. At least he was supposed to be demanding. His voice sounded scratchy and faint. He cleared his throat and tried again. "Who are you?" he asked, squinting against the bright afternoon light streaming through two large windows on either side of the four-poster bed.

"I heard you the first time. I'm not deaf." The woman stepped next to him and smiled slightly. She had gray hair and was probably old enough to be his mother. He sent up a brief prayer that he hadn't been so drunk that he'd tried to—

He shook his head. Another serious mistake he realized when spots appeared. A familiar rushing sound filled his ears. He fought to stay in the room and not float away into the black cloud circling through his mind. Gritting his teeth, he concentrated all his effort on keeping focused on the woman. Even if he *had* bedded her, the thought of which at any other time would have made him swear off whisky for a week, facing the consequences was better than the mind-numbing darkness that kept him trapped between sleeping and being awake.

"We'll have none of that," the woman said, sitting down next to him on the bed and leaning forward to support his swimming head. She reached over to the nightstand and spooned something hot and flavorful into his mouth. The broth got his attention and the fog receded.

"Who are you?" he asked when he'd swallowed.

"Fayre."

She offered another spoonful and he took it gratefully. "Fayre. That doesn't help much. You are . . . ?"

She grinned, which made the lines around her pale blue eyes deepen. He found himself smiling back.

"Why, Mr. Tyler, I'm surprised you don't remember. You paid ten dollars, in gold, for the pleasure of my company last night." She gave him a broad wink. "We made this old bed rattle, I'll tell you that."

Jackson clenched his jaw, then made himself relax. He studied Fayre, ignoring the gray hair and lines. All in all, she was still a fine figure of a woman. She seemed pleasant enough, didn't smell bad, and had an appreciation of his skills in the bedroom. It could be worse.

A voice in his head asked how.

"You'll have to forgive me, Fayre," he said, trying to sound gracious. "I don't remember much after I started southwest from Kansas." He felt the bandage on his leg, then the small one on his left arm. "I seem to have run into some trouble somewhere."

Fayre stood up. "You don't remember any of it, do you?"

He knew better than to shake his head. "No."

She laughed, then touched the side of his face. "I've cared for you these past four days, Mr. Tyler. You're a fine specimen of a man, but you don't hold a candle to my Hank. I was just having some fun with you. I saw the look on your face when you thought we'd been together. I couldn't resist. It sorta makes up for all the trouble you've been."

"Four days?" That was a long time to have spent in bed. Alone. The relief tasted better than any broth she could have fed him. "So why am I here, and how did I get shot?"

She planted her hands on her hips. "Does the name Regan O'Neil mean anything to you?"

Regan! He tried to sit up, but his body didn't cooperate. His muscles screamed in protest and the fog returned, threatening him with more blackness. Fayre pressed her hand on his shoulders.

"Don't try anything yet. You've lost a lot of blood. If that weren't bad enough you hit your head on something and you have a lump there the size of a prize-winning pecan. I suspect it's going to take some time for your brains to get unscrambled. I'll go get some tea and toast and we'll see if you can tolerate that."

He heard her leave the room, then the fading sound of her footsteps. Regan. He closed his eyes as the memories returned. They bounced around like a storm of June hail, hitting him with painful intensity. When the flow of images was too much, he tried to focus on something else. He glanced around the room, at the large well-made armoire and the foot of the four-poster bed. Wallpaper covered the walls with an ivory-and-yellow floral print, and a marble-topped stand for the basin and pitcher stood in the corner. None of it distracted him from what had happened four days before.

The stream, his bath. His own stupidity that had let those men sneak up on him. Then Regan. Son of a bitch. She'd shot him. Twice!

Why? Damn. He couldn't remember everything. She'd thought he was working with Daniel O'Neil. Then he'd mentioned his son and she'd—

The footsteps returned. He stared at the door, waiting. Seconds before the handle turned he realized the sound was different. Fayre wasn't the one bringing him his tea.

"Come in, Regan," he called, folding his arms over his bare chest. Bare? He adjusted the sheet over his nakedness and wished for trousers. Or even the strength to sit up.

There was a moment of hesitation, then the door pushed open and she entered the room. "Good afternoon, Jackson. Fayre told me you were awake."

The sunlight caught Regan full in the face, illuminating her tanned skin and the freckles across her nose and cheeks. Her wild curly red hair had been partially tamed into a braid. The split skirt and work-worn boots had been replaced by a blue calico dress and fashionable ladies' shoes. Except for the angry glint in her eyes, he would never have guessed the woman in front of him was capable of shooting an unarmed man.

"How kind of you to be concerned. It's a little late, though, don't you think? If you'd had your way, I'd be six feet under."

The tray in her hands shook slightly, betraying her tension. Judging by her white knuckles, she was fighting strong emotions. Did she want to finish what she'd started, or did she fear his reprisals?

She stepped into the room and set the tray on the nightstand. There was a teapot, one mug, and a piece of dry toasted bread. Jackson wished he had the strength to sit up on his own. He figured he would starve before asking her for help.

She poured the tea, then straightened and folded

her hands together in front of her. "If Pete hadn't jerked my arm, I would have killed you," she said coolly, her blue eyes meeting his. "I admit that. However, you're alive. I'm willing to put the past behind us. When you're able to leave, you may do so. No one here will try to stop you."

He couldn't believe she was standing there telling him he was free to leave. "When I'm able, Miss O'Neil, I'll be on my way to the nearest sheriff's office to tell him there's a madwoman on this ranch and that you should be locked up."

She didn't even have the courtesy to look embarrassed by what she'd done. Regan shrugged and sat on the edge of the bed. "Go ahead. My men will say you threatened me and that I was defending myself."

"Threatened you? With what? I was buck naked."

She smiled then. He was flat on his back and that made it worse.

"Damn you, woman," he said and tried to sit up. Pain tore through his leg and arm, causing him to catch his breath. His vision blurred and something loud pounded in his head.

"Here, let me help you." Regan grabbed the two pillows from the far side of the bed, then slipped her hand behind his neck. He found himself in the particularly interesting position of having his face pressed into her bosom. She smelled sweet and womanly and her curves were a temptation, even in his weakened condition.

He bit back a curse. Womanly or not, she'd tried to kill him. If she had the only bosom in Texas, it couldn't make that right. She could dress like a lady all she wanted but he knew she was a female demon

in disguise. Which explained why he couldn't figure
out if he wanted to wring her neck or have her help
him again. Another few minutes with that bosom
and he would be his old self again. He sighed.
Looked like the last six years hadn't taught him a
damn thing. He was in this mess all because he
hadn't been able to resist Elizabeth's charms. Even
he shouldn't be foolish enough to think about getting
friendly with her gun-toting sister.

She adjusted the pillows behind him and resumed
her seat on the edge of the bed. When he settled back
he was still slightly below her eye level, but there
wasn't anything he could do about it. She stared at
him, her full mouth pulled into a straight line.

"How do you feel?" she asked.

"How do you think I feel? I've been shot. Twice. I
feel like somebody stuck red-hot pokers into my leg
and arm. Right now they're twisting 'em around and
around and dancing on the ends."

Her gaze slipped away. "I'm sorry."

"About what?" he asked. "About my being shot, or
your doing the shooting?"

She drew in a deep breath. "I'm sorry I lost my
temper and I'm sorry you're in pain."

"I expected that."

"What does that mean?"

He adjusted the sheet over him before answering.
"You're not sorry you shot me."

"Why should I be? You were trespassing on private property."

He raised his eyebrows. It didn't hurt too much.
He was getting better. In a couple of days he just might
be able to use his left leg again. "Unless you've spent

the last six years buying up free land, I was on your public grazing land, not near your private property. And when exactly did it become a shooting offense to take a bath?"

She was sitting close enough that if he inhaled deeply, he could catch the scent of her body. He hated that she'd grown from a coltish young lady into a woman. Even more he hated the fact that he could still feel the warmth of her bosom against his cheek. He didn't want to think of Regan as anything but a half-mad killer. He glanced at her face, at those damn freckles that should have been ugly as sin, at her big eyes and too-big mouth. She was no more a killer than a jackrabbit. So why had she shot him?

"You're a liar," she said softly. "I couldn't let you say those things about my sister."

His temper flared, but he fought it down. "Let's leave Elizabeth alone for now. I hadn't said a word about her when your men got the drop on me. They were hell-bent on protecting something. What is it?"

"Don't concern yourself, Jackson. Like I said, you should ride out of here as soon as you're able." She twisted her fingers together on her lap.

"I deserve to know why I was almost killed."

"Does it matter?" she asked, glaring at him. "I didn't kill you. Stop complaining about a gunshot or two. You're worse than an old woman."

He studied her, the proud set of her head, the stubborn tilt of her chin. He pushed down the anger and the pain. He ignored the memories and everything else in his mind, concentrating only on what his gut would tell him. The feeling had kept him alive for eleven years in a profession where the foolhardy died young.

"You had men patrolling the ranch for a reason," he said, hazarding a guess. "When they told you they'd found someone, you came riding out like the barn was on fire." He paused and let that sink in. The angle of her chin didn't dip, but she swallowed hard. "You wanted to know if I was working for your cousin. Daniel's giving you trouble again, isn't he?"

"It doesn't matter."

He tapped the bandage on his arm. "It does to me."

"My father died two months ago." Her chin dropped slightly and her shoulders hunched.

"I'm sorry."

She looked as if she didn't believe him.

"I am," he said. "Sean O'Neil was a good man. One of the few I knew who wanted to stop trouble but wasn't willing to kill to do it."

Her smile was sad. "He didn't change. After you fixed things with Daniel, my cousin pretended to get along with my father. Everything was fine until Sean died. Now Daniel wants to get control of the ranch."

"Which your father left to you."

She nodded.

"So if Daniel can't legally claim what he sees as his rightful inheritance, he's going to make sure he gets it another way?"

"So far he's made some threats and beat up a couple of the cowboys. Nothing too serious. But we're keeping watch. I know he won't do anything rash like set grasslands on fire. He wants the land and the cattle intact."

"What are you doing about it?"

She opened her mouth to answer, then clamped it shut. The shoulders went back, the chin went out, and he waited for the lash of her words to strike him.

She didn't disappoint. "Thank you so much for your interest, Mr. Tyler. However, I have the situation under control. There are six hired guns on my property and they are more than enough protection. Even if I'd wanted to hire another, you wouldn't be my first choice. After all, who would trust their safety to someone as easily caught as yourself?"

The last sentence made him wince. He raised his hands in a gesture of surrender. "I know. It's my own fault for wanting to take a bath. What can I say? Water will be the death of me."

One corner of her mouth trembled, as if she fought a smile. Her anger faded and with it her tension. "How did they do it?" she asked, leaning toward him. Curiosity brightened her eyes. "You can't be that bad if you've stayed alive all this time."

"Thanks for the compliment," he muttered. He hated to think about it. It was damned embarrassing. "I knew I was close to O'Neil land," he started, by way of an explanation. "I wasn't expecting any trouble, so I took a bath."

"But how did they get the drop on you? You'd left out your rifle. I saw it. I know Pete and the other men are good cowboys, but didn't you hear them coming through the bushes?"

"No, I didn't. Now I'm a little tired. If you'll excuse me?" He folded his arms over his chest and closed his eyes.

She didn't budge. Not only didn't the mattress shift from her standing, but he could still hear her breathing.

"I'm not going anywhere," she said. "Not until I know."

"Why is it so important?"

"Jackson!"

It was the way she said his name. It reminded him of something from long ago. Back when he was young and cocky enough to believe he could be a gunfighter forever. Back before he realized how many of his friends would die and how quiet the world would be after they were gone. Back to when his ma was still pretty enough for him to know why his pa married her.

"I was singing," he said without opening his eyes. Then he waited for the laughter, because damn it all, it *was* funny.

She made a choking sound, which was quickly muffled. And then he remembered that he'd always liked Regan. She wasn't the kind of woman who made a man think of being alone with her in the dark, but she was someone a man would consider trusting and laughing with.

He grimaced. He was softer than a goose-down pillow and about as dangerous. Good thing he'd already decided to give up gunfighting. The way his mind was turning to mush, he would be laid out in a pine box before collecting his first pay.

He opened his eyes to find her watching him. "It's my own fault," he said.

She reached toward him and touched the bandage on his arm. "Does it hurt bad?"

"Yeah."

Her touch was light and didn't make the throbbing worse, so he didn't mind when she left her fingers on his skin.

"I didn't mean to lose my temper."

"But you did mean to shoot me." He pulled his arm away.

She drew her hand back to her lap. "Jackson, I—" She bit her lower lip and glanced down.

Irritation burned in him. "You can't even apologize, can you? Must make it difficult to run this place. Everybody makes mistakes, or do you find other people to blame for what you've done?"

Her head snapped up. "You have no right to say that to me."

"I'm not surprised," he said. "You never were one to take responsibility for what you'd done. You got too used to your daddy looking out for you."

"Me!" Regan rose to her feet and glared at him. "Don't you dare speak to me about responsibility. You're the one who was hired on to do a job. But that wasn't enough for you. No, you also had to seduce the innocent daughter of your employer."

"I never touched you, Regan. Not even when you asked me to." What had happened by the stream wasn't all he remembered when she walked into the room. He'd been able to fill in the hazy moments from his last visit to the O'Neil ranch, particularly that night when he got drunk to keep himself from taking what was being offered to him on all sides. Regan with her longing glances and adoration, and Elizabeth with her practiced seduction. He'd managed to ignore Regan, but Elizabeth hadn't left him much choice.

Regan's eyes widened at his statement. Color flared on her cheeks. He thought she might flee, but something, probably pride, held her in place.

"How dare you?" Her voice was low and angry. "How dare you continue to sully the reputation of my late sister. You seduced her, you bastard. I know. She told me how you promised to marry her and told her you loved her. Elizabeth was very susceptible to what men said to her and you took advantage of that."

"The hell I did." He braced his arms to push himself into a sitting position, but the muscles in his left arm cramped and refused to cooperate. He sagged against the pillow. "Elizabeth was as innocent as a milk cow, Regan. Grow up and see your sister for what she was. I didn't seduce her. I didn't have to. You came in that barn looking for kisses and nothing else. She came in half-naked and looking for trouble. Her latest lover had moved on a few months before, leaving her hotter than a cat in heat. If I hadn't given her what she wanted, she would have gotten it from one of the cowboys the way she'd been getting it for years."

She drew her arm back to slap him, but he grabbed her wrist before her palm made contact with his face.

"Stop," he said, holding her tightly enough to make her bite her lower lip. "You had your chance down by the stream. You should have killed me then if you meant to, because you won't get the chance again." She pulled away from him, but he didn't release his grip.

"No," he said, and jerked her hard toward him.

She fell across his legs, her knee connecting painfully with his injured thigh. He grunted but didn't release her. She lay on her left side struggling against his grip.

"Let me go."

"Not until we get this cleared up. I have some questions I want answered."

"Not until you let me go."

She tried to tug her arm free. He used more force, knowing he was bruising her, but she wouldn't give up. Her knee shifted away from his wound and he was able to draw in a clear breath. Several strands of hair pulled free of her braid and drifted across her face. She tossed her head to get them out of her eyes.

"Damn you, Jackson Tyler."

"I thought ladies didn't swear in front of a gentleman."

"You're no gentleman." She shifted and tried to get leverage to push up. Her free hand landed directly on his privates. Her fingers curved over his pecker while her thumb dug hard into his sensitive parts. He yelped and released her at the exact moment she jerked her hand away from him. The unexpected freedom made her lose her balance and slide off the opposite side of the bed.

She landed hard on her rear, her back to him.

He shifted uncomfortably, wanting to rub the injured area but holding back. Regan rose to her knees, then stood up. She turned to face him.

More strands of hair drifted around her face. She wasn't the proper young woman anymore. She looked more like a hellcat bent on revenge. Fire flared in her eyes. For a moment he wondered if the flames had ever burned as brightly for a man. Bad timing, he told himself as pain continued to pulse between his legs.

"My sister loved you," she said. "She believed you cared about her. She believed you were coming back to marry her."

He swore. "Elizabeth wanted what I was offering, but she had plans to marry a rich man."

"You're wrong. She waited for you, and when you didn't come back, she married Daniel."

He sat up straight, ignoring the throbbing in his arm and leg. "What?"

Regan smiled faintly. "My sister married Daniel after you left."

"She couldn't have. He was her first cousin." Daniel was also a yellow-bellied coward and first-class bastard, but he didn't have to point that out to Regan.

"Not by blood," she said. "My uncle adopted Daniel when he married Daniel's mother."

"Elizabeth married him for the money," he said, thinking aloud.

Regan took a step toward him. "Don't you dare say that. Stop saying those things. Stop lying about her. She married Daniel because you broke her heart."

"I'm not lying about the letter. Where's my son?"

"You have no son. Elizabeth never had a child, by you or anyone. Ever." She brushed her hair from her face and stared down at him. Her chest rose and fell with each breath. "You can ask the cowboys or even the sheriff on your way out of town. Elizabeth never had your son. If you cared so much, why are you just coming here now? My sister died almost a year ago. Where were you then? Where were you when she needed you?"

All the blood had fled her face leaving her pale under her tan. Her freckles stood out across her nose and cheeks.

Her stark pain made him feel uncomfortable. "Regan—"

"He killed her," she said, interrupting. "She told me she'd found a way to leave Daniel. I'd been begging her to come back to the ranch but she wouldn't. She was afraid of what he'd do to me if she did. I wondered how she thought she was going to escape. It must have been her letter to you. You were her last hope. But you waited all this time to come and now she's dead."

Jackson stared at her. Regan obviously believed what she was saying, but none of it made sense with what he remembered about Elizabeth O'Neil. She was tempting enough to get any man for a ten-county radius. Why Daniel? He was rich, but not that rich. And why was Regan so sure that he, Jackson, had made promises to her sister? He hadn't. He didn't make promises to any woman. He never had. Life as a gunfighter had been too uncertain to plan much past the next twenty-four hours.

"I only got the letter a month ago," he said. "I came right away."

"No." She shook her head. "I don't believe you. Elizabeth trusted you. You seduced her and left her alone. Then when she begged you to help her, you wouldn't come." She clamped her lips shut and walked to the door. Without turning back to him, she said, "As soon as you're able, I want you out of my house."

Regan was still shaking when she leaned against the closed door and stood in the darkness of the hallway. Visions of Elizabeth and the way she looked when she was found lying dead filled her mind. Regan fought against the tightness in her chest. She'd long since learned that tears solved nothing, so she refused to give in to them. Crying didn't change the past.

Her fingers curled around the doorknob, squeezing tightly. She hated Jackson Tyler with every part of her being. He was responsible for Elizabeth's death. He had to be.

He was the easiest person to blame.

Regan grimaced. Sometimes she hated that her father

had spent many hours tutoring her in the skill of looking at something from both sides. She hated knowing that Jackson might not be as irresponsible as she wished him to be. Elizabeth had cared about him and been in love with him, but her sister had never spoken of Jackson's promising to marry her. She'd confessed that when Regan suggested asking their father to send out a group of men to hunt him down and force him to come and marry her. Elizabeth hadn't wanted that at all.

Regan stepped away from the door. No wonder Jackson was confused. Her accusations were a careful combination of lies and truth. The truth was he *had* seduced her sister. Her mouth twisted with anger. Shooting was too good for him. The lies were that he'd promised to marry her and come back for her. Truth, that Elizabeth had sent a letter, and she had mentioned a child. Not a son, as he'd claimed. Just a child.

His child.

For a short time Regan had allowed herself to be lulled into a sense of security. With Jackson unconscious, it had been easy to forget the danger he represented. He'd come searching for his son. Pray God that was all he looked for. If her lies confused him enough to blind him to the biggest truth of all, it was worth the black marks against her soul. She would do anything to protect that which she loved. She would sacrifice every ideal, every teaching in the world, to save Amy.

As if her thoughts had drawn her daughter to her, Regan heard childish laughter floating down the stairs. Amy danced down after it.

"Mama!" she called. Her brown hair was pulled into two braids and they bounced in time with her exaggerated steps. Amy had the energy of a whole barnful of calves and twice the ability to get into trouble. There was a smudge of dirt on her cheek and a new rip in the skirt of her dress.

"What have you been up to?" Regan asked, easing away from Jackson's closed door.

"I think there's a mouse in my room," her daughter said, her hazel eyes gleaming with excitement. "I was trying to catch it."

Regan crouched down and held out her arms. Amy moved close and held her tight. The familiar scent of her child, the feel of her strong, growing body, brought a rush of gladness and joy to her. It was worth anything, she reminded herself. She would die for this child. If necessary, she would kill for her.

"Maybe we should let one of the barn cats do the catching," Regan said.

Amy frowned. Her eyebrows, the exact shade and shape of her father's, pulled together. "No. Barn cats *eat* mice, Mama. I want to keep this one for me."

"Why?"

"To take care of."

"You take care of your dolls."

Amy looked up at her as if she was slow-witted. "They're not real."

Regan smiled. "Then why did I have tea with them last Sunday?"

Amy wiggled free and grinned. She hadn't lost her baby teeth yet and her smile made her beautiful. Regan took her child's hand and studied the small fingers and trimmed nails. She needed a bath, but then Amy spent her days getting dirty. She wasn't a young lady yet, and she wasn't a baby. She was caught in the middle, partially grown but still needing so much.

"My dolls are real sometimes," Amy admitted. "I wouldn't mind about the barn cat catching the mouse if I had a horse to ride."

The familiar argument made Regan shake her head. "You're not big enough."

Amy planted her hands on her hips. "I *am* big enough. Pete said so."

"You'd fall off and get hurt." Regan brushed her daughter's bangs from her eyes. "I don't want that to happen."

"I'd be real careful." Big hazel eyes pleaded.

Regan felt a tug at her heart. Amy might not look like Elizabeth, but she sure had her late sister's charm. "You can't control accidents."

"I don't have 'cidents no more. I'm a big girl."

"I'll think about it," Regan said, wondering why she bothered to resist in the first place. Amy almost always got her way in the end. She rose to her feet and glanced to her left when she heard Fayre coming down the hall from the kitchen.

"There you are, Amy," the housekeeper said. "I'm about to make a cake for tonight. Do you want to help?"

Amy practically quivered with excitement. "Can I have some crumbs to feed to my mouse?"

Fayre's gray eyebrows rose toward her hairline. "Mouse?"

Regan grinned. "No, Amy. No mouse feeding. Now you run on to the kitchen."

Amy eyed the closed door. "When's that man coming out? Maybe he wants to see my mouse."

"You stay away from him," Regan said. "He's very sick and doesn't need to be disturbed by a noisy little girl."

"I'm not noisy. I'm quiet."

Despite the panic fluttering in her chest at the thought of Amy and Jackson meeting, she couldn't help smiling. "As quiet as a mouse, yes, I know. Now go wash your hands if you're going to help Fayre."

Her daughter scampered away. Fayre stared after her. "A mouse?"

"She thinks there might be one in her room. She wants to keep it for a pet. I think she's trying to use the mouse to persuade me to let her learn to ride."

"I don't care why it's in the house. I want it gone." Fayre shuddered. "I'll get one of the barn cats in there this afternoon. The last thing I need is some critter in my supplies." She glanced at the closed door. "Did he finish his tea?"

"Tea?" Regan thought for a moment before remembering that she was supposed to make sure Jackson could keep down tea and toast. "I, ah, I don't know. I didn't stay to find out."

Fayre looked from the door to Regan and back again. "I'm sure he'll manage on his own," was all she said before she turned back toward the kitchen.

Regan watched her go. Fayre didn't say much, but Regan suspected the older woman knew more than she let on. She might be the only one who had guessed the truth about Amy.

Regan sighed. Fayre would never say anything. All that mattered was that Jackson didn't figure it out.

She glanced over at the closed door, then climbed the stairs to the second floor and walked into her bedroom. It was the same one she'd had as a child. The narrow bed, the beautifully carved dresser and vanity, the wardrobe between the two windows, were all familiar fixtures of her haven. She'd recently picked out new wallpaper in soft roses and blues. It contrasted with the cream-colored quilt she and Fayre had made this past winter.

After she crossed the room to the vanity, Regan took a seat. She pulled open the narrow drawer on her right and removed the worn letter. How many times had Jackson read those words? Had he pictured Elizabeth as he studied them? Had he remembered his time with Elizabeth? Had he thought of being with her, touching her?

Regan opened the paper and stared at the familiar handwriting.

Dear Jackson,

I hardly know how to address you. It's been six years since we were last together. I've thought about you often.

The ranch is much as you remember, yet there are a few changes. Those nights we shared together produced a child. Your child. I have come to see keeping the truth from you was wrong. I hope you'll forgive me. Please come back to me, and to your child. We need you very much.

Elizabeth

The date of the letter was October. Eighteen months ago Elizabeth had written this letter and sent it without saying a word to Regan. Why? Had her life been so desperate that she needed to risk so much to escape from Daniel?

"You could have come here," Regan said aloud. But she'd made the offer many times, and each time Elizabeth had refused.

"I won't have his temper turned on you," her sister had told her, her blue eyes darkening with some remembered pain. "Not after what you did for me."

There had been nothing Regan could say to that. Elizabeth's marriage to Daniel had been an act of absolution. Daniel had wanted to marry one of Sean's daughters and Elizabeth had sacrificed herself to save Regan. At the time Regan had thought her sister really loved their adoptive cousin. Now she knew better.

Outside, the sounds from the corral drifted up in the warm afternoon. Regan folded the letter and slipped it back in the drawer. She'd gone through Jackson's saddlebags. He'd had books and clothes, ammunition and a large sum of cash. The letter was all she'd taken. She couldn't let him keep it; the danger was too great.

Lies and truth woven so carefully together that she was having trouble telling one from the other. If she tried to separate them now, if she pulled away a single thread, she would find her world in tatters around her.

If she allowed questions, she would lose her daughter.

She stared into the mirror and studied her familiar features. Amy looked nothing like her. She looked nothing like Jackson either, or any of the O'Neils. It was a blessing that had enabled Regan to claim her as her own without anyone guessing what had really happened. As far as the ranch hands and her friends knew, as far as the good citizens of Hampton, Texas, were concerned, Amy was hers by a man she'd refused to name. There was no one left who knew the truth.

That Amy wasn't hers at all. That Elizabeth and Jackson had never had a son. They'd had a daughter instead.

4

She'd just spent ten hours in the saddle and every part of her ached. Regan paused by the back door of the house. She could feel the grit and dust coating her skin. Tight curls clung to her damp forehead. She was dirty and hungry, and she wanted nothing more than to crawl into bed and sleep for three days.

Spring was coming. She wouldn't get a full night's sleep from early April through some time in July. There was so much to be done. First the calving, then the roundup to decide which cows would be sent north, which bulls brought in. Hiring extra men, planning for the winter, praying for good weather, worrying about fire and Daniel.

It had been so much easier when her father had still been alive. They'd shared the burdens and that had made them seem if not lighter, then at least something she could manage.

She drew off her hat and slapped it against the porch railing. Small clouds of dust rose up. She coughed twice, then clapped her hat back on her head and moved toward the door.

"Supper'll be ready by the time you wash up," Fayre said from the stove. She had a large apron pinned to the front of her worn dress. Steam from the stew had added a flush to her cheeks.

"I was going to tell you I was too tired to eat," Regan said, then inhaled deeply. "But I think I'll dig up the strength from somewhere."

"You do that. And while you're at it, you'd better have a talk with your daughter."

"Amy?" Regan set her hat on the peg by the door and hung her pistol up next to it, then walked toward the metal sink. Fayre had already prepared a basin of warm water for her. She started rolling up her cuffs. "What's she done today?"

Fayre opened the oven and poked at her biscuits. "Nothing worth getting het up about. Except I found her playing outside Mr. Tyler's room twice this afternoon. She was being quiet enough, but she's curious about him. I shooed her away, but she kept going back. While she was helping me with the biscuits, she asked lots of questions about him."

Regan rolled up her other sleeve, then washed her hands. She performed the familiar task mindlessly, her thoughts focused on the danger Jackson presented to her and to Amy.

"What did you tell her?"

"That he was sick and didn't want his rest disturbed by someone who got in as much trouble as she did." Fayre smiled as she closed the oven door. Then her

smile faded and her mouth straightened into a worried line. "What happens if the two of them meet?"

Regan met her friend's gaze. She had no answer to
that question. What happened if Jackson found out
about his daughter? "Nothing will happen, because
they're not going to meet." She rinsed her hands with
a pitcher of cool water, then reached for the folded
towel on the counter. "I'll speak to Amy tonight and
remind her to leave him alone. Once he's gone, it
won't be a problem anymore."

"Amy's determined to make his acquaintance,"
Fayre said as she opened a cupboard and pulled out
the tray she'd been using to serve Jackson his meals.
"I can't blame the child. She never sees a new face,
except the extra hands you hire at roundup. It's no
wonder she's as curious as a pup near a beehive."

"And the results will be just as dangerous," Regan
murmured. She knew it was her fault the child was so
isolated. But it wasn't safe for Amy to accompany her to
town on those few occasions Regan was forced to go.
She knew what people thought about her in Hampton.
She'd heard the whispers. She shook her head. They
didn't even whisper anymore. Last time she'd gone to
town someone had yelled out. She couldn't let her
daughter know that the town of Hampton had never
forgiven her for having a child out of wedlock. They
considered her little more than a whore, and Amy
nothing but a bastard brat. Better for her child to see
the same faces and know those people loved her than
to experience the cold condemnation of strangers.

"You can't protect her forever," Fayre said. Her
pale blue eyes didn't judge. They didn't have to. She
and Regan had discussed this before.

"I'll keep her safe as long as I'm able."

"She needs room to grow, to make mistakes."

Regan sighed. "I just want her to be happy."

The older woman nodded. Regan knew she should listen to Fayre's counsel. But Fayre didn't know everything. Or did she?

Regan watched the other woman ladle stew into a bowl. Fayre had been so close to both the O'Neil girls when they were growing up. But she'd never said anything. Not when Regan and Elizabeth had left, and not when they'd returned fourteen months later with Amy. She'd accepted without question the story that the child was Regan's.

Still it didn't matter if Fayre knew or not. She wouldn't say anything to jeopardize Amy.

Too many secrets, Regan thought as she poured herself a glass of cool water and drank it down. Too many lies and stories. So much hidden.

"If you don't mind, I told Amy she could come and have supper with Hank and me."

"Good idea," Regan said. "It'll keep her away from Jackson."

Fayre pulled the golden-brown biscuits from the oven. "I invited her because we like her company, not just to keep her away from Mr. Tyler."

"I know. I appreciate that." Regan glanced at the wooden table beside the window. The cloth covering it had been freshly pressed. It was set for one. She would eat alone tonight. For some reason the thought of solitude disturbed her. It shouldn't. She'd done it many times before. Enough times, in fact, that she'd convinced herself she preferred it this way. Just as well—it wasn't as if she was ever likely to marry.

She walked over to the table and stared out the window toward the corrals. This was her land. She owned the acreage around the house and out toward the grazing land. No man controlled it. No man told her what to do. The ranch was all she'd ever wanted. If the price of that was solitude, so be it.

At one time she'd thought of marrying, of course. What young woman didn't? Until Jackson's arrival six years ago, she'd even thought she might marry Pete. She'd imagined them growing old together on this land. Raising cattle together, building an empire. Pete would have been willing to be her partner, not her superior. But after Jackson left, her broken heart hadn't wanted to heal. Pete's gentle smile hadn't made her feel special anymore and she'd known she couldn't marry a man without loving him. She hadn't loved Pete that way.

After she claimed Amy as her child, no one else had wanted her. She was ruined in the eyes of the town and the local ranchers around Hampton. Just as well, she consoled herself. She didn't have the time or temperament to marry. She was too used to getting things her way. Besides, if she did become someone's bride, he would find out the truth about Amy and she couldn't risk that.

The situation was so perverse, she almost smiled. She was branded as a fallen woman. No decent man would want her for herself. Even if one was willing to marry her for the ranch, she couldn't risk it. How could she explain to her bridegroom that despite supposedly giving birth, she was still a virgin?

So she would stay alone. Because it was easier for all of them. A small price to pay for her daughter's happiness.

"Mr. Tyler is getting stronger every day," Fayre said as she placed five rolls on a plate. "He's gonna limp for a while, but he's handsome enough to carry it off. I doubt the ladies will mind any."

"You talk as if his famous charm is beginning to work on you," Regan said, trying not to sound disgruntled.

"Oh, I'm young enough to appreciate the gifts God gave that young man." Fayre winked at her. "I'd have to be blind not to."

Regan thought about pointing out the fact that *she* had no trouble ignoring their guest's charms, but she didn't bother. It was one thing to avoid the truth about Amy. It was quite another to flat out lie to a close friend. Besides, if she protested too much about Jackson, Fayre might guess why. She might suspect that Elizabeth's heart hadn't been the only one touched by the handsome gunslinger.

"At least he didn't lose his leg," she murmured.

"Praise be for that," Fayre agreed. "Bad enough to have shot him the way you did. I doubt you could have stood being around yourself if you'd caused permanent damage."

"I would have found a way to get over it," Regan said, wishing Fayre wasn't so willing to speak her mind all the time.

"Oh, sure, you would have because you've got your responsibilities and all, but it would have stayed with you, sticking tighter than a starved leech. Yes sir, in a few months you would have been grumbling at the world, all the while knowing you only had yourself to blame. As much as you try to be like the men, you're just a woman and hurting creatures goes against a woman's ways. If you ask me—"

"I don't believe I did." Regan met her house-keeper's even stare. "His dinner's getting cold," she added, glancing at the full tray.

"So it is." Fayre sniffed. "So I guess you'd better be taking it to him."

"Me?" She set her glass of water on the table in front of her. "I won't."

"I think you might." Fayre's expression turned sly. "Mr. Tyler mentioned he wanted to speak to you tonight."

"He can damn well wait until morning."

Pale blue eyes glared at her. "Just because you work with those cowboys don't mean you can talk like 'em. I won't have you swearing at me, missy."

Regan swallowed. "Yes, ma'am. Jackson can wait until morning. I'm too tired to deal with him now."

"He won't be here come morning. He said he was pulling out come sunup."

"He's leaving?" Relief filled her chest making her heart beat faster. "As simple as that? He's just going to ride out of here without . . ." Without asking any more questions? Without finding out about Amy? It was too good to be true.

"He wasn't that specific with me," Fayre said, picking up the tray and thrusting it at Regan. "He said he was leaving first thing and that he wanted to talk to you tonight."

Fayre unpinned her apron and walked toward the back door. "I'll have Amy back here before her bedtime," the older woman said. "Now get on with you. No sense in his supper getting cold while you stand there with your mouth hanging open."

Regan took the heavy tray. "You're a bossy old

woman," she said, but the tone of her voice was affectionate.

"That I am. It's one of the benefits of my years. I intend to take advantage of every one of them. Next I'm planning on getting crotchety, so you just be prepared."

Regan smiled as Fayre left the kitchen. The house was silent without Fayre, as if Regan had been left alone in the world. Regan's smile faded slowly. She wasn't that lucky. Just a few feet away, on the other side of the kitchen and down the hall, lay Jackson Tyler. If he was really leaving in the morning, she would find it in herself to be pleasant to him before he left. If he planned to make trouble—her fingers tightened on the tray—she would protect what was hers, no matter what the cost.

She moved quickly through the kitchen and dining room, then turned down the hallway. According to Fayre, Jackson had grown stronger every day. It was hard to believe it had been ten days since the shooting. She'd avoided him since the first night he awakened from his four-day sleep. The ranch had kept her busy and away from the house, and what time the ranch didn't use up she filled with other necessary chores. She had no desire to spend her time with Jackson. Unfortunately staying away from him had meant not spending much time with her daughter.

The bedroom door was closed. She balanced the lip of the tray against the chair railing and knocked once. When she heard the deep-voiced "Come in," she turned the knob, then grabbed the tray and stepped inside.

The sun had already dropped below the horizon,

so only the last rays of orange-gold slipped into the large room. Lanterns had been lit on the dresser and beside the bed. Jackson sat in front of the window, looking out toward the fading sunset. His hair hung just past the edge of his collarless white shirt. He'd rolled his sleeves up to his elbows, exposing tanned arms. His shoulders were broad, his back strong.

Her gaze flickered over him, taking in dark trousers and the slight bulge around the middle of his left thigh from the bandage he wore.

He didn't turn around, so she continued to study him. His jawline was clean, as if he'd recently shaved. She inhaled deeply, smelling something faintly masculine. Her palms grew damp. It wasn't the weight of the tray that made her step quickly to the bedside table and set it down. Rather it was her sudden need to shove her hands into her pockets so he couldn't see her trembling.

"Fayre said you wanted to talk to me."

He didn't start at the sound of her voice. Nothing about his posture changed. She wondered if he'd known it was she when she knocked. It made sense. Her step was bound to be different from the housekeeper's. Fayre wore lady's lace-up shoes, while Regan was still dressed for her day on horseback. Her boots clattered on the wooden floor.

"Please, sit down," Jackson said, motioning to the bed.

She didn't move. She wasn't about to sit there. Not with him in the room. "I'll stand."

He turned slowly until his eyes met hers. She'd been so afraid and angry the last time she was in this room. Too distraught to notice the odd gray-green coloring of his eyes, or the way his thick gold lashes framed them.

She hadn't taken the time to study the shape of his mouth, still tempting, as it had been all those years ago.

Now those eyes flickered over her face, then dipped lower to her blouse and skirt. She drew her hands out of her pockets and twisted her fingers together. Today she'd helped the men pull a pregnant cow out of a mud hole. The activity had left a darker streak on her already dirty skirt. Grass, sweat, and bits of cud stained her blouse. Her hair had long since escaped from its braid and now fluttered around her face in carrot-colored corkscrew curls.

Jackson, on the other hand, looked as if he'd just stepped from his weekly bath. For a moment she wished she'd taken the time to put on a clean dress and comb her hair. Then she raised her chin slightly and met his gaze. What did it matter how she looked? She wasn't that foolish young woman who had wanted to give her heart to Jackson Tyler. She wasn't interested in a man like him, and he certainly wasn't interested in her. He wanted his woman to be like Elizabeth. Pretty, delicate, feminine.

"You had a hard day," he said, motioning to her hands.

She glanced down. One of her knuckles was scraped, with a scab just beginning to form over the raw part. Her rolled-up sleeves exposed a bruise by her left wrist and a healing cut on her right forearm.

Without even closing her eyes she could see Elizabeth's pale skin and long, elegant nails. Different from her own tanned, freckled arms. She thought about thanking him for reminding her of all the things she would never be, then thought the sarcasm might let him think his assessment of her mattered.

"Some of us have to work to keep a roof over our heads," she said.

One gold-blond eyebrow raised. "And I don't?"

"That's not exactly what I meant."

"What did you mean?"

"Nothing."

"You could wear gloves," he said. "That scrape looks painful."

It was. It throbbed in time with her rapidly beating heart. But he didn't have to know that. "I don't always have time to put them on. Besides, what does it matter? On the ranch no one cares what I look like."

She would never be Elizabeth and she would never be like the ladies in town with their layers of petticoats and with umbrellas held high to protect them from the sun.

She looked around the room, but Jackson had taken the only chair. She was more tired than proud so she sat on the edge of the bed and crossed her arms over her chest. "Fayre says you're leaving in the morning."

He nodded. "As soon as I get the rest of my things, and what I came for."

She ignored the last part of his statement. If she had to hold off every man in the state of Texas, he wasn't getting her daughter. "All your things are there," she said, pointing at his saddle and saddlebags in the corner of the room. "Your horse is in the barn. I believe that's everything you arrived with."

"The letter's missing."

Regan stared at her scraped knuckle, then at the bruise. Finally she noticed that one short nail had torn off sometime during the day. She rubbed the uneven edge, reminding herself she would have to file it that night.

"What letter?" she asked, not meeting his gaze.

"You know damn well what I'm talking about. Elizabeth's letter."

The one upstairs in her dresser drawer. Yes, she knew which letter. It was wrong of her to keep it from him but much more dangerous for him to have it. If he stared at it long enough, if he read it over and over again, he might realize her sister had written the word *child*, not *son*. He might see his mistake and then start asking questions.

She drew in a deep breath and cleared her mind. Forcing herself to smile slightly, she glanced up at him. "I'm afraid I have no idea what you're talking about. No one has touched your belongings, Jackson."

"You're not a good poker player." His eyes darkened. "Why are you lying?"

"I'm not." She jumped to her feet. She had to convince him. She glanced frantically around the room looking for proof. The armoire stood where it always had, since her father had slept in this room. Of course. She should have thought of it sooner.

She crossed the room and opened the wooden doors. On the top shelf was the old family Bible. She pulled it out and walked crossed over to Jackson. He took it from her.

"What are you trying to trick me with now?" he asked and opened the book. He flipped through until he came to the list of births and deaths in the O'Neil family. His tanned finger moved down the list, past Regan's and Elizabeth's births, past their mother's death, to a single entry.

Amy Beth O'Neil born May 5th, 1869.

"What's this?" he asked.

Her breath caught in her throat. How could she have forgotten? Oh, God, now what?

Her hands fluttered slightly. She wanted to pull the Bible back and run. Instead she stiffened her spine.

"Daniel's cousin," she said, willing her voice to remain calm. "You know how important family is to my father."

He eyed her suspiciously, then looked back at the list. Next was the entry of Elizabeth's marriage to Daniel.

He slapped the book shut and glared at her. "Son of a bitch. Where the hell is my son?"

Something painful flickered in his eyes, something that made her feel a flash of shame for what she was doing. She'd spent the last six years living a lie, but it wasn't her nature to be dishonest. She didn't want to hurt Jackson, not deliberately, but she couldn't risk Amy. She couldn't risk the world she'd carefully woven together from truth and falsehoods.

He was still holding the family Bible. Drawing in a deep breath, she placed her right hand on top of the worn cover and looked into his face.

"As God is my witness, I swear you have no son, Jackson Tyler. Not here, or anywhere that I know of. Elizabeth never bore you a son."

He looked as shocked as he had when she'd shot him.

"You thought I was lying," she blurted out, snatching her hand back as if she feared he might cut it off.

"Of course," he said, his voice low and angry. "Why

not? The damn letter said—" He broke off and glared at her. "Again. Swear again. I want you to say it a second time and promise to burn in hell if you're lying."

She closed her eyes briefly. "All right." She fixed her gaze on him, on his gray-green eyes, on the emotions boiling just below the surface. Her moment of fear surprised her. She wondered if she was headed for the fires of hell, then reminded herself she wasn't lying. Withholding the truth wasn't the same as a lie. Everyone knew that.

She placed her hand back on the Bible. He set his on top of hers, as if to hold hers in place. The pressure distracted her as she felt the heat of him, his dry palm and rough calluses from holding the reins. Then she shook off the feelings. They weren't important. All that mattered was getting Jackson as far away from the ranch as quickly as possible.

"Now," he ordered. "Swear it again." His well-shaped mouth pulled straight, his gaze narrowed.

"I swear on this Holy Bible," she began, her voice shaking slightly. The pressure on her hand increased. She wanted to pull away, but she forced herself to stand before him. "If I'm lying, may I burn in hell for all eternity. Elizabeth O'Neil, my sister, never bore your son, or any man's son. When you left here those years ago, she was not carrying your son. I swear before God that I've spoken the truth."

He pushed her away from him. The quick thrust of his hand against her arm sent her stumbling into the bed. She grabbed the metal footboard for balance, then stared at him. He looked past her to something she couldn't see. The lines of his face tightened with rage.

Slowly, she started moving toward the door. She'd almost reached the handle when he noticed her.

"You wouldn't be thinking of leaving me already, would you?" he asked.

She lunged for the doorknob. Despite his injured thigh, he moved quickly, crossing the room in three limping strides. She would have made her escape if she hadn't stayed to watch him walk, assessing the damage she'd done.

Her hand reached for the knob as his fist connected with the door. She pulled it open slightly, but he slammed it shut. His breath fanned over her face, stirring the curls around her forehead and cheeks. He smelled clean, unlike herself. She smelled like sweat and the cows.

He moved closer, she moved back. They repeated their awkward dance twice more until he wedged her between the dresser and the corner. She had nowhere to go. She stared at the scar on his chin and swore she wasn't afraid.

Long, lean fingers cupped her jaw, squeezing until she looked at him. His touch was hard and unfriendly, threatening to bruise her. "I want my letter," he said.

"I—I don't know what you're talking about." She licked her dry lips.

"You wouldn't be willing to swear on that as well, would you?"

"No." She wouldn't swear to a lie. Not unless she had to.

"I thought not."

She could feel the heat of him and the strength. Funny how, with him so injured and lying in bed all this time, she'd forgotten about his strength. Now that he was recovering, he was regaining it quickly. A few days ago, she would have had a chance against him, but not now.

The fingers tightened. "Why are you doing this? What does it gain you?"

She bit back a cry of pain. "I don't know what you're talking about."

He shifted so that his forearm pressed against her neck. She kept her hands at her sides. She wouldn't let him see that she was afraid. This was her house, her ranch. He wouldn't dare hurt her here.

"What the hell is going on?" he asked. "I came back here because of the letter. Now you claim I have no son. Then why did Elizabeth write me?"

"I don't know." He hadn't applied any pressure yet. He was barely touching her neck. Still, it was hard to breathe, as if the threat was enough to block off her supply of air. She swallowed.

"That's not good enough." He glared at her. "Why did you shoot me?"

"I told you. I thought you were working for Daniel. There's been trouble between us since my father died."

"Why don't I believe that?"

She tried to shrug, but in her position, she couldn't move. He touched her nowhere but at her neck, where his forearm barely brushed against her throat.

"There's more than you're willing to tell me," he said. His soft, almost caressing voice didn't reassure her. He moved forward so that his thighs whispered close to hers and his chest hovered a bare inch from her breasts. "Shall I make you talk?"

She didn't answer. She focused on the scar on his chin and refused to look higher.

"When I leave here, I'm going straight to the sheriff," he said. "I don't give a rat's ass about what your cowboys say. I'm going to tell him what happened and make sure you get locked up before you kill someone."

The first tendril of fear curled through her belly and up her chest. Coldness leadened her legs, and weakened her knees. Involuntarily, she looked up. There was nothing in his eyes. Not anger or disdain or triumph. The emptiness was more frightening than any threat he might have made.

In that moment, before she drew in a sharp breath and turned away, she remembered he was a killer. His trade was death, and men paid him to commit murder.

A small voice whispered that it wouldn't be so bad if she gave him back the letter. But she couldn't. She knew in her heart it was just a matter of time until he figured out the ruse. Then he would return, this time searching for his daughter.

Would the sheriff put her in jail? She swallowed hard.

The fear grew and with it, her imagination. Would there be a trial? How much of the past would come out? Would people guess the truth? They couldn't. Oh, please, God, they couldn't ever know. Jackson would take Amy and then—

She could apologize. She tried to ease away from him, but the walls left her no room. Her shoulder blades pressed into the corner. She could tell him it was all an accident. It had been really. She'd never intended to shoot him. If he hadn't said those things about Elizabeth.

Her eyes slowly closed. No, she couldn't lie to herself. Everyone else, yes, but not herself. Her rage hadn't all been about Elizabeth. Some of it, most of it, had been about herself. About her pride. About the fact that he'd rejected her so long ago and that her young heart had never recovered.

If she was in jail, Daniel would get control of the ranch. Her eyes flew open. She stared at Jackson's scar and his mouth. Dammit, she couldn't let her cousin have the ranch. Everyone was depending on her.

"They'll lock you away," he said, pressing slightly against her throat. "This is Texas, darlin'. They aren't going to care that you're a woman."

She wanted to scream at him that this was all his fault to begin with. If he hadn't chosen Elizabeth—if he'd chosen her instead of her sister. Her breathing grew slightly labored. She fought the fear, ignored the pressure, the tightness at her throat. But he hadn't chosen her. No man had. Elizabeth was the one they'd all wanted. Regan wasn't pretty enough; she didn't know how to flirt or be charming. She didn't get kissed in barns on hot summer nights.

"Damn you, Regan."

"Yes, damn me all you want. That's the only satisfaction you're going to get."

He leaned harder, his arm digging into her throat more. Her thoughts jumped around like an unbroken horse. She would have to send someone ahead to the sheriff to warn him about Jackson. She dismissed the idea. What was the cowboy going to say? "I'm sorry to have to report this, Sheriff, but Miss Regan seems to have shot a man."

Of course. She smiled slightly. That startled Jackson enough to make him stiffen. She reached her hands up and grabbed his forearm. He let her pull him away. She grimaced, wondering if she could have done that at the beginning and not had to endure his closeness. Her pride had always gotten her in trouble.

She ducked under his arm and spun to face him. He turned leisurely and crossed his arms over his chest. The action pulled his white shirt tight across his shoulders, emphasizing his strength.

He was handsome enough to make her want to weep. He'd been her ideal from the first moment she saw him riding up on his bay gelding so long ago. How innocent she'd been. Full of hopes and dreams.

They were all gone now, scattered like fire ashes in a breeze.

"I believe this is what they call a Mexican stand-off," he said slowly. "You give me what I want and I'll be on my way."

"If I don't, you'll go to the sheriff?"

"That's about it."

"I see." But that wasn't about it. She wished it could have been different. She wished he could have once thought of her as a woman. She wished a lot of things. None of that mattered anymore. Wishes were a waste of time. What she had to do now was survive.

To that end she would destroy everything, including the past. Including Jackson. Fayre was right. A man could forgive a lot of things, but not what she'd done to him. Certainly not what she was about to do.

She forced herself to shake her head as if in amazement, then smiled. "Go ahead. Tell the sheriff. I'm sure he'll be impressed. As will the town." She walked toward the door.

"What are you going on about?" he asked, obviously confused.

She clutched the doorknob, then glanced at him over her shoulder. "I'm not concerned about your empty threats. You can't go to the sheriff. What are you going to say? That you were shot by a woman while standing buck naked in a stream?" She chuckled. The dark flush on his cheeks told her he hadn't noticed the false sound of her amusement. "You'll be laughed out of town. Good-bye, Jackson. I'll tell the men to have your horse ready at dawn."

The door closed quietly behind her. Jackson would have felt better if she'd gone ahead and slammed it shut. He swore under his breath. First she'd shot him, then she'd outsmarted him. She was right, damn her sorry hide. There was no way he was going to go to the local sheriff and admit what had happened.

He turned from the door and limped back to the window. He lowered himself into the chair and stared out into the darkness. Nothing made sense. Not Elizabeth's letter, Regan's reaction to seeing him, her stealing his letter and refusing to admit it, and most of all, the apparant absence of his son. With Elizabeth's willingness to give her favors easily, he hadn't been completely convinced the child mentioned in her letter was his. Yet six years ago Elizabeth had feasted like a starved creature, draining him dry again and again. She'd complained that she hadn't had a man in months. So he'd been willing to come see the boy. He'd even been intrigued by the thought of having a son.

He glanced at the Bible resting on the bed where he'd tossed it. Regan might be a lot of things, but she wasn't the type of person who could swear to a lie. He turned back to the window and shook his head.

How did he know that? Six years ago Regan wouldn't have sworn to a lie, but she'd changed since then. She'd grown up and taken charge of her daddy's ranch. She wasn't the gangly half-grown kid he remembered. Nothing was as it had been.

Her eyes hadn't lied. He comforted himself with that fact. He would have been able to see it if she'd been withholding the truth. Being able to sniff out the difference between truth and falsehood had helped keep him alive.

So he didn't have a son. But she had stolen Elizabeth's letter. Why, if what he'd come back for didn't exist?

He leaned against the chair and closed his eyes. It didn't matter. He would leave in the morning. Leave this sorry place and never come back. He had enough money to buy his own spread, somewhere far from the O'Neil ranch. Maybe southern Wyoming. He'd liked it the few times he was there. Maybe he'd—

There was a knock at the door. Jackson didn't bother opening his eyes or turning around.

"What do you want?" he called.

The person didn't answer. There wasn't any sound at all. The hairs on the back of his neck stood up. He opened his eyes and watched the glass in front of him.

Lamplight reflected on the panes, creating a mirror image of the room behind him. He saw the door open slowly, then a tall man dressed entirely in black started to enter the room.

Jackson smiled. He raised his right hand toward the image, curling his last three fingers toward his palm so his thumb and forefinger formed the outline of a gun.

"You're dead, McLane," he said quietly.

The man behind him stopped for a moment, then met his gaze in the reflection. "Hard to shoot with a knife in your back."

"I'd have gotten you first."

"Big talk for a man shot by a woman."

Jackson grimaced. "What are you doing here, you old bastard?"

Gage McLane entered the bedroom and closed the door behind him. He crossed to Jackson's chair and stared down at him. A slow grin cut across his hard, chiseled features, momentarily erasing the threatening expression from his eyes. "Looking better than you. I heard what happened. So a woman really shot you?"

"Yeah, I don't want to talk about it."

"I can't blame you." Gage stuck out his hand. "I wouldn't want to either. I heard she caught you with your pants down. She was so unimpressed by your size she decided to kill you and put you out of your misery."

Jackson stood up and shook the other man's hand. "You'd be grateful to have half of what I've got."

"I see you're still delirious with fever."

"And you're still crawling out from the strangest places."

Gage's grin faded. His hold on Jackson's hand tightened slightly, then he pulled hard once, yanking Jackson toward him. The men hugged briefly.

"It's good to see you, old friend," Gage said quietly, when Jackson had settled on the chair he'd turned toward the room and Gage had taken a seat on the bed.

"You, too." Jackson took in the black hat and jacket, the worn trousers and dusty boots. He'd never seen Gage dressed in anything else. "Don't you have anything in another color? What about brown boots? And you should cut your hair. You look like a renegade half-breed."

"You sound like my mama. I see you're feeling better."

Jackson nodded. "Good enough to be moving on. I'm leaving in the morning."

"Then I'm glad I came by tonight."

Jackson studied his friend. It had been over a year since they'd last worked together. Gage was one of the few men he trusted enough to let cover his back. The respect was mutual, although at last count, Gage owed him.

"Regan hire you?" Jackson asked.

"Me and some others. Bennett, Ives, Quincy. A few more you don't know."

Jackson grimaced. "Ives and Quincy are lazy bastards switching sides according to who has the most money."

"Right now that's Miss O'Neil." As always Gage's expression was unreadable, but that didn't bother Jackson. He knew the other man well enough to be able to sense what he was feeling.

"For how long?" he asked.

"She doesn't have many choices," Gage said. "Most men don't like working for a woman. Fewer yet want to work for a whore."

Jackson sprang to his feet. A sharp pain in his healing thigh screamed that he shouldn't have done that, but he ignored the pulsing muscle. He stared at Gage not sure if he should punch him in the face or ask him to apologize. A stupid reaction, he told himself. In Jackson's weakened condition, Gage would reduce him to a bloody carcass in about two minutes. Besides, why the hell did he care what Gage called Regan?

His friend took off his black hat and stared at the brim. "Of course I don't believe the talk," he said, flicking away a bit of dust. "Miss O'Neil's no whore. If you ask me, I think she's—"

"What are you talking about?" Jackson asked, cutting him off. "Who's calling Regan a whore?"

It didn't make sense. Another woman maybe, but not Regan. No way she could inspire that kind of talk. She wasn't the type to make a man want her bad enough that he would sully her reputation to get her. Besides, he couldn't imagine her unbuttoning enough to bed a man. She would probably spend the entire time giving orders with that bossy mouth of hers. Not that she wasn't sort of attractive. She had a nice-enough bosom, he reminded himself, thinking of how it had felt against his face when she'd helped him sit up. But a whore?

Gage's gaze narrowed. "You've been here over a week, Jackson. Why are you asking me questions?"

"I've been in this damn room. The only people I've seen are Fayre and Regan."

"Sit down before that leg gives out and starts bleeding. Unless you plan on hitting me for bad mouthing your lady friend."

The statement was said deliberately. Jackson didn't rise to the bait. Gage was curious about why Jackson was here and why Regan had shot him. "She's not my lady friend."

"Uh huh."

Jackson lowered himself into the chair and began to massage his thigh. The area around the gunshot was still swollen and red, but the wound itself had started healing. There wasn't any more infection. In another few days he would be able to walk without much of a limp.

"I guess if you're leaving in the morning, you won't be joining us."

Jackson shook his head. "I was just passing through." He wasn't about to get involved with this. Regan had made it clear what she thought about his skills and he was in no hurry to spend more time with her.

"I thought you might be here to take charge."

Jackson glanced at his friend. "Is there a problem?"

Gage continued to turn his hat in his hands. Dark hair fell onto his forehead. He looked relaxed as he shifted his weight and leaned against the footboard. Jackson knew better. Gage didn't relax. He could go from sound sleep to firing a deadly shot in less than a heartbeat.

"Regan's a lot smarter than most of the men I've worked for," Gage said. "Like I said, it's not a problem for me. Some of the hired guns are getting a little restless, though. They want to see something happen, soon. Or they'll make their own trouble."

Jackson knew what that meant. She'd hired men who lived in the shadows of polite society. Men who killed and destroyed for a living. They stayed outside the law and preferred it that way. When things didn't go their way, they had less reluctance than most to exact their own kind of revenge. Boredom was tolerated only a little more than horse stealing.

"Daniel hasn't made a move?" he asked.

"Not since I've been here. There've been a few incidents with the cowboys, but nothing worth mentioning.

That's part of the trouble. The cowboys are insulted that Miss O'Neil hired the men to begin with. The gunslingers make trouble with the cowboys."

"Regan doesn't know what kind of danger she's playing with here," he muttered.

"You could tell her."

Jackson glared at his friend. "*You* tell her. You're her employee."

"I tried. The lady's stubborn."

"I know." He leaned back in the chair and folded his arms over his chest. He refused to let it matter. In the morning he would ride out of here and never look back. He would forget about Elizabeth and Regan, about his son and the letter. He would get on with his life.

"Why do they say she's a whore?" he asked.

Gage placed his hat on his head. "Because of her daughter."

Jackson felt as if he'd been kicked by his horse. "What?"

"You didn't know? She's got a daughter, a real pretty little thing. There's no husband, and as far as everyone knows, no father. You know what ranches are like. Word spreads fast. A child with no husband makes Miss O'Neil a—"

"Don't say it." Jackson slammed his hands down on the arms of the chair. Regan? A daughter? No. "Are you sure it's hers?"

"Who else's would it be? What's wrong with you, Jackson? Why are you so stirred up about this? I thought you were leaving in the morning."

"I am. None of this matters to me. It just doesn't make sense."

"That's because you're slower than a frozen snake."

Jackson grinned. "So why did I save your sorry ass the last time we worked together?"

"You were lucky."

"I was better than lucky."

Gage stared at him for a long moment, then grinned. "That you were, old friend. I still owe you for that one." He rose to his feet. "I've got to get back. It's almost time for my watch. Come by and see me before you leave in the morning."

"I will," Jackson promised.

He watched his friend leave, then leaned back and listened to the silence. Questions whirled around inside his head. He rubbed his temple, but that didn't help settle anything. This was worse than the time he'd gotten sick on bad tequila down Mexico way. At least then the confusion had been imaginary. The images inside his head had faded. Now, every time he learned something new, everything made less sense.

First there was Elizabeth and her damn letter, then Regan, then the fact that she had a daughter. He tilted his head against the chair back and smiled. That bitch. She was smart, he would give her that. Daniel's new cousin. She hadn't even had to lie. He'd never thought that the girl—what was her name?—might have belonged to Regan herself. He remembered odd noises he heard in the house. Fayre had said it was the dog. Instead it had been Regan's daughter. Yup, not a damn thing made sense.

In the midst of all of this, he'd seen Gage again. At least Regan had done one thing right. If anyone could keep her safe, Gage could. Not that he cared, he reminded himself. He didn't give a hoot about Miss Regan O'Neil. He didn't care if she survived this or . . .

His eyes drifted closed. He thought about moving to the bed, but he was too tired. If he slept in the chair, he would be stiff in the morning, but he didn't bother moving. He exhaled a deep breath as weariness washed over him, then gave himself up to the silence. Only a faint scratching by the door disturbed his descent into—

His eyes popped open as he straightened in the chair. A scratching by the door? Gage wouldn't come back. Was it one of the other men? Regan? No, he would have heard her footsteps. She had never learned to walk with the mincing steps of a lady. She clomped around like a cowboy, even in her daintiest shoes. So if it wasn't Gage and it wasn't Fayre or Regan, it must be trouble.

He leaned over to the nightstand and slowly opened the drawer. As soon as he'd been able, he'd moved his pistol close by. His right hand reached for the gun as his left gripped the chair, ready to spring up if necessary. He reminded himself if he hit the floor to roll to his right so his injured leg didn't have to take his weight.

The doorknob turned. He waited, not even bothering to breathe. It wasn't necessary. All he had to do was react.

The door opened, creaking slightly. A small head poked around the edge of the frame. Without thinking Jackson tucked the gun behind him, between the small of his back and the chair.

When the child saw him looking at her, she smiled and entered the room.

"Mama said you was sick, but you don't look sick to me."

He stared at her, not believing his eyes. He didn't know whether to laugh or yell with rage. Damn Regan to hell. She'd tricked him.

The young girl moved closer. Her medium brown hair had been pulled back into two braids that hung over her shoulders down the front of her dirty blue dress. She had wide hazel eyes and a generous smile. Without thinking, he smiled back.

The girl looked exactly like his youngest sister Lily had at that age. He supposed it was his own fault. He'd assumed *child* meant *son*. Regan hadn't lied when she'd sworn on the family Bible. He and Elizabeth hadn't had a son. They'd had a daughter.

5

"Can't you talk, mister?" the child asked.

"I can talk just fine. Who are you?"

The girl smiled engagingly. Jackson grinned in return. She did look amazingly like Lily, although now that she was moving closer, he could see the differences. She had freckles on her nose, which his sister had never had. Her mouth was shaped a little differently, too. More like Elizabeth's.

Even as he made the comparison, there was a part of him that was stunned. A daughter? He had a daughter? He'd assumed his child was a son. He'd even imagined a boy, although one much bigger than the girl. But now that he saw her, he felt as giddy as a two-day-old colt.

"I'm Amy."

"How do you do, Amy? I'm Jackson." He held out his hand.

She hesitated by the foot of the bed, then walked toward him, giggling. Hazel eyes held his as she squirmed a little closer, then offered him her hand. They shook, then she jerked her hand back and tucked it into her skirt pocket.

"I'm not supposed to be here," she whispered loudly, twirling the fingers of her free hand through her left braid.

"Why not?" he asked in the same mock whisper.

"'Cause you're sick and you don't need to be 'stirbed."

"You said I don't look sick."

She dropped her hand to her side and shook her head causing her braids to flip back and forth in front of her face. "You look nice." She tilted her head slightly to one side. It took him a moment to figure out all the fidgeting meant she was shy.

"Mama would yell at me if she knew I was here," Amy told him. She skipped to the side of the bed and leaned against the coverlet. "I heard Fayre telling Uncle Hank that you're gonna leave in the morning, so I came to see you. If you're leaving you can't be too sick to be 'stirbed."

"That makes sense. How old are you?"

"Almost five." She held up her right hand and splayed her fingers. "I'm gettin' big, but Mama won't let me ride a pony. She says I'm still too small."

Amy did look kinda short, but then he didn't know how big five-year-old girls were supposed to be. She was a pretty thing, with a smile that was going to break hearts from here to Kansas City. Something tight knotted in his chest. He had a daughter.

Who apparently knew nothing about him.

"Your mother," he began slowly, careful to keep

the tone of his voice light. He didn't want his sudden burst of temper to scare her off. "She's Regan, right?"

"Uh huh." Amy slipped one leg around the bedpost and leaned against it. She grabbed the round knob at the top with both hands, then swung out and back, pivoting on her standing foot. "Regan O'Neil. I'm Amy O'Neil."

"I sorta figured that." He frowned. "What about Elizabeth?"

Amy stopped suddenly. Her hazel eyes widened. Thick lashes swept down toward her freckled cheeks, then back up. Her small mouth twisted slightly. "Auntie Elizabeth went to live with Baby Jesus in heaven. She's watching me all the time, just like an angel. She likes me best of all the little girls in the world."

She spoke with the confidence of someone who has been told the same story countless times. He didn't know whether he should congratulate Regan on a job well done, or strangle her for spouting lies.

What was going on? Why was she claiming Amy as hers? Apparently she'd never bothered naming a father, and no one had thought to ask. Did she really think she could get away with this? He shook his head. She had gotten away with it. For almost five years. But why had Elizabeth allowed it? And how had they pulled off their deception? Hadn't anyone noticed that Elizabeth had been the one with child, not Regan?

He looked at Amy and saw her glancing past him toward the night stand. The tray Regan had brought still sat there untouched. Amy didn't seem to have a lot of interest in the stew or biscuits, but the pie was clearly fascinating.

"Help yourself," he said, leaning back in the chair.

She licked her lower lip. "Could I?"

He nodded.

She moved closer, along the side of the bed, then grabbed the plate. The fork beside it bounced off the tray to the floor. Amy froze, staring at him. He smiled slightly, then bent forward and picked up the fork. When she figured out she wasn't going to get into trouble, she picked up the piece of pie and took a big bite from the pointy end.

"'licious," she murmured as she chewed.

"Fayre is a good cook."

"I help sometimes," she said, before taking another bite.

"What else do you do?"

"Fayre teaches me reading. I can read by my whole self. I can count to twelve." She licked her fingers thoughtfully. "Sometimes I go in the barn with Pete and he lets me groom horses. They have big feet."

"Yes, they do."

Her little pug nose wrinkled. "I have a mouse in my room. Mama wants to bring in one of the barn cats to catch it, but I want to keep it because she says I'm too small to ride."

He was sure in some way that all made sense, but he couldn't figure it out.

Amy looked around the room. "Grandpa used to sleep here." Her happiness faded and she set the rest of the pie down. "He's in heaven with Auntie Elizabeth. I miss her 'cause she used to bring me pretty ribbons for my hair and she smelled nice. But she always cried a lot and I don't like Uncle Daniel. Grandpa used to read me stories and tell me secrets." She smoothed her dress down with her hands. "I can't tell you none, 'cause then they wouldn't be secrets. I miss him the most of everyone."

She sighed, then glanced up at him through her lashes. "One time he took me fishing. We caught seven whole fish, and I got one all myself. Mama let me cook it for dinner and . . . "

She continued to chatter on about her fishing trip. Jackson stared at her, not quite sure if this was really happening, or if he would wake up in the morning with a headache and only a faint memory of a night-time visitation.

He leaned forward in the chair so that he could study Amy more closely. Lamplight made her brown hair gleam. It had been parted neatly before being braided. Her bangs were long, to the edge of her delicate eyebrows. She had lightly tanned skin that looked as soft as a fawn's belly. She was his child.

He wanted to gather her up in his arms and hold her close. He wanted to proclaim her to the world as his. The swelling of pride surprised him. But he didn't care. She was his.

Regan would have let him ride away without saying a word. He cursed her silently, all the while nodding as Amy chatted on. She'd played him perfectly. He felt like a patsy who'd lost his stake to a rigged game.

"I swear on this Holy Bible that you don't have a son."

She'd never said anything about a child. Or a daughter. He was going to make her pay for this. Maybe he would ride to the sheriff in the morning. Not only had she shot him in cold blood, but she'd kept his child from him for all these years.

"Now that Grandpa's gone to be in heaven, Mama runs the ranch herself," Amy was saying. "She's very busy and important." She sighed. "She can't always tell me a story before I go to bed, but if she comes home early, she usually does."

Amy was as pretty as Lily, and just as bright. A real charmer. He fought a frown. Thank God she hadn't turned out like her lying, cheating aunt.

Amy paused, seeming to expect some praise of Regan from him.

"Ah, I'm sure she works very hard to keep everything running smoothly."

She nodded vigorously. "Uncle Daniel's a damned menace."

He burst out laughing.

Amy drew her eyebrows together. "It's not funny."

"I know, darlin', but I don't think anyone wants you to go around saying things like that."

"Like what?"

"Damned menace."

"Is menace a bad word?"

"Ah, not really. It's the other one."

Her eyes widened. She leaned forward on the edge of the bed. "Really?"

He nodded.

"I won't say it no more."

"Good for you. No more eavesdropping either."

She flushed. "I know," she said, hanging her head slightly. "Mama tells me that all the time. I can't help it, though. 'dults are more 'tresting than anybody."

He understood the 'dults part, but 'tresting? "Interesting?"

"Uh huh."

He had to agree. He was very interested in having a conversation with Regan. "I'll speak to her before I go to town," he said without thinking.

"You're going to town?" Amy's pink lips parted slightly. "Golly."

"Sure. Haven't you been before?"

"Never. Mama doesn't want me to go." Amy glanced toward the closed door, then leaned closer. "Something bad happens in town. I heard Pete talking about it one day. They say things, but I didn't understand 'xactly what."

Amy wasn't the only one who was confused. What bad thing could be happening in town? Maybe the townspeople didn't take kindly to Regan claiming Amy as her own without marrying the father. But that answer put him back at the top of his list of questions. Why would Regan deliberately ruin herself to claim a child that wasn't even hers? Had Elizabeth forced her so that she could claim to be innocent? Jackson snorted. Elizabeth? Innocent? According to her, she'd discovered the wonders that could occur between a man and a woman about the time she'd turned fourteen.

"Do you think the people in town don't like my mama?" Amy asked.

The question caught him off guard. "I'm sure they like her fine."

She didn't seem satisfied by his answer. "She's the best mama ever." She glared at him. "Do you like her?"

"I don't know her very well."

"She's very nice."

"I'm sure she is," he said between gritted teeth. Nice wasn't the word he was thinking. He swore to himself that before he left her, he was going to know the truth. All of it. Somebody somewhere had to have answers.

"What about your father?" he asked Amy, wondering what lies Regan had told her. "Where's he?"

Amy drew in a deep breath, as if it was a long story. "He's gone."

Somehow he'd expected more. "Do you know where?"

She nodded. "He's in heaven, too. Heaven sure has a lot of people."

"It seems that way."

She smiled. "My daddy was a very handsome cowboy. Mommy says he had a special smile and big eyes. She says I have his eyes. I never saw him. He died before I was borned."

He looked closely at her face. The hazel color reminded him of Lily, but Regan was right, Amy had inherited the shape from him. He returned her smile, feeling slightly mollified by what she was telling him. At least Regan hadn't told his daughter that her father was a part of a prison chain gang. He wasn't surprised at the claim of death. No doubt Regan never expected to see him again.

"One day he was herding cattle across a river. It was a long way from here." Amy shifted on the bed so that she was sitting on her heels with her knees out in front of her. "The water was very cold and deep. One of the cows slipped. He went to help it. The rushing water pulled at him. His foot got stuck, but he still tried really hard to save the cow."

Jackson bit back a groan. He didn't like the way this story was going. He should have figured Regan wouldn't have his best interest at heart.

"Then what happened?" he asked, not sure he wanted to hear the rest of it.

"He couldn't get his foot out, and the water came faster. He pushed really hard and got the cow out. But it turned around in the swirling water and sat on him."

"What?" Jackson roared, half-rising from the chair. Amy ducked away from him. He saw the flicker of fear in her eyes. He forced himself to sit back down. "I'm sorry," he said more quietly. "Go ahead."

"He drowned."

Jackson closed his eyes. A cow sat on him and he drowned? Was that the best she could come up with?

"It's not the cow's fault," Amy said gently. "When Mama told me what happened, I got angry at the cow, but Mama said it was just an 'cident. That Daddy should have watched what he was doing." She smiled brightly. "It's hard work to be a cowboy."

"I know," he muttered. He was going to kill her. He didn't care if she was a woman. He was going to find her and strangle her. No, strangling was too good for her.

How dare she tell Amy such a stupid story? He understood why Regan would want to say Amy's father was dead, but did it have to be so damned ridiculous? Couldn't it have been a noble death, maybe saving someone in a fall wildfire, or even a quick broken neck from being thrown off a bronco?

Sat on by a cow and drowned! By God, he would make her pay for that and everything else she'd done to him.

Amy sighed. "I should go. Fayre is cleaning up the kitchen, but she's going to want to put me to bed soon." She looked up at him. "Mama had to go to the barn and be with a sick horse, so she couldn't tell me a story tonight, but talking to you has been almost as nice."

"Thanks," he said. He liked her as well.

"Maybe you don't have to go in the morning and we can talk some more."

"I'd like that."

"Really?" Her eyes widened. "I'll show you my mouse if you'd like." Her voice dropped to a whisper. "But don't say nothing to Fayre. She doesn't want a mouse in the house."

"I won't say a word."

She slipped off the bed and skipped to the door. Once there, she turned back toward him. Fidgeting as much as she had when she'd first come in, she twisted a braid between her fingers.

"Night," she called as she opened the door and stepped out into the hallway.

"Good night, Amy," he said as he sat in the room alone.

He rose slowly to his feet, ignoring the pain in his thigh. A daughter. He had a daughter. A grin split his face. "Hot damn and hallelujah." Then his smile faded and his gaze narrowed. Since he showed up here he'd been shot at while naked and unarmed, stolen from, lied to, found out he had a daughter, and had her tell he'd died like a fool. All in all, Regan O'Neil had a lot of explaining to do.

The kitchen was empty, but the lights were still on. He sat down at the table and waited. Shortly he heard rapid, light footsteps on the wooden floor. Seconds later Fayre entered the kitchen.

At first she didn't notice him. When she looked up and saw him by the window, she gasped, then put her hand against her chest.

"Lord have mercy, Mr. Tyler, you about scared me out of year's life. And I don't have that many years left."

"I doubt that, Fayre. You're going to outlive us all." Especially Regan, he thought, tightening his hands into fists and thinking about how hard he was going to squeeze. He should have done it while he'd had the chance.

"You're looking fine this evening," she said, moving to the counter and pouring water from the stove into a large metal basin.

"My leg is much better."

"I'm glad to hear it. I'll pack you up some food to take with you in the morning." She added soap flakes and stirred the water until it got frothy. Then she started washing the cups.

"I won't be leaving in the morning."

The mug in her hand slipped into the basin. It bumped hard against the metal bottom but didn't break. Slowly she turned and looked at him.

"I thought you were feeling better."

"I am." He rose to his feet, towering above her slight height. "I met Amy tonight."

Fayre held his gaze steadily, then returned to her washing. "I hope she wasn't a bother."

"Not at all." He moved closer. "We had an interesting chat. She's a very charming little girl."

"Full of trouble, that one."

"So like her mother?" he asked.

Fayre didn't answer.

He leaned against the counter, leaning on one

hip and resting his weight on his good leg. "Where's Regan?"

"She's out in the barn with a sick horse. She could be all night."

"I've got time."

He limped back to the table and sat down. Fayre continued to work in silence. When she was finished, she poured two cups of coffee and brought them with her. She took the seat opposite him. After smoothing back a strand of hair, she studied him.

"Why'd you come back, Mr. Tyler?"

"Don't you think it's time you called me Jackson? After all, we had that one night."

She laughed. "I told you I was teasing you about making that old bed screech. But all right. Jackson. What are you doing here?"

"Elizabeth sent for me."

"Elizabeth's been dead for quite some time."

"I know. She sent a letter." He picked up the mug of coffee and leaned toward her. "Didn't Regan tell you about this?"

"No, and I didn't ask. I'm just the housekeeper here. I don't make it my business to know everything that's going on."

He grinned at that. "Of course you don't, Fayre. Elizabeth sent me a letter. Probably just before she died. She said that we'd had a child together and asked me to come back for her and the child."

Fayre's gray eyebrows rose. "You don't say. Elizabeth never had a child."

"What about Amy?"

"Amy belongs to Regan. I thought you were sweet on Elizabeth."

Sweet wasn't exactly the word he would have used to describe what happened between him and Elizabeth all those years ago. But he didn't want to upset Fayre. Mostly because he suspected she knew everyone's secrets, even if she wasn't supposed to and didn't want to admit the fact.

"You're right," he said. "Elizabeth is the one I was sweet on. So don't you find it odd that Regan is the sister claiming to have had a child?"

Pale blue eyes turned icy. Fayre pushed to her feet. "Seeing as you're feeling so spry, I think it would be best if you left right now."

"I'm not leaving until I get some answers."

"I have none to give you."

"You're lying."

"Perhaps, Mr. Tyler, but you can't prove it."

Jackson watched her walk out of the kitchen, then he settled back in his chair. He was going to get his answers tonight—no matter how long it took.

Regan climbed the back porch steps. If she had been weary when she returned home in the early evening, now, near dawn, she was exhausted. The effort of putting one foot in front of the other had her thinking about simply sleeping on a sofa in the parlor. She didn't have the strength to climb the stairs.

There was a light on in the kitchen. Fayre had left coffee on the stove, but Regan couldn't imagine picking up the pot and pouring a mug. She'd already washed outside, as best she could. Her hair was loose around her face, her split skirt dirty, her boots caked with straw and horse manure. She smelled bad and felt worse. But the horse would survive.

Regan leaned against the entrance to the kitchen and braced herself. She bent down and pulled off her boots, then left them by the door. She didn't want to think about it, but she had no choice. In the morning she would have to talk to Mike about what had happened in the barn. The door to the gelding's stall hadn't been secured and the animal had gotten out. He'd wandered into the feed bin and eaten too much grain before he'd been caught. They might have lost the animal completely. She couldn't afford to lose a good horse. If Mike did it again, Regan was going to have to let him go.

She sighed heavily, hating that part of her job. Before her father had died, she'd had him beside her when she'd fired people. His quiet, strong presence had given her the strength to handle the unpleasant chores. Now she had no one to lean on.

She pulled her hair off her face, then rubbed her burning eyes. At least Jackson was leaving in the morning. That was a blessing.

She inhaled deeply, then froze. There was something in the air. A faint male scent. It was as if her thoughts had brought him to her. She dropped her arms to her sides, her right hand bumping her pistol. At first she thought the kitchen was empty, but then she spotted him sitting on a chair in the shadowy corner. He had his bad leg propped up on a stool. The pool of light cast by the lamp on the counter fell far short of his figure. She couldn't read his expression, but the knot in her gut told her he wasn't smiling.

"You're up early," she said, wondering why he was

waiting for her. Please, Lord, she didn't want to know if it was bad.

"I haven't been to bed yet."

His voice was quiet enough to match the late hour, but there was a sharp edge to his words. As if the sounds had been formed by honed steel instead of air. She forced herself to cross to the stove and pour herself some coffee. Taking the full mug with her, she moved the lantern closer until its soft glow swept over the kitchen table. Only then did she risk looking directly at Jackson.

She wished she hadn't. He looked much as he had earlier, with clean clothes and freshly washed hair. However, something cold and deadly stared out at her from his eyes. Tonight, in this hour closer to dawn than midnight, the color had fled his irises, leaving behind expressionless gray. A single lock of the gold blond hair fell across his forehead. But brushing it away made as much sense as tangling with a wildcat.

The fear was a tangible thing. An icy whisper that blew across her skin and made her shiver. She reminded herself she'd seen this man naked and shot him. As he'd pointed out, she'd had her chance with him. She wouldn't get another one.

The fear moved up her spine, across her chest to her throat, where she suddenly felt the pressure of his forearm against her skin. She didn't know whether to stay or leave. She wanted to run more than she wanted to draw her next breath. So instead she crossed the room and sat across from him at the table.

His gaze flickered over her, dismissing her. She should have been relieved. Instead she was disappointed. He'd never seen her as a woman. Not that she blamed him tonight. She was dirty and smelly, her hair loose and tangled, her face smudged with grime and sweat. New scrapes and scars marred her hands. She was no man's ideal, while Jackson could cause the sternest of female hearts to beat faster.

"Are you eager to be on your way?" she asked, after clearing her throat. She was pleased her voice sounded so calm.

"Not as eager as I was."

Uneasiness flickered along side the fear. "Did—" She licked her lips. "Did something happen tonight?" Had he changed his mind? Oh, please, not that. She couldn't bear to think what would happen if he stayed.

"I had an interesting conversation with Gage McLane."

She frowned, confused. That wasn't what she'd expected him to say. "The gunfighter? Why would you talk with him?"

"Gage and I have been friends for a long time."

That made sense. Why wouldn't gunfighters know each other? She knew that's what Jackson did; it was why her father had hired him in the first place. But when she thought of Jackson it had always been here, on the ranch, not outside in the world killing people.

"You seem surprised," he said.

"That you would know Mr. McLane? I suppose I am. I've heard he's very good."

Jackson shifted in his chair. He tilted his head forward slightly so that the light and shadows cast by the lamp shifted, hiding his eyes. "Gage is the best. And dangerous."

"That's why I hired him."

"Daniel has you running scared."

"I don't see anyone running." Except maybe you. But she didn't say that. She didn't have to. Jackson was leaving in the morning. They both knew he wasn't going to go to the sheriff and report the shooting. Once he was gone, she would be free of him. He couldn't hurt her or threaten her anymore. She should feel better about everything. But she didn't. She watched him as cautiously as she would watch a rattler sunning on a rock. At any moment he could strike out at her.

Why was it so easy for her to forget how dangerous he was? Maybe it was because she wanted to. Because she couldn't reconcile the danger with the man who had, so long ago, stolen, then trampled her heart.

Even now, even when she knew he could destroy her world, she felt herself responding to his masculine presence. She spent her days surrounded by men, yet only Jackson had this power over her. Only he could make her breathing quicker, her heart beat faster, her body lean toward his. Only he could remind her of her inadequacies, make her long to be pretty and feminine. Only he made her forget what was important in her world.

"Gage said you have a daughter."

He made the statement so calmly, she thought she'd misheard him. Regan caught her breath, then swallowed hard. The pressure on her throat seemed to increase. A daughter. Not that. Anything but that. She would rather lose the ranch than risk Amy.

Schooling her features into polite indifference, she glanced at her hands and studied the scrape on her knuckles. "Yes?"

"I find that fascinating. You, of all people, Regan. Giving in to passion. I'm impressed."

His mockery hurt her. She bit the inside of her lip to keep from lashing out at him.

"What's the child's name?"

"Amy."

"It's so curious, don't you think? That you would have this child. A daughter. And you and I never shared a bed."

He knows. She felt it in her bones. She felt it in the reminder of his rejection and the flash of pain that followed. She felt it in the panic as she wondered what she was going to do now. Could she run? Just get a horse and ride until all of this was behind her.

"I should think not," she said, her voice shaking. "You're far from my type, Jackson. You're not Amy's father."

"Liar."

Did he mean both statements, or just the last, she wondered frantically.

He stood up and moved toward her, his limping stride menacing. "Amy visited me tonight. She is mine, Regan. Mine and Elizabeth's. I'll see you in hell for keeping her from me."

6

Her first instinct was to demand he tell her who had exposed her secret. But she didn't. No one knew. Fayre suspected, but she would never say anything. She loved Amy as much as Regan did. She would never risk the child. There wasn't a soul on the entire ranch who could betray her. So how had he found out?

She stared up at him, praying he couldn't see the fear in her eyes. She had to tilt her head back to see his face, the coldness there, the promise of retribution. She had to be strong enough to save her child. He could never really know. He'd made a guess. She would convince him otherwise.

"I told you earlier. You and Elizabeth never had a child. I swore on the Bible. Why do you doubt me now?"

"You swore we had no son, you lying bitch." He leaned down and grabbed her loose hair in his hand.

Before she could pull away, he twisted the curls around his fingers, jerking tight. She cried out in surprise, then clamped her lips together.

"Why?" he demanded. "Why did you do it? Why did you lie?" He pulled hard, forcing her to her feet. Once she was standing, he grabbed her right upper arm with his free hand and held her fast. "Tell me, dammit!"

She thought he might rip her hair from her head. Tears sprang to her eyes. She fought them back, as she did the whimper of pain that hovered on her lips. His fingers dug into her skin, branding her. She was close enough to feel his breath on her face, close enough to smell his rage.

She refused to be intimidated. She forced herself to stare at him, at his cold gray eyes and stern mouth. "You and Elizabeth had no child together. No son, no daughter."

His expression was as friendly as a wildcat's snarl. "Are you willing to swear to that? On the family Bible?"

Up until she'd brought Amy back and claimed her as her own, Regan had spent most Sundays in church, weather permitting. She knew about the fires of hell and the risks to her immortal soul. She knew the price of swearing to a lie in the presence of God. She also knew the value of her child.

She looked up at him, forcing all her hatred and anger into her glare. "Yes, I will."

He surprised her by dropping his hands to his sides and stepping back. "What is going on here?" he asked. "What are you doing? Are you trying to convince me I'm crazy? Hell, lady, I don't need your help for that. Coming back here was about the dumbest thing I ever did. I wish to hell Elizabeth had never sent me that letter."

"So ignore it," she blurted out. "Leave in the morning. Put all of this behind you and get on with whatever you were doing before you came here."

"At least you've admitted the letter exists."

She almost stomped her foot in irritation. How had he done that? She would have to be more careful. "So what if it does? Amy is my child. As you already pointed out yourself, you and I never shared a bed."

He reached out toward her. She started backing up, then stopped herself. No matter what, she wouldn't show fear. Not to him. Not if it killed her. He touched a single finger to her cheek. The soft contact sent a shiver racing to her feet where her toes curled inside her thick woolen socks. It was good that Jackson saw her as less than a woman. If he knew how she reacted to his slightest attention, all the advantages would be his.

"So who did?" he asked.

She blinked. "Who did what?"

"Who shared your bed? Who took your innocence, Regan? What man dared steal Sean O'Neil's favorite daughter's most prized possession? Who played the old man for a fool?"

He baited her perfectly, playing on her love for her father and family pride. She wanted to scream out that no one had. She wouldn't have done that to her father. Only she'd done much worse. She'd broken her father's heart when she'd returned with Amy. He'd asked her once. Asked the name of the man. She'd refused to say and he'd never asked again. She'd seen the questions in his eyes as Amy grew, but she ignored them. What could she have done? The lie had been spoken, her path chosen. Even if she'd wanted to explain the truth to her father, she couldn't have. Elizabeth had already married Daniel. Regan was afraid that her father might think Amy belonged with Elizabeth. Regan would have done anything to keep the little girl away from Daniel's evil influence.

The finger on her cheek drifted slowly to her chin. She tried to ignore the feeling skittering along her arms and down her back. A single touch by this man reduced her to a quivering, mindless female.

"There wasn't a man, was there?" he asked softly. "I'd bet my last silver dollar that you're still a virgin."

She was so caught up in the sound of his voice, in the way his eyes held hers that she didn't really pay attention to what he was saying. When the words sank in, she blanched, then drew away from him.

"How dare you say that to me? This is not a discussion I choose to have with you or any man."

Jackson's eyebrows drew together. "Yup, my last silver dollar for sure. You think if I took all this information to the sheriff, he'd order you to be examined by a doctor? I suspect they might be able to tell that sort of thing."

Regan swallowed hard and started backing up. That was the last thing she needed. What if the doctor *could* tell she hadn't been with a man? If everyone knew she was a virgin, they would know Amy wasn't hers. Jackson would be able to take her child.

She tasted the fear and fought the panic. "He was a drifter. A cowboy hired for the roundup. We fell in love. He had brown hair and hazel eyes, just like Amy."

She'd expected several reactions from Jackson, but

not a self-satisfied smile. Not a slight relaxing of his posture as he shifted his weight to his good leg.

He folded his arms over his chest. "Then explain to me why she looks so much like my youngest sister."

The room swept around her, fading to black. Regan clutched at the table, then sat heavily in one of the chairs. His sister? Amy looked like his sister?

"No," she said softly. "No, she doesn't. You're just saying that to frighten me. I refuse to believe it."

"I don't care what you believe, it's true." He bent toward her. "What I want to know is why. Why didn't someone get in touch with me? Why didn't Elizabeth write sooner?"

Because she didn't want you to know, you bastard, Regan thought, glaring at him. But she couldn't say that. She couldn't tell him the truth. Too many lies to remember. Too many stories to keep straight.

"Amy isn't yours," Regan said. "Even if she was, you have no right to come back after all this time."

"I didn't know before," he said impatiently. "I came as soon as I got Elizabeth's letter."

"How convenient." She glared at him. She didn't care that his green-gray eyes flashed anger. She had some rage of her own to share. "You're so fired up ready to blame people for what's happened to you," she said, pointing a finger at his leg. "What about what you brought on yourself? You seduced my sister, then rode away without giving a single thought to how you were leaving her. You didn't bother to find out if you'd broken her heart or—"

She pressed her lips together. She'd been about to say "left her with child." That would have given it all away. After so many years of keeping silent, talking about what happened with Amy was difficult. She wasn't used to having to share part of the truth. Everyone had always believed the lies.

Jackson threw up his hands. "What the hell are you talking about? Seducing your sister? Elizabeth? Darlin', your sister was giving it to every unrelated man under the age of fifty."

Regan sprang to her feet. "Get out," she said loudly. "Get out right now, Jackson Tyler, or I won't be responsible for what I do."

"We all know what you do when you don't get your way, little girl," he said, moving closer to her. "You shoot anyone who doesn't agree with you."

She flushed but refused to back down. "You'll apologize for the filth you said about Elizabeth."

"Damned if I will."

Their faces were inches apart. She could see his individual whiskers, the shape of his mouth, the changing color of his eyes. His temper should have frightened her, but it didn't. It made her feel alive. She wanted him to take her in his arms and kiss her. She hated herself for her weakness. She hated him more.

"I want you out of my house and off my property. Either you leave now, or I'll force you to." Even as she made the threat, she could feel the weight of the holster against her left hip. She didn't think she could shoot him again. Pray God she didn't have to find out what she was capable of.

"I'm not leaving until I know exactly what's going on here. I want the truth."

"The truth is six years ago you left and didn't bother coming back." Her loose hair tumbled over her shoulders and onto her chest. It rose and fell with her rapid breathing.

Jackson reached toward her and took a strand in his fingers. He rubbed it, as if testing the texture and softness. The bright red curl slipped around his hand as if it was as eager to be close to him as she was.

"Why?" he asked quietly. "Why the lies? Why do you claim Amy as your daughter? Why does everyone believe you? What did Elizabeth have to gain, and why did you sacrifice yourself for her?"

If he'd continued yelling, she might have been able to resist him, but the gentleness was her undoing. She swayed toward him. No one had ever asked that before. No one knew to bother with questions at all. They accepted what she'd told them. Even her father hadn't suspected the falsehood. Why would he? Regan had never lied to him before.

"Was it worth it?"

Yes. But she didn't speak the word aloud. She couldn't. "Go away," she whispered, pleading.

"Not until I get some answers."

"You'll destroy everything if you stay."

"I don't care. I want to know what happened here. I want to find out the truth."

His expression didn't change, nor did he stop rubbing her hair. But she knew then. His gentleness was just another trick. He didn't mean it. He didn't care about her sacrifice, or the past. This was all for his benefit. He didn't care about her or the lives he would ruin. He wanted his answers. At any price.

She closed her eyes briefly. Amy flashed through her mind. The sweet little girl was the innocent in all of this. She was the one who would suffer the most. What if Jackson wanted to take her away? What if he went to the sheriff? Could she, Regan, be put in prison for what she'd done? What would happen to the ranch then? What would happen to Amy? Would he take her child away from all that she'd known? She couldn't let that happen. No matter what. She would save Amy at any price.

Without thinking, she moved her right hand across the front of her body toward the pistol. With one fluid, practiced reach, she drew out her gun and pointed it at Jackson's belly.

"I won't let you take Amy," she said. "I'll kill you first."

Jackson stared at her, mad enough to wrestle a grizzly bear. He cursed loudly. Every time he and Regan were together, she got the drop on him. If he tried hiring out as a gunslinger now, he would be laughed clear to Canada.

He'd known she was carrying a pistol. He'd seen it when she walked in the kitchen. But he'd been too busy arguing about Amy to bother taking it away from her. Which was why he was now staring down the barrel and wondering if she was really going to do him in. He didn't doubt she had the skill and the courage.

He'd never been so humiliated in his entire life. Not counting the time she and her men had gotten the drop on him while he was naked.

Why had he thought coming here was a good idea?

"I mean it," Regan said.

He looked at her, disgusted with himself. Something caught his attention. Some whisper of an idea. He kept his gaze on her, all the while focusing, trying to figure out what exactly his finely honed senses were trying to tell him.

He studied the shadows under her eyes and the

lines of exhaustion around her mouth. The pistol trembled slightly, even when she clamped her other hand around her wrist to steady herself. She'd been up all night with a sick horse, not to mention worrying about Daniel and having unexpected, unwanted company in the house.

"All right, Regan," he said, slowly raising his hands to shoulder level. "You win this round."

"You'll be out of here by morning?" she asked.

"Why make me wait until then. I can find my way in the dark."

"I'd rather wait and have one of my men escort you to the edge of my property."

"That's fine. Whatever you think is best."

While they talked, he kept his attention on her. He watched the barrel dip slightly.

"You can sleep in the barn for the rest of the night," she said.

She was relaxing. He could see it in the way her shoulders slumped slightly. He was close enough. Now!

He lunged toward her. He grabbed the hand gripping the pistol and jerked it up toward the ceiling. She spun away, trying to break free of his hold. It didn't help. Before she could call out, he'd squeezed her hand cruelly, forcing her to release the gun. He caught it as it fell and tucked it into the waistband of his trousers.

She tried to break away, but he held her fast, one arm around her waist, the other at her throat.

"Didn't we already do this?" he asked. When she didn't answer, he laughed humorlessly. "No one's going anywhere tonight, Regan, so just relax. I mean to get my answers."

"Never. I won't give you the satisfaction."

"Then maybe I'll have to take what I want." He grabbed her shoulders and jerked her around until she was facing him. He'd meant to frighten her into telling him the truth, but when he saw the terror in her eyes, he realized she'd thought he meant something else. Something ugly, like rape.

He felt lower than the slime on the bottom of a rock. Jesus, he'd never deliberately forced a woman in his life. Without thinking, he released her and backed up slightly. "I didn't mean what you're thinking. I—"

Before he could finish, Regan rushed at him. She raised her knee and jabbed him hard in the crotch, then reached behind him for the pistol. Pain exploded in his balls, forcing the air from his chest and making his stomach seize up as if he might retch. His bad leg buckled and he fought against going down.

Regan's arms around him actually saved him. He pushed off her, struggling for balance. She twisted around him, trying to reach the gun.

"Enough," he said, barely able to force the word out past the pain. He was tired of being nice. Of playing fair. She didn't give a rat's ass about anything except what she wanted. So it was time to get her attention.

He straightened and grabbed her wrists. She struggled against his strength, but he simply held her arms until she'd tired herself. It didn't take long. Using his body weight, he forced her to turn, then walk backward toward the kitchen counter. When she pressed up against the cupboards, he stepped right in front of her so his lower body pinned hers in place. Then he took both her arms and drew them behind her. He held her wrists with one hand and took her face in his other.

Her bright hair fell loose over her dusty ivory

blouse. Her face was pale, her expression wary. She licked her lips, then glared defiantly.

She was a wild woman. Untamed. Fearless in the presence of danger but terrified at the thought of being taken by a man. She was tough. He had the bullet holes and bruises to prove it. And she was smart. If she wasn't being such a pain in the rear, he might have liked her for her tenacity. But he didn't trust her.

He tightened his hold on her jaw. "Now we talk," he said.

"I have nothing to say." She pushed against him.

Her hips and belly moving against him would have been pleasant—at any other time. Right now all the brushing and thrusting made the aching worse.

"If you're trying to get me in the mood, darlin'," he said provocatively, "you should have thought about that before you tried to damage my privates." She flushed. "But if you keep moving like that, I might still be able to work up some interest."

"You're disgusting."

"And you're a lying bitch."

His switch from teasing domination to pure anger shocked her. Her eyes widened and she flinched from him.

"Amy's mine," she said. "I won't let you have her. Ever."

"Then I'll have to force things. I'll wire my sister in the morning. She could be here in less than a week. One look at her, and everyone would know the truth."

"By the time she got here, Amy and I would be gone. You'd never find us."

"Don't be so sure. Finding people on the run and bringing them to justice is what I do best."

"I'm not afraid of you."

"You've always had more guts than sense."

She jerked her head back, trying to break free of his hold. He let her go because it suddenly disturbed him to see her held captive, even by him. He wasn't a complete fool, though. He continued to hold on to her hands and press his lower body firmly against hers.

"What are you going to do now?" he asked. "I'll find you wherever you go. How far do you think you'll get with a five-year-old girl? How long can you keep her on the run? Even if I don't find you, someone else will."

"What will you do with her?" she asked.

"What do you mean?"

"I'm asking you the same question you asked me. What are you going to do with a five-year-old girl? Are you going to take her with you on your next job? Do you plan to teach her how to be a gunfighter? She's a little small to be able to hold a pistol, let alone a rifle. I guess she could take care of the ammunition for you. That's something."

He opened his mouth, then closed it. He didn't have an answer for her. What would he do with Amy if he took her away?

"You show up here after all this time, looking for your son. What were you going to do, Jackson? You must have had some kind of plan." She shook her head, then went on. "Did you ever stop to think your son might have a family here that he cared about? Did you think you would just take him away from everything he'd ever known? Did you think he wouldn't care or miss everyone? What about the people who love him? Were they just to be left behind? Were you going to rip him away without another thought?"

Again he had nothing to say. Regan was right. He hadn't thought it through. He'd gotten the letter and reacted.

"I don't have a son," he pointed out. "I have a daughter."

Her blue eyes filled with scorn. "You have nothing. No child, no home, no honor. You're a hunter and a killer. Nothing more. Is that the legacy you want to pass on to your child?"

"Easy for you to say. Honor sounds nice when you have a big house and your belly's full, but honor doesn't build that house or pay for the food."

"Honor keeps a man alive when he has no hope," she said. "If you had a scrap of it, you would ride away and forget about all of this. After all, you've been gone for six years and we've gotten along fine without you."

"I have a child."

"No, you don't. Besides, even if you did, you never cared enough to show up before now."

"I didn't know before now," he reminded her. "I didn't know until I got Elizabeth's letter. I came back as soon as I knew."

"Why didn't you bother finding out the truth before you left? If you'd taken the time to know whether or not Elizabeth was carrying your child, we wouldn't be talking about this now."

"You're right." He stared at her. "If I'd taken the time to find out, as you pointed out, I'd be married to your sister right now, wouldn't I?"

The last bit of color fled her face. She hadn't thought about that. "What, Regan? Wouldn't you want me for a brother-in-law? I couldn't be worse than Daniel."

She looked away from him, but not before he saw a trace of pain reflected in her eyes.

"Now what?" she asked, still not meeting his gaze.

Good question, he thought. Now what? His plan had been vague at best. He'd assumed he would ride onto the O'Neil ranch and claim the son who had been waiting patiently for him. He'd never thought the child would be a girl, or that she would be so young. In his mind, his son was eleven or twelve. It made no sense; he'd only been gone six years. But he hadn't put the facts together. He'd been too caught up in the daydream to think about what had really happened.

He wanted to start a ranch somewhere. He had the cash, the experience, and the time. Amy changed everything. What was he going to do about her?

Blue eyes bore into his. He met Regan's gaze, then looked at her face, really studying her for the first time that evening. She had freckles across her straight nose, but if he remembered correctly, her father had had freckles as well. Her mouth was well shaped, fuller on the bottom than on the top. Her skin was tanned, but smooth. It had felt soft when he touched her. Soft and warm. She smelled of horses and sweat. Not unpleasant, just different from the ladies he usually chose.

Something stirred in his groin. He ignored the sensation, knowing there was no way in hell he was going to get interested in Regan O'Neil. She was ten kinds of trouble he didn't need, not to mention more likely to castrate him than take him willingly to her virgin bed.

"You don't look anything like Amy," he said.

"She doesn't look anything like Elizabeth, either. That doesn't prove anything."

"She does look like my sister. That's proof."

Regan shook her head. "No, it isn't. I won't let it matter. You can't do this, Jackson." She struggled against him, pulling with her arms, trying to free her wrists. "I won't let you do this. You can't have Amy." Her chest rose and fell with each deep breath. Her voice shook, as if she was close to tears. "She's my daughter. You can't take her away. I'll kill you first. I swear I'll kill you."

"No!" He grabbed her shoulder and held her still. "No more killing. No more drawing guns. No more threats. I mean it." He shook her slightly. "No more. I'm tired of it, Regan. You've had your way in this for six years. Now I get a say."

She stared at him in mute pain. There weren't any tears, but that didn't mean she wasn't suffering. He thought about letting her go, but he didn't. Not until he said his piece.

"I know you're right," he said. "I can't just take Amy and leave."

"I'm glad you see that."

"But I'm not going to walk away from her either."

"You're not staying here!" She tried to twist free of him.

"Dammit, woman, stop your jumping around. Despite your attempt to change the fact, I am still a man."

She glared at him. "It's not enough that you hold me here as if I were some untamed horse, now you have to insult me as well? If you don't like me touching you, then let me go." The last three words were accompanied by even more vigorous movements. She tugged at her wrists, leaning forward to get more leverage. Her breasts brushed against his chest. Instantly heat flared in his groin. He was hard in a heartbeat. Hell, he ought to let her just keep on what she was doing. At least one of them would end this night with a smile.

Her head moved back and forth with her effort. Her hair flew over her shoulder exposing her neck to view. He was about to lean forward and taste her when the lamplight caught something shiny by the corner of her eye. His breath caught in his throat. A single tear clung to her lower lashes.

He let her go instantly.

Regan moved away from him. She rubbed her wrists, then quickly brushed her fingers against her cheek.

"I need a few days to think about this," he said. "I want a truce between us."

"No."

"Be reasonable."

"I don't have to be. I have the law on my side."

She turned away from him and faced the back door. Pride made her square her shoulders. He watched her, knowing pride was about all she had left.

"You have nothing on your side and we both know it," he said. "I'm not asking you, I'm telling you."

"You think you can come in here and order me around?" She turned toward him, her temper giving her the strength to keep going. He admired her ability to dig deep and come at him fighting. "I've got a bunkhouse full of cowboys and half a dozen hired guns on my side. As I see it, I'm the one who decides, not you."

"If you push this, Amy is the one who's going to get hurt. A truce," he repeated. "Is that so bad?"

"I can't," she said, staring at him. "You don't understand. I can't risk it."

The pain in her expression reminded him of another time, another moment of hurt. He'd been the cause of it then, as well. She'd been young. Too young and too damn innocent. She'd come to him looking for a little excitement, for stolen kisses on a hot summer night. Nothing else. He'd always told himself he did the right thing by sending her away. He wasn't the one to give that to Regan. Maybe he did the right thing, but he acted all wrong. He'd hurt her. Even now he could see the flash of pain, feel the heat of her humiliation. She'd fled from him, from his cruel words. For the rest of his stay on the ranch, she avoided him. He wanted to apologize, but he'd been young himself. Too young to willingly pay the price of an apology. Easier to take Elizabeth and forget everything between her silky thighs. Easier to ride away without looking back.

He wanted to tell Regan he was sorry, but it would be too little too late.

"I'm not going," he said. "You can't make me go. If you try, I'll tell everyone the truth. It won't be so bad to have me around. Most people like me, once they get to know me."

"I just bet they do. Especially the ladies."

Why had he thought coming back would be so easy? Still, he was here. He didn't have a choice, but to figure out what was best. One thing was sure. He wasn't walking away from Amy. Not when he'd just found her. From what he'd seen so far, the kid needed a father.

That reminded him of something. "Give in, Regan, if for no other reason than the fact that you owe me."

"I don't owe you anything."

"You're wrong. I spoke with Amy tonight and she told me a lot of interesting things."

Regan clutched the counter behind her, as if needing it to stay upright.

"I asked her about her father. You told her I was dead."

"So?"

"You told her a cow sat on me and I drowned," he roared. "Did you have to make it so stupid?"

Her lips twitched. She glanced down, then back at him. The twitching got worse, then she grinned.

"It was humiliating."

"I had to tell her something about her father." She cleared her throat. "The drifter, I mean."

"Yeah, right. The drifter."

He liked how she looked when she smiled. He liked the sweetness in her expression and the way her eyes crinkled at the corner.

"So as I see it, you owe me," he said. "I won't do anything or tell anyone the truth, but I'm going to stick around for a while. You can make it tough if you want, but we don't have to be enemies."

"I don't trust you."

"Fair enough. But if you let me stay and don't try to trick me, I won't send for my sister."

She looked at him for a long time, weighing her choices. He knew she was smart enough to figure out she didn't have any. It was his way or not at all.

"All right," she said at last. "You win. I'll tell everyone you're going to give me advice on how to handle Daniel. That will give you an excuse to stay for a few days. But don't try anything, Jackson. I meant what I said. I won't lose my daughter."

He nodded. "I understand." He watched her leave the room. It was a victory of sorts. It should have made him feel better, but oddly enough, it didn't.

7

Fayre had already started breakfast when Regan came downstairs. Regan thought she would have trouble waking up this morning after staying up so late, but it wasn't a problem because she'd never really fallen asleep. Long after she left Jackson in the kitchen, she thought about what had happened between them. She'd been unable to forget his words or his request for a truce.

He wasn't leaving any time soon and there was nothing she could do about that. She would have to trust that it would all work out, that she would be able to keep Amy safe from her father and the ranch safe from Daniel.

She entered the kitchen. Fayre was bent over the stove, sliding in a baking sheet of biscuits.

"Coffee's all ready," she said, then straightened

and closed the oven door. She wiped her hands on her apron, then turned toward Regan. Her mouth twisted slightly. "I can see you washed up and put on clean clothes, but don't look any better than you did yesterday. You feeling poorly?"

"Just tired." Regan poured herself a cup of coffee, then leaned against the counter. She'd just adjusted her weight when she realized this was the same place Jackson had trapped her. She moved a little to the left, closer to the sink.

The morning looked bright and clear. She peered through the window, noting the faint pink at the horizon. By the time she ate breakfast, the sun would be up and the cowboys hard at work. She had to join them, even though every part of her ached for sleep.

Fayre bustled around, turning bacon, counting out eggs. There was something odd about her movements, almost tentative. And she was unusually quiet.

Regan exhaled softly, then stared at her cup. She'd hoped it wouldn't come to this. Looks like she didn't have a choice.

"How much did you hear?" she asked.

"Just about all of it." The older woman set the eggs down in the bowl and glanced at her. "How much of it's true?"

"You really want to know?"

Her friend studied her. Faded blue eyes softened with emotion as she shook her head. "Better if I don't. I can't tell anyone what I haven't heard from you. As far as last night goes, well, I did have an extra slice of pie before bed. I dare say it gave me some colorful dreams."

"Thank you," she whispered.

Fayre paused and patted her on the shoulder.

"He's staying for a while. What are you going to do about him?"

"I don't know. Nothing unless I have to. I won't let him take Amy, no matter what."

"I don't think it'll come to that. Jackson doesn't seem the ornery type, despite what you did to him."

"You call him Jackson?"

Fayre cracked an egg open and spilled the contents into a skillet. "He asked me to. As long as it's harmless, it makes sense to give him what he wants. A dog's less likely to piss on the chair he sleeps on."

Despite her exhaustion, Regan smiled. "What does that mean?"

"If Jackson feels welcome here, if he's not angry, then he won't have anything to prove by taking away his daughter. You're gonna have to watch yourself. Don't provoke him."

Regan thought about what had happened the previous night, the way she pulled a gun on Jackson and then kicked him in the . . . She cleared her throat. "It sounds as if you're taking his side."

"There aren't any sides. There's just Amy. We've got to think of what's best for the child."

"The best thing for her is to stay right here with everything she knows and loves. We can protect her and keep her safe."

"How much longer can you keep her from going into town?" Fayre asked quietly.

Regan walked to the window and stared out. "As long as I have to."

"She's bound to want to go sometime. She's not a puppy. You can't keep her tied up forever."

"She's just five. We'll deal with that when it happens."

"It's going to happen sooner than you want it to. She's growing up. She needs other children to play with."

"She's happy here." Regan pulled back the lace curtains. "She has everything she needs."

"Not a father."

The pan sizzled as Fayre dropped in another egg. Regan ignored the sound and the smells. She didn't want to think about anything or do anything. She was overwhelmed by the last few days. Three months ago her life had been perfect. Her father had been alive, her world in place. Now, such a short time later, everything had changed for the worst.

Regan moved toward the back door.

"What about your breakfast?" Fayre asked.

"I'm not hungry."

"Watch yourself. I'll leave some food out in case you get hungry later."

Regan nodded, then opened the door. It was a measure of Fayre's concern that she was letting her skip breakfast. The housekeeper didn't take kindly to missed meals.

"Oh, Regan? Look out for Daniel. It's been a while since he made trouble and he's due. That boy was always consistent."

"You're right. I'll warn the men."

She stepped out into the morning and closed the door behind her. She shared Fayre's feeling. Daniel would strike again, soon. She wished she knew where and how. At least she could be prepared for him. Now, the best she could do was wait and pray.

The sky was quickly changing from pale gray to pink, then light blue. Birds chirped in the trees. The air was cold, but it would warm soon. Another perfect Texas day.

Already the cowboys were at work. She could hear them calling to each other and the rattle of bridles and saddles being carried to the horses. She should go saddle up her gelding and get started. Instead she sat down on the top step of the porch and sipped her coffee.

Her gaze moved past the barn to the other outbuildings. To her right was the garden, to her left, the corrals. A small creek wound through the property, close to the house. Black willows, their yellow flowers just starting to bud, lined the damp bank. Pecan trees shaded three sides of the house, although they were still standing bare this time of year. Come fall Fayre and Amy would harvest the sweet nuts for baking and eating. Past the pecans were the other orchard trees her father had brought with him to the ranch.

For as far as she could see, she controlled the land. The cowboys answered to her, the cattle bore her brand. She ran the stock, determined the bloodlines, decided which cows would be kept, and which sold. When her father had died, he'd entrusted it all to her. At the time she assumed she knew enough, that he'd trained her well and that she would be fine. Now she knew how false that assumption was. Despite years of training, of doing all the jobs herself, she knew nothing. Making a decision with her father hovering in the background, knowing he would help her if she took the wrong step, was far different from doing everything on her own.

She couldn't let him down. She refused even to consider that possibility. So when she was afraid, she kept going forward because the alternative was unthinkable.

Movement by the open double doors of the barn caught her attention. She shifted so that she was leaning against the railing and watched as a man led his bay gelding out of the building. The horse was beautiful, his coat gleaming in the morning light. The man, equally stunning, despite the limp as he walked. His wound was obviously giving him pain. She wondered how much of that discomfort came from her actions the night before.

She hadn't planned to knee him in his private parts. Regan took a big swallow of coffee, but it did nothing to ease her embarrassment or the flush she felt on her cheeks. She'd just reacted, lashing out in order to get away from him. He'd been wrong, but what she did had been unforgivable. She sighed. Jackson could add it to her list of sins.

He and the horse entered the main corral. He stopped the animal, then swung into the saddle. Even from this distance, she could see his grimace as he settled his weight. He didn't wear a hat, and long hair fell to the bottom of his collar. He needed a haircut. Her fingers curled around the mug as she thought about trimming his hair, touching the strands, feeling the warmth of him so close to her.

He adjusted his seat, then took the reins. Without a visible command, the horse moved forward, first walking, then trotting. They moved together, man and beast, in perfect harmony. She was used to cowboys who rode their ponies as if they'd been born to the saddle. She worked with hard, lean men who stripped down to jeans and boots, or less if they thought they were alone by the horse trough or the stream. Yet none of them had caused her to look a second time. Not the quiet moody ones, or the good-looking strangers. No one had captured her attention or her heart the way Jackson Tyler had.

It wasn't his fault, she acknowledged. Or even her own. He'd come out of nowhere, a handsome gun-fighter with a smile that made her want to follow him around like a lost puppy. She'd been caught between girlhood and being grown-up. He'd stolen her heart with his easy laughter and teasing ways. He'd sealed her fate with unconscious gentleness.

All for nothing. He'd never noticed her, had never looked at her as a man looks at a woman he wants. He'd never kissed her. Even though she'd begged him to. Even though he'd bedded her sister.

Regan drained the mug, then set it next to her on the top stair. She glanced down at her hands. Her short nails were clean, but otherwise, her hands had nothing to recommend them. The scrape by her knuckles was healing. There were bruises and scars, bits of missing skin and calluses. She didn't have the hands of a lady. She didn't smell of sweet perfumes and baking bread. Her arms weren't pale and soft.

She looked up at him. He'd reined in the horse and turned him so he was facing the house. As she glanced up, their eyes met. He was too far away for her to know what he was thinking, but she sensed it wasn't anything she would like. He saw her as the one person in the way of what he wanted. If she wasn't around, he could have Amy.

She should hate him for that. She should see him as her greatest enemy and think only about the danger he represented. She didn't. In all the time he was gone, she'd never been able to forget. Now that he was here all those old emotions came back to life, all the old desires and needs. It didn't matter that he would never see her as a woman. It didn't matter that he would try to steal her daughter away as surely as the sun would come up in the morning. It didn't matter that he would pity her if he suspected her feelings. Nothing had changed for her. She'd spent the last six years trying to convince herself she didn't care about Jackson. Unfortunately she still did, and it looked as if she always would.

She told herself to look away, but she couldn't. Jackson's stare compelled her as much as the man himself. She would have stayed there, frozen in place forever, if she hadn't heard footsteps headed her way.

She turned and saw Pete walking toward her, his long, easy stride quickly covering ground.

"You look terrible," he said by way of greeting. He took off his hat and slapped it against his thigh a couple of times before settling it on his head. "You need to see a doctor or something?"

"Always the compliment," she said, smiling up at him. "I'm fine. Just tired. Max got into the grain last night and I had to stay up with him."

"You could have told me. I would have taken care of it."

She shook her head. "It was my turn. You can't stay up every night and then work the next day any more than I can. It's better if we share." She glanced at her mug and wished for more coffee, but it was too much trouble to stand up and get some. "What are you doing today?"

"I should be out with the cattle," Pete grumbled. "Instead I'll be out scouting fence lines."

Despite her weariness, Regan smiled. "I know you don't agree with what I'm doing."

"It's a fool waste of time and money. Range land is free. Why tie up cash buying what the government is happy to give you?"

"What if it isn't free forever? More people are coming here every year, Pete. My father believed it wouldn't be that long until we were fighting for places to graze our cattle. If I buy it up now, while no one wants it, it'll be cheaper than waiting until everyone else figures out the best solution."

Her friend stared at her. "If you're wrong, you've lost a lot of money."

"My father was rarely wrong."

Pete's mouth spread into a familiar grin. "I'll give you that. Sean had enough sense for three men." His grin faded. "Two of the hired guns got into a fight last night."

She closed her eyes briefly. She didn't need any more trouble. "Did they kill each other?"

"Nope. One's got a black eye, the other a busted nose, but otherwise they're fine." His brown eyes met hers. "They're getting as dangerous as Daniel."

"I know." She rested her elbows on her knees then propped her chin on her hands, watching Jackson as he rode his horse around the corral. "Gage mentioned they were getting restless. Have they been to town?"

"Not yet."

"Send them in, three at a time. They can be gone for two days. But only give them half their wages. They'll have to come back if they want the other half."

"Sending 'em to town is only going to rile 'em up."

"Maybe they'll get it out of their system," she said. "They can get drunk."

"They're doing that anyway," Pete mumbled.

She ignored him. "They can get drunk," she repeated,

"play cards and visit the whores. After two days, they should be ready to work."

Pete was used to her frank language, but even he raised his eyebrows at her comment.

"Yes, Pete, I know what whores are for. Who would know better than me?"

He leaned against the railing and placed his hand on her shoulder. "You shouldn't let them bother you. They don't know anything about you. It's just talk."

"Talk has a way of hurting a body, even if it's not supposed to." But she didn't want to think about that. Not this morning. She stood up and stretched, then started toward the barn.

Pete followed her. "You should ignore what they say."

"I try. Sometimes it's difficult." She'd expected problems when she brought Amy home and claimed her as her own. She'd known her father would be disappointed and people shocked, but she hadn't expected the town to turn against her. She hadn't thought that even after all this time they would still turn away from her, shunning her and her family, refusing to have anything to do with the ranch.

"I meant what I said," Pete reminded her as they reached the barn. "I'll marry you, Regan."

She stopped and looked up at him. His face was as familiar as her own. She knew she'd been about Amy's age when Fayre and Hank had adopted Pete and brought him to the ranch, but she had no memories that didn't include him. For as long as she could recall, they'd been the best of friends.

She reached out and took his hand. His skin was as tanned, as callused, and as bruised as hers. They worked hard for this ranch.

He stared down at her, his brown eyes kind, his expression open. There were few secrets with Pete— none if she didn't count Jackson and Amy. He knew the best and worst about her and he still cared for her.

"I always assumed I would marry because of the ranch," she said.

He shook his head angrily. "You know I'm not doing this for the ranch. You'd still run it. I'm not looking to claim your inheritance."

"I know," she said. Other men weren't as honest with their intentions. "But I thought I would be willing to do it all the same." She stared down at their joined hands, then up at him. He had a nice face. Regular features with an easy smile. Nothing mysterious lurked in his brown eyes. He was good-looking enough to get noticed in town, but he'd never made her heart beat faster just by looking at her. He'd never been swept away by his affections for her either.

"You deserve better," she told him. "Find some girl and marry her because you can't imagine living without her. Don't marry me so that people in town won't talk."

Pete reached back and tugged on her braid. She smiled up at him. "You're as stubborn as your father," he said.

"Thanks."

Jackson reined in his mount so he could watch what was happening between Regan and her foreman. They looked mighty friendly, holding hands and making calf eyes at each other. He snorted. It wasn't getting the day's work done.

He dismounted, grunting when his bad leg took his

weight. After loosely tying the reins around the corral fence, he strolled over to where Regan and the other man were in conversation.

Regan flushed slightly and stepped back, tugging her hand free as she moved. "Good morning, Jackson."

He tilted his hat toward her, then glanced at the other man. "Morning. I'm Jackson Tyler. I don't think we met the last time I was here on the O'Neil ranch."

"Pete Nash." They shook hands.

Jackson liked Pete's grip. It was firm without trying to prove anything. The foreman seemed the sensible sort. He met his gaze straight on, which Jackson liked. What he wasn't too fond of was how cozy Pete and Regan had been. He didn't care what she did with her cowboys, but if she planned on keeping Amy around, then any man she hooked up with would be his daughter's father. Unless he was to take Amy with him, which was more than he could think about right now. Questions like that had kept him up all night. He was damn tired of thinking.

"You seem fit enough," Pete said. "When are you going to be moving out?"

Jackson glanced at Regan. She ducked her head, avoiding the question. Jackson rubbed his chin. "It seems that I'm going to be staying around here for a while. There's a matter of—"

"I asked Jackson to stay," Regan blurted out, interrupting him. She focused on the center of Pete's chest. "To help out. With Daniel, I mean. He helped my father with him before, and I thought he might—" She drew in a breath, then smoothed her hands over her split skirt. "We need the extra help."

"I thought I was handling everything," Pete said, obviously irritated.

She raised her head and squared her shoulders. "You are, Pete. Of course you are. But Jackson can help, too."

She looked different this morning, Jackson thought. Just as tired. The shadows under her eyes were darker. But she'd cleaned up pretty good. Her bright red hair had been pulled back into a braid. Her skirt and blouse were tidy. The dull beige-and-brown fabric did nothing to improve her looks, but her breasts thrust out provocatively as she straightened, and the split skirt outlined the feminine curve of her hips. Regan's face might not be beautiful, but the rest of her seemed to be in fine order.

"You could have told me," Pete muttered.

"I was going to."

"We just decided it last night," Jackson said. His tone indicated he was trying to help, but the look Regan flashed him told him she didn't believe that for a second. He grinned at her. She was right.

"I thought you were up with one of the horses last night," Pete said suspiciously. He folded his arms over his chest and looked down at her.

"I . . . uh . . . I was."

"Perhaps I should have been more specific," Jackson said. "It was early this morning, rather than last night. I waited up for Regan. We had lots of things to talk about." He hesitated just enough before the word *talk* to make Pete bristle.

"Then I'll let you two get on with your conversation. I've got fence lines to ride." Pete tilted his head slightly. "Regan, I'll see you later. Mr. Tyler, enjoy your visit." He emphasized the last word.

Jackson watched the other man walk away. He could feel Regan's temper rising. "Did you have to act like that?" she asked, as soon as Pete was out of earshot.

"No, I didn't have to. I wanted to."

She stomped her foot in the dirt. "What is wrong with you?"

"I could ask you the same thing." He stared after the cowboy. "You gonna marry him?"

"What?"

"You heard me. Are you and Pete going to get hitched? Before you start steaming up and telling me it's none of my business, I'd say Amy makes it my business. What kind of man you have in your life affects my daughter."

She stared at him as if he'd started talking a foreign language, then she threw back her head and laughed. He waited. Her blue eyes were bright with humor, her tanned face slightly flushed, her lips parted. For a moment, before she composed herself, he saw past the freckles and pale imitation of Elizabeth's perfect features. He saw something else. Something unique. A kind of beauty that caught him off guard and left him feeling strangely drawn. Before he could figure out what had happened, or what he was feeling, she sobered. Her expression changed and she was just Regan again.

"This time yesterday you didn't even know Amy existed, and now you're worried about who I'm going to marry?" Regan shook her head. "Get over it, Jackson. We've survived all this time without you. I think we can continue to muddle along without your help."

"It wasn't my fault I wasn't here," he reminded her.

"You didn't bother staying long enough—" She

clamped her mouth shut as if she'd just figured out
what she was saying. "What I meant was, even if Amy
was your child by Elizabeth, which I won't say she is,
you should have worried about what might have happened long before now."

It was an argument they'd had before. He was
saved from responding by the slamming of the back
door. They both turned toward the sound. Regan's
breath caught in her throat, but Jackson grinned.

"Morning, darlin'," he called.

Amy came skipping down the stairs, then ran across
the yard toward them. She wore a yellow calico dress
and sturdy brown shoes. Her hair had been pulled into
two braids that flew out behind her as she moved
toward him. He bent over and held out his arms.

Amy launched herself in the air. He caught her and
spun her around. Her laughter spilled over, making
his chest tighten.

"You're still here," Amy said, obviously delighted.
"I thought you was leaving."

"Nope. I'll be around for a while." He slowed his
turns, then pulled her up against him.

Her legs went around his waist and she rested one
arm on his shoulder. "Mama, did you hear? Jackson's
going to stay with us for a while. He's nice."

"I'm glad you like him," Regan said. "But that
doesn't change the fact that you went to see him yesterday after I told you to leave him alone."

Amy's chin dropped to her chest. "I know. I
couldn't help it. The door wasn't 'xactly closed, so I
just sorta peeked inside. And there he was."

"I'll bet."

The sun had moved high enough in the sky to cast

shadows across the yard. Regan stood in the shade of the barn. Her expression was two parts resignation, one part fear. He wanted to tell her he wouldn't do anything to make her unhappy, but he couldn't. It felt right to hold Amy close and listen to her chatter. He had a lot of years to make up for.

Amy wiggled slightly, so he bent over and put her down. She moved close to Regan and stared up at her. Regan sighed, then touched the girl's face. Amy grinned.

"I saw my mouse again, Mama."

"Did you?"

Amy nodded vigorously. "Last night, afore I went to sleep. He came out and sat by my window."

"The answer is no."

"But, Mama."

"No, Amy, you can't ride. You're too little."

Amy glanced at him slyly. "Jackson doesn't think I'm little."

Regan glared at him. "Thanks a lot."

"Wait a minute." He help up his hands. "I don't want to get involved in this. I never said you weren't too little."

"Well, I'm not!"

Now both females were glaring at him. He took a step back. As usual, he was with Regan about fifteen minutes, and she was attacking him. The woman was dangerous to his health.

"A-my, time for lessons," Fayre called from the back door.

"Go on," Regan urged her, gently touching her shoulder. "We'll talk about this later."

Amy stared up at her, as if she wanted to argue the point. Regan dropped to her knees and held out her arms. Amy flung herself at her and held her tight.

"Go do your lessons," she told the child. "Tonight I promise I'll come tell you a story."

Amy nodded once, then darted toward the house. She stopped midway, turned, and grinned at him. "'Bye, Jackson." Her smile was contagious.

He waved.

"She's already a little flirt," Regan muttered.

"Just like her mother," he said without thinking. At Regan's glare, he shrugged. "Sorry. I didn't mean to start anything." He stared after Amy. "She reminds me a lot of Lily, too, at her age. My sister was a charmer."

Regan started for the barn door. He followed.

"How long are you going to pretend she's not mine?" he asked.

"Forever," she answered, not stopping.

He grabbed her arm. She turned, her hands raised, as if prepared to fight.

"What happened to our truce?" he asked.

She glanced pointedly at the place he was holding her. "I'd like to amend it to include you not physically handling me all the time."

"What about what you've done to me?"

He wasn't just referring to last night when she'd kneed him, and they both knew it. Some of the fire faded from her blue eyes, leaving her looking slightly ashamed.

"What do you want from me?" she asked.

Answers, he thought. He wanted to know how Elizabeth had convinced her to claim the child as hers. But they'd called a truce.

"Why won't you let her ride?" he asked.

"She's too little."

"She's five. You were younger than that when you got on your first horse."

"That was different." She moved toward the barn.

He followed. "How?" She kept walking, stopping long enough to grab a halter from the tack room. "You can't protect her forever," he said. "She's got to fall on her fanny eventually."

"Not if I can help it." She walked back to the last stall on her left, then entered. He heard her soft crooning, then she led out a bay gelding. The horse wasn't as big or as dark as his but was still a strong animal. She controlled him easily, tugging gently on the halter as she led him to the front of the barn.

"You can't keep her locked away here. She's going to grow up."

Regan glared at him. "You've been her father for exactly one day and you're telling me what to do?"

"I'm just saying—"

"I don't care what you're saying." She secured the horse, then glanced up at him. Pain filled her blue eyes, darkening the irises to the color of a coming storm. "It's easy for you to show up and tell me what's right for my daughter. Maybe I was riding when I was her age. Maybe I had more freedom than she did, but it was different."

"You keep saying that. Different how?"

Regan ducked under her horse's head so that she was standing in front of him. He could smell the scent of the hay and the animals. It was all familiar and pleasant. Under that, so faint he wasn't sure he hadn't imagine it, was a whispering sweetness that could only be a woman. A soft flicker of heady aroma designed to drive a man mad—or to his knees.

She glared up at him, eyes flashing. Her temper lent color to her face, highlighting her cheekbones. She wasn't a beauty like her sister, but she would age better than Elizabeth could have. Time would carve away at her face, reducing it to strong lines and bone, leaving her spare but stunning. She would be one of those bad-tempered, straight-backed old women with hair that refused to gray and a tongue that wouldn't be still for man or God. She would shake her fist and terrify the local children who dared to stray onto her property. She would never be boring.

"It's different because my father had Elizabeth and me," she said, then twisted her hands together. "This probably sounds silly to you, but Amy is all I have. I couldn't bear it if something happened to her."

"So you keep her wrapped up, like a fragile bit of glass?"

"What's the alternative?"

"Let her do what she wants. She's a kid. She deserves to run wild."

She shook her head. "Why am I having this conversation with you? You know as much about raising children as I know about being a gunfighter. But like a typical man, you think you can offer your superior opinion and I'll be so grateful for your advice." She leaned forward and poked him in the chest, punctuating each word with a sharp jab. "Don't think that I am. As far as I'm concerned, you can take your opinions and—"

"I thought the truce meant no physical contact," he said teasingly. Truth was, riling Regan was the most fun he'd had since that time in Dodge City when his straight flush won him not one but two saloon girls for the night.

She jerked her hand away and tucked it behind her. "Excuse me. I got carried away."

"If you expect to run the ranch, you're going to have to control yourself."

She puffed up, her chest swelling until he wondered if the buttons on her blouse might pop. He wouldn't mind witnessing that. He waited expectantly, but she exhaled loudly and her chest returned to its normal, perfect size.

"I do a fine job of running this ranch," she said slowly, carefully pronouncing each word as if he was a half-wit. "I haven't had any complaints."

"I have one. You shouldn't go around shooting innocent men."

Fire flashed from her eyes. "Damn you, Jackson Tyler. Why the hell did you have to come back here now?"

He grinned. "Temper, temper, darlin'. And swearin'? My, my. What will the cowboys think if they hear you yelling like this?"

Her gaze narrowed. "You're doing this on purpose. You're deliberately baiting me to make me angry."

Rather than deny the obvious, he winked.

"Why?"

He bent at the waist, leaning toward her until the sweet scent of her surrounded him and her breath fanned his face. He stared at the freckles, half deciding they might begin to grow on a man. Not him, of course, but someone else. "Because it's so easy."

"I—I—"

"You what?" he asked, focusing on her mouth. She kept opening it and closing it, but no sound came out. It occurred to him that keeping her temper hot wasn't in his best interest. Entertainment or not, if she got upset enough, she just might take a shot at him. Of course, he'd always been one to play the odds.

She sure wasn't Elizabeth. She wasn't even the woman-girl he remembered. She'd been so innocent then. So intent on giving him her heart. He'd had no interest in hearts, or feelings, although he wouldn't have objected to sharing a little of her heat. But she'd been a virgin and he hadn't been quite drunk enough to forget his good sense.

She was still a virgin, he thought as she grew very still. She backed up slightly and bumped into her horse's shoulder. The gelding whinnied.

A shaft of sunlight slipped through the open door and touched her hair, turning the bright red to the color of fire. Even as he told himself he was a fool and this was a mistake, he reached up to touch her head to see if he could feel the flames. Her hair was soft beneath his questing fingers, but cool to the touch. She caught her breath.

If she'd gotten mad he would have backed off. If she'd said something, or hit him, he would have moved away. But she didn't. She breathed rapidly, as if she'd ridden for hours. Her chest rose and fell, those damn buttons tightening, then releasing as if to taunt him.

"Dammit, Regan, stop that," he murmured, moving his head those last few inches.

"Stop what?"

Instead of answering, he brushed her mouth once with his. He did it to make her angry. At least that's what he told the voice inside his head that was screaming at him to stop. That's the excuse he used as his instincts ordered his body to pull away. But his body didn't listen. Instead it stayed in place as his lips swept once across hers.

He'd expected the softness. He hadn't met a woman yet who didn't have a soft mouth. He'd expected the heat. Anyone with hair the color of Regan's had to be hot-blooded. He hadn't expected the passion that nipped at him unexpectedly, or the impulse to kiss her again. He hadn't expected his blood to run faster, pooling in the spot she'd injured the previous night, and he sure hadn't expected to like it.

Regan kept her eyes open during the entire kiss. She thought about closing them, but the sensation of his lips against hers was so shocking, she couldn't have closed them if she'd wanted to. She'd wasted too much time wondering if she would ever be kissed by a man, so she sure wasn't going to waste experiencing it all by not being able to see what he was doing. Of course there wasn't much to look at. Just the side of his face—his eyes *were* closed—and the barn wall beyond. Her hands fluttered at her sides. She wasn't sure what to do with them. Frankly she wasn't sure exactly what was happening.

One minute he was baiting her, then next he was kissing her. Just like that. As if he did that sort of thing all the time. No doubt Jackson did. He was the kissing sort. Elizabeth had said as much. Her sister had told her he kissed better than anyone. Regan knew she was going to have to take Elizabeth's word on it. She didn't have anything to compare it to.

The contact was fleeting but intense. His skin was smooth and warm, the pressure slight, yet she could feel all of it. Her mouth tingled slightly, her body grew warm. It was harder to breathe, or maybe that was because he was standing so close. He didn't hold her in his arms. Regan told herself she was glad. She wasn't a hold-in-the-arms sort of woman.

He raised his head and smiled at her. A stupid smile, but she didn't tell him that. His eyes held hers. He had beautiful eyes. This morning the green color dominated, standing out against his tanned skin. She was close enough to see his clean-shaven jaw and the tiny lines created by his smile. He was handsome enough to tempt an angel.

"You're staring at me," she said when he didn't look away. She tried to move back, but the horse behind her didn't budge. To slide past him would risk more physical contact. She just noticed he'd braced one hand against the gelding and angled his body toward her, effectively trapping her.

"What'd you think?"

"About what?" she asked, sure he couldn't be talking about the kiss. Her face flushed. People didn't actually talk about kissing, did they?

"The kiss."

"Oh." They did talk about it. Why hadn't Elizabeth warned her? She didn't know what to say. "It was very nice." She cleared her throat. "Thank you," she added, hoping it was enough.

Apparently it wasn't. He didn't budge. She didn't know what to do with her hands, so she tucked them behind her back, feeling the warmth of the gelding behind her. She focused on Jackson's neck. His shirt wasn't buttoned to the collar. She could see his skin there, as tanned as his face, and a few stray hairs. They were the same gold-blond color she adored.

Now what? What did he want of her? This was so

awkward. She glanced at his face, then away because, dammit, he was still staring at her.

"I'm going to kiss you again," he said casually, as if he'd just asked her to give his horse an extra measure of grain.

"Why?"

"Two reasons. First, because I want to." He moved closer so that his thighs brushed hers and his chest was perilously close to her breasts. She sucked in a breath, but that made them move the wrong way . . . toward him. She hunched her shoulders and leaned more against the horse.

"What's the other?" she asked, hoping to distract him.

"Because kissing seems to make you nervous. For once you're not yelling orders and telling me what to do. I like that."

She opened her mouth to tell him exactly what he could do, but before she could speak, he brushed his mouth against her cheek.

"Close your eyes," he said.

"I don't trust you enough to close my eyes."

"What are you afraid of?"

She stiffened. "I'm not afraid."

"Prove it."

She had a funny feeling he was twisting her around to suit his purpose, but she couldn't say that without admitting he was also successful at it. So she closed her eyes, then opened them quickly.

"If you try anything, I'll kick you again."

His smug grin was annoying.

"Close your eyes," he whispered, then placed his hands on her shoulders.

His fingers kneaded her skin through her blouse. She could feel his warmth and strength. It relaxed her and she did as he asked.

She waited, breathless, wondering if he was again taunting her. In those moments she spent staring at nothing, insecurities overwhelmed her. Then his mouth settled against hers, pressing, probing, as if searching for the most comfortable spot in which to remain.

A small sound hovered at the back of her throat. Part pleasure, part surprise. She didn't know whether to lean forward or away, so she stayed still, hoping he would give her a hint as to what he expected.

His mouth parted slightly, then she felt the warm moistness of his tongue brushing against her lips. She stiffened in surprise. Why was he doing that? It didn't make sense . . . and yet it felt delicious.

She leaned toward him while her toes curled inside her worn boots. She brought her hands up toward him, then let them hover near him, not sure if she should touch him. Her fingers flexed several times before she tentatively, carefully placed her palm against his side.

It was just to keep her balance, she told herself, in case she had to explain her actions to him. Just for a moment. She felt the lean line of his muscles and his heat through his shirt. He was hard and strong, straight lines to her curves. She'd never been this close to a man for this long. Even as she told herself it was just a kiss and Jackson had kissed more women than she owned cows, she couldn't help feeling special.

He moved his head slightly so that his lips pressed against her cheek. He brushed against her jaw, her chin, then down on her throat. Damp heat sent hot sparks shooting through her chest and arms. Her muscles seemed to relax until she wondered if she would be able to remain standing. His hands moved from her shoulders down to her back. He pulled her hard against him. She hadn't expected the action so she didn't have time to fight against it. One minute she was standing in front of him, the next they touched from shoulder to thigh.

Her breasts nestled against his chest, her thighs brushed his. He was broader, bigger, yet their difference in size wasn't frightening. She raised her hands to his shoulders, liking the way he felt against her palms.

He nibbled on the skin under her left ear. She caught her breath. His teeth teased her, finding her earlobe. Shivers raced to her thighs making her legs tremble. Her breathing increased. For the first time in her life, she thought she might faint.

Slowly, he moved up her jaw toward her mouth. Once there, he pressed hard, then sucked on her lower lip. She gasped, her eyelids flying open. Sensual pleasure swept over her. She gazed at the side of his face, at the gold-blond hair and his thick lashes resting against his tanned cheek.

Jackson Tyler was kissing her. Honest to God kissing her. His tongue swept over her damp mouth. She arched toward him, wanting more.

"Open your mouth," he murmured against her warm skin.

She thought about asking why, then decided she didn't care why. It felt too wonderful to question. She parted her lips slightly. Instantly he swept inside, brushing against her sensitive inner lip before touching the tip of her tongue with his own.

All she'd felt before, the warmth, the tingles, the

excitement, hadn't prepared her for that most intimate contact. It was as if every bit of her body held its breath and focused its attention on that tiny point of pleasure. Hot passion boiled up inside of her, making her want more. Much more. She leaned closer to Jackson, wanting him to teach her as he'd probably taught—

Even as his tongue moved across her own, sending heat and need skittering down her spine, she grew cold. He'd done this with her sister. He'd tempted, then seduced Elizabeth and who knows how many other women. Jackson had never noticed her before. He couldn't like her, not after what she'd done to him and the secrets she'd kept from him. Which left only one reason for the kiss.

She jerked her head back, then pushed hard on his chest. Her unexpected force sent him back two steps. She glared up at him, hating the way passion had brightened his eyes. His mouth was parted and damp. Damp from her. In her heart, in the place where her dreams still dared to live, she knew she would hold on to the memory of this kiss forever. But she couldn't let him know. Not when he was playing her for a fool.

"I won't be used," she said, her temper fueled more by sorrow than outrage. Six years ago she would have sold her soul to have Jackson want to kiss her. Despite the passage of time, in some part of her heart, she still felt the same. Better to have not known the sweetness than to have been played false this way. "I won't be a substitute."

Wariness replaced the passion, dousing the fire and leaving his expression carefully shuttered. "What are you talking about?"

"Elizabeth."

"What has she got to do with anything?"

"You bedded my sister. Despite your despicable behavior, you must have loved her at the time. I won't have you kiss me and do those things all the while knowing you're thinking about Elizabeth."

He drew his eyebrows together in confusion. "While I'll admit to bedding Elizabeth, love never entered into it."

She couldn't have been more shocked if he'd slapped her. "You didn't care for her at all?" That made it worse. "You're nothing but a—a rutting stallion."

His slow, teasing smile did nothing to cool her temper. "That's right, darlin'. Nobody ever said anything about love. It's kinda like having an itch."

"You're saying you used her to scratch your itch?" Her voice was getting louder and higher, but she didn't care.

"No, I'm saying she used me."

She stared at his handsome face and wished she could slap him hard enough to make his ears ring. But she didn't bother. Jackson was healing fast and he would stop her before she even got close. She wanted to call him out for slandering her sister. She wanted him off her land and out of her life before he did any more damage.

Worse, she wanted him to kiss her again. She didn't only despise him, she despised herself.

"Aren't you going to waste your breath defending her virtue?" he asked.

She shook her head. "You're not worth the trouble." With that she turned to walk away.

She hadn't gone two steps when he grabbed her arm and turned her back toward him. "Listen, Regan. It's not what you think."

She opened her mouth to tell him exactly what she thought of him. Before she could speak, one of the cowboys, Billy, ran into the barn.

"Miss Regan?" he said between breaths. His face was flushed, his hat askew.

"Billy, what's wrong?"

"On the north range. There's been trouble."

Panic hit her. She jerked free of Jackson's hold and faced the man. He was about two years younger than she was, but a good worker. "What happened?"

"There's a dozen dead cattle by the watering hole."

"Damn." She and Fayre had been right. Daniel had tried something else. "All right, I'll ride out and see what happened."

"There's more, ma'am."

She waited expectantly.

"One of the men is there. He's dead, too."

8

Regan closed her eyes for a moment, fighting for strength. Then she drew in a deep breath and stared at Billy. "Who?"

"George, ma'am." He took off his hat and twisted it in his hands. Billy had dark hair and eyes. Most of the time he was easy-going, always ready with a joke or a smile. This morning he gazed at her solemnly.

She nodded. George was an older man. He'd been with the ranch since she was a little girl. Dead. Their first casualty of the range war that had sprung up between her and Daniel. She had hoped it wouldn't come to killing.

"Get one of the men to ride to town for the sheriff," she said. "Then have Zeke bring a wagon out to carry George's body back. Get yourself a fresh mount. I want you to show me where this happened."

Billy hesitated. "Should I go get Pete?"

"Why?"

"For protection. Excuse me for saying so, but you shouldn't be riding out there by yourself."

She wanted to point out that he, Billy, would be with her, but she suspected he didn't want that kind of responsibility. "Pete's already left to ride fence lines. I don't want to wait for him to come back."

"Take care of the wagon and your horse," Jackson said, speaking for the first time since the cowboy had interrupted them. "Regan will be safe. I'm going with her."

The young man smiled gratefully, then walked out of the barn.

Regan glared at Jackson. "I don't need your help."

"I don't care what you think you need. I'm coming with you."

"The way I've gotten the drop on you twice in the last ten days, I don't think I should trust your abilities."

His mouth twisted. "Can't blame you for that, but you're going to have to risk it. You're not going alone."

She would have argued, but in truth, she was pleased for the company. Daniel might still be lurking out in the foothills. She didn't doubt she could take him if she had to, but not if he was with several others. And despite her comments to Jackson to the contrary, she knew he was good at his job. She'd gotten the drop on him because she was a woman, and like most men, he tended to underestimate her abilities.

"Can you ride with your injury?" she asked, pointing to his left thigh.

"Worry about trying to stay out of trouble. I'll take care of everything else."

He walked out of the barn, his long stride broken
only by the slightest of limps. She stared after him. A
few minutes ago he'd been holding her in his arms,
kissing her. Now he was concerned about her safety.
She wished she could trust him, but she didn't. He was
here because of Amy and no other reason. He'd kissed
her because . . . She didn't know why he'd kissed her.
If he hadn't loved Elizabeth, then he wasn't using her
as a substitute. What was he doing, then?

She shook her head. It didn't matter. Walking into
the tack room, she collected her saddle and moved
back to her bay gelding.

Five minutes later she, Jackson, and Billy rode
northwest away from the ranch. Billy led the way,
with Regan in the middle and Jackson at the rear. In
less than a hour, they crested a slight hill that led
down to a small valley. A stream cut through the
north half, making this a perfect spot to graze cattle.

The sun was rising in the blue Texas sky, the temperature approaching pleasant. The smell of fresh
grasses and spring flowers filled the air. Regan reined
in her horse and stared down at the scene below.
Wildflowers covered the land. Bluebonnets, butter-
cups, blossoms of white, orange, and pink. Their delicate petals fluttered in the slight breeze, dipping and
swaying in a dance of beauty. Bright green grass fed
by sunshine and the recent rains provided a dark
background for the paler flowers.

Down by the creek banks, in ugly contrast, twelve
cows lay on their sides, their bodies stretched out,
contorted, as if invisible hands had left them twisted
and broken. There was no blood, no sign of violence,
just the scattered cows and the wildflowers.

"George is over there," Billy said, pointing to the far side of the valley.

Regan nodded, but she didn't look in that direction. She didn't want to see his body.

Without saying anything, Jackson broke away and rode off toward George. Regan kneed her mount, then rode the horse down to the first of the dead cows. She slipped onto the ground and examined the dead beast. There was no blood, no signs of a gunshot wound. The animal's stomach was distended, its mouth flecked with spittle, its eyes oddly colored.

All of the cows looked the same. By the time she'd studied the last one, Jackson had returned. She stood up and looked at him.

"There's no sign of his horse," Jackson said. "He's dead. There's a bump on the back of his head and his neck is broken. He could have fallen off."

"Or been hit on the head and pushed off," she said.

"Maybe." Jackson. He squinted at the sky. "It'll take the wagon a couple of hours to get here. I'll wait if you want to head back."

She shook her head. "I'll stay, too." She looked at Billy. "You can go to the ranch."

"Yes, ma'am." He touched the brim of his hat, then mounted his horse and started out of the valley.

Regan watched him until he disappeared over the rise, then she walked toward the fast-moving stream. In summer the creek slowed to a trickle, but with the spring runoff, the water flowed quickly.

There were several flat rocks on the bank, and a cluster of mesquite trees. Regan could see the first hints of leaves on the bare branches. She sat down on one of the rocks and stared at the water.

"He was bound to do something," Jackson said from behind her.

"I know." She rested her elbows on her knees, and her chin on her hands. "Fayre and I even talked about it this morning. I've been expecting him to act. Killing a dozen cattle warns me he means to have his way, but it doesn't damage the ranch. He won't destroy it because he wants it so much. But killing George, that's what I don't understand."

"Maybe it was an accident."

"How do you mean?"

"Maybe George discovered his men poisoning the salt lick or putting out tainted feed. It might have been an accident."

"That doesn't make George any less dead."

"You shouldn't blame yourself."

"Who else can I blame? I knew Daniel was angry about the will. I knew there would be trouble. I guess I didn't want to believe he would resort to murder."

Jackson walked around in front of her and settled on the rock beside hers. It was slightly lower, putting him at her eye level. His black hat hid most of his hair from view and shaded his eyes, but his good looks still had the power to make her heart beat faster. She wished he was more of a distraction so that she could stop thinking about the dead man.

"What happened after I left?" Jackson asked. "Did Daniel give your father any more trouble?"

She frowned, trying to remember that time. She'd been heartbroken to learn Jackson was leaving, then devastated when Elizabeth confessed her guilty secret. For weeks Regan was unable to think about anything but Jackson bedding her sister. By the time she recovered from her feeling of betrayal, Elizabeth found out she was pregnant.

"After you broke up the ring of cattle rustlers, Daniel stayed away from the ranch. He'd already told my father that it was all the other men's doing. He wasn't really guilty of anything." She leaned forward and picked up a blade of grass and studied it. "Of course my father believed him. Sean always wanted to think the best of family. ' 'Tis only family you can depend on.' " she said, imitating his Irish brogue. "I think he was wrong about Daniel. I think Daniel was involved from the beginning."

"I'm surprised you knew why I was here at all," Jackson said. "Your father wanted it kept from you."

"He did, but I asked around." She glanced at him, then smiled faintly. "It was obvious you weren't just another cowboy. After a few weeks, my father started inviting Daniel out to the ranch. All was forgiven and we went on as before."

"You sound as if you don't believe that."

"I don't think I ever did. Daniel was always nice to Sean and Elizabeth, but he didn't trouble himself to be kind to me."

"Maybe he knew he couldn't hide the truth from you."

"If that's another comment about my sister—"

"It isn't," he said, interrupting her. "I'm just pointing out that you're pretty smart. Sean saw what he wanted to, about family anyway, and Elizabeth was only concerned with—" he cleared his throat, "—other things."

Regan stared at him. Why did he insist on making up lies about her sister? Jackson had never been untruthful before. Even when a lie would have been welcomed. She thought about that night in the barn when he pushed her away, telling her he wasn't drunk enough to want to kiss her, and he wasn't likely to ever get that drunk.

So why had he kissed her today?

"How does Amy fit in all this?" Jackson asked casually.

For one brief moment, Regan forgot whom she was talking to and opened her mouth to speak the truth. She caught herself just in time. Jackson sat on the rock, his relaxed position—elbows on knees, hands hanging loosely—reminded her of a wild cat resting in the sun. The animal looked gentle enough, but when you got close, it was tensed up ready to have you for dinner.

"There was this handsome drifter," she began.

"Yeah, I've heard all that. Did Elizabeth go away to have her?"

If he was going to be stubborn enough to insist Elizabeth was Amy's mother, she was going to be just as stubborn in withholding the truth. "I went away when I found out I was with child. To a place back east. A sort of home for unwed women."

"So you went with Elizabeth."

"She came with me."

"How generous of her. So she had the baby and you brought her back, claiming her as yours. Then what happened?"

"When we came back, it was different."

She turned away from Jackson, but that wasn't enough to erase the past. She'd known it would be difficult to come home and face her father. She'd always been his favorite. It had bothered her for years until Elizabeth had laughingly told her it was a fair exchange. Regan was the favorite and Elizabeth was the pretty one. Her sister hadn't meant to be cruel, Regan knew, but the dig had hurt all the same.

On the train east, they'd come up with the plan. When they returned fourteen months later, Regan was the one carrying Amy. They waited until the infant was weaned before returning to the ranch. Regan spent time with Amy, holding her, changing her, acting like the mother she claimed to be.

She'd known she would disappoint her father. She'd expected a scandal in town. She hadn't thought her world would be forever changed. She hadn't known her father would look at her as if she meant to wound him. She hadn't known he would say all the right things, promise love and forgiveness, then hold a piece of himself apart from her. She hadn't known how much that distance would hurt her.

"When we came back, Elizabeth decided to marry," she said, not wanting to talk about Sean. If she mentioned her father, Jackson might see the truth in her eyes. She couldn't risk that.

"And leave Amy behind?"

"She was a very good aunt."

"But not much of a mother."

Regan willed herself to keep her temper. "She never had the opportunity."

"I'll let that go. Why did she marry Daniel?"

Regan glared at him. "She married Daniel because you broke her heart."

He swore loudly.

"Deny it all you want, but she was heartbroken when you left."

"If she was so *heartbroken*," he said the word with a sneer, "why didn't she send for me when she found out she was pregnant?"

"I—" She pressed her lips together. She didn't

know. Regan had suggested that, but Elizabeth had refused. She'd said Jackson didn't really love her, that he'd only been using her. Regan was appalled. She didn't understand how a man could treat a woman like that. But she agreed to keep silent, even when Elizabeth found out she was pregnant.

"She didn't think you cared for her."

He muttered something under his breath, but she didn't ask him to repeat it. This conversation was dangerous enough. They were dancing close to the truth, then moving away. She would have to be careful to keep her story logical and her facts in order. If she made a single mistake, Jackson would pounce on her, like the wild cat she'd likened him to.

"Several men in town wanted to marry Elizabeth, but she chose Daniel," she said.

"Was he rich?"

She spun toward him and placed her hands on her hips. "If you want to continue this conversation, you must stop saying bad things about my sister. I don't know what complaints you have about her, but I loved her very much. If you can't respect the person she was, at least respect my feelings."

"Why should I? You're the one who told my daughter I drowned after being sat on by a cow."

His disgust was a tangible thing between them. Outrage darkened his eyes. His lack of sleep must be close to her own, but he still managed to look handsome enough to befuddle her senses. They were supposed to be talking about serious things. She couldn't help smiling.

"See," he said pointing at her, "you're not even sorry."

"I had to tell her something. I'm sorry if you don't like what I chose."

"You chose it *because* you knew I wouldn't like it."

He was right about that. "I am sorry."

"Yeah, sure you are."

"No, really." Without thinking, she reached out and placed her hand on his forearm. He was warm beneath her palm. Warm and strong. Her body was angled awkwardly away from him but she didn't dare turn toward him. Their knees would bump. It would be too intimate, too much like their kiss.

At the thought of it, she bit her lower lip and withdrew her hand, lacing her fingers together on her lap. She stared at the stream.

"So why did Elizabeth marry Daniel?" he asked, as if nothing had just happened.

"I don't know. I want to think she loved him. I used to believe that, but I don't anymore. Father gave them money to add on to the house and several of our best cows to start upgrading their herd. We even shared a blooded bull."

"Daniel probably thought if he married Elizabeth he would be sure to inherit."

"My father would never do that," she said automatically, then paused. He never would have in the past, but things had been different after she came home with Amy. Perhaps Jackson was right. Maybe Daniel had seen that as an opportunity to get in Sean's good graces.

Regan remembered how hard it had been to live with her father. She'd wanted to tell him the truth, but she couldn't. She'd given her word. And once Elizabeth married Daniel, she couldn't risk her sister's happiness or her marriage. Not that their marriage had ever been perfect. Regan had been uneasy about the situation from the first mention of an engagement, but Elizabeth wouldn't listen.

"Daniel used Elizabeth to get what he wanted," she said slowly.

"You sound surprised."

"I suppose I shouldn't be. I don't think he was a good husband."

"He was a complete bastard. Any man who beats his horses is bound to fail at keeping a wife happy. And don't tell me not to criticize your relatives. You've already said Daniel wasn't related by blood."

She turned to look at him. His body was stiff, his hands tight fists. "You don't like him."

"Of course not. He was stealing cattle from your father. When I finally confronted him about it, he begged me not to hurt him. I have no time for bullies like Daniel O'Neil."

Overhead, several birds called to each other. The scene was peaceful. Yet just out of her line of vision, twelve cattle and one man lay dead. Was George the first person Daniel had killed?

"I think he might have hurt my sister." She said the words quickly, then hunched over waiting for him to laugh at her. Or worse. She'd said the same thing to her father once, but Sean hadn't wanted to know that Elizabeth's marriage wasn't what it appeared to be.

"I'm not surprised."

"You believe me?"

"Why not?" Jackson took off his hat and studied the crown. "When I caught up with Daniel, he blamed all the rustling on his friends. Said he never once took part."

"And you think he did?"

"The rustlers were too lucky not to know exactly where the cattle were going to be and where the cowboys weren't. He fingered them, and got himself a bride and more cattle in the process."

"What happened to his friends?"

"Hanged."

"What?"

"Most likely. I didn't stick around to see what happened, but most cattle rustlers end up that way if they're caught." He glanced at her. "Why are you shocked? You're the one with hired guns at the ranch. There's twelve cows and one cowboy already dead. What do you think is going on with Daniel? He's not just going to go away. It's going to get a lot more dangerous."

She didn't want to know that. She shivered. "You sound so calm."

"I'm used to this sort of thing. I'm a gunfighter. I don't sit around talking people out of their problems. By the time I show up, it means there's going to be killing."

"I don't think of you like that." The Jackson she knew smiled easily and was gentle with his five-year-old daughter. She didn't want to know that he was also a killer.

"That's because you got the drop on me." The grin was familiar but the haunted light in his eyes gave her pause. "It's my own damn fault. I should never have stopped for a bath."

Her inability to see Jackson as a killer wasn't just because she'd shot him. It was also because he'd kissed her. Even thinking about it made her heart beat faster and her body feel warmer. She told herself it was just the sun and the approaching afternoon.

But how did she reconcile the Jackson who'd held her so sweetly with the cold-blooded killer or with the man who wanted to take her daughter away? She was a fool for even trying. No matter how this ended, she wasn't going to like the outcome. She sensed it with an inevitability she couldn't ignore. After all, Jackson had left her innocent sister to face the consequences of what had happened between them.

Of course he'd come back as soon as he found out about the child. He'd come back for Amy, but not for Elizabeth. Perhaps he hadn't been lying about not loving her sister.

But he'd stolen Elizabeth's innocence.

But he was nice to Amy.

She pressed her fingers to her temples to block out her thoughts. Nothing made sense. She didn't know what to believe about him. She tried to tell herself it didn't matter, but it did. She'd never stopped caring about Jackson.

"Gage is a good man," Jackson said. He dropped his hat on the grass and braced his hands behind him on the rock. After stretching his long legs out in front of him, he leaned back and turned his head to the sun. "I can't say that for some of the men you've hired. A couple of them are real wild sons of—" He opened one eye and looked at her. "You know what I'm trying to say."

"I know." She thought about telling him he couldn't use a word she hadn't heard before. Being around cowboys all her life had made her immune to swearing, but she liked his attempt at protecting her delicate sensibilities. "Sometimes I wonder who's worse. Daniel or the hired guns."

"Daniel. I'm sure of it. There's nothing he won't do to get his way." He pushed up into a sitting position and turned to face her. "I'm not saying that to scare you but because it's true. The more you can learn about your enemy, the better."

He unbuttoned the right cuff of his white long-sleeved shirt, then started rolling it up toward his elbow. His wrists were wide and strong looking, his forearms muscled and tanned. She watched his elegant fingers at work. He had some calluses from holding the reins, but few other scars. So different from her own battered hands. She curled her fingers toward her palms and hid her fists in the folds of her brown split skirt.

"Do you think Daniel could kill someone?" she asked, voicing a question that had bothered her for months.

"Yup."

"Do you think—" She drew in a deep breath. A strand of hair had escaped from her braid. She pushed it off her face. "Do you think he could have killed a woman?"

Jackson looked at her. His eyes met her own. He hid his emotions well, concealing any surprise at her question. "Why do you ask?"

"I think he killed Elizabeth."

Jackson started on his other sleeve. "Why?"

She'd held back her feelings for so long that they all spilled out in a rush. "She'd been sick for a long time before she died. Elizabeth was never ill before the marriage. But she couldn't keep food down and she was always tired. She looked horrible. I tried to get her to see the doctor, but she kept saying it would pass. I thought he might have been poisoning her."

"Probably."

"Why do you say that?"

He pointed past her to the dead cattle lying by the stream. "They were poisoned, too."

Of course. She should have figured that out. She supposed she'd done her best to put it out of her mind. She didn't want to know that her cousin and brother-in-law had poisoned his wife. She didn't want to think that if she'd tried harder to get Elizabeth away from him, her sister might still be alive.

"They found her lying in a gully between the two properties," she said quietly. "Daniel said she'd been thrown from her horse, but I never believed him. She'd been too sick to ride. She was all bruised and broken. None of his men were out looking for her. I think he did it himself, then left her for us to find."

Anger flickered across Jackson's face. "What did the sheriff do about it? Did he arrest Daniel?"

"No. He didn't do anything. He said it was a riding accident."

"Did you tell him your concerns?"

"Of course." She looked up at him, liking the fact that he believed her. Even her father hadn't wanted her to talk about it. She'd gone to him after Elizabeth died and told him she thought Daniel might have been responsible. He'd refused to listen. "The sheriff and my father both believed I was overreacting because of grief. Sheriff Barnes thinks I'm an emotional woman given to fits of hysteria."

Jackson laughed out loud. The clear sound rolled over the valley and drifted back with a slight echo.

"Sheriff Barnes doesn't know you, does he?"

She smiled "I guess not."

Placing one booted foot on the rock she sat on, Jackson leaned toward her. There was a scar on his temple. She reached toward it but didn't have the courage to actually touch him. "What happened?"

Before he could answer, she heard the rattling of a wagon. They stood up and turned toward the sound. Zeke drove a spring wagon down the hillside. A man on horseback rode beside him. She shaded her eyes and squinted, then raised her arms.

"Pete, over here."

The man on horseback rode toward them. As he got closer, Regan could see he was angry. His usually smiling mouth was pulled straight. His gaze took in Jackson, then settled on her.

"I found out what happened," he said as he got close enough to be heard. "Why didn't you send for me?"

"You'd already left to ride the fence lines. I thought—"

"What if Daniel had been waiting here?"

"I can handle Daniel."

Pete reined in his horse and dismounted. He stalked over to her, stopping when he was in front of her. For the first time in as long as she could remember, he looked down at her as if trying to use his greater height to intimidate her. "What if Daniel hadn't been alone?"

"That's why I came along," Jackson said, his calm voice a contrast to Pete's obvious temper.

Pete ignored him. "Until this is settled, you can't go riding off like this on your own."

She was about to remind him that she was the boss and no one, not even he, could tell her what to do. Then she noticed that Pete was spending more time glaring at Jackson than at her. Realization dawned. Pete was more upset about Jackson's accompanying her than he was about her running into Daniel.

She wanted to tell him exactly what she thought of his lack of sense, but she didn't. Pete wouldn't appreciate being yelled at in front of Jackson. She didn't want the two men circling each other like stallions fighting for the herd.

"I didn't go off by myself," she said at last. "But I appreciate your concern." She glanced at the wagon and the driver. "Where's the sheriff?"

"He couldn't make it."

"What?"

"He sent a message saying dead is dead. He's too busy to make time today, but he'll be here first thing in the morning."

Looked as if Pete and Jackson weren't the only stubborn males she was going to have to handle. "That's just like him. If one of the other ranchers had had this problem, he would have been out before spit could dry on a rock. But because it's me, he can't even bother to show his face until tomorrow. Does he know one of my men is dead, too?"

"Yeah, he knows." Pete looked disgusted. "I don't understand what Sheriff Barnes has against you, Regan."

"Me, either."

"Where's George?"

She pointed to a slight depression on the hillside. Pete led his horse toward the spot and called for the wagon driver to join him. Together they bent over the fallen man.

"The sheriff really does think you're stupid," Jackson said.

"Apparently so. You can see for yourself in the morning."

Her bay gelding was grazing nearby. She grabbed the reins, then swung up into the saddle. Jackson hesitated.

"You coming?" she asked.

He looked at the dead cattle. "You going to post a guard?"

"Why? No one's going to steal them. As the good sheriff pointed out, dead is dead."

9

The spring morning had dawned just as perfectly as the one before. The sky was clear, the air pleasantly warm. None of that had made a damn bit of difference, Jackson thought as he rubbed the back of his neck. He had a bad feeling about this whole thing and no matter how he tried, he couldn't shake it.

Regan led the way, with Sheriff Barnes right behind her. Jackson was third, mostly because Pete seemed determined to keep an eye on him. Just what he needed. Some overeager cowboy guarding Regan's back. What Pete didn't realized was that Regan didn't need protecting. After being shot, kicked, and left senseless from a kiss that was supposed to teach *her* a lesson, Jackson had learned to be wary of Regan O'Neil. She could bring a man to his knees faster than a slippery creek bottom.

The riders approached the rolling hills and angled north. Pete kept pace with Jackson, occasionally casting him searching glances. Jackson didn't know how much Regan had told her friend, but it seemed to be enough to put Pete on guard. That wasn't a bad thing. Jackson knew if his sense for trouble was right, everybody was going to need to be alert. They weren't going to get any help from the sheriff.

He looked up at the older man riding ahead of him. Barnes was closer to fifty than forty, with graying hair and piercing black eyes. He was wiry, with the rolling stride of someone who had spent his life in a saddle. Jackson figured he was probably good at his job and intended to keep the peace. The problem was that Barnes thought Regan was some swooning female given to fits of fancy and fainting. That had been obvious from his reluctance to even visit the valley. He'd looked at the dead cowboy laid out in a spare shed and had determined he fell off his horse. Nothing sinister about that.

Jackson glanced around at the blossoming countryside. He didn't need this kind of trouble. He should collect his things and ride off. Somewhere up north there was a ranch waiting for him. There was nothing keeping him here in Texas.

Except for one bright-eyed little girl named Amy.

Just that morning, before they left, she'd come out to the barn and shyly invited him to have tea with her dolls when he got back. Her appeal wasn't just that she reminded him of Lily. Part of it was that she genuinely seemed to like him. There was a sweetness about her. She was quick, pretty, and, by God, his daughter. So even if leaving made the most sense, he couldn't do it yet. Not until he knew what was going to happen.

Would he take Amy with him or leave her behind? Which was best for the child? Part of him believed

Amy would be better off around people she'd known all her life. Yet something inside of him balked at the idea of giving up his daughter.

Regan was out in front. She crested the slight rise first. He watched as she suddenly reined in her horse and stared. Sheriff Barnes moved next to her. Jackson rode up and looked down into the valley. The feeling of uneasiness grew.

Grazing on the rich green grass and drinking from the stream were thirty-five or forty head of cattle. The brand on the animals showed they belonged to Regan O'Neil's herd. Jackson looked around the shallow valley. There were no dead bodies, no sign that anything had ever died here.

Pete stopped beside him. "Damn Daniel's hide."

Jackson squeezed his thighs. His horse leaped forward. He cantered down the sloping hill toward the creek. After circling the small herd, he found what he was looking for. Drag marks and hoof prints, heading west out of the valley. If he remembered correctly, Daniel's spread was west of here. Someone had come by late yesterday and dragged the dead cattle off. Then this new herd had been brought over to graze. He looked toward the trail made by the dead cattle. It would be easy enough to go over and scout out the situation. He glanced back and saw Regan arguing with the sheriff.

One of the grazing cows lifted its head and stared at him. Jackson frowned. This had to be the craziest thing he'd ever seen. Why would someone want to make Regan look bad? He frowned, then adjusted his hat. Why go to all that trouble? Unless Daniel planned to take advantage of it later. Maybe he wanted the sheriff to think Regan was unbalanced so that when she reported a more serious crime, Barnes would have reason not to believe her.

He rode back to the top of the rise.

"They were dragged off," he said. "There's some marks by the creek." He pointed in that direction. "There's too many hoof marks, though. They blur everything."

Barnes looked at him as if he was crazy. "So you saw these dead cattle, too?"

"Yes. There were twelve of them. They'd been poisoned."

Barnes shook his head. "Regan, I've known you a long time. Your daddy, too. I've got to tell you, I'm worried. This is a big spread. It was difficult enough for Sean to keep everything going. You're just a woman. It seems to me that losing your sister, then your father, has been too much. Your brain is addled."

Regan stiffened. Fire shot from her blue eyes. "There's nothing wrong with my brain, Sheriff. Or any part of me. Just because I'm a woman doesn't mean I can't see dead cattle when they're lying in a field."

"I suppose you saw them, too?" Barnes asked Pete.

The cowboy nodded. "All twelve. They were dead all right."

"You've got them all seeing dead cows," Barnes said. He took off his hat and smoothed down his hair. "Your men have always been loyal to you, Regan. I'll grant you that. You've done your best, girl. No one can ask more than that. There's no shame in failing, either. Why if you were a man, you'd be able to make a go of it."

Jackson saw Regan lean forward. For a second he

thought she was going to pull her gun on the sheriff. He grabbed her arm and gave her a warning glance. She glared at him, then relaxed slightly. The faint twist of her mouth told him he'd read her intentions perfectly.

Jackson turned to the sheriff. "I saw those cattle. Are you calling me a liar?"

Barnes's bushy eyebrows drew together. "I don't know you. Are you new to these parts?"

"I'm a friend of the family."

"What's your name?"

"Jackson Tyler."

"Why is that name familiar?" Barnes asked quietly. He rubbed his chin.

"I was here six years ago to help Sean with some trouble he was having. With Daniel O'Neil."

Barnes's gaze narrowed. "You're a gunfighter. We don't take to your kind around here. You best not be making any trouble."

Jackson was surprised. Apparently the good sheriff hadn't figured out Regan and Daniel already were in the middle of a range war. Unless he was turning a blind eye to Daniel's part in the problem.

"You didn't answer my question. You calling me a liar?"

Jackson wasn't worried. The sheriff was old and wily. He wouldn't start trouble with a gunfighter over something as foolish as a few dead cows. But Jackson wanted to make a point. They'd all seen the cattle; they all knew Daniel had done it. Jackson wanted the sheriff to acknowledge something had happened here.

Barnes looked at the shallow valley, then back at

Jackson. "I'm saying there aren't any dead cows there now. No dead cattle, no crime."

"What about George?" Regan blurted out. "He's dead. Aren't you going to do anything about that?"

"Like I said before, there's no gunshot or knife wound. Near as I can tell, he fell off his horse and broke his neck. It's a sorry thing, to be sure, but nobody's fault." Barnes wheeled his horse around. "Regan, you'd best be thinking about what I said. It's time you got married and let a man take over this place. It's too much for you."

"Of course," she said bitterly. "And Daniel is my best choice, right?"

"He's concerned about you and willing to overlook certain matters of your past."

"I'm so grateful for that." She glared at the older man. "He killed my sister, and now he's killed George. How many people have to die before you realize how dangerous he is?"

Barnes stared at her for a long time. "I'm sorry you feel this way, Regan. I suggest you see a doctor as soon as you can. He'll be able to give you a tonic to settle your temperament." He nodded at the other two men, then rode off toward town.

Jackson watched him until he disappeared over a rise. His own temper was mighty close to the surface. His word had never been questioned before.

"If that's what you put up with when you go into town, it's no wonder you don't bother," he said.

He'd expected some sharp comment from Regan. Instead she studied her hands. Pete moved his horse closer to her.

"You all right?" he asked.

"I'm fine." She raised her head slightly and glanced at Jackson. "Yesterday you said you wanted to post a guard. How did you know this was going to happen?"

"I didn't. I just had a bad feeling about it."

"Next time I'll trust your feelings. If we'd left somebody here—"

"He'd be a dead man right now," Jackson interrupted. "Daniel wants to get this ranch, and he wants to make it as hard on you as he can."

"He's doing a good job." She sighed. "Sometimes I feel as if I can't win at this."

"Regan . . . " Pete touched her arm.

She smiled at him. "Don't worry. There's no way Daniel is going to get his hands on my ranch. Now don't you have some fences to ride?"

Pete looked at Jackson. "What are you going to do?"

"I want to look around here a little more," he said.

"I'll be back later, too," Regan added.

Pete didn't want to ride off and leave them. Jackson wasn't sure if it was because Pete didn't trust what Regan would do, or if he didn't trust Jackson. Probably both, Jackson thought.

"You know where to find me if you need anything," Pete said, then turned his horse back toward the ranch.

"You should go with him," Jackson said.

"Why?"

"Don't sound so suspicious. I have a couple of things I want to check out."

"Like what?"

He frowned at her. "Nothing I want to talk about. And the last thing I need is you tagging along."

"Let me guess." She fluttered her lashes. "A poor little woman like me might swoon in the saddle, or get in your way." She pressed the back of her hand to her forehead. "I swear, I feel a faint comin' on right now."

He smiled. "Yeah, that's it." He rubbed his thigh, feeling the bandage he still wore and the ache from the wound. He would be in a lot better shape if she was more like a typical female. "At least we know you can shoot if things get bad with Daniel."

Her gaze dropped to his leg. "Did I tell you I was sorry?" she asked.

"No."

She sighed. She was stubborn and had the temper of a wounded bear. She would rather be publicly flogged than admit she'd been wrong. He knew that because he shared a lot of her more imperfect traits. Maybe that was why they butted heads so much. It was also why he knew exactly how much it cost her to apologize.

"I am," she said, her voice low. "It was wrong of me to shoot you like that."

"How should you have shot me?"

She looked at him. Today she wore a dark blue blouse tucked into a rust-colored split skirt. She'd slept enough to make the shadows under her eyes fade. There was color in her cheeks and only a few loose strands of hair drifting around her face.

She smiled—slowly. The curve of her lips and the flash of white teeth caught him by surprise. Mostly because he wanted to smile back. Worse, he wanted to urge his horse to close the few feet between them and touch her face. He wanted to find out if her freckles felt any different from the rest of her face.

His gaze dropped to her chest. She couldn't wear a corset and ride as much as she did. So what exactly was under the blue blouse that was—he noticed, much to his chagrin—the exact color of her eyes?

He shook his head. No way. He refused to be attracted to Regan O'Neil. The way his luck was running, the next time she aimed, she would hit something more important than his thigh.

"I shouldn't have shot you at all," she said.

"What about kneeing me in the—" He motioned to his crotch.

She colored slightly but didn't look away. "You deserved that."

He grinned. "I suppose I did. I accept your apology. Now get on home."

"Where are you going? I want to come with you."

"Why? Don't you trust me?"

"Not really."

That was honest. "You're a helluva woman, Regan, but you've got no business trailing after me. If I'm right, I'll tell you about it when I get back. If I'm wrong, you won't have to worry about me wanting to take Amy away."

She wouldn't budge. He could tell by the stubborn set of her shoulders. "I'm coming with you," she said. "You might as well get used to the fact."

"All right, if you're determined to tag along, then I'm not going to stop you. But stay out of trouble."

He turned his horse west and started across the valley. She followed, her bay gelding easily keeping stride with his.

"You're going to Daniel's, aren't you?"

"I just want to have a word or two with him." He didn't have a plan exactly, but that was fine. He often

If you have a passion for great historical romance, here's an offer you'll love...

4 FREE NOVELS

Reader Service.

Yes! I want to join the Timeless Romance Reader Service. Please send me my 4 FREE HarperMonogram historical romances. Then each month send me 4 new historical romances to preview without obligation for 10 days. I'll pay the low subscription price of $4.00 for every book I choose to keep--a total savings of at least $2.00 each month--and home delivery is free! I understand that I may return any title within 10 days and receive a full credit. I may cancel this subscription at any time without obligation by simply writing "Canceled" on any invoice and mailing it to Timeless Romance. There is no minimum number of books to purchase.

NAME

ADDRESS

CITY   STATE   ZIP

TELEPHONE

SIGNATURE

(If under 18, parent or guardian must sign. Program, price, terms, and conditions subject to cancellation and change. Orders subject to acceptance by HarperMonogram.)

Indulge in passion, adventure and romance with your

4 FREE

Historical Romances.

TIMELESS ROMANCE
READER SERVICE

120 Brighton Road
P.O. Box 5069
Clifton, NJ 07015-5069

didn't have a plan. He preferred to work things out as he went. "I want to see if he's changed."

"He has. For the worst."

"Anybody in town share your opinion of him?" They rode abreast through the valley, then over the far hill, following the trail left by the dead cattle. Jackson wondered if they should have insisted Sheriff Barnes see this, then realized the old man had already made up his mind about Regan. It would take Daniel holding his cousin at gunpoint to get Barnes to change his feelings about the situation.

"No, they think Daniel is wonderful. He can be very charming when he wants to be. After all, he charmed Elizabeth."

He was about to point out that it didn't take much doing, but he held in the words. He liked his truce with Regan better than he liked her hating him.

"At some point, she figured out the truth about him," he said.

"Probably about the time he started hitting her." Regan sounded matter-of-fact.

"What?" Jackson reined in his horse and stared at her. "Daniel hit Elizabeth?"

"I saw the bruises. I went over to their house once, and she had a black eye and split lip." Regan stared past him. "There were marks on her neck. In the shape of a man's fingers."

Emotions flickered across her face. Sadness for her sister, and maybe for herself.

"What did she say happened?"

"That she'd had an accident in the barn. It wasn't likely. Elizabeth didn't go in the barn if she could help it."

Unless she wanted a man. The thought came unbidden. Jackson remembered Elizabeth approaching him late at night. She'd complained about being in the barn, but since he wouldn't come to her, she hadn't had any choice.

He'd been too drunk to get out of her way, but not too drunk to enjoy her performance. She'd taken off her clothes slowly, exposing her perfect body, and then showed him everything she'd learned. He'd been impressed.

He blinked and was back with Regan. He saw her studying him, then witnessed her flash of shame. She remembered that night, too. He wanted to tell her he was sorry he'd sent her away. He had a feeling that an apology would only make it worse between them. She continued to compare herself to Elizabeth and find herself wanting. But Elizabeth had been nothing but a vain, selfish young woman who thought only of her own pleasure.

He looked at Regan's hands, scarred, bruised, battered. Her clothes served a function rather than fashion. She cared more about the ranch and Amy than about her looks. Her entire life was spent in service of something other than herself. She worked harder than any man he knew, for little reward. She deserved better than his statement that her sister was a slut, better than his confession that he hadn't thought enough of her to want to kiss her, so he said nothing. He urged his horse forward, and Regan's moved into step next to him.

"Given all that happened to Elizabeth, you can understand why I don't want to take Sheriff Barnes up on his suggestion that I marry my cousin," she said.

"Has he proposed?"

Regan laughed, but her humor was edged with bitterness. "I haven't seen much of him since my father died. Daniel came over after the funeral and told me he would have the ranch. He didn't care what he had to do to get it. Then he offered to marry me." She looked at Jackson. "He told me his was the only proposal I was likely to get and that I should be grateful for it. I told him despite his generous offer, I wouldn't marry the man who'd murdered my sister."

"How did he take that?"

She ducked her head so that her hat hid her expression.

"He threatened you." It wasn't a question.

"He said I would live to regret my decision."

"I know Barnes is a fool, but he does have a point. If you were married, Daniel wouldn't be able to get the ranch away from you. It would belong to your husband."

"It still wouldn't be mine," she snapped. "This is O'Neil land and I intend to keep it safe for my daughter. I wouldn't trust anyone who would marry me just to get the ranch. He might be worse than Daniel."

"I didn't mean that you should marry just for the land."

"What other reason is there?" She turned to look at him. The sun hit her fully in the face, illuminating her features. "That land out there is more appealing than I am. I don't have what men want. I'm not Elizabeth."

"That's true," he said, thinking Elizabeth had little to recommend her outside of her obvious physical charms. Regan would always challenge a man. She would never make it easy, but the ride would be interesting as hell. "But I think that—"

His words died in his throat. Regan had straightened

in her saddle and was staring straight ahead. Her head was high, her chin thrust forward, her spine as stiff as a fireplace poker. Something had her tail feathers in a bunch.

He thought about their conversation. She'd said she wasn't like her sister and he'd agreed. She wasn't. He didn't mean she was less than Elizabeth, but she hadn't taken it that way. She thought he'd insulted her.

In a situation like this, the best thing to do was compliment the woman on her pretty eyes or smile. Women usually forgave a man anything if he said something nice about how she looked. He had a feeling that Regan wasn't most women and that she wouldn't believe him even if he could think of something nice to say. It's not that she was ugly. She wasn't. She was just—different. Most women of his acquaintance didn't ride astride, carry a gun, and know how to use it, or successfully run several thousand head of cattle. She didn't spend time keeping her skin white and her hair tamed. He liked her spirit; he admired her ability to work hard. And she was a damn fine kisser.

He darted her a quick glance. Her stiff posture hadn't changed. He didn't think talking about kissing would make her feel better. Next time he would think before he spoke.

Jackson grimaced. He'd made that promise before.

"Did anyone else believe Daniel murdered his wife?" he asked, to change the subject.

"A couple of the men agreed with me. Pete, of course. Fayre and her husband. But they weren't enough for Sheriff Barnes. My father didn't believe us either. He didn't even want to hear me talk about it. I suppose he couldn't bear to think that someone he'd accepted into the family had turned on him like that. He always thought the best of Daniel. Even when he was rustling cattle. In a way I'm glad he died before he found out the truth. It would have destroyed him. He'd already been disappointed enough."

Before he could ask by what, they entered a grove of trees. The leaves of the oaks weren't completely unfolded yet, while the cedar elms were already covered with green and offering shade. He recognized the path and knew the house was just up ahead.

Unlike Regan's big white two-story house, Daniel lived in a smaller place. Six years ago it needed repairs and Jackson didn't doubt it still would. Regan had mentioned something about her father giving Daniel money. If her cousin hadn't changed, and men like him rarely did, the money had gone for gambling and whiskey, rather than repairs and breeding stock.

The grove of trees ended. Jackson reined in his horse and stared down at the house. A couple of rooms had been added. Black oaks surrounded the building.

Jackson had waited in this very spot back then to confront Daniel. When the younger man finally rode up, Jackson went down to say his piece. He still remembered telling Daniel he had proof that Daniel was rustling cattle from Sean. Daniel went for his gun, but he was shaking too hard to fire straight. The single bullet went wide.

Jackson didn't have the same problem. He aimed his pistol, then told the other man he could confess or die. Daniel had defied him, Jackson recalled. He'd laughed and said Jackson couldn't kill him.

"I know about Sean's orders," Daniel had said, his black eyes flashing with triumph.

"But there's only the two of us here," Jackson had replied. "And you fired first. I told your uncle I'd follow orders, but not at the expense of my life. I could explain your death as self-defense."

He could hear the other men riding up; Sean and his cowboys had been a half mile behind. "You have less than a minute to decide," he'd said. "Confess or die."

At that moment, he'd wanted to kill Daniel. He could smell the other man's evilness. If Daniel wasn't destroyed, he would continue to prey on others, a human vulture searching out the weak.

Daniel had read his intentions in his eyes. The dark-haired man had fallen to his knees.

"It was them," he'd said, pointing in the direction of the barn. "They forced me to give them information about my uncle's cattle. I didn't want to have anything to do with it. It was them."

They both knew he was lying. Daniel played his part well. By the time Sean and the other men rode up, he was in tears, protesting his sorrow and his innocence. Even as Daniel told his stories and was forgiven, his gaze had locked with Jackson's. Hatred had flowed between them. Jackson had known one or both of them would die if they ever met again.

Which made riding onto Daniel's ranch a pretty stupid idea.

"What are you going to do?" Regan's question drew him back to the present.

"Hell if I know. You stay here while I figure it out."

"I don't think so." She urged her horse forward so it stayed in step with his. "Whatever you do, you're going to need help."

"And that's you?"

She looked at him and raised her eyebrows. "I was good enough to shoot you. I think I can handle the situation."

"I was naked and unarmed. Can you react the same way when someone's holding a gun on you?"

"Let's find out."

Jackson mumbled something under his breath. Regan wasn't sure what it was, and she didn't ask him to repeat it. No doubt he was calling her ten different kinds of fool. She didn't blame him. She *was* a fool for coming with him. She didn't want to confront Daniel right now. Truthfully, she didn't ever want to confront him, but Jackson had forced her hand. She couldn't let him go riding in there by himself. Who knew what would happen? If nothing else, she could count on herself to keep a firm grip on her temper and make sure the situation didn't flare out of control.

She stiffened her spine and squared her shoulders, hoping Jackson wouldn't figure out she was scared. She didn't like direct confrontation, especially with a murderer. Daniel had already killed Elizabeth and one of her men. Who would be next? Fayre? Amy? Herself? The knot in her belly told her Daniel wasn't going to stop until he got exactly what he wanted: the ranch.

What was he going to say when he saw Jackson? Six years ago, after everything had settled down about the rustling, Daniel had wanted to go after Jackson. He'd had a heated conversation with Sean about the gunslinger. Sean had told her cousin that Jackson had simply been doing his job, but that wasn't good enough for Daniel. He'd wished Jackson in hell.

Still smarting from his rejection, Regan had agreed. Now she knew better. Jackson might not be interested in her as a woman, but she trusted him to protect her. Any slight to her female pride didn't matter when compared with keeping her family alive.

She leaned forward and untied the leather thongs that held her rifle in place. With one long, swift motion, she pulled it out, set it stock down on her thigh, and supported the barrel with her right hand. Jackson did the same.

Their eyes met. "That loaded?" he asked.

At first she was insulted, then she saw the teasing glint in his eye. "Want me to shoot your hat off to prove it?"

"Lady, I wouldn't trust your aim. You were less than twenty feet away and you still missed my heart by a good three feet."

"And you're damned grateful."

He winked. "That I am."

They rode out of the trees and toward the house. Regan saw several men around the house and main barn. They weren't working. Instead they seemed to be waiting for something. They were all heavily armed.

"Looks like we're expected," he said.

"There's more of them than us."

"Is that a problem?"

She looked at Jackson. He was calm, even relaxed. He was the professional. "Not if you don't think it is."

"We can't turn back," he said, pointing to one of the men standing by the house. The man looked up and saw them, then called to the others.

"You think a retreat would look bad?"

"Can't let Daniel know he's got us running scared. Besides, nothing is going to happen."

"How do you know?"

Jackson grinned. The flash of white teeth gave her courage. "Explaining away drugged cattle is one thing. Explaining bullet-filled corpses on his front porch is quite another."

She wanted to ask what would happen if Jackson was wrong, but she agreed with one thing he said. They'd come too far to turn away. Dealing with Daniel had taught her never to show her back or her fear. Besides, she trusted Jackson to keep her safe. They might not agree on certain issues, such as Amy and Elizabeth, but he was, at heart, an honorable man.

It was silent as they rode toward the house. Even the birds stopped calling to each other. She wondered if they'd had the good sense to fly off, or if they were watching, waiting to see who won.

The corral in front of the barn had some railings that needed mending. The barn itself needed a good coat of paint. She didn't understand why Daniel let his place get so run-down. Her father had given him money to fix everything up when he married Elizabeth. The good breeding cows should have brought him lots of cattle to sell up north. But somehow it hadn't worked out the way it was supposed to. She wondered if it was because Daniel was bitter, or if he was inept at running the ranch. The latter thought gave her pause. Bad enough to lose everything Sean had worked for; worse to lose it to someone who wouldn't treat the ranch with respect and help it to grow.

In the time it took them to ride down the slight slope toward the sprawling one-story house, she counted eight armed men watching them. Her heart started beating a little faster and her palms grew sweaty. She brushed them, one at a time, against her skirt. Her hat sat low on her head, shielding her eyes. The rifle felt heavy, so she shifted, cradling it in her arms like a baby.

The path widened as they reached the house. In the shadows of the wide porch she saw two more men standing, armed and ready for trouble. She didn't recognize any of them, although she knew most of Daniel's cowboys. But she knew what they were. She was familiar with the sharp-eyed gazes, the restlessness, even as they stood still, the casual poses that kept their shooting hand free and within easy reach of their pistols.

Hired guns. She knew them because she'd hired a half dozen just like them herself.

The men watched her and Jackson as they reached the house. Something cold slipped down her spine. She knew it was fear, but she refused to give in to it. She wouldn't run, wouldn't show it in any way. So instead of cowering on her saddle, she sat taller and raised her chin slightly. When she reined in the bay, she shifted the rifle just enough so she would be able to shoot it in a second, if she had to.

The front door opened slowly and Daniel walked out. He looked nothing like the O'Neils. He was medium height and wiry, with black hair and small dark eyes. The slightly swarthy cast to his skin always made her wonder if he had Indian blood, or perhaps that of a Spanish conquistador. Daniel had never mentioned his past. He was four when Regan's uncle adopted him and if he remembered anything about that time, he didn't say.

Regan stared at her cousin and wondered how they'd come to this moment. Why was he so determined to make trouble? They could have lived peacefully, side by side, each ranch growing bigger, better, because of the other. She exhaled softly. That had never been good enough for Daniel. He was determined to have it all.

Daniel looked at her, then frowned at Jackson. Regan glanced to her left. She realized Jackson wore his hat pulled low. The wide brim cast shadows on his face, hiding his features. Daniel wasn't going to be happy to find out Jackson was back.

"I know it was you," she said, not bothering with a greeting.

Daniel smiled slowly. She hated his smiles. They reminded her of a small vicious dog pretending to be friendly right before biting. He walked to the edge of the porch and leaned against the railing. The wood was worn, parts hanging loose. She sent up a quick prayer that the part that supported him would choose this moment to give way.

Unfortunately, the prayer went unanswered.

"I'm sure I don't know what you're talking about," he said, his evil smile staying in place. Around him several of the men grinned at each other. They'd all been part of the destruction. It sickened her.

"I'm sure you do. The dozen cows are no great loss, but George was a good man." She shook her head slowly. "I suppose even murder doesn't disturb your conscience."

Daniel's smile faded. "That's a serious accusation. If you think I killed your man, where's the sheriff?"

"You know damn well after the trick you played—" She clamped her lips together. She didn't want to give him the satisfaction of knowing how much he'd upset her. She leaned forward in her saddle. Daniel's dark eyes met and held her own. She stared at the man, trying to find the boy she'd known. She'd never liked Daniel very much, but there was a time when he hadn't been so evil.

Maybe not, she told herself. Perhaps he'd always been this way, but he'd kept it hidden.

"You won't win," she said loudly, looking at her cousin but speaking to all the men. "The ranch is mine. My father left it to me, and I intend to keep it."

Daniel folded his arms over his chest. "Don't be a fool, Regan. I'll have your ranch. Making it easier on yourself is your choice. But no matter what, I'll have what's rightfully mine."

"Yours?" She dismissed him with a flick of her hand. "You're no one, Daniel. Not an O'Neil by blood. You'll never get what you so want. I swear it on my life."

His gaze narrowed. "As you wish. I had hoped it wouldn't come to killing you, but if it does . . ." He shrugged and let the sentence trail off.

Regan caught her breath and glanced at the men around them. The trickling fear intensified. She hoped Jackson had been right when he said Daniel wouldn't risk killing them on his property.

"I see you're still a bully," Jackson said. "What kind of man enjoys threatening a woman?"

Daniel jerked his head toward the other man. He peered at him, obviously trying to place the voice. Jackson reached up and shifted his hat back on his head, exposing his face. Daniel paled, then swore under his breath.

"What the hell are you doing back here?" he asked, his voice not as confident as it had been just a moment before.

"Taking care of some business I should have finished

the last time I was here." He shifted on his saddle. "If anyone's going to die, old friend, it's going to be you."

Daniel took a step back, then halted suddenly as if he just realized what he'd done. His eyes flared with rage. "Not this time, you bastard. This time you'll be the one."

"I don't think so."

Jackson moved so quickly, Regan didn't see the actual action. One second he was sitting on his horse, his hand resting on his thigh, the next he was holding a pistol pointed directly at Daniel. She glanced around them. Most of the other men had drawn guns as well.

"They have more guns than we do," she said quietly, making sure there was no fear in her voice.

"I'm not surprised."

"You're going to kill him? Despite the consequences?"

Jackson didn't even spare her a glance. "I should have done it years ago."

"If you do, they won't have any trouble explaining bullet-riddled corpses."

Jackson gave her a quick glance. She wasn't surprised to see pure gray irises. His expression was cold, distant. He had the eyes of a killer. If he hadn't been on her side, she would have been terrified of him. As it was, she was a little nervous.

"I told you to stay behind."

"Maybe if you told me why, I would have listened."

"Yeah, right." He returned his attention to Daniel.

Her cousin had backed up closer to the house. He was obviously shaken. His men circled around like vultures waiting to see who died first. She prayed they wouldn't fire. Daniel had a pistol strapped to his hip but didn't seem inclined to pull it out.

She watched the gunslingers move closer. Her heart pounded hard in her chest and it was difficult to breathe. Something bad was going to happen here, unless she stopped it. The problem was she didn't know how. She was involved in a situation she didn't understand and she had a feeling they were all going to die. Jackson didn't seem to care. If anything, he was willing to destroy Daniel at any cost. She didn't want that. She just wanted to be left alone to run the ranch.

Something inside of her flared up at the thought of having her choices taken away from her.

"No!" she said loudly. All the men turned to look at her. She pressed her thighs against her horse, moving him between Daniel and Jackson. She turned to Jackson. "Put your gun away."

Gray eyes met hers. He didn't work for her. She probably didn't have any right to tell him what to do, and she wasn't sure he was going to bother to listen. But she had to try. It couldn't end like this. If it did, Daniel would win.

Jackson met her gaze. She read his anger and indecision. She pleaded silently. He nodded slightly and shifted his pistol so it pointed at the ground. She sighed her relief, then turned her attention to Daniel.

The pure hatred on her cousin's face made her recoil slightly in her saddle. She swallowed hard. "It's over, Daniel," she said quietly. "No more killing, no more trouble."

"You're wrong, Regan," Daniel said, moving toward the edge of the porch. "None of this will stop until I get the ranch. You can make it easy on yourself, or you can make it hard." His words were a snarl. "I would like it better if you made it hard. That way you'll suffer more."

She wondered how they'd all been so blind to his rage. "You mean to kill me," she said. "The same way you killed my sister."

"No, Regan, I'll kill you a different way."

She sucked in her breath. Oh, God, she'd been right about him. Her heart squeezed tight in her chest. She'd wanted to be wrong. She could feel the burning pressure behind her eyes, but she wouldn't give into tears here. She wouldn't give Daniel the satisfaction.

"You bastard," she said. "You lying, murdering bastard. I'll see you in hell for this."

Daniel laughed at her. "Strong words coming from the sister of a slut."

Regan stiffened. "Don't you dare talk about Elizabeth that way."

"Why not? Everyone knew it." He glanced at Jackson. "Even your hired gun there had his way with her. Everyone did. Elizabeth deserved to die, and you do, too. The proud Sean O'Neil, always talking about his precious daughters. It must have killed the old man to know he'd sired whores."

She heard his words through a haze of rage. Without thinking, she raised her rifle toward him. Daniel drew back in horror. The men around him scattered.

Before she could aim, Jackson swept off his hat and slapped it against her horse's rump. The bay gelding jumped forward, nearly unseating her. She hung on with her thighs. The tight pressure urged her horse to go faster. She grabbed the reins and turned him back the way they'd come. Only then did she notice Jackson riding between her and Daniel's men.

They made their way back through the trees, then up to the top of the rise. There they paused.

As she slipped her rifle back in its scabbard, she tried to catch her breath. Lingering fear made her cold.

"We both have a little trouble with our temper," Jackson said, staring down at the way they'd come. "We'll have to remember that for next time."

"Next time?" she echoed, trying to gather her thoughts. "Of course. It's not over. It will never be over. This will go on until—"

She didn't want to think about the "until."

She wondered if she could destroy her cousin. She wanted to believe she could. Heaven knew he needed killing. But her father had raised her to respect family above all else. She could hear her father's voice in her head telling her it was wrong.

She grimaced, recalling her recent behavior. Of course if Daniel made her furious again, she would probably do it herself.

"That's twice now I've pulled a gun in anger," she said, ashamed. "I was never like that before."

"You've never had your back to the wall. You're a strong woman, Regan. You're willing to do anything necessary to protect what's yours."

"It's not just the land," she said, glancing at him. "It's Amy. I won't let her be harmed by this."

"I know. You're a good mother."

She should have been pleased by his words. Instead they made her wonder if she was. Perhaps it would be best to let him take his daughter. At least then Amy would be safe from Daniel. She closed her eyes against the pain. Giving up her child would destroy her. She might as well hand Daniel the ranch.

Without her child, she would have no reason to keep fighting.

"It will never end, will it?" she asked.

Jackson leaned over and touched her arm. It was silly, but the pressure of his hand gave her comfort. "It'll end when Daniel is dead."

Dead. That was so final. Another person destroyed. Did it always have to come to that? Wasn't there another solution?

"What are you thinking?" Jackson asked as he urged his horse forward.

Her bay gelding moved into step beside his. "I was wondering why it always comes down to killing. There has to be another way out of this problem."

"If you believe that, why did you hire gunslingers?"

"To keep the peace."

"You know Daniel. That's not possible. He wants what you have. He won't stop until he gets it. Our little visit there didn't help things."

"What do you mean?"

"I mean instead of calling, he just raised the stakes. Unless you give him what he wants, he's going to kill you."

10

The ride back to the ranch was silent. Jackson could feel Regan watching him. He tried to ignore her. Things had gotten out of hand at Daniel's ranch and he had only himself to blame. Seeing that bastard there, knowing what he'd done and what he still planned to do, he'd reacted without thinking. It was stupid. Worse, it was deadly. He could have gotten Regan killed. He knew better. If he didn't, he wouldn't have survived all this time. A gunslinger with bad instincts made for a very young corpse.

Finally, she glanced at him one too many times. "What's wrong?" he asked.

"I was just wondering why I didn't see what was going to happen. When Daniel first started making trouble, I thought I could handle it on my own. I thought he would be reasonable. I see now that's not going to happen. It's never going to end." She motioned toward him. "I'm afraid you're right."

He didn't want to be right. Unfortunately, he knew he was. "I'm sorry," he said.

"Don't be." She stared straight ahead. "You must think I'm a fool."

"No. It's hard for people who get involved in this kind of situation to really understand where it's going to lead."

"I agree. I had no idea. I hired Mr. McLane and the other men, but I didn't really think about the killing. I wasn't frightened of you before."

"Are you now?"

They'd crossed through the shallow valley where the dead cattle had lain, then rode up the other side. She reined in her horse. The early afternoon sun was bright overhead. She wore her hat low, but he could see her face. Concern darkened her blue eyes. She worried her lower lip as she thought. Her fingers twisted around the reins.

He studied her hands. Her fingers didn't move gracefully through the air as she spoke, they didn't slip softly on the keys of a piano creating beautiful music on warm summer nights. If she was still awake when the moon was high, she was probably dealing with a sick horse or helping some cow give birth.

"Are you afraid of me?" he asked again, not sure he wanted to know the answer. He'd come to the O'Neil ranch to claim his son. Instead he found a daughter and Regan. In the last six years, something had changed. He didn't know if it was himself, Regan, or the situation. He didn't want to know. But he was sure he didn't want her to be afraid of him.

"You talk about living and dying so easily," she said. She loosened her grip on the reins. Her horse bent down and began cropping grass. She patted the animal's shoulder absently. "As if the taking of a life was as easy as breathing."

He stared out past her, at the grassland and cattle, wondering if he'd ever seen anything so peaceful. "Killing a man is never easy, but if you're a gun-slinger, you have to get the job done."

"I shot you easy enough," she said. "If Pete hadn't jerked my arm down, I would have killed you."

He met her gaze. "I understand what happened."

"I don't," she said loudly. "I don't understand at all. How could I have done that? What's worse is that I almost did it again today. If you hadn't hit my horse—" She shook her head. "What's happening to me?"

"You've got your back against a wall and you're willing to do anything to survive."

"Anything?" Her dark blue eyes widened. "Oh, Jackson, I don't want to do *anything*. Not for myself. Life is precious. I've learned that over these last two years. I've lost Elizabeth and my father. Amy is all I have left. I've been thinking I'll do anything to keep her safe, but now I don't know if I should."

"If you don't, Daniel will take the ranch away from you. If he kills you in the process, he'll get Amy, too."

She flinched at that. He thought about reaching out to offer comfort, but he didn't. He'd already touched her once today. Bad enough he wanted to protect her, worse that he might start thinking of her as a woman. He didn't need that kind of trouble in his life.

"It's not a sin to protect the people you love," he said.

"I wasn't protecting anyone when I shot you," she blurted out. "I certainly wasn't protecting anyone when I pointed the rifle at Daniel. It's all about my stupid pride. I hate it when people say bad things about my sister." Her voice dropped. "I hate it more when they say bad things about me."

It wasn't his fault, Jackson reminded himself even as he fought off a twinge of guilt. She'd chosen to claim Amy as her own. He wasn't to blame for the town's reaction to that. Just as he wasn't to blame for the loss of her sister and father. It wasn't his business that, except for Amy, Regan was alone in the world. It became his business if he took Amy away.

Before he could figure out an answer to that, Regan urged her horse into a walk. He followed along, trying not to think about anything. He didn't have to decide what to do today.

A few miles later, she broke the silence. "Why did you do it?" she asked. "Why did you pull a gun on Daniel?"

"To find out if he was still a coward."

"If he wasn't, we could have both been killed."

"I know. But I was pretty sure he hadn't changed."

"Pretty sure doesn't help when you're dead."

He started to agree, then stopped. He swore under his breath. What the hell kind of a game had he been playing? Jesus, he'd just reacted, but Regan could have been killed. He'd long ago made his peace with death. In his profession there wasn't always time for thoughts about the hereafter. A man went in and got the job done. If he was lucky, he walked away. If luck was against him, then he met the good Lord and hoped for a little mercy.

But Regan hadn't made the same decision. She had a child and a ranch. She wasn't prepared to die today, or anytime soon. What would have happened to Amy if Regan had been killed? He'd gambled with Regan's life. He didn't have the right.

"I'm sorry," he said. "It was stupid. I was pushing Daniel to find out where he'd break. With all that happened between us six years ago, hell, maybe I was pushing myself."

"I think I'm starting to understand why I'm having so much trouble with the hired guns," she said. "Those men and I don't understand each other at all. We don't believe the same things or have the same desires."

"You got that right."

They reached a small creek and crossed it together. The sun was warm overhead. His stomach growled and he remembered he hadn't bothered to eat yet that day. He hoped Fayre had put something by for him.

"Why do they do it?" she asked.

He heard her real question. Why did *he* do it? "It's all I know. I didn't set out to be a gunfighter, if that's what you're asking. I don't know that anyone does."

"How does that sort of thing happen?" She paused and lowered her voice. "You didn't mean to kill someone? It was an accident?"

He thought back to the first man he'd killed. The man was an overseer during the War Between the States. Jackson had been all of fourteen, but there was no older man around to protect his mother and the other woman left behind.

"It wasn't an accident," he said flatly. "I meant to kill him."

"And you did?"

He looked at her. He could smell her fear, even though she tried to keep it from him. "Yes."

She stiffened. "As easily as that?"

"It wasn't easy," he said. "But it was the right thing to do."

"How can you know it's right?" she asked. "How can you be sure?"

He shrugged. He didn't know for sure. He believed. It was enough.

"I find your world frightening," she said as they neared her ranch.

He was the most frightening part of that world. In the past he'd used his air of danger to entice women. They'd found it irresistible and he'd taken advantage of that.

But Regan wasn't like those other women. She wasn't tempted by the scent of death or his life in the shadows. She lived hers in the light, with her child.

He glanced at her. For the first time since he returned, she avoided his gaze. For the first time, she didn't defy him.

For the first time, he saw himself as she must see him. A killer with no conscience. A threat to all she knew.

He glanced around at the ranch land, at the out-buildings barely visible through a grove of trees. This was her world. It was all she'd ever known. He'd hoped to find something like it for himself. Now he wasn't so sure. He'd thought it would be easy to walk away from the killing and the death. Would it? For the first time he wondered if he would be able to walk away from who he was.

They rode silently up to the barn and dismounted. Pete came out of the building.

"What happened?" he asked. "Did you see Daniel? Was there trouble."

"We saw him," Regan said, still not looking at Jackson. "There wasn't any trouble, but there's going to be." She looked at Pete. Jackson hated the way her mouth trembled slightly. "He's not going to stop until he gets what he wants. He doesn't care what it costs, or who gets hurt."

"What are you going to do?" Pete asked.

Jackson dismounted. He told himself he should just walk away. This wasn't his fight. There was no point in getting involved here.

"I don't know," Regan said. "We should talk about it and come up with some sort of plan. Jackson—" she drew in a deep breath, "he's made me see that we've underestimated Daniel and his men. Get Hank and meet me in my office."

"But Regan—"

Before Pete could continue, Amy came out the back of the house and skipped down the stairs.

"Mama, Jackson, you're back!"

The sight of her brought a tightness to Jackson's chest. He had a daughter. He smiled as Amy danced closer. She was constant movement, twisting and turning on a whim, always laughing or smiling. A happy child. So much like his sister. Seeing her made him miss his family. Since that day he killed the overseer, he hadn't been back to their small dirt farm. He'd sent money until his sisters married and Lily took their mother to live with her.

"Amy, you're the prettiest little girl west of the Mississippi."

"Really?" Amy danced to a stop and grinned up at

him. Her hazel eyes glittered with pleasure. "Did you remember about our tea party?"

Before he could answer, Regan stepped between him and the child. She shielded the girl with her skirts and stared up at him, as if daring him to push her away. It was at that moment he realized Regan had learned to be afraid of him. She saw him as a killer of innocents.

Their gazes locked. He searched for something more in her expression, something that would make sense, something that would ease the knot tightening in his gut.

"Mama, what's wrong?" Amy asked, peering from around Regan's split skirt.

"Stay back," Regan said. "Jackson won't have time for your tea party today."

"But, Mama—"

"Hush."

Jackson stared at her, then at the troubled child. He would never have hurt Amy. But Regan was reacting to what she believed to be true. From what he *knew* to be true. He was a killer. Perhaps not of innocents, but did that matter?

He turned on his heel and limped away.

Hank had been with the ranch from the beginning. Regan had heard the story of his accidental meeting with her father in Boston. For years it had been a bedtime treat, told over and over again. She'd gone to sleep imagining both her father and Hank as young men with dreams of a ranch in a beautiful land called Texas.

If Fayre had been Regan's second mother, then her husband, Hank, was a second father. The kindly man had taken the time to teach a small child to ride almost before she could walk. Now Regan stared at Hank's grizzled features, at his gray hair and the wrinkles around his eyes and mouth. It still surprised her that he'd grown old. In her heart, she carried a picture of him as he'd been in her childhood. She hadn't noticed the gradual change until her father's unexpected death slowed Hank's step and put a stoop in his shoulders.

The old man leaned over his cup of coffee in the kitchen of the ranch house. She sat at the head of the wooden table, with Pete on her left.

"Daniel isn't going to let anything keep him from what he wants," she said.

"This means a range war." Hank's voice was still as strong as she remembered. He glanced at her, his once piercing blue eyes now faded, as if the sun had bleached away the color. "Range wars mean men are going to die."

"I don't want that," Regan said. "I'm just not sure how to prevent it."

"These new rules will help," Pete said. He didn't look at her as he spoke. So far he hadn't looked her in the eye since she came back from Daniel's ranch. She knew he was angry, she just wasn't sure why.

She glanced down at the list she'd written as they devised ways to keep everybody safer. No cowboys were to go out alone, or even in pairs. Only in groups of three or larger. Cattle in the fields closest to Daniel's herds were to be moved. Hired guns were to start regular patrolling. Not just of the immediate area, but of some of the grazing areas as well.

"The men aren't going to like this," Hank said, pointing at the last rule. "They don't care for the gunslingers. Can't say I blame 'em. I don't much like 'em myself."

"I know," Regan said. Now that she'd spoken with Jackson, she understood the cowboy's reluctance. Her men had lives they enjoyed. They hadn't made their decision to die yet. The gunslingers expected each day to be their last. Life was cheap, death easy and quickly forgotten. "But it can't be helped. They have skills our men don't. They'll be able to react quickly to any danger. The cowboys would hesitate before firing. That could mean the difference between living and dying. I've seen Daniel's men. Not one of them is going to think twice about killing. We can all believe that."

"How long do you think we can keep this up?" Hank asked. "We've got cattle to run. Roundup'll be here before we know it. Spring is busy. What if something needs doing and there aren't two other men around?"

"Then it goes undone. Hank, I mean that." Regan laid her hand on the older man's forearm. "I don't want to lose any more of the cowboys and I sure don't want to lose you. I know it's going to be difficult, but I don't see that we have a choice."

"Maybe I should go talk to the boy," Hank muttered, stroking his chin. He thought for a minute, then shook his head. "Nope, that would be as silly as a pig lecturing the devil on keepin' clean. He hasn't listened to me since he was ten years old."

"We have to keep the ranch and everyone on it safe," Regan said. "We've already lost George. I'm worried about everyone, especially Amy."

"Now don't you fret, little girl," Hank said. He leaned over and kissed her cheek. Then he pushed back his chair and stood up. "We'll keep you and Amy safe from Daniel. You have my word."

He nodded at Pete, then left the kitchen in search of Fayre.

Regan stared after him, praying he was right, that they would be able to keep Amy safe. Since Jackson arrived, she'd sworn she would do anything to protect her child. She still believed that; however, she'd come to see the price might be much higher than she expected.

"You all right?" Pete asked.

She glanced at him. He was staring at his mug of coffee. "I'm fine."

"You aren't acting fine."

"Neither are you."

He looked at her then. His shaggy hair fell across his forehead, almost to his eyebrows. His mouth was straight. Everything about him was familiar. "I don't understand you anymore, Regan. You're different."

"How?"

"Riding off to Daniel's place like you did. Why?"

He really wanted to know why she'd gone with Jackson rather than him. "I'm not sure. I didn't want Jackson to go alone."

"Jackson can take care of himself."

"I suppose, but I wanted to be sure. I'm glad I went. I learned something important. Daniel will do anything to get what he wants."

"Why'd he let you go?" Pete asked.

Regan wasn't sure about that. "Jackson says it would have been too hard for Daniel to explain bullet-filled corpses to the sheriff. I suppose he's right. Although when Jackson pulled a gun on Daniel, I thought it was over for sure."

"He what?" Now Pete wasn't just looking at her, he was glaring at her. "Are you both crazy? He pulled a gun on Daniel?" He stood up suddenly and waved his arms in the air. "Was he trying to get you killed?"

"I think he was trying to make a point."

"He sure as hell made one."

"Perhaps." She thought about all she'd learned that afternoon. "Daniel is crazy, too."

Pete reached down and grabbed her hand. He pulled her to her feet. "If Daniel knew he couldn't get the land, maybe he'd leave you alone."

She knew what he was getting at. "Pete—"

He cut her off with a quick shake of his head. "Regan, think about it. If you were married, Daniel couldn't get hold of the ranch. You know how I feel about you and Amy. I wouldn't expect to control you or the land. You can trust me."

She searched his face. He'd been her best friend for years. She'd loved her sister, Elizabeth, but they'd had little in common beyond the bond of blood. Elizabeth was interested in feminine things. Regan wanted to learn everything she could about the ranch. She was more excited by roping her first steer than her developing bosom.

"I do know how you feel about Amy and me," she said, reaching up to lay her palm against his cheek. She could feel the stubble there. It prickled slightly but didn't ignite any feelings other than that. Her heart didn't race fast, her thighs didn't tremble. She didn't want to do more than be kind.

"You're the best friend I've ever had," she said.

"We're more than friends."

He turned his head and pressed his mouth to her palm. The touch of his lips was sweet. Sweet and quiet and friendly. Nothing more. Her life would be so much easier if she'd fallen in love with this gentle man.

She forced herself to smile. "No, we're not," she said softly. "I know you want us to be more. I'll admit I want that, too. But it doesn't make it so. You're my best friend in the world. I love you. But not that way."

He started to pull his head back. She squeezed the hand he still held. "No, Pete, you must listen to me because you know what I'm saying is true. You care about me. We care about each other. But it's not the right kind of love. You can't marry me. One day you'll find the girl who's right for you. What would happen then, if you were already married to me? You would be miserable. I know that's true, and you do, too."

He studied her face for a long time. The kitchen was silent except for the ticking of the clock in the hallway. He smiled slightly. "You're pretty smart— for a girl."

She grinned. "I know."

He pulled her close then, pressing her face against his chest. She wrapped her arms around his waist. The sound of his heartbeat, the scent of his body, even his warmth, comforted her. When Pete held her in his arms she felt safe. It wasn't exciting. It didn't make her feel tingly. She wished it could have been enough. For both of them.

"It's Jackson, isn't it?" he asked. At first she didn't know what to say. When she tried to pull back, he held her tight. "I've known from the beginning,

Regan. From the first day I came back that summer six years ago. You were different. Grown-up maybe. I was mad 'cause I wasn't the reason you'd changed."

"Nothing happened," she said, her voice sounding strained even to her own ears. "Nothing at all."

"That didn't change how you felt about him. Or how you feel."

She pulled back slightly so that she could look at Pete's face. His expression was curious but not judging. "I'm sorry," she whispered. "I never meant to hurt you."

"I know that. But it is him."

"Yes."

She didn't know why. It wasn't fair, of course. It should have just been a schoolgirl infatuation. She should have outgrown it. But the more time she spent with Jackson, the less she was able to believe she'd forgotten. If anything, she cared more about him now than she ever had.

What would happen when he was gone? Would he go back to what he was doing? He couldn't keep up that kind of life forever. Eventually someone would catch him when he wasn't looking and shoot him in the back. He would die alone somewhere. Unnoticed, unmourned. And she would spend the rest of her life wondering if he was still alive. Always waiting, hoping he would find a reason to come back.

She shook her head. That image was pure imagination. Jackson wasn't going to walk out of her life. For one thing, she still had Amy, and they hadn't come to any sort of an agreement about that.

The situation frightened her. Not just the potential for losing her daughter, but coming to care more about

Jackson. He affected her as no other man could. He made her want things—he made her glad to be a woman.

She still didn't know why he'd kissed her. No one wanted her, not the way men had wanted Elizabeth. Pete was willing to marry her because she was his friend and he cared for her but not because the thought of loving her kept him up nights. Daniel was willing to marry her to keep her quiet, and probably to get her out of the way. A couple of other men had, years before, offered marriage, with the clear understanding that their only interest was the ranch.

"He'll break your heart, Regan," Pete said as he released her and stepped back. He reached for his hat. "You know he will."

"I know." There was nothing she could do about it. It had been too late the first time she saw him. In a way she had Daniel to thank for that. If he hadn't started rustling cattle years ago, she and Jackson would never have met.

"We'll get through this," he said, as he walked to the door. "You'll see."

She hoped he was right.

Pete pulled the door open. She remembered something else Daniel had said. At the time it had angered her. It still did. But it was so close to the accusations Jackson had made. It couldn't be true, and yet—

"Pete, can I ask you a question?"

"Sure." He paused in the doorway.

"Was Elizabeth . . . loose with men?"

In her heart she expected Pete to burst out laughing and say of course not. Instead he stared at her, then quickly looked away. But even ducking his head slightly didn't stop her from seeing the blush that crawled up his face.

"Pete?"

He cleared his throat. "Elizabeth was a lady, Regan. Don't believe what people say." He stepped outside and closed the door behind him.

Regan stared after him. She should have been reassured by his comments. Except for one small thing. How did Pete know what people were saying unless he'd heard the talk himself? Why hadn't he told her about the lies being spread around? Why was there talk in the first place? She was the one with the illegitimate child. As far as anyone knew, Elizabeth had gone to her marriage a virgin.

Unless Daniel was right. Which meant Jackson was right. Elizabeth? Regan shook her head. She didn't want to know. Not now. Not with everything else going on.

She turned away from the door and tried to put the questions from her mind. But it was too late. The seed had been planted.

11

After telling Amy her promised story and staying until the child fell asleep, Regan walked down the stairs and paused in the hallway. Fayre had gone back to spend the night with Hank. Jackson was in his room. The house was still, waiting. She wanted to forget her troubles in a dreamless sleep, but she knew her concerns would follow her into the darkness. As they had for weeks, the nightmares would haunt her. She would be standing alone against an enemy she could neither see nor hear. Only the fear told her he was near. There was no way to fight him off, no weapon strong enough, no one to offer assistance.

She knew what the dreams meant. Her enemy was Daniel and the fear was very real. She knew he wouldn't stop until he'd won. It wasn't just about the ranch anymore. She'd learned that today. He wanted her punished, as he'd punished her sister. She didn't know why. Perhaps because she and Elizabeth had the O'Neil name by virtue of birth rather than charity. It didn't matter. Daniel was more of a threat than she'd been willing to admit. Her plans with Hank and Pete weren't going to be enough. They needed more. Someone who understood how Daniel thought and what his men would do. To win she needed someone like those men. She needed Jackson.

But she didn't want to acknowledge that part of him. She didn't want to have to think of him as a killer. It frightened her. Today, she'd instinctively pulled her child away from Jackson. When she'd had time to think, she'd known he wouldn't hurt Amy. But she hadn't thought. She only felt the fear. It was beginning to be her most constant companion.

Without giving herself time to regret her decision, she walked briskly to her father's old bedroom and knocked once on the door.

"Come in, Regan," Jackson called.

She entered. He stood by the window, looking out into the darkness. He was still dressed as he had been that morning, in dark trousers and a white shirt. His hat was on the dresser, so she could see the gold-blond of his hair. It hung long, to the bottom of his collar. The lantern light caught the individual shades, some fair, some darker, all beautiful.

"How did you know it was me?" she asked.

"Your footsteps," he said without turning around. "You're wearing boots. They sound different from Fayre's shoes. But even without them, I always know it's you. You have a distinctive stride."

She glanced down at her worn brown leather boots. They were a year old and she'd long since given up trying to keep them shiny. "I don't walk like a lady," she admitted.

He didn't answer. She continued to study him, the broad shoulders, the length of his legs. He was a powerful man. That shouldn't make a difference. Most of the cowboys were powerful men. They had to be, to do their job. Yet there was something about Jackson. Or maybe it was just her. Perhaps every woman made a fool of herself over one man.

He took the ladderback chair by the window and turned it neatly with one hand, then sat, straddling it. He rested his forearms on the back.

"Have a seat," he said, motioning to the bed.

She sat down and folded her hands in her lap. "I'm sorry about today," she said. "About Amy. I knew you wouldn't hurt her. I was just scared. You'd been so different with Daniel, like you were really ready to kill him."

"I was."

She looked at him. Conviction burned in his eyes. "Just like that?"

"You don't agree the man needs killing?"

"Yes, I do. I think that makes it worse. I don't want to believe it, but I can't ignore the truth. There's going to be trouble."

"Trouble?" Jackson laughed. "Trouble doesn't even begin to describe it. Daniel isn't going to rest until he's taken everything that ever belonged to you."

"We've made some changes." She outlined the plan she, Pete, and Hank had come up with.

Jackson listened, then when she was finished he shook his head. "Regan, having your cowboys going out in threes isn't going to accomplish anything except not getting the work done."

"It'll keep them from being killed."

"For now." His gaze was steady, his voice filled with conviction. "You need more."

"I agree. I don't have the experience to handle this." She rubbed her palms together. "I asked Mr. McLane to lead the men, but he refused."

"He would. He doesn't work that way. He's a loner by nature as well as by choice. Most men are smart enough to stay clear of him."

"You're his friend."

"No one ever said I was smart."

She tried to return his smile, but she couldn't. There were too many questions and not enough answers.

"Listen, Regan, Gage owes me. We had some trouble in Kansas a year or so back. I saved his sorry life. If I ask him to take charge, he will. You couldn't ask for a better shot, or a cooler set of nerves."

She stood up and walked to the armoire. She touched the smooth wood and inhaled the scent of cedar. Her father had brought this piece of furniture with him when he returned with his bride. It was beautiful, old, elegant, a part of her past.

She understood the cattle. She was learning to run the ranch on her own. Not a day went by that she didn't mourn her father. She would survive—if Daniel gave her the chance.

"I appreciate the offer with Mr. McLane," she said, "but I had something else in mind. I wondered if I could hire you to handle the situation and the men."

Jackson stared at her. She could feel the heat of his gaze boring into her back. She didn't turn around. She couldn't bear to know what he was thinking.

"I'll pay you. This ranch has been profitable for a long time. I need someone to protect the ranch, Jackson. I need someone to keep Amy safe. I don't think I'm enough anymore."

It was wrong of her to use the child as leverage, but she didn't have a choice. She needed his help. Their meeting with Daniel had shown her that.

"I won't work with my hands tied, the way I did with Sean. It's my way, or not at all."

Which meant men would die. Perhaps even her men. She turned to face him. His face was expressionless, his eyes distant.

"I don't want my cowboys hurt."

"I'll do my best."

The blood would be on her hands, as surely as if she'd pulled the trigger herself. Could she do it? Could she let Jackson kill Daniel? Worse, could she risk Jackson's life? What if he didn't get lucky this time?

A small bit of colored cloth by the armoire caught her attention. She bent down and saw one of Amy's rag dolls lying against the large piece of furniture. She picked it up and studied the stitched face, worn from frequent hugs and dirty from Amy's spirited play.

While Daniel was alive, her child was in danger.

She looked at Jackson. "Do what you have to. I want the ranch and my child safe from him. Forever."

Jackson raised his eyebrows. "All right, Regan. You've got a deal."

She set the doll back on the floor then reached in her skirt pocket. "This is for you," she said, pulling out a folded, worn letter. Elizabeth's letter. "I thought you might want to have it back."

His expression was still unreadable. "A peace offering?"

"Maybe. You're all I've got to keep us alive and to keep Amy safe."

"I won't let you down," he promised.

She believed him because the alternative meant giving up. "I know," she said softly.

He was a damn fool.

Jackson leaned against the barn and squinted at the night sky. No, damned fool didn't even begin to describe himself, but he couldn't think of anything better, so he thought it again and sighed. Was he crazy? Getting soft with old age? Why had he agreed to do this? Working for Regan O'Neil wasn't smart. Deliberately facing down Daniel wasn't smart. No sir, it was plain stupid. Probably the stupidest thing he'd ever done.

He was supposed to be walking away from all this. That's why he was at the ranch in the first place. He'd wanted to collect his son and be on his way. So there wasn't a son. Fine. He could accept that. Why didn't he just take his money and his sorry self and ride off? But no. He had to stay around and be a hero. He had to believe he was the only one who could keep Regan and Amy safe. He had to go get suckered into caring about his daughter, not to mention kissing her prickly mother. Aunt. Whatever the hell Regan was to Amy. Jesus, even *he* was getting confused.

Sticking around was a mistake. A big one. He could feel it in his throbbing thigh, not to mention in that place in his gut that had never let him down. It was the same feeling that kept reminding him that one kiss had changed everything. No matter how he tried, he couldn't look at Regan the same way. His body got hard remembering how she felt all pressed up against him, and his brain went soft. While she stood there offering him a job, instead of remembering how frightened she'd been of him, he'd been telling himself he didn't really mind her freckles. That in the right light, with her hair all loose and her eyes wide, she might be downright pretty.

He needed a drink. More than that, he needed to hightail it outta here before he did something even stupider, although right now he couldn't imagine what that would be.

The slight scratch of a match, followed by the hiss of burning sulphur, caught his attention. He turned toward the sound, although he couldn't see the flame. He inhaled sharply, then smiled.

"You bring one of those out for me, or are you still keeping them all to yourself?"

"I brought one."

Gage stepped out from behind a nearby pecan tree. A faint glow from the house outlined his silhouette. He moved with the easy grace of someone more comfortable with shadows than light.

As usual, he was dressed in black and wore his hat pulled low on his head. He stepped toward Jackson and handed him a thin unlit cigar.

"Thanks." Jackson took the offered match as well and flicked it against the side of the barn. In a few minutes, when his cigar was going nicely, he leaned back against the building and stared at the sky.

"You on patrol?" he asked.

"Yup."

"Any sign of trouble?"

Gage leaned against the barn as well, although he watched the darkness rather than the stars. "Not yet. But it's coming. I can feel it."

"Me, too."

"I heard you've had the pleasure of meeting Daniel O'Neil."

Jackson nodded. "He means to have his way in this. He wants the ranch. He's also crazy."

"That makes him more dangerous."

"That it does."

"I also heard you've hired on."

Jackson sighed. Word traveled fast in a small community. "I guess I have."

"Weren't you going to walk away from all of this?"

"A few things got in the way." Mostly finding out he had a daughter, although some of the problem was Regan.

"You ever think about getting out?" Jackson asked, then bit down on the cigar.

"No." Gage exhaled a puff of smoke. The scent of the cigar seeped into the night. "I always figured I'd end my days the way I started 'em. Sometime, somewhere, there's going to be somebody faster than me. Or smarter."

"Why not walk away?"

"It's all I know."

It was all Jackson knew, too. "I'd thought about getting a spread somewhere. Maybe Wyoming. There aren't a lot of people there. Maybe raise some cattle and a few kids."

Gage straightened and stared at him. "You fixin' on getting married?"

"I thought I might."

"Anyone particular in mind?"

"Nope." He hadn't gotten that far with his plan. "I never had trouble with the ladies. I'll find someone."

"Getting your pecker looked after and getting married are two different things," Gage said. "The one willing to do the first isn't the kind you'd want for the second."

He hadn't thought of it quite like that, but Jackson had to admit Gage had a point. Marrying kind of women were different. They were more serious. They had plans and dreams. They expected more from a man. Kinda like Regan.

That thought brought him upright. He inhaled and choked on the cigar smoke. Damn it all to hell, he was *not* going to get involved with Regan O'Neil. She wasn't pretty enough, she was too loud, too feisty, too everything. Besides, she already had this ranch and it mattered more to her than any man ever would. The only thing she cared for more was Amy.

Thinking of his daughter calmed him some but didn't give him any more answers. "You know anything about being a father?" Jackson asked.

"Nope."

"You reckon a man sort of learns as he goes, or is it something you either have or don't have?"

"I suspect it's like riding. Everyone can learn how, but only a few are born to it."

That made sense. Jackson leaned back against the barn. "You ever think about the killing, Gage?"

"Sometimes." His friend propped one foot on an old crate beside the barn.

"I thought I could walk away from it. Forget what I'd done. Now I don't know."

"Working on the railroad is a job a man walks away from," Gage said quietly. "The killing gets into a man's blood. Becomes who he is. I don't know if you can walk far enough or fast enough to get away from that."

Jackson nodded. He had a feeling his old friend was right. So where did that leave him? He didn't want to die a gunslinger. There had been a time when the excitement, the challenge of always being better, was enough to keep him going. He hadn't cared about the money. But all that had changed. Maybe because he was getting older. Maybe because the souls of the dead had gotten so loud.

He'd seen so many friends fall to an unexpected bullet. As Gage had pointed out, eventually someone else was faster or smarter.

"What happened the first time?" Gage asked.

"There was a man who needed killing."

"How'd you know you were the one to do it?"

"There wasn't anyone else."

Gage puffed on his thin cigar, causing the tip to glow red in the night. "There's always someone else. Something inside told you that you were the one. Maybe we're born with it in the blood."

Jackson didn't want to think about that. "At first there was the glory," he said. "Then I was better than everyone else."

He'd never been interested in building a reputation. He'd worked quietly, without anyone but his boss knowing his name. People had referred him to friends who were having trouble. Other gunfighters had come to respect him.

"Some men can't do it," Gage said. "They can't pick up a gun and end a man's life." He was silent for a moment. "Or maybe they won't. I'm not saying the willingness to do it is bad. But I don't think you can walk away from that."

Jackson remembered the fear in Regan's eyes after their confrontation with Daniel. It was as if she hadn't known him until that moment, as if she'd never seen him before.

"Not many people would accept a man with that kind of past," Jackson said.

He said "people" but he really meant women. Regan had stood up to him, she'd even shot him, but at that moment, she was filled with fear. She'd instinctively kept her daughter from him. His daughter. Regan had been afraid of him. He'd thought she wouldn't be afraid of anything.

What did that make him?

"Maybe there aren't any answers," Gage said. He shifted, placing both feet on the ground. "Maybe there's just the doing and the living with what's been done."

"Maybe." Jackson dropped his cigar and ground the butt out with his heel. He didn't know what was going to happen next. He didn't know where he was going to end up or even if he could walk away from the killing. He did know one thing for sure. He wasn't going to let Daniel O'Neil get his hands on Amy, the ranch, or Regan.

12

It was still early when Regan went searching for Jackson. He was in the supply shed behind the barn, counting bullets.

The door stood propped open by a rock. She could see him bent over boxes. Sunlight streamed into the small room, highlighting the supplies and glinting off Jackson's hair. She reached up and touched her neat braid. Her bright red curls were tamed for the moment. In time, with the help of wind and riding, they would escape and frame her face in a mass of corkscrew curls. She hated her hair. Not just because the color was ugly and it was unmanageable, but because it wasn't normal, like Elizabeth's hair. It didn't fall to her waist in auburn waves. She couldn't sweep it up into fancy styles. It hung down in thick ringlets. Her hair was too much like herself—awkward and out of place.

Jackson moved to his left. She stared at his body, his long legs and broad shoulders, the strength in his arms, the grace of his movements. She'd always thought he was beautiful. Perhaps it was the wrong word to use to describe a man, but she couldn't think of another. It was as if God had kept her blind to the inherent perfection of the male form until she saw Jackson. His face was lean and handsome, his hair the color of gold. Even his eyes were stunning, the gray-green that shifted with his moods. She could spend her lifetime watching him and never grow tired of the view. Except for yesterday when he'd stared at her with the eyes of a killer.

A chill swept through her. She hugged her arms to her chest and shivered. He'd frightened her then. She hadn't known what to say or how to act. Her mouth twisted. At least she was used to feeling that way around Jackson.

"How long you going to stand there gawking?" he asked without turning around.

"I was waiting for you to finish."

He straightened and turned to face her. Her breath caught in her throat. It was probably a sin to admire a man's features as much as she admired his. Elizabeth had thought him good looking but had insisted several men in town were handsomer. Regan disagreed. She'd never seen anyone who made her feel the way Jackson did. She liked how her heart beat faster and her mouth grew dry. She liked that he made her palms sweat. Around Jackson she knew she was alive. She knew she was a woman. Not that any of that mattered to him. She didn't know what he thought of her, but it wasn't going to be flattering.

She wanted Jackson to see her as more. She wanted him to see past the sensible, dull blouses and split skirts, past the heavy boots. They were necessary for her to get her job done, but they weren't all of her. She had other sides, other feelings, just like a regular woman.

She sighed. She was wishing for the moon.

"I went through my father's books last night," she said. "I'm going to double what he paid you."

Jackson leaned against the doorframe of the shed. "That's not necessary."

"I think it is. Last time you were here to stop trouble without anyone getting hurt. I would think under those circumstances, your life wasn't in danger. This time is different. We both know that."

She searched his eyes, but the killer was absent this morning. She couldn't read his feelings, but she knew the man. This was the Jackson who had stolen her heart so long ago. She wondered if hiring the killer would make her care less for the man.

"You're putting a price on my life," he said.

She swallowed. She hadn't thought of it quite like that. "I suppose you're right."

He nodded. "Then I'll accept the money."

He would lead the men well. He wasn't just working for the money. He was also helping her to keep Amy safe. Jackson had a stake in what happened at the ranch. He wouldn't want Daniel to get his hands on Jackson's child.

For a moment, as she stared at him and he gave her a half-smile back, she wanted to believe there was more. That Jackson was doing it for her. Because he cared. For that single heartbeat, she allowed herself to believe he saw her for herself. That he understood how hard it was for her to be alone, that he knew she had a woman's heart and a woman's needs. She allowed herself to imagine he might be glad she was falling in love with him.

Then she glanced down and saw her hands. The cuts and bruises, the calluses. She was not the kind of woman to inspire affection in a man. Especially not in one like Jackson. He was strong and loyal, honest, funny, charming, and handsome as sin. Even her daughter was infatuated with him. He could have any woman he chose. Regan didn't stand a chance against those odds.

She nodded at the ammunition behind him. "Do we have enough?"

He shook his head. "I was going to talk to you about that. We need more."

Before she could respond, Pete came out of the barn and started toward them. The set of his head told her he wasn't happy about something. She had a feeling she knew what was wrong.

"Is it true?" Pete asked, barely acknowledging Jackson. "Are you going to town?"

"Hank told you," she said.

"I'm damned glad someone did. What are you thinking of?"

She avoided his gaze. "I have to get money from the bank to pay the men. Jackson told me we need more ammunition as well. Fayre is putting together a list of supplies. You know I'm the only one who can get money out of the bank. I can't hide here forever."

Pete glared at her. She wondered how much of his

anger came from her decision to hire Jackson. She'd told him briefly, earlier that morning, but hadn't stayed to hear his opinion. She knew he wouldn't approve. Unfortunately, she didn't have another choice.

Pete glared at Jackson, then turned on her. "I'm coming with you."

"You can't. I need you to act as the go-between for the hired guns and our cowboys. I don't want there to be any trouble."

"You can't go by yourself. Or don't you remember what happened the last time you went to town?"

She didn't want to think about that. The shame was too horrible. Even now she could feel the color crawling up her cheeks. She raised her chin. "I'll be fine."

Jackson pushed off the doorframe and took a step toward them. "What happened the last time Regan went into town?"

"I had a little trouble."

Pete snorted. "Someone threw a rock at her and hit her in the back."

Jackson's gaze narrowed and his eyes turned icy gray.

"I'm sure they didn't mean to hit me," she said, not wanting him to find out more. "It was only a bruise." She turned back to Pete. "I'm not afraid. I have as much right to go to Hampton as anyone."

"Regan!" he started.

"No. I don't want to hear it."

"Why did someone throw a rock at you?" Jackson asked.

She glanced at Pete. He stared at the ground. She could feel his concern, and his embarrassment for her. She hadn't wanted Jackson to know. Stupid of her, really. Why would he care one way or the other? She didn't matter to him.

She sighed. It was a small point of pride. She should get over it.

She turned so that she was facing him, then forced herself to look him in the eye. She squared her shoulders. "I'm surprised you haven't heard. I'm a fallen woman, little more than a whore. The good people of Hampton don't like to see me in town. It sets a bad example for their daughters." She smiled and smoothed her hands over her split skirt. "Of course Daniel's played on this. He's let it be known he's willing to marry me, despite my past sins. Isn't that sweet of him? The town thinks so, especially after Elizabeth up and died without having the courtesy to bear him a son."

She tried to keep her voice calm, but it started shaking before she'd finished. Emotions she tried to ignore welled up inside of her. It wasn't fair. She hadn't done anything wrong. Yet she was the one being punished. Daniel was a murderer, he was the danger, yet they all adored him.

"Some of the townspeople have taken it upon themselves to discourage me from visiting." She could feel her body starting to tremble. Pete moved close to put his arm around her. She shook him off. She *would* be strong. Jackson could never know what the masquerade cost her.

She tossed her head and tried to stare him down. The silence lengthened. He didn't look away. His eyes stayed cold, his mouth unyielding. Finally he stepped out of the storage shed and closed the door behind him.

"I'm coming with you," he said flatly.

"No." She didn't want that. She couldn't stand to have Jackson as a witness.

He jerked his head back toward the shed. "We need more supplies and I want to make sure we get the right ones. I'm in charge of your protection, Regan. I'm coming with you to town whether you like it or not."

Regan opened the armoire and stared at her four dresses. They were all simple, lacking ruffles and lace. She'd always told herself she wasn't the lace type. Even when Elizabeth wanted to help her make something pretty, she'd refused. She'd known there was no point in trying to call attention to herself. There was no one to notice.

Now, as she pulled out a plain dark blue wool dress, she wished she'd listened to her sister. She would like to spend one day looking pretty. It didn't seem like too much to ask. But it wasn't going to happen. Try as she might to be someone else, she could only be herself.

Her bedroom door opened. Fayre stared at her, then slowly shook her head. "You're a foolish child."

"I know. But you're going to help me anyway."

"That I am."

Fayre stepped into the room and closed the door behind her. While Regan slipped out of her blouse and split skirt, Fayre took petticoats off of hooks and shook them. Regan reached past her for the corset on a shelf. She placed it against her midsection and held it there. Her friend began tightening the strings.

"Which dress are you wearing?" the older woman asked.

"The blue one."

"You're going to need this tighter, then."

"I know." A small vanity. She was giving up her ability to draw a deep breath solely to wear a dress that matched the color of her eyes. She wouldn't look very special if she fainted on the journey into town. But she didn't complain as the laces were pulled tighter. She drew in a breath and held it, as if she could fill her lungs once and it would last for the day. The boned corset tightened around her ribs and waist, drawing in more.

Fayre held the strings with one hand and with the other, she measured her waist. "Another half inch or so."

"All right." Regan grabbed the armoire shelving and held on. "Pull."

Fayre jerked the strings tighter. Regan gasped. The room spun suddenly and started to go dark. She forced herself to take slow breaths, pulling in as much air as she could. Her vision cleared.

She raised her hands above her head while Fayre slipped the corset cover down her arms. Next came three petticoats, each tied at the small of her back. The dress was last. The older woman settled the yards of fabric over her petticoats while Regan fastened the buttons up the front. When she finished, she held out her arms to have the cuffs fastened. Moving slowly, wondering when she would get used to not having enough air, she settled on a stool while Fayre loosened her braid.

"I still don't know why you have to go into town," Fayre said as she brushed out her tangled curls.

"The men have to be paid, we need supplies, and the money from the last cattle sale is just sitting in the bank. No one else can get it."

Fayre continued to stroke the brush firmly down the length of her hair. "You're asking for trouble."

She met her friend's gaze in the mirror. "I don't want the trouble, Fayre. They don't give me a choice."

"Oh, child." Fayre bent down and kissed the top of her head. "Whatever am I to do with you?"

"Love me."

"I already do. More than you can imagine." They smiled at each other. Fayre sniffed. "Enough of this nonsense. If you're stubborn enough to go to town, you'd better get going." She grabbed Regan's hair and twisted. After coiling it at the base of her neck, she secured it with several pins, then stepped back and studied her handiwork. "You're pretty enough to turn a blind man's head."

"Thanks, Fayre."

"You take care of yourself."

"I will."

The older woman squeezed her shoulder, then left the room. Regan stared at her reflection, wishing Fayre was right. Perhaps being pretty would bring her a measure of confidence. As it was, she was already nervous and frightened, and they hadn't even left yet. If only—

If only her hair wasn't so bright. She reached up and touched her smooth head. By the return trip, the curls would be flying around her face. She wrinkled her nose. Freckles. There were freckles everywhere. And her mouth was too big.

She studied her eyes. They were her best feature.

Wide, expressive, and the color was nice. She liked her eyes. Her gaze dropped to her chest. The corset made her waist look smaller. By comparison, her bust seemed bigger, but she knew it was an illusion. She'd never filled out the way Elizabeth had. Her shape wasn't enough to entice a man. All the boning and lacing couldn't make her bosom larger.

She glanced at her hands, then lowered them and stared at her palms. She tried to hate her hands, but she couldn't. They served her well, allowing her to keep the ranch going. She didn't have the hands of a lady, but they were her badge of honor. Still, no one would understand that. She opened a drawer in her vanity and pulled out a pair of gloves. They were cotton, and the same blue as her dress. She tugged them on, wincing as the fabric caught on a healing cut, then snagged on her calluses.

She was pretending to be a lady, and no one would be fooled.

Before she shut the drawer, she saw a piece of paper tucked in the back. She picked it up, then smiled when she saw what it was. Recipes. Forbidden recipes for beauty potions. Elizabeth had given them to her several years ago. At the time Regan had thought she might try them, but then realized there was no reason to bother. No one cared if her skin was soft and white, or if her hair smelled like flowers.

She started to shove the paper back in the drawer, then hesitated. There still wasn't a reason to go to all the trouble. Jackson wouldn't care. But maybe doing it for him wasn't the right reason. Maybe she should do it for herself.

Without giving herself time to think, she wrote

down a list of ingredients from two of the recipes, then shoved the sheet into her reticule. She glanced over her shoulder as if she was afraid someone was watching her, witnessing her foolishness. But she didn't remove the list.

It didn't matter if she would never find anyone. She'd grown used to being alone, and being lonely. She'd had to. Her dream of finding someone to love her for who she was had remained a dream. Jackson would never see her that way. No one in town had taken the time to find out whether she was good or bad. They'd all simply accepted what they were told.

She glanced back at her reflection. If she didn't have to work so hard, she might find the time to be pretty. Perhaps make a few changes, use a few of the recipes. But she didn't have time. Amy and the ranch consumed her until there was nothing left.

She closed her eyes briefly and wished for more. Then she shook her head. Wishes like that never came true. She reached for her small blue hat and placed it on her smooth hair. She tied the wide ribbons in a bow under her chin, then rose to her feet.

She didn't recognize her reflection in the mirror. If one didn't look too closely, she might even pass for a lady. If only Jackson noticed. She turned toward the door and knew wishing for him was the most foolish dream of all.

13

Jackson was leaning against the spring wagon when Regan came out the back door of the house. He knew it was she because he recognized her face and her size, but little else of her resembled the woman he thought of as Regan.

The sensible, dull-colored blouse and split riding skirt had been replaced with a dark blue dress, the same color as her eyes. It hugged her breasts and trim waist before flaring out and settling gracefully over layers of petticoats. Her usually unruly hair had been tamed at the base of her neck, and partially hidden by a wisp of a hat. From the top of her head to the tips of her gloves she looked like—a lady.

He blinked, then blinked again. "Regan?"

The glare she gave him was pure ice. "Don't say anything," she snapped. "Not a single word."

Her flare of temper surprised him. He almost shot a remark back at her. Almost. Then he saw the haunting flash of fear in her eyes and knew the anger was a disguise.

He straightened and stepped to one side. She approached the wagon, still glaring. "Fayre said since we're going to town, we might as well stock up on supplies. I have her list." She patted the reticule hanging from her wrist.

"Fine with me."

She sniffed, as if she didn't believe his agreeable response. When she was in front of the wagon, she reached up and grabbed the side. He moved next to her and pulled her hand away.

She turned on him. "I'm perfectly capable of getting myself into the wagon."

He looked at her face, at the flush of color and the firm set of her mouth. Even through her gloves he could feel the warmth of her fingers against his. He squeezed them gently.

"I know you can, Regan. There's just no call for you to."

Her gaze narrowed as she eyed him suspiciously. Some of the tension seemed to leave her. Slowly, he released her hand and placed both of his on her waist. She flinched from his touch, then relaxed.

"Put your hands on my shoulders," he said.

She did as he asked. The color in her face burned brighter. With one easy lift, he raised her to the seat. She released him instantly, turned, and started smoothing her skirt. He stared at her for a long time. He'd never really thought of Regan as a woman. As feminine. The dress didn't change who she was. He knew that. Yet there was something about her wearing it that made her seem different. Or maybe the difference was in him.

He shook his head and walked around the wagon. After climbing up next to her, he flicked the reins and they were on their way.

The journey was silent. Jackson mulled over the change in Regan. Then he told himself not to think about it. He worked on the problem of how to handle Daniel instead. But time and again his gaze was drawn back to her.

She sat stiffly, as far away from him as she could get. She twisted her fingers together and pulled on her gloves. Her chin was tucked close to her chest, her small hat˙shaded her from the sun peeking through the morning clouds.

The dark blue ribbon contrasted with her skin and her freckles. Her mouth was firm. The corner moved slightly, as if keeping time with her changing emotions. His gaze drifted lower, to the small collar lying flat, then lower still to the swell of her breasts outlined by the trim fitting bodice. Her ribs and waist were smaller than he remembered them being. Was it the dress? He sucked in a breath. She was wearing a corset.

It was a mistake to think that. He realized it as his blood suddenly flowed faster and hotter and the first prickling of interest made itself known between his legs. What the hell was he thinking of? He stared fixedly at the horse in front of him. It didn't help. He could still imagine Regan standing in the center of a room, wearing nothing but a camisole, pantaloons, and a corset. He could feel the tight laces loosening beneath his roving fingers, hear her sigh of relief, then her soft breath fanning his face as she turned to him and—

"Stop it," she ordered.

He was so shocked, he jerked on the reins. The horse slowed instantly. Jackson flicked the reins again, then looked at Regan. How had she known what he was thinking?

"Stop what?" he asked, then had to clear his throat.

"You keep staring at me. I know you've never seen me dressed up like this, but I can't believe I look that different."

He sagged against the back of the seat. She hadn't known. Thank God. He couldn't imagine what she would do if she knew he'd been thinking about bedding her. She'd probably haul off and shoot him again, only this time she would deliberately aim low enough to make sure he never had those thoughts again.

"I was just thinking how pretty you look."

She snorted. "Sure."

"I was. You look very nice."

"Save your compliments for your fancy women," Regan said. She didn't look at him as she spoke, instead staring out at the green grasses and wildflowers scattered around the trail.

"I don't have any fancy women."

She snorted again.

"If you're going to keep making that sound, I'm going to have to take back the nice things I said."

Her mouth curved up slightly.

"Come on, Regan. Is it so hard to believe I think you look nice today?"

She mumbled something under her breath.

"What?"

She turned on him. "No. It's not *so* hard. There, are you happy?"

He grinned. "Yes."

"Why do I bother?" she asked.

"You can't help yourself. You find me charming and hard to resist."

He expected some quick comment, a line or two designed to squash his male pride into dust. Instead Regan shifted on the seat and smoothed her skirt. "Pay attention to the horse or we'll end up in the middle of a field," she said.

He obliged her, giving her quick glances instead of staring openly. He'd always prided himself on his success with the ladies. He'd never lacked for female companionship and didn't have trouble finding the right words. With Regan it wasn't that simple. He could set her off without trying to, and she was suspicious of the nice things he tried to say. The woman was as prickly as a porcupine, and he knew better than to tangle with her. He'd likely end up bruised, watching her shapely behind scurrying off in the opposite direction.

He forced his thoughts away from her form, from her scent, and the way the weak sunlight turned her hair to flame. Instead he watched the frown pulling her eyebrows together and the lines of worry beside her mouth.

"From what I've heard, you don't get to town much. They really give you trouble about Amy?"

"What do you think? Hampton is very small. Everyone knows everyone else's business. There's no place to hide an illegitimate child."

"This has been hard on you," he said, his voice quiet.

She glanced at him. The mistrust in her eyes darkened the blue to the color of a midnight sky. "Amy's worth any trouble."

"You've been a good mother to her."

Some of the mistrust faded. "I've tried."

"How long are you going to lie about Amy being yours?"

She jerked her head away from him and stared straight ahead. "Forever."

"You're the most stubborn woman I've ever met."

"With the number you've likely known, I'll take those as words of high praise."

Her smugness fanned his temper. "Dammit, Regan, when are you going to look around and see what's really happened here? You've ruined your life for nothing. Elizabeth wasn't worth it. She was about the easiest, most willing—"

"Stop it!"

Regan turned quickly on the seat and raised her arms. Before he could do more than shift the reins to his outside hand, she'd started beating on his chest with her fists. She was strong. The blows didn't do any damage, but he felt them. He raised his free arm in front of him. She simply went lower and around, peppering him with quick shots.

"Don't say that about my sister," she cried. "Don't you dare."

Her sharp voice and rapid movements startled the horse. The animal reared up slightly and started to canter.

Jackson swore. He shoved Regan away, not caring that he might hurt her, then turned his attention to the horse. After bringing the animal back under control, he glared at her.

"You trying to kill us both?" he demanded. "You know better than to risk spooking the horse. We could have both been hurt. Where would that leave Amy?"

She huddled on the far edge of the seat. Her chest rose and fell with each rapid breath. He wondered if she might be crying but knew that wasn't possible. Regan wasn't the type to give in to tears.

"Don't say that about my sister ever again. Do you hear me?"

Her gaze locked with his. He saw determination there. And something else. Something that did more damage than all her blows combined. He saw a flicker of hurt. Regan really believed in Elizabeth's innocence. He didn't know how she'd avoided the truth for so long, but somehow she had. In that moment, with her eyes meeting his and the corner of her mouth trembling with emotion, he knew he wanted her to continue to believe. It was foolish. Thinking Elizabeth to be the innocent made him the seducer. All the blame fell on his shoulders. It should have bothered him, but it didn't. Better him than Elizabeth. He didn't want Regan hurt more than she had been.

Son of a bitch. When had he started caring about her feelings? He had a bad feeling in his gut, the kind of tight ache that warned him it was going to get a lot worse before it got better.

"I'm sorry," he said, knowing he was a fool because he would do anything to get rid of that hurt look in her eyes.

She was silent. He would have felt better if she'd delivered one of her unladylike snorts.

"Really," he said. "I am sorry. I didn't mean to say anything bad about your sister." *I didn't mean to hurt you.* Except he couldn't say that, exactly.

"I've already told you not to waste your pretty

words on me," she said, staring past him toward the horizon. "They're all lies, anyway."

"Are my lies better or worse than yours?"

She didn't answer. They rode on in silence, the quiet broken only by the sound of the horse's hooves on the narrow dirt road and the calls of birds from the trees lining the trail. If there was a heavy downpour, the way would be impassible for a wagon. He glanced up at the sky. There were clouds, but he didn't smell rain.

The miles passed quickly. With each one, he could feel Regan's tension increasing. Her body got stiffer and her hands twisted together until he thought she might pull her fingers right off.

His gaze slipped over her dress, pausing at her narrow waist. Something wasn't right. He drew his eyebrows together.

"You're not wearing a pistol," he said.

"There's a rifle under the seat." She shrugged. "Daniel isn't about to shoot at me while I'm in town. Besides, the holster doesn't hang right over the petticoats."

"You're always practical."

"Someone has to be."

She said the words without looking at him. In a way, he was glad. Her body gave away her concern and apprehension. He hated knowing even that. Better for both of them if he thought of Regan as strong. He liked her that way. Practical, competent, quick, and a hell of a good fighter. For a female.

He grinned. She'd have his hide for the last thought. Regan was tough. He wouldn't mind having her on his side during a fight. She would hold her own and take care of whatever needed doing.

But who took care of her?

He didn't like the question and he sure didn't have an answer. Before he could mull it over any, he saw the faint outline of buildings up ahead.

As they rode closer, Regan's hands twisted faster and faster. He wanted to say something to comfort her, but his usual glibness deserted him. Besides, she would likely rather face a bear unarmed than hear something friendly from him. She didn't trust him. He couldn't blame her—he was a scoundrel through to his black soul, a killer, and one of two men who threatened her possession of Amy.

As they got closer to town, he heard Regan's breathing increase. The short, shallow sounds reminded him that with her corset, she wouldn't be able to draw in a full breath. Her shoes would prevent her from running fast, the petticoats would keep her off-balance. Between her clothes and being unarmed, she was as vulnerable as an upended turtle. He gripped the reins tighter and held back a curse. He didn't like that one bit.

The first buildings were houses set just outside of the main section of town. When he last rode through Hampton, he'd seen lots of people on the streets, children playing in the dirt and the general business of a growing community. Today he heard the silence. As they rode past, curtains fluttered at windows. Young boys stopped to stare.

Jackson shook his head. He was acting as nervous as an untried filly. Hampton might be small, but it was still a sizeable community. No way everyone knew about Regan. He glanced at her and saw her sitting straight in the seat. Her chin tilted up proudly.

Her hair was like a beacon, drawing the eye. She was a fine figure of a woman; she would be noticed wherever she went. After wearing her sensible skirts and boots, she wasn't used to that kind of attention.

They turned onto the main street. Every third storefront was a saloon.

"The bank is up there," she said, pointing to a building on the left.

He saw the sign and urged the horse forward. Out of the corner of his eye, he noticed people stopping on the boardwalk. Stopping and staring. Whispering. One of the saloon doors banged open.

"Hey, Regan. Four bits for a fuck."

Jackson spun toward the voice, but no one stood there. The saloon door swung back and forth as if pushed by an invisible hand.

He'd barely turned back to face front when something hard hit the side of the wagon.

"Go home, whore."

With one smooth movement, Jackson transferred the reins to his left hand and reached for his pistol with his right. Before he could draw his gun, Regan reached over and placed her hand on his forearm.

"Don't," she whispered. "Please. It won't make any difference." Her eyes were wide and dark with pain, her face pale. "You'll only make it worse."

The sneers continued. Jackson hung on to his temper, even though he wanted to throttle every man who dared to call her names. He kept his eye on her, but her stiff spine never wavered. She looked straight ahead, ignoring them all.

When they reached the bank, she left him by the wagon.

"Are you sure?" he asked.

For the first time since leaving the ranch, she smiled. "I have a large sum of money here," she said. "I'm one of their best customers. If the price is right, they don't mind dealing with the town's fallen woman. Don't worry, Jackson, they'll even offer me tea."

With that, she swept into the building. He stood with his back to the wagon, watching the citizens of Hampton go about their business. Several had the courage to glance at him, but their eyes quickly averted when he stared them down.

Cowards, he thought grimly. Stinking cowards. It was easy to call a woman names. He wondered how brave they would be if they faced Regan on her terms. He'd barely imagined her pulling a gun and sending them all running when she reappeared, holding her reticule close to her body.

"All done?" he asked.

She nodded.

He helped her up into the wagon. She stared at him, as if gathering strength. When he climbed up beside her, she held out several gold coins and a stack of bills.

"Half the amount we agreed upon," she said. "The remainder to be paid when the job is finished."

He took the money.

"Aren't you going to count it?" she asked, her voice slightly high pitched.

"I trust you."

"What? Trust a whore? Jackson, are you mad? There are several people standing on the other side of the street who would be happy to tell you exactly what's wrong with my character."

He looked at her. "The hell with them."

She closed her eyes briefly. "You're right. The hell with them. The general store is right down there." She pointed back the way they'd come. "I have Fayre's list, plus some things for myself. I shouldn't be more than a half hour."

He flicked the reins, then turned them in a wide half circle. When he stopped the horse in front of the store, Regan jumped down without waiting for him.

"I imagine you have a few things you'd like to do without me," she said, looking up at him. "Why don't we meet here when I'm done."

He did have a couple of things he wanted to take care of. He glanced around at the people watching them, then back at her. "Will you be all right?"

"They're just words. They can't hurt me."

"That rock was more than words."

"I'll be fine."

Before he could respond, she turned and disappeared into the store. He watched her go. Regan O'Neil was some kind of woman. She had more courage than most men he knew, more brains, too. He wasn't sure he would have kept coming to town, knowing what was going to happen when he got here. But she didn't back down.

He looked up and down the street, then saw the sign for the blacksmith. With one last glance at the store, he tied up the horse and walked toward the building. He ignored the feeling of uneasiness knotting his gut. It was only for a half hour. What could possibly happen in that short amount of time?

14

Regan pushed open the door and stepped into the store. While her eyes adjusted to the dim light, she inhaled the mixture of scents. Vanilla, coffee, salty brine, tobacco, herbs, teas, spices, and the faint musty odor of dusty corners and sawdust floors.

The square building was filled from top to bottom with shelves and rows of merchandise. As a child Regan had spent hours in the store, exploring the outside world through the things available to buy. She'd seen India on the maps in her father's office, then had inhaled the fragrance of imported tea. She'd read about sugarcane, then bought sugar. The store had always been a magical place to her—until coming to town turned ugly and she could no longer count on the people she'd once thought of as friends.

She reached in her reticule and pulled out her list.

Mrs. Vander, the woman who ran the store, was a cold and difficult woman with a sense of right and wrong only slightly smaller than her greed. She allowed Regan in the store because she bought lots of supplies and paid in cash, something few store owners could resist. Yet she made sure Regan knew her sins had not been forgotten. It would have been easier to allow Fayre to do the shopping. Most of the time Regan gave in to what was easy rather than face Mrs. Vander. However, she'd had to come to town to get money from the bank. She couldn't justify having Fayre make a special trip. She would buy the supplies and endure what she had to. Thank goodness Jackson had business that took him elsewhere. At least he wouldn't witness her shame.

Holding the list tightly, she walked toward the counter. But instead of Mrs. Vander's large frame and gray hair, she saw a younger woman. Her relief was instant.

"Maureen?"

The pretty blond woman looked up, then smiled. "Regan. I haven't seen you in so long."

Maureen slipped from behind the counter and hurried toward her. Regan hung back, cautious. Maureen paid her no mind and engulfed her in a hug. The brief embrace made Regan feel welcome. Her eyes burned, although she blinked back any tears that dared to threaten.

"I didn't know you were working in the store," Regan said. If she had, she wouldn't have been so nervous about coming by.

"I don't usually." Maureen's blue eyes danced. "Mama doesn't think it's right for a married woman to have employment. But she's been ill and Alfred is too young to take care of things himself."

As if hearing his name had summoned him, Alfred, Maureen's younger brother, appeared from the back room. He was a slight boy, about sixteen or so. His eyes widened as he saw Regan. Something flared in his gaze. Regan tried to ignore the male response to a woman with a bad reputation.

"Now let's see what you need." Maureen plucked the list from Regan's hand. She scanned it, then nodded. "This shouldn't take long." She turned to her brother. "Alfred, start loading sacks of flour in the wagon out front. Regan needs ten. Then bring out sugar."

Maureen leaned close. "He hates working for me. A young man of his age taking orders from his older sister. He can barely hold his head up for the shame." She giggled.

Regan was surprised to find herself joining in. It had been a long time since she laughed with a friend. Back when they were in school together, they'd often laughed. So much so that one day they were sent home for talking. It seemed to have happened a lifetime ago.

Maureen collected two large baskets. She handed one to Regan, then slipped the other over her arm. Together they started up the aisle. Maureen glanced at the list, then tossed a few cans into her basket. The next half dozen went into Regan's, and so they moved through the store.

Maureen chattered about her marriage to a local rancher. "I think it does Robert good to have me away for a few days," she said. "Having to eat his own cooking and take care of the house himself will remind him how much he needs me."

Regan grinned. "You sound like Fayre. She's always saying Hank appreciates her more when she's been too busy to pay attention to him."

"It's true." Maureen scooped up an armful of canned peaches, then carried them back to the counter. Once there, she began unloading their baskets. She glanced around, as if checking to make sure Alfred was out of earshot. "How's Amy?"

"She's growing fast." Regan allowed herself to smile slightly. "She's very pretty, and is already reading."

"I wish I could see her." Maureen smiled sadly. "But I know it would be hard on her to come to town. Mama would have a seizure, anyway." Blue eyes met and held her own. "I wish you'd come to town more often. I miss seeing you."

Regan nodded. She missed her old life, too.

Maureen squeezed her forearm, then started listing the supplies and their cost. As she worked, she hummed softly under her breath.

Regan admired her pretty rose dress and the white lace-trimmed collar and sleeves. Maureen had always dressed like a lady. Despite her mother's small-mindedness, Maureen had never said anything mean about Regan's daughter. She was one of the few people in town who was kind. Regan had received an invitation to Maureen's wedding two years ago, but she hadn't attended. She didn't doubt her friend had wanted her there, but the price would have been too high. She'd sent along a fine piece of crystal instead and hoped Maureen would understand.

Alfred came by carrying a sack of sugar. His gaze boldly raked over Regan's bodice. She sucked in a breath and stared him down, determined that he be the one embarrassed, rather than she. His eyes met hers and skittered away, then he returned his attention to her breasts. No doubt being so close to a fallen woman was exciting to a boy his age. He would tell his friends about her that night. She shuddered and wished she was safely back on the ranch.

When the front door slammed shut behind him, Maureen looked up. "I have a secret," she said softly. Her mouth spread in a wide smile as she leaned forward. "I'm going to have a baby in September."

"That's wonderful. Robert must be thrilled."

"He is. We were beginning to despair. It's been almost two years since we were married. Not that we weren't trying." A blush stole across her face. "Mama would wash my mouth out for sure if she heard me say that. Robert wants a boy, but I'm hoping for a little girl. You're so lucky to have Amy."

"I know."

Maureen chattered on about her pregnancy. Regan was pleased for her friend; she would be a good mother. But a part of her felt distant from the conversation, as if the obvious joy was painful to be near. Maureen was happy, with a husband who loved her. She would bear this child, perhaps others as well. Her life would go on as before. No one would call her a whore. The women of the town would gather around her when her time came. They would deliver food, offer advice and heirloom lace for the christening gown. She wouldn't be shunned and ignored. No one would throw rocks at her or call her names. Young men wouldn't boldly assess her figure, trying to catch a glimpse of something forbidden.

Regan loved her daughter more than anything in the

world, including the ranch. She counted her a blessing. But there were times when the burden was too heavy, the shame too endless to bear. She wanted to be the carefree young girl who had given her heart to a handsome gunslinger all those years ago. She wanted to be Sean's favorite daughter, Pete's best friend. She didn't want to worry about what people thought, or about raising a child on her own.

Maureen planted her hands on her hips. "Here I am going on about myself." She grinned. "I'm getting as self-centered as my mother. Tell me about the ranch. Are things going well?"

Regan fought back laughter, because she knew it would have a hysterical edge. How were things? Should she mention the range war, the dead cowboy, or perhaps the fact that the sheriff thought she should marry the man who had murdered her sister? "Everyone is doing well."

"Good. Your handsome cousin was in here a few days ago. He seems sweet on you."

Regan turned away. "Daniel has a way of being charming," she said, fingering a can of peaches.

"It's not my business," Maureen said slowly.

Regan turned back toward her friend. "What isn't?"

"It's silly, but I never trusted him. There's something odd about his eyes. I'm only saying this because if you were going to marry him, you would have done so already. You're not going to marry him, are you?"

Regan leaned forward and kissed Maureen on the cheek. "You're lovely," she said, grateful someone else had seen what she always sensed. "No, I'm not going to marry him."

"Good. You'll find the right man, Regan. I know you will. Someone sensible enough to see how special you are."

"You're a romantic, Maureen. It's not that simple."

"Isn't it?" Maureen smiled knowingly. "We'll just see. When you find him, I shall say 'I told you so.'"

Gladly, Regan thought, wishing Jackson was sensible enough to notice her. But he hadn't. And he wouldn't. She was like a child crying for the moon. Her dream would always be out of reach. She sighed. At least she had his child.

Alfred stalked back to the counter. "I've put out the flour and sugar."

"Then go get a couple of crates for the canned goods." Maureen bent over the list. "All right, let me figure out the total."

While she counted, Regan continued to circle through the store. She paused by the bolts of fabric and pretty ribbons. Her blue dress might match her eyes, but it was several years old and as plain as her face. She fingered a length of lace, then glanced at Maureen. A row of ruffles hemmed the bottom of her skirt. It didn't take too much to make a dress over, perhaps turn it into something attractive.

A bolt of dark blue satin caught her eyes. She touched the smooth, cool fabric. How she would love to wear something like this. She closed her eyes and imagined what it would feel like against her skin. She could see herself gliding down the stairs, her petticoats rustling, Jackson waiting for her, admiration glowing in his eyes.

She shook her head. Jackson didn't see her that way. Besides, he wouldn't be around long enough for the dress to be made, let alone worn. What would she do with it when he was gone? Wear it to break the horses? She would do better with some sensible cotton and wool in colors that didn't show the dirt.

Regan moved past the fabrics and stopped in front of a display of wooden toys. There were carved animals, a wagon, and a train set.

"There," Maureen said, setting down her pencil. "I've added it twice, so it should be right. Is there anything else?" She turned and saw the toys. "Isn't the train wonderful? Robert wants us to buy it if we have a boy."

Regan picked up a small wooden pony. "I'll take this for Amy."

Maureen wrote down the price. When she looked up her usual smiling expression was sad. "I would so love to visit you sometime. Robert wouldn't mind, but Mama is difficult. When I suggest it, she has these spells. Sometimes I think she's pretending, but the doctor told me too much excitement would be bad for her."

"I understand," Regan said.

Maureen nodded. "I know that you do. I supposed I just wanted you to know that I think about you." She glanced toward the back. "What is taking Alfred so long? I'll be right back." She disappeared behind the curtain.

Regan held on to the toy and continued down the aisle. Next was a row of bottles. She read the hand-lettered labels and remembered the recipes Elizabeth had given her. Oil of rosemary, lavender oil, rose water. She glanced around guiltily, then picked them up. Her fingers lingered over a small jar. The label proclaimed the cream was guaranteed to fade freckles overnight. She touched a gloved finger to her face. Was it possible? Could a cream make her despised freckles go away?

Before she could decide, the scrape of a boot against the wooden floor made her turn quickly. Alfred had entered the main room. He stood next to her—close, too close—and stared down. He had his sister's blue eyes, but their faces were different. Maureen was feminine and pretty while Alfred looked like his mother.

"Good afternoon, Miss Regan," Alfred said, crowding her.

Regan swallowed, feeling vulnerable. She didn't like the way he was staring at her. His gaze focused on her bosom and he licked his lips. He was younger than she, barely sixteen, but he towered over her by at least a head. She didn't have her gun. Between the bottles she was holding and uncomfortable heeled shoes, she would be hampered if she tried to run.

She forced herself to stare at him, never acknowledging the fear. This was little Alfred. He wouldn't hurt her. He was just a boy.

"I've been savin' up," he said, his dark blond hair falling across his forehead. "I've got a dollar and two bits. Some of the boys said you've got a real special way of makin' a man of someone."

She couldn't have heard him correctly. No, it wasn't possible. They weren't lying about her that way. Her breath caught in her throat, her corset squeezing tight against her ribs. She was cold and hot at the same time. The shame overwhelmed her. Please, Lord, not that. Don't let Alfred be asking what she thought he was.

In some hysterical part of her brain, she acknowledged that her worth had more than doubled in the space of an hour. She should be pleased. A strangled sound escaped her mouth before she clamped her lips shut.

The boy sighed. "I can get another two bits if I have to, but I don't think you'd be worth much more. From the looks of it, you ain't got much up here." He reach out to touch her breast.

She shrieked and started backing up. She bumped into the glass display case behind her. Alfred followed. She was ready to throw the bottles in his face, when she heard loud footsteps.

Jackson swept down upon them like an avenging angel she'd read about in the Bible. He grabbed Alfred by the back of his shirt collar and shook him.

The boy swung his arms, trying to get him to let go. Jackson let him down and spun him around. Alfred took one look at Jackson's blazing eyes and blanched. "Lookee here, mister, there's been a mistake."

"I ought to kill you right now, you little shit."

"I'm sorry," Alfred mumbled. "I didn't know she was your—"

Regan wasn't sure what he was going to say, but Jackson didn't bother waiting. He backhanded the teenager, sending him stumbling across the floor and into a pile of cans. Alfred and the tins crashed to the ground, then Alfred scrambled to his feet and ran out the front.

Maureen came through the curtain and into the store. She glanced at the mess on the floor, then at Regan. "What happened?"

"Some little bastard—"

Regan jerked on his sleeve. "Alfred is her brother, Jackson. He didn't mean anything. It was my fault."

Jackson glared at her. She saw the cold determined stare of a killer and knew why Alfred had paled. "He offered you money for the pleasure of your company. How is that your fault?"

She didn't dare look at Maureen. She could feel the color on her cheeks. "I'm sorry," she mumbled. She should have handled it herself. It was being in town and wearing these unfamiliar feminine clothes. They made her forget what she was capable of. If Alfred had come on her at the ranch, she would have taken care of him in about ten seconds. But here, she was out of her element.

Maureen approached her. She touched Regan's cheek. "I apologize for what my brother said. He's young and stupid." A slight smile pulled at her mouth. "If it makes you feel any better, I plan to whip his backside when he gets the nerve to come back here."

"It's all right," Regan insisted.

"No, it's not. No one has the right to say that to you. Least of all my brother." Maureen glanced at the bottles in her arms. "Do you want me to add those to the bill?"

Before Regan could answer, she heard footsteps in the storeroom. Maureen stiffened. "Oh, Lord," she murmured.

The curtain parted and a large gray-haired woman

walked into the store. "What's going on here?" she asked, her voice shrill. "I heard things falling about. Maureen, what exactly is going on here?" Mrs. Vander glanced at Jackson, then dismissed him without a word. Her gaze fixed on Regan and her eyes widened. "You! You—"

"Mama," Maureen said. "Regan is buying a few things. We're almost done. Why don't you go back to bed and rest."

"Rest? Rest? While that whore is in our store?" She glared at her daughter. "And you've been speaking with her, haven't you?"

"Mama—"

"Don't 'Mama' me, young lady. You might be married, but you're still my daughter. How dare you sully your reputation by allowing this woman to converse with you?" Mrs. Vander drew herself up to her full height. It was an inch or so less than Regan's, two inches less than Maureen's but that didn't stop her friend from flinching slightly. "Maureen, go into the back room. I mean it, I . . ."

Her voice trailed off and she clutched at her chest. Maureen gave her a worried glance, then smiled at Regan. "It was good to see you."

"Now, Maureen," Mrs. Vander ordered.

Regan watched her friend walk away and disappear behind the curtain. Mrs. Vander picked up the receipt on the counter. "Is this everything?"

"No. I have these, too." She placed the carved horse and the bottles next to the few cans Alfred hadn't taken to the wagon.

During her time away from town, she often forgot that shame had a particular flavor. It was bitter and salty, almost like blood. She swallowed the taste in her mouth and wished to be anywhere but here. She didn't dare look at Jackson. She didn't want to know what he thought of her. Bad enough to have him witness her shame without making it worse by seeing the pity in his eyes.

Mrs. Vander wrote down the price of the horse, then picked up the first bottle. She frowned at the label, then moved to the next two. Her small dark eyes fixed on Regan's face. She willed herself not to flush, but she could feel her cheeks flaming.

After writing down the prices, she announced the total. Regan dug in her reticule for her money, then passed the woman several coins.

"I won't assist you in plying your trade," Mrs. Vander said. "If you wish to buy these things again, talk to your sisters in the saloon."

Out of the corner of her eye, Regan saw Jackson move toward the older woman. She put up a hand to stop him. Mrs. Vander counted out the change.

"All the potions in the world won't change who you are," Mrs. Vander said. "Nothing can hide your black soul. You're a whore and you always will be."

Regan caught her breath as if she'd been slapped. Before she could respond, the other woman threw her change at her. Several coins hit her in the chest. They bounced off her and dropped to the ground. Regan stood frozen, listening to them roll, then spin to silence.

Jackson took another step.

"Don't," Regan ordered, not looking at him. "She's not worth it."

She grabbed her bottles and the carved horse.

Jackson reached past her for the remaining cans. She ran to the door as quickly as her heeled shoes and corset would let her, then pushed out into the sunlight.

It was hard to breathe. She realized she was shaking. People collected nearby on the wooden boardwalks. They stared. She wanted to collapse and sob at the unfairness of it all. She wanted to scream to God and demand He tell her why she was the one chosen to suffer. She wanted to explain her innocence. She had proof of it. She was a virgin, and they branded her a whore.

But she did none of those things. She placed her bottles and the carved horse in the back, securing them with soft straw. She waited for Jackson to drop the last few cans into a crate, then lift her into the wagon. She hated the feel of his hands on her waist. She was dirty, disgusting. What must he think of her? Her throat tightened. She swallowed against the pain knowing they must never know how they hurt her.

Tears blurred her vision. She blinked them away. She would be strong. Pride was all she had left.

Jackson climbed up next to her. Instead of reaching for the reins, he glanced at the crowd, then at her. She could hear the mumblings of conversation. Go, she thought. Just let's go.

"Does this happen every time you come to town?" he asked.

She nodded. She lowered her chin slightly and twisted her hands together. She wanted to be anywhere but here. Her body shook. She thought she might throw up. Despite the heat of the sun, she knew she would never be warm again.

Slowly Jackson picked up the reins. She leaned forward, urging him to go. He didn't.

"They're watching," he said, staring straight ahead. "Through the curtains from across the street. The old hag in the store is, too."

Regan glanced around and confirmed what he'd said. They'd won. Wasn't it enough? Did they have to witness her shame as well?

Jackson held out his arm. She stared at him, then at his arm. What was he doing? She studied the crowd again. She saw the contempt in their expressions. Slowly, fearful of what she might see, she looked at Jackson. His gray-green eyes burned with anger. Not at her. And search as she might, she couldn't find any pity or condemnation. There was only understanding, and something she didn't dare identify.

Slowly she scooted closer to him, then adjusted her skirts. She straightened her spine and raised her chin high. With a deep breath for courage, she slipped her hand through the crook of his arm. He smiled down at her.

Only then did he flick the reins and start the horse moving toward home.

15

Clouds had rolled in. *Jackson* could smell the threat of rain. He stared at the darkening sky, at the horse walking in front of them, then at the lush wildflower-covered grass on either side of the road. He looked at everything except Regan.

He didn't want to know. He couldn't bear the thought of her shame, of her embarrassment. She'd shot him, lied to him, called him names, and taunted him, but he didn't want to see her hurt. Not by some old biddy in town, and not by a young pup offering money for her.

At the thought of what had just happened, he curled his fingers around the reins as if squeezing the strips of leather would ease his frustration. She'd told him there was trouble in town. That was the reason she hadn't let Amy leave the ranch. He'd thought she was being over-protective. Now he knew why. If they would say those things to a grown woman, imagine what they would do to a helpless child.

He wanted to find out who had called the ugly words, then beat that man into unconsciousness. He wanted to whip Alfred until he couldn't sit down for a month. He wanted Regan to taunt him, or yell at him. He wanted to know she hadn't been broken.

"How long has it been like this?" he asked.

She didn't pretend to misunderstand. "Since I came back with Amy. I knew that people would be surprised. I even expected a few not to accept me, but I never imagined the whole town would turn against me. Elizabeth thought it was because my father was so successful. There aren't a lot of Irish settlers in this part of Texas. He was fresh off the boat. Perhaps people were glad to see the family fail in this way if no other."

"I'm sorry," he said.

"I'm used to it. The first inkling I had of trouble was when we wanted to baptize Amy. There was an outcry, and the minister refused to allow us in the church. Papa had to bribe him to come out to the ranch to perform the ceremony." She sighed softly. "Amy wore the same gown Elizabeth and I wore. There was just family and a few of the cowboys. I told myself God wouldn't mind that we weren't in a church. It was very beautiful outside. Perhaps He wouldn't even hold our sins against Amy. It wasn't her fault. She's always had a sweet spirit."

"I've seen this sort of thing before," Jackson said, not wanting to picture the makeshift ceremony conducted on the front porch of the ranch house. Amy deserved better than that. So did Regan. "Small towns are the worst. The women work so hard to be civilized that they lose all sense of what's important."

"They value their virtue and purity above all." Regan shifted on the seat. "It was as if I would sully them just by being in the same room. No one's come calling since then. A few people would like to, I think. Maureen is always very sweet to me when I go into town. But her mother is cruel."

Jackson hated the resignation in Regan's voice. He much preferred her yelling at him to the dull sound of defeat.

"Why do you go back?" he asked. "Send someone else or go to another town."

"I should, I suppose. The next nearest town is two days away. Sometimes I send Fayre in for supplies, or even Pete. But if I don't go, it's too much like they've won." The smile she gave him didn't reach her eyes. "I don't want them to think I'm going to hide forever. That's why I keep going back. To show them I still can."

He studied her face, the familiar lines, the curve of her cheek, the shape of her wide mouth. The freckles looked darker, then he realized it was because she'd paled. The strain of the morning had left her looking weary. There were tiny lines around her eyes.

Since leaving town, she'd moved away from him and allowed her shoulders to slump. Guilt overwhelmed him until he couldn't bear to look at her. She was ruined because of him. He'd never touched her. If his gut was right, she was still a virgin, but the town treated her like a fallen woman. Because she'd taken in a child—his child.

It wasn't fair. It didn't even make sense. If she'd

cried, he might have been able to ignore her hurt feelings. In his experience, women used tears to get their
way. They used them as tools to bend men to their
wills. But not Regan. Even in pain, she kept her hurt
to herself.

She could run several thousand head of cattle, control the ranch and the men on it, yet the words of a
few mean-spirited people could destroy her pride and
leave her soul in tatters.

He wanted to hunt them down and hurt them. The
overreaction startled him. Fights weren't personal to
him. He killed because it was his job; he refused to
get involved. But something had happened today.
Maybe because he'd known Regan before. Maybe
because he'd always admired her. How could he not?
She'd gotten the drop on him.

She didn't have time to pretend. She lived her life
honestly, working hard each day to achieve something. She wasn't content to be an ornament. No one
took care of her. Instead she took care of others.
Especially his daughter.

"Why do you do it?" he asked. "Why do you keep
taking the blame. Why not tell them you're innocent?"

"As if they would believe me?" She paused then,
as if considering what she'd just said. It was a confession of sorts, but he wasn't going to call her on it.
Not today.

"Where was Elizabeth in all of this? What did she
have to say about the town?"

Regan turned to glare at him. "Are you asking how
Elizabeth would have handled the situation if you'd
ridden off and left her with child? Is there concern in
your voice, Jackson? After all, you stole her innocence,

then left her to deal with the consequences of your actions."

Now it was his turn to hunch forward. He rested his elbows on his knees and held the reins loosely. The temperature had dropped with the coming clouds. He wished he'd brought a coat.

She twisted lies and truth together so tightly it was difficult to tell them apart. He had taken his pleasure with Elizabeth and not thought about the consequences. Elizabeth hadn't been innocent. But he had left her pregnant.

"I would have come back if I'd known," he said

"For your *son*, not for Elizabeth."

"I never cared about your sister."

"That makes it worse, not better. If you didn't care for her, how could you—"

She didn't finish the sentence, but he knew what she was saying. How could he have bedded her without having feelings for her? What would Regan say if she knew how easy that was for a man? He could close his eyes and be anywhere, as long as the body beneath him was soft, tight, and willing. It was about finding ease, not finding comfort. He could bed someone without liking her, and like someone without wanting to bed her.

Regan was an example of that. He respected her, enjoyed her sharp wit and quick mind. But he didn't think about taking her clothes off and tasting her sweet flesh.

Jackson rubbed his hand on his jaw and shifted on the seat. The temperature of his blood had risen to uncomfortable as the first ripple of need swept through him. Maybe he'd been a bit hasty in dismissing Regan's physical charms. They might not be as obvious as Elizabeth's, but they were there, waiting for the right man to discover them.

"You should have loved her," Regan said. "She loved you."

Elizabeth hadn't. They'd wanted the same thing. But he couldn't explain that to Regan. She wouldn't understand. To her, passion and love were the same thing. She believed in a world that didn't exist, at least he'd never had any experience with it. But her innocence didn't protect her. He'd taken what Elizabeth offered without thought to the consequences, but it wasn't Elizabeth who paid the price. It was Regan.

Why? he wanted to ask. If she would just tell him why. But he didn't push her. He didn't want to see her shattered more than she was.

"It's not too late to tell the truth," he said.

"No."

"But—"

"No." She looked at him, her eyes blazing with fire. "I won't have Amy's life made into a lie."

"It already is."

"It's not. I'm her mother and no one can change that. Not ever. I'll do anything to protect her. I'm not afraid of you or the town or Daniel. I'll keep Amy safe, even if I have to die to do it."

He didn't doubt her. Her chest rose and fell with her deep breathing. Twin spots of color stained her cheeks. She looked ready to battle a battalion of warriors. He would put his money on her, too.

"I agree that Amy is worth the sacrifice," he said. "But not Elizabeth."

"Despite your practiced seduction, you never knew

my sister." She tossed her head. "I would have done anything for her. We're family."

Regan led with her chin and her heart. He supposed he should dismiss her as a fool. Life would chip away at that determination until there was nothing left. But instead of feeling sorry for her, he wondered what it would take to inspire that kind of loyalty in someone. He'd been looking for a place to belong when he decided to give up gunfighting. Perhaps he would have done better to look for a person to belong to.

Jackson stared at the road ahead. His parents had cared for each other that way. He remembered his mother's grief when his father had died. Her sobs had torn at his heart. He'd thought she would perish from her sorrow.

She'd forced herself to go on because she had children to care for. But she changed. He saw it in her eyes. As if some part of her was missing, and she would spend the rest of her life with a hole inside.

He grimaced. He was thinking with all the clarity of someone who had just polished off a bottle of whiskey. He should just let it go. Regan wasn't his problem.

Only she was. It was his fault she was in this situation. He might not have bedded her, but for reasons that made no sense to him, they had a child together. He had to make it right for her. But how?

Up ahead he could see the buildings of the ranch. He tugged on the reins to slow the horse. He needed a few minutes to think before they were surrounded by her cowboys, not to mention Amy. There had to be a solution. He could give her money so she could go away. No, she wouldn't leave the ranch. He could take Amy and— No, she wouldn't give up the child.

Damn it all, why did she have to take the responsibility in the first place?

He knew what the answer was. He didn't like it, but like all perfect solutions it was simple.

"You could marry me," he said, not looking at her. "It'll protect you in town and take care of Daniel."

He waited for her acceptance. The knot in his belly tightened. Married. To Regan O'Neil. He shuddered. She might be halfway attractive, and he was willing to admit he'd admired her shape more than once. It wouldn't be a hardship to bed her. But marriage? She would make his life—

"Are you crazy? Perhaps your hat has a hole in the top of it and the sun has been beating down on your brain."

He slowly turned toward her. He'd expected gratitude, maybe even a little surprise. He sure hadn't expected her to be glaring at him as if he'd just suggested they take off their clothes and parade around naked.

"Regan—"

She cut him off. "Marry you? So you can give up gunfighting and become a rancher?"

Fire flared in her eyes. Her body trembled with rage. She didn't seem real happy with his sacrifice. In fact, he was beginning to think he might have misjudged the entire situation.

"Isn't that convenient," she said, leaning forward and jabbing her index finger against his chest. "You get all this." She motioned to the land around them. "You don't even have to go to the trouble of finding your own place, or the expense of buying it."

"That's not what I meant," he mumbled, wondering

how she'd misunderstood his offer. "It's not about the ranch. I'm not even sure I can quit gunfighting." He hadn't finished wrestling with that problem. What if Gage was right and it did get in a man's blood? Would he ever be able to leave it behind?

"But won't it be lovely if you do?" She poked him again. "Don't for a second imagine I'm that foolish, Mr. Tyler. I might be merely a woman, but my father made sure I understood what was important."

They were getting closer to the ranch. Within a few minutes they would be in earshot of the men working around the barn. He reined the horse to a stop.

"Dammit, you're twisting my words all around. I don't want your ranch, Regan. It's not about that. I just want to give you and Amy a name. Is that so terrible?"

He'd hoped she would soften. Once again, he misjudged her. She drew her eyebrows together. "A name? We have a name. O'Neil is good enough for us."

His temper snapped without warning. "It's a fine name. I never said it wasn't. But I thought if you married me you wouldn't have to be alone. You could be a wife, instead of a whore with a bastard child."

He knew it was a mistake as soon as he said it. She drew back as if he'd slapped her, then stood up. He reached for her, but she pushed his hand away.

"I'd rather be a whore with a bastard than marry a gunfighter."

With that she turned and jumped out of the wagon. Her skirt tangled around her feet. She stumbled, caught her balance, then walked briskly toward the barn.

Jackson stared after her, wondering how the hell everything had gone so wrong.

16

Regan paced in her bedroom, the sound of her bare feet on the wooden floor muted by the steady pounding of the spring rain. If she were feeling fanciful, she might think that the heavens cried for her pain. But she knew better. She refused to give in to tears, and she doubted anyone else cared enough to cry for her.

A bolt of lightning illuminated the room. She waited for the echo of thunder. When it came, the house shook slightly. She was glad Amy was spending the night with Fayre and Hank. The older man would tell Amy stories to keep her from being frightened, then they would tuck her in bed and keep her safe.

When Regan returned from town, Fayre had taken one look at her, then had simply held out her arms, offering comfort. Regan had allowed herself a few

moments reprieve. Her friend's silent support had
helped her get through the day, as had the promise of
privacy tonight. She'd managed to smile at Amy's
chatter and had even listened to Pete's report on the
fence lines. Only when it grew dark was she free to
slip into her room and hide.

She didn't usually allow herself to act like a coward,
but tonight was different. She walked to the window.
She'd left the curtains open. The sky was black. She
could hear the rain but couldn't see it until lightning
illuminated the night. Then she saw the individual
drops hitting the window. The *boom* of the thunder
made her fold her arms in front of her chest and hug
herself. Storms usually made her feel alive. Tonight
the darkness only made her feel more unsettled. Her
skin prickled, as if it had grown too small. She felt
jumpy, wishing she were anywhere but here, anyone
but herself.

If only she didn't have to remember.

She turned and walked to the vanity, then felt for a
match and lit the lantern sitting there. After adjusting
the flame, she sat down and stared into the mirror.

Her hair had long since escaped from Fayre's careful
attentions. Corkscrew curls framed her pale face and
tumbled down her back. With only the single lamp for
light, the color wasn't as bright. She was almost
pretty—if not for the freckles and the too wide mouth.

She reached up and touched a curl. It coiled
around her finger. Her hair was soft. She brushed it
off her face and peered closer. In her white cotton
robe and simple night shift, she looked young and
afraid. Innocent. Still the memory of their words
filled her brain.

"Whore." "The boys say you've got a real special way of makin' a man of someone." "Four bits for a fuck."

She pulled the sleeve of her robe up to her elbow and stared at her skin. She'd worn her sleeves down all winter, so her arms were pale. She couldn't see anything there, but she felt dirty. The bath she'd taken couldn't clean away their insults.

She blinked back the tears. There was no kindness in the town, no forgiveness. She was trapped by the lies. A virgin whore.

It wasn't fair. It had never been fair. If only—

If only Jackson hadn't bedded Elizabeth. If only Elizabeth hadn't gotten with child. If only Elizabeth had told the truth. If only she could find peace.

She swept her hair off her shoulders. Most of the curls bounced back to frame her face. She grimaced. It wasn't just about what had happened riding into town. Alfred had upset her. She'd known him when he was a young boy. She'd bought him sweets and told him stories. He'd kissed her cheek and called her Auntie Regan. How had that all changed?

Worse than Alfred's actions, worse than the crude words and Mrs. Vander's behavior, was the fact that Jackson had witnessed it. Regan ducked her head and placed her hands against her flushed face.

She would have been able to put it behind her if he'd ignored it. But to propose? Not that. When he said the words, oh, she'd wanted to believe. Just for that moment, she dared to hope that he'd come to care about her. That he didn't mind that she wasn't beautiful like her sister. That he'd seen she was more inside, that she could be a good wife to him. She would never bake pies or sew beautiful quilts, but she could keep the ranch running, even if times got bad. She didn't need him to love her very much. Just enough to keep him close by.

Instead he pitied her. He knew it was his fault she was shunned by the town. He couldn't take back what had happened, so he did the next best thing. He'd offered to marry her. Not because he loved her, but because it was the right thing to do.

She raised her head slightly and smoothed her fingers against her cheeks. She was still strong. She would survive this, as she'd survived everything else. She would go on, because she didn't have another choice.

As she reached down to grab the brush, her fingers bumped the bottles she'd purchased earlier that day. She took the largest in her hand and stared at the label. Rosewater. She'd bought it to rinse her hair, to make herself smell sweet. She thought about the freckle cream, then met her own gaze in the mirror. Freckle cream wouldn't help. Nothing would erase the hideous spots on her face. She grabbed her hair with her free hand and yanked it hard. Rosewater wouldn't make it a different color or take away the curls. She sneered at herself. Nothing would change the way she looked.

"I'm not a whore," she said softly, to her reflection.

That didn't matter either.

With a harsh cry of "No!" she hurled the bottle across the room. It hit the wall by the window and splintered. The shattered bits of glass fell to the wooden floor as the liquid dribbled along the wallpaper.

Instantly the scent of roses filled the room. Mrs. Vander had accused her of buying tools for her whorish trade. The fragrance of flowers surrounded her, mocking her.

"I'm not a whore," she said louder. "I'm not."

She stared at her reflection. Her eyes were wide and unfocused, her mouth parted. There was a wildness about her. She hated it, hated what she saw. Hated what she'd become.

"Then I'll be a whore," she said. She tore open the center drawer and grabbed the scissors. "I'll look the part, so they have something more to whisper."

She took a hank of hair in one hand and with the other used the scissors to chop off her hated curls. They drifted silently to the floor. She reached for the next section, then heard rapid footsteps on the stairs. Frozen, she stared in the mirror, watching the door behind her.

It flung open and Jackson stepped inside. "What happened?"

He'd obviously been asleep. The crash of the bottle must have woken him. He wore trousers, but no shoes. He'd pulled on a shirt, but it was unbuttoned. He carried a pistol in one hand. He glanced around the room, searching, then inhaled sharply. The scent of roses was stronger now.

"I threw a bottle of rosewater against the wall," she said tonelessly.

He glanced at the damp wallpaper. Already the pattern was bleeding into the background.

"You all right?" he asked.

"Fine."

He studied her in the glass, then he saw her cut hair and his eyes widened. "Regan?"

She started shaking, but she didn't want him to

know. She tucked her hands together, holding the scissors tightly. "I cut my hair. Whores wear it short." She tried to laugh. The sound came out more like a croak. "You probably know that. I thought I should look more like them. Satin and lace will be impractical around the ranch, but my hair will be enough, don't you think?"

He swore under his breath, then moved toward her. She stiffened, not wanting him to touch her or see her this way. She felt exposed, as if her protective self had been peeled away, leaving only her most pitiful secrets. She didn't want to know what he must think of her now. At least before she'd always been strong. Now she was nothing except defeated. They had all won.

When he stood directly behind her, he leaned forward and set his pistol on the dresser. Then he placed his hand on her head. She could feel his warmth and strength. If she could borrow that strength for a moment, she might survive. But she couldn't ask.

He stroked her head, on the side she'd already cut, then fingered the ragged edges. "You don't know what it means to be a whore," he said. "Even if you sold your body, you would never be less, Regan."

"I can't be less than I am. What does that make me? A most feeble creature?"

"Never that." He placed his other hand on her head and drew her hair back from her face. "You're very special."

This time the laugh was genuine. "You've been drinking. I'm not special. Elizabeth—"

"No. Not Elizabeth. You. You're honest and determined. You risk everything for people you care about."

Ah, her best qualities. The good minister would be proud, should he ever stoop low enough to speak to her. She'd retained her innocence and her goodness. She would trade them all for a day of being pretty.

She looked into the glass, at Jackson's reflection. He was the perfect one. Even at this late hour, with his cheeks and jaw dark with stubble, with his shirt partially open. Her gaze slipped over the exposed skin, slightly tanned despite the fact that it was only spring. She saw the hair that darkened as its pattern narrowed at the waist of his trousers. She could feel the heat of him against her back. He was as stunning as a black stallion posed against a sunset. As awe-inspiring as the storm that raged beyond her window. As promising as the first step of a newborn foal. He was all things.

The single tear slipped off her lower lid and trickled down her cheek. She blinked the rest back. She didn't cry because she was sad, but because she was in the presence of all that she'd ever desired. If she could have one wish, it would be for a single night with him. That he would be the one to show her the secrets his kiss had only hinted at. That for a few hours he would find her as perfect as she found him.

He turned her on the stool until she was facing him, then knelt in front of her. With his index finger, he brushed away her tear.

"Sweet Regan," he murmured. His fingers lingered on her cheek. "I knew you'd be this soft."

Lies, pretty lies. As if he'd thought of touching her. As if he'd ever thought of her at all. But tonight she didn't mind. She would believe the lies because they were better than the truth. In the morning she would have her regrets. In the morning it would once again matter.

He slipped his hands through her hair, again drawing it away from her face. "I love the color of your eyes," he said, staring at her. "And the shape of your mouth."

Her trembling increased. Her lips felt dry. She moistened them with her tongue, a quick darting flick. His gaze followed her actions and he swallowed.

Something flared to life in the pit of her stomach. Heat grew, then radiated out along her arms and legs. Even her fingers and toes tingled. She was naked beneath her robe and night shift.

Then he clenched his jaw and his expression hardened. "I'm sorry," he said. He released her hair. "So damn sorry for everything. I swear I didn't know what would happen today."

It was as if he'd doused her with water from the stream. She straightened, then tried to move away. She was trapped between him and the dresser. Her feet had settled between his knees. She didn't think she could get past him without touching him, and she didn't think she could bear to touch him without confessing her feelings.

"How could you have known?" she asked, forcing her voice to sound calm.

His eyes looked gray in the lamplight. Mysterious. Sometimes she knew what he was thinking, but not tonight. "If I could go back and change things, I would. I would erase everything."

"I don't want your regrets," she said quickly. "Besides, even if things could be changed, I wouldn't want them to be. I love Amy as much as I would my own child. I wouldn't give her up for anything."

"Hell of a time to confess."

She frowned. "What are you talking about?"

His smile was weary. "You said you couldn't love Amy more if she was your own. She's my daughter, isn't she, Regan?"

She closed her eyes for a moment, then opened them. There was nowhere else to hide. "Yes. For tonight I'll speak the truth. Amy is the child you had with Elizabeth."

He stared at her as if she'd handed him a fortune in gold coins. His intensity, not to mention the bare chest rising and falling not three inches from her fingers, made her nervous. She tossed her head, then felt the short ragged edges of her cut hair brush against her shoulder.

"Oh, no," she whispered, and turned toward the mirror. She stared at her reflection in horror. On the right side of her head, her curls tumbled down her back, almost to her waist. On the left, her hair barely touched her shoulder. A few strands hung longer than the rest. She wanted to cry, but there weren't any tears.

"It'll be all right," Jackson insisted.

She shook her head mutely. It would never be all right. "I look like someone from a sideshow." She raised the scissors to her hair so she could cut off the rest and at least make it even. She drew in a deep breath, then shuddered and dropped her hand to her lap. "I can't do it."

Their gazes met in the mirror. She asked silently. He nodded in response and held out his hand. She placed the scissors on his palm, then watched as he cut off her hair. In just a few minutes almost two feet of curls lay tangled on the floor. Her head felt light. She tossed her shoulder-length hair back and forth, watching it sway in time with the movement.

Jackson set the scissors on the vanity, then placed his hands on her shoulders. She could feel the warmth of him. His fingers squeezed her gently. "This doesn't make you a whore."

She didn't disagree because she thought if she tried to speak, he would know how much this hurt.

He gathered her hair in his hands and held it at the base of her neck. Then, as she watched in the glass, he bent down, near her ear. His lips whispered against her skin.

"Why, Regan? For the love of God, tell me why."

She closed her eyes because she couldn't stand to see him so close and know that it was pity. She closed her eyes because then she could pretend that this was real, that he cared for her. She closed her eyes because she was afraid of what he would see there, and pride was all she had left.

"Elizabeth was convinced our father would throw her out if he knew the truth," she whispered. "I had always been the favorite. Elizabeth knew that. She said if he thought the child was mine, she would be able to stay home until she got married. I knew she was right. I suppose I felt guilty because Papa preferred me. I never understood why."

"Maybe because you were a better daughter."

She opened her eyes. Jackson stood behind her, staring at her. He began to move his hands, smoothing them over her shoulders, rubbing small circles on her neck and upper back. Some of the stiffness there eased.

"I wasn't," she said. "Not really."

"Why did you agree? It couldn't have been just out of guilt."

"No. I knew Elizabeth would find a husband and move away. I thought Papa might eventually marry again. I was afraid—" She swallowed and lowered her chin toward her chest. "I was afraid I would be alone. I knew that I might marry, but it would only be because a man wanted the ranch. I needed more than that. I thought a child would care about me if she thought I was her mother. I agreed because I got Amy."

"You paid a big price for that."

She glanced up at him. "You mean my father?"

His hand grew still as he nodded.

"He was very upset. More angry than I'd imagined. I hated to disappoint him." She sighed. "I wanted to tell him the truth, but I'd promised Elizabeth I wouldn't. Then after she married Daniel, I was afraid. If Sean knew Amy was Elizabeth's, he would insist she take the baby. I didn't want Daniel anywhere near Amy."

He turned her until she was facing him again, then crouched down in front of her. "I'm sorry for my part in this. I want to say something or do something that will make it better for you."

She reached out toward him, to touch him, then caught herself and pulled her hand back. He grabbed her wrist and drew her close to his cheek. He pressed her fingers against his skin. She could feel the stubble and his hot flesh.

"Keep us safe, Jackson," she said. "That's what you can do."

Dark eyes met and held her own. Her breathing quickened. "I never wanted Elizabeth," he said. "Not the way you think I did."

She ducked her head. He was referring to his rejection of her that night in the barn all those years before. She'd been so young. No wonder he'd turned her away.

He touched his knuckle to her chin and forced her to look at him. "I wasn't interested in getting hitched," he said.

"It would have been just a kiss."

"No. It would have been more than that. You can refuse to believe I didn't care about your sister, or that I didn't promise her anything, but that doesn't change the truth. I wanted it to be easy. You would have made things complicated."

"How?"

"Because you're nothing like your sister."

She jerked her head free of his gentle hold and drew her hands back to her lap. Of course. It always came back to Elizabeth.

"You misunderstand me," he said impatiently.

"I understand perfectly." She spread out her hands, turning her wrists to expose her palms. She had calluses by the base of her fingers, a partially healed blister, several cuts and bruises. She didn't look or act like Elizabeth. "I don't have the hands of a lady."

"Thank the Lord." Jackson took her fingers in his. She was too startled to protest or pull back, and then she didn't want to. He brushed his thumbs against her suddenly sensitive palms. He traced her calluses and gently touched her healing cuts.

She watched, barely able to breathe. His head bent over her hands as he studied her short nails. She should have been embarrassed, but she wasn't. She was too caught up in the wonder of being close to him. To Jackson. She could inhale the masculine scent of his body. He shifted, kneeling in front of her. His almost-bare stomach was inches from her knees. She could feel his warm breath on her fingers, then he bent his head and pressed his mouth to her right palm.

She gasped softly as sensation shot up her arm. The fleeting pressure, soft and slightly damp, left her hand tingling.

"Pretty white hands are one thing ladies and whores have in common," he said, then glanced at her. "Remember that the next time you're ashamed of your bruised knuckles."

She laughed. "Jackson, that's a terrible thing to say."

"Maybe. But it's true." His eyes darkened, the gray-green irises deepening to the color of spring grass. Several strands of hair fell over his forehead. She would have sold her soul to brush it back. Instead she curled her fingers toward her palm, only to trap his hand against hers.

Her chest tightened. The fragrance of roses didn't seem so overpowering. In that instant she knew instead of reviving bad memories of her horrible day in town, the scent would forever recall this moment with Jackson.

He reached up his free hand and touched her face. He gently pressed his fingertip against her skin, as if tracing the pattern of her freckles.

"I never knew," he said quietly. "Is it just today, or have you always been beautiful?"

She jerked her head back. Some of her happiness faded. "Don't tease me."

"I'm not. Look at you." He moved his hand down her neck, then up through her hair. "Look at you. Your skin is soft and smooth. Your mouth would tempt a man into hell. Your eyes make promises that drive a man wild."

"I don't—"

"Good," he said, cutting her off. "Better if you don't do anything at all. Don't think, don't question, don't move."

He slipped closer, so that her knees bumped his broad chest. His face was near hers.

"I don't need your pretty words," she blurted out.

"Of course you do, but that's not why I'm saying them. I'm saying them because they're true, and six years ago I was a damn fool."

Her breath caught in her throat. She desperately wanted to believe him. How could she? a voice in her head screamed. How could she not?

Then the hand that had nestled with hers slipped up her forearm to her waist. Jackson angled his body between her legs, separating her thighs. He slipped between them, closer still, so that she straddled his hips. His fingers tightened around her curls and his mouth touched hers.

This time he didn't have to tell her to shut her eyes. Her lids fluttered closed and his lips pressed softly against her sensitized skin. He was still for a moment, then he began moving back and forth, teasing her with his touch. Her body heated. Perhaps it was from him being so close, perhaps it was from the flames she felt flickering in her belly.

Heat traveled down her legs to her toes, which curled against the bare floor. Her hands fluttered. She wanted to hold him, to touch him back. She raised her arms, ignoring her apprehension, then gently rested her palms on his shoulders. His shirt was thin. She could feel his hard strength, the rippling of his muscles as he moved closer. Her legs parted even more as he pressed flush against her—from her breasts all the way to her most feminine place.

A blush climbed her neck to her face, then continued to her hair. She could feel it. Worse, she could feel him, that male part of him, against her. *There.* She swallowed. She remembered what her father had told her about men and women together. She was naked under her night shift, and Jackson didn't have that much on.

He pulled back. "Relax."

"I can't," she blurted out. "I'm scared."

"About what?"

She inched her hips back, then winced when he grinned at her. "It's not funny."

"Yes, it is. You'd rather face an armed gunslinger than risk being this close to a man."

It wasn't just any man, it was Jackson. And it wasn't that she was scared of being close, it was that she didn't know what he wanted from her. She wished she could believe his words and know that he really thought she was pretty. But it wasn't true. He was trying to make her feel better.

"Oh, Regan, I can see the doubt," he said, touching her cheek again. "Stop thinking so much."

"What else am I supposed to do?"

"Feel."

He pressed his mouth against hers. Instead of staying still, he moved back and forth. He cupped her jaw, tilting her head slightly, so their noses didn't bump. She liked the movements. They made her feel giggly inside, as if someone were tickling her heart.

His tongue traced the seam of her lips. She sighed her acceptance, and he slipped inside. He tasted sweet, and a little like brandy. He swept around her mouth, circling. Everywhere he touched seemed to ignite with heat. Her fingers tightened their grip on his shoulders, her body strained toward his.

The tip of his tongue delicately danced against hers. She caught her breath. She felt the urge to respond but didn't know what to do. He moved again, a quick flicker, then he retreated. She waited, wanting more, needing to know how he was making her legs tremble and her breasts ache. Every part of her quivered with anticipation. In her deepest heart, she'd never understood how Elizabeth could have given herself to Jackson. She'd never known why her sister just didn't stop him before he took her innocence. But now, with his lower half nestled against her feminine place, with her breath coming quickly and her body straining to understand the confusing and exciting sensations flooding her, she knew. It would be easy to forget, so easy to give herself up to him and his magical ministrations.

He gently drew her lower lip into his mouth and sucked. When he released her, she arched her head back. He kissed her chin, then moved down her throat, leaving a damp trail of need. She felt both hot and cold. The bottom of her feet burned, her hands closed around his shoulders. She moved her palms back and forth until she touched the strong column of his neck.

With one quick, fluid movement, Jackson shrugged out of his shirt, then grabbed her hands and placed them on his bare chest. Her eyes flew open. He leaned toward her, his mouth caressing the base of her throat. She could see his gold hair gleaming in the lamplight, and the tanned skin of his shoulders and back. As his hands returned to settle at her waist, she watched his muscles bunch.

Slowly, she moved her fingers. His skin was smooth under the crinkly blond hair, his strength hard, his heat intense. She could feel the steady beating of his heart. It thumped against her palm. Her eyes burned suddenly, and she blinked away the tears. Tenderness overwhelmed her. His life's blood flowed beneath her fingers, hot and ready, so very alive.

He raised his head and smiled at her. As always, his male beauty left her silent and wanting. He took the hand covering his heart and brought it to his mouth. Still holding her gaze, he kissed her palm, then used his tongue to trace a line from the base of her thumb to her smallest finger. In that moment, as his eyes held hers and delicious languor crept down her arm, she knew she loved him.

Whatever happened in the morning, whatever happened with Daniel or Amy, with the ranch and the town, she would always love him. A schoolgirl infatuation had ripened into a woman's affection. It never occurred to her to tell him; it was enough to know it herself.

"Kiss me back," he murmured, then bent toward her.

His mouth claimed hers, his tongue plunging inside. This time there was no slow exploration. He circled around her, moving deeper, touching her as she'd never been touched before. The heat in her belly grew.

Cautiously, tentatively, she responded to him, mimicking his movements, dancing with him, after him, even when he retreated to his mouth. She followed, then paused to savor the different tastes and textures. She leaned into him, moving her hands up and down his bare back, sweeping across his skin, clinging to him as the room spun.

She couldn't catch her breath, then decided it didn't matter. Nothing mattered but the moment and the man. Nothing would ever be the same again. She felt a sharp jolt of need between her thighs. Her hips arched forward, and she brushed against something hard. In her mind's eye, she pictured him by the stream, standing naked in front of her. He *had* grown and changed. Her hips arched toward him again and he groaned.

Before she could pull back to ask if he was all right, his hands at her waist began to move up. Slowly, steadily, they slid up her ribs before cupping her breasts.

She gasped. All her attention became focused on his fingers and the way they moved against her robe and nightgown. Her head fell back. He bent lower and kissed her neck. She still couldn't breathe, but it mattered even less.

Her breasts grew more sensitive, more aware. Her heart pounded harder, her thighs trembled. He touched her nipples with his thumb. Now it was she who moaned. Her chest arched toward him. She wanted, no *needed,* more. More of his heat, more of his touch, more of everything.

Over and over again he stroked the hardened points until she thought she might perish from the pleasure. Between her thighs, in her woman's place, she felt a dampness. A musky scent rose from their bodies, far sweeter than the fragrance of roses lingering in the room.

He dropped his hands to her thighs and began pulling up her robe and nightgown. She felt the material moving up her legs, baring them to him. It seemed foolish to protest. This was the man she'd always cared about; what did it matter if she showed herself to him?

He breathed her name, then buried his face in the crook of her neck. As she reached up to stroke his head, her fingers got tangled in her own hair. She brushed it aside, then stilled when she felt the short length of her curls. Events from the day flashed through her mind—the ride into town, the people calling her a whore, Alfred's proposition, Jackson's proposal.

He'd pulled the fabric up to the tops of her thighs. She placed her hand on his to stop him.

"Why are you doing this?" she asked, her voice a whisper.

He raised his head. His eyes were dark, his gaze unfocused. "Because I want you. Because it's right."

"Are you trying to trick me into marrying you?"

His smile was sad. "Sweet Regan, will you ever trust me?"

She searched his face, the familiar lines of his jaw and nose, the unreadable expression in his eyes. The faint guilt twisting his mouth. "You are, aren't you? You think if you bed me, I'll be forced to marry you."

He took her hand and placed it against his groin. She felt the outline of his arousal. Long and hard, it surged against her untutored touch. "There are other reasons to bed you. Do you know what this hardness means?"

"I think so."

"Then you must know that I want you."

If only she dared to believe him. "Have you been thinking about Elizabeth?"

He reached up and cupped her face, then closed his eyes. "You have eleven freckles on your right cheek, seven on your nose, and thirteen on your left cheek. There is a tiny scar by the corner of your mouth. Right here." He bent forward and, with his eyes still closed, touched the place with his tongue. She thought she might swoon.

One hand moved down to her breast. "You fill my hand," he said. "You smell like heaven." He opened his eyes. "No, I haven't been thinking of Elizabeth."

"I believe you," she whispered, because if she didn't believe she would die.

"Then marry me."

The pain was so sharp, so entwined with her hunger for him, that it was almost sweet. She inhaled, feeling it grow in her chest. If only he'd said a single word about loving her, or even liking her. The wanting wasn't enough. He told her himself he'd never loved a woman he'd bedded. His arousal meant nothing to his heart.

She told herself it didn't matter why she married him. It was enough that he'd asked. She should accept. Jackson would be good to her and to Amy. He might not stay long at the ranch, but he would likely return. He would share her bed. Many marriages survived on less.

"I can't." It was knowing he didn't love her back, that he never would. If he could have anyone, why would Jackson want a woman like her?

He groaned in frustration. "You're the most stubborn, pigheaded . . . Damn." He kissed her hard on the mouth. "Be that way if you must." He moved close and drew her into his arms.

She pushed him away. "No."

He frowned. "What do you mean . . . 'no'?"

"I can't do this." She motioned to his naked chest.

"Why?"

He wouldn't understand. She knew that. But she had to say it anyway. Because, as she'd long ago realized, pride was all she had left.

"If I let you stay with me tonight then I *am* nothing more than what they called me today. I'm sorry, Jackson. I can't be your whore."

17

Jackson closed the door silently behind him. Regan stared into the shadows of the room. The pain had ceased being sweet, now it simply robbed her of breath.

Mercifully, there weren't any tears. She didn't want to cry. It made her feel weak and out of control. Bad enough that her heart had been shattered and her insides left trampled. Worse to cry over it.

She drew in a deep breath, then winced at the sharp pain in her chest. It had been so hard to let him go, even though she knew it was the right thing to do. At least she thought it was the right thing. She pressed her fingertips to her temples. It had to be right; it hurt too much to be wrong.

For the first time in many years she allowed herself to wish she wasn't so alone. If only there was someone to talk to. She couldn't go to Fayre. If her old friend knew of Jackson's proposal, she would want Regan to accept. In her heart, Regan knew how everyone who cared for her had been hurt by the situation with Amy. It wasn't easy for Fayre and Hank, or even Pete, to know what had happened when she went into town. Everyone missed being invited to the town socials and seasonal dances. It was lonely to be on the O'Neil ranch, cut off from everyone around them.

She rose and walked to the window. The storm had passed, leaving behind a light rain. She opened her window and leaned out, breathing in the clean, cool air. She wouldn't think about it any more tonight, she told herself. She would fix her mind on something else. Something pleasant.

But no other thoughts came to mind. Her arms ached to hold Jackson close and her mouth hungered for his kisses. There wasn't a part of her that didn't quiver in anticipation of his touch. It would have been so easy to say yes, to both the proposal and the night together. Easy, but wrong.

Without wanting to, she remembered the first time a man had ridden in from town to talk to her father about her. She'd watched him from behind the barn, hating the way he glanced around at the outbuildings and the stock, as if assessing their value. In her heart, she'd long ago accepted the fact that a man wouldn't want to marry her for herself. Elizabeth was the one the boys all wanted. She was the one they stole kisses from.

But the moment it happened, and her father told her about the stranger's proposal, she'd felt dirty. She'd refused his suit. Her father had understood.

She'd known he would. He'd always loved her and cared about her. Even as a child she'd wondered if anyone else would ever love her as much.

She stared up at the sky and watched the clouds part, showing a bit of the crescent moon. Life had been simpler then. Her place secure. She'd adored the ranch, and her father. She'd known—

Regan sucked in a breath. The pain in her chest grew until she thought she might explode. She closed her eyes, then opened them again, not wanting to face the darkness, not wanting to know if it was true.

Had her father loved her best because he'd always known no one else would? A sob caught in her throat. She swallowed hard and refused to give in to it.

"Nonsense," she said aloud. "None of that matters now."

She turned from the window and returned to her vanity. Two small bottles sat where she'd left them. She opened them and sprinkled a few drops on her brush, then sat on the stool. The scent of rosemary and lavender blended with the roses. She hoped Elizabeth's recipe was correct, that the oil would leave her hair silky. Maybe it would even darken the color to something normal.

She smiled faintly, then raised her hand toward her hair and her gaze toward the mirror. Her eyes widened with shock. She'd forgotten. Her hair was gone, cut off at her shoulders. She stared at herself, at the hideous image in the glass. When the tears came, she didn't have the strength to fight them. They poured down her cheeks. A single harsh sob split the silence of the night.

*   *   *

Jackson leaned back in the chair and frowned. He hated the waiting. It had always been the worst part of his job. Waiting for Daniel to act was harder still, because he knew the man was crazy. Planning a defense against any enemy was challenging. The problem with Daniel was that Jackson didn't know which way he would go. He knew Daniel wanted the ranch. He wouldn't risk too much stock or land. He probably wouldn't attack the house directly.

He tilted the kitchen chair back on its two rear legs and rested his booted feet on the windowsill. Would Daniel kidnap Regan? Jackson grinned. He didn't think even Daniel would want that kind of trouble. Nope, Regan was safe as well. So what would Daniel come after?

Jackson looked around the kitchen as if the warm, friendly room would provide him with answers. A stew bubbled on the stove. There was a stack of dishes on the counter, and Amy's carved pony next to the bread box.

Amy. Daniel would come after what Regan valued most. He would have to talk to her about having someone guard the house. Assuming she was still speaking to him.

He'd barely seen her in the last week. They'd never discussed it, but by silent agreement, they'd stayed out of each other's way. It was probably easier for both of them. No doubt Regan had some regrets about that night, as he did. Although he doubted their regrets were the same. He was sorry he'd been so clumsy trying to get her to see it would be better for everyone if they married. The funny thing was, once he'd proposed, he had kind of gotten used to the idea.

She would no doubt regret confessing her secrets and having him see her at her most vulnerable.

He wanted to tell her it would be fine between them. He didn't have any intention of using what he knew against her. He wasn't sure what was going to happen with Amy, but his time on the ranch had shown him the child was happy here. He didn't want to lose track of his daughter, but he wasn't planning on riding off with her, either. It wouldn't be right. This was Amy's home.

Which left him with a whole lot of questions and not too many answers. Not that it mattered. Right now, they had to figure out what to do with Daniel.

"You mark up my clean windowsill, Jackson Tyler, and I'll make you lick up the dirt."

He lowered the front chair legs to the ground, then dropped his feet to the floor. Only then did he glance at Fayre standing just inside the pantry door. She wiped her hands on her apron and glared at him.

"Don't you think I'm not big enough to do it, neither," she said. "I've wrestled cowboys bigger than you."

"But not cowboys more handsome," he said giving her his best smile.

Her gaze narrowed. "You can flatter me all you want. I meant what I said about the windowsill."

He winked. The corner of her mouth twitched. Jackson stood up and stretched. "You're a bully," he teased. "All talk and no action."

"If it takes reminding you I've seen you as naked as the day you were born to put you in your place, I'm not above doing it."

He walked toward her, then grabbed his hat from

the peg by the door. As he got close to her, he bent slightly, so he could whisper in her ear. "You liked looking at me, didn't you?"

She swatted his arm. "Get your sorry behind out of my kitchen. Regan thinks she hired you to work, but the way I see it, you spend the day sitting around preening for the ladies."

"Just for you, Fayre. Just for you." He was still laughing as he stepped outside.

It had rained for almost a week. Yesterday was the first dry day, and this morning the sun shone brightly in the blue Texas sky. Birds swooped down from the budding pecan trees. The fields were green, the cattle giving birth. It was hard to believe that less than three miles away Daniel plotted his revenge.

A shout came from the corral. He headed in that direction figuring one of the men would know where to find Regan.

His boots sank slightly in the mud. The puddles had dried up, but the ground was still soft. Spring rains would come for the next month or so, before the summer sun parched the land.

He rounded the barn and saw several cowboys beside the main corral. A few of them were leaning against the railings, others had climbed up to sit on the wooden slats. Jackson strolled over to see what they were watching.

He nodded his greetings, then looked in the center of the ring.

"Holy shit," he said loudly.

The men next to him laughed. "Don't fret, young man," the gray-haired cowboy said, then pounded him on the back. "She can ride with the best of 'em."

Maybe, but he sure didn't want to watch it. Jackson clutched the railing and stared at the large black blindfolded gelding circling nervously in the ring. Pete controlled the animal while Regan held a saddle. Every time she got too close, the horse jerked away or reared. She jumped back, but the hooves still slashed dangerously close.

He drew in a deep breath, then wiped the sweat from his brow. What was she thinking of?

Before he could ask, Pete pulled the horse's head down. The animal bucked several times, then paused. In those few moments before he started up again, Regan tossed the saddle on his back, then reached under and grabbed the cinch. In about ten seconds, the horse was saddled.

As soon as the animal figured out what had happened, he tossed his head wildly and started bucking. Regan stepped back to let him wear himself out while Pete continued to hold the bridle.

"Are you crazy?" Jackson called when she was out of reach of the horse's hooves.

She glanced up at him, then grinned. "Yes, of course. What did you think?"

"You're gonna break your fool neck when he throws you," he said, jerking his head toward the horse.

"It's not going to happen, Jackson."

He raised his eyebrows. "Five bucks says it does."

Several of the men around him chuckled. Regan walked toward the railing and tipped back her hat. Her short hair was secured in a braid that ended at the collar of her light blue blouse. She wore the familiar split skirt and worn boots. Gone was the lady he had accompanied to town a week ago. Gone was the sweet-faced innocent he'd kissed and touched long into the night.

That was another of his regrets. That they hadn't continued what they started. Not so much for his own release, although he had been hard and needy since he first kissed her, but because he wanted her to know he really did think she was everything a man desired. He'd seen her doubt. He would have continued, knowing he might have seduced her into doing what she resisted. Her pain had stopped him. He would never trick Regan into anything. He respected her more than he'd ever respected anyone.

This morning her blue eyes were wide and bright, her expression smug. "Are you saying I can't stay on that horse?"

"My five bucks is willing to do all my talking," he said.

"Five dollars doesn't sound like you're very sure." She smiled.

He was tempted to up the bet, just to call her bluff. Only he wasn't interested in more money. He glanced around at the cowboys watching them. Damn. He couldn't say what he was thinking because neither she nor the men would ever forgive him for it. He couldn't take away her authority.

He turned his attention back to her. "On what you're paying me, five bucks is all I can afford."

Several of the men laughed out loud. Regan grinned. "Liar."

He reached into his trouser pocket and pulled out a gold coin. "I might be willing to bet more," he said, fingering it, then glancing at her.

Their gazes locked. Although her face was tanned,

a slight flush highlighting her cheeks. Her mouth was parted, her expression happy. He imagined her as she'd been that night, dressed all in white, innocent and alluring. He remembered her hot kisses and the way she'd clung to him, responding to his every touch. He allowed his eyes to say what he could not.

He saw the exact moment she figured out what he was thinking. She licked her lips, then swallowed.

"Five dollars is plenty," she said, stepping forward and taking his coin. She handed it to Pete, who looked back at Jackson.

"Hope you can afford to lose it," the cowboy said, as Pete removed the horse's blindfold. "Regan's one of the best."

"I haven't seen anything to prove that yet."

Regan ignored him. She approached the horse, murmuring softly. The animal had quieted some, although he shook occasionally, as if trying to dislodge the saddle. The horse was huge, outweighing her by hundreds of pounds. Jackson cleared his throat. He had to trust that Pete was right. If Regan wasn't the best—

He couldn't even think about that. He wanted to turn away and not watch. He wanted to tell her it was a stupid bet, and not to do it. Instead he saw how her men waited eagerly for her to mount the gelding. She had to prove herself to them.

With a movement so quick he almost missed it, she stepped into the stirrup and swung herself up into the saddle. The horse stood still, as if too shocked to move. Pete got out of the way. The horse started to buck.

Regan clung to the saddle as the animal hopped, kicked, bucked, and reared its way around the ring. The men cheered. Jackson thought he might lose his breakfast. Small clods of dirt were kicked up as the gelding circled around and around, trying to dislodge the small woman on his back. She held on, her hands clinging to the horn and the lead line, her thighs hugging the animal's sides.

Jackson's heart pounded hard in his chest. He kept swallowing. Was this what his mother had felt when he and his brother did something stupid? If it was, he owed her a big apology.

The men cheered every contortion of the gelding, they whistled loudly as Regan continued to hold on. The sun beat down on the crowd. Jackson wiped away more sweat, but he had a feeling it had nothing to do with the temperature.

At last the animal quieted. She continued to hold on to the horn but began to guide the horse around the ring. He trotted politely in a large circle, then she drew him to a stop in the center. While the gelding stood still, she raised her hat toward the men, but her smile was just for Jackson.

"The best five bucks I ever spent," he called.

She nodded.

One of the men whistled loudly. The shrill sound cut through the morning. The gelding rose up on its back legs, front hooves pawing the air. Regan was holding the lead line and her hat. She scrambled to grab the horn, but it was too late. Silently, she sailed off the back of the animal and fell to the ground.

Jackson was through the rails and into the corral almost before she hit. Pete ran after him.

"Grab the horse," Jackson ordered, kneeling down beside her still body. He didn't want her trampled. "Regan?"

She opened her mouth and inhaled harshly. He touched her head, feeling for bumps, then checked her shoulders and arms. Finally he ran his hands down her legs. Nothing seemed broken.

Gently, he touched her face. Her eyes were closed. She made the gasping sound again. The ground was soft from the recent rain, but she'd hit it pretty hard. Oh, God, had she hurt herself inside?

"Regan? Dammit, say something," he demanded.

She raised one hand to her chest, as if trying to catch her breath. He helped her into a sitting position, kneeling next to her and supporting her back with his arm. From the corner of his eye he could see the men hovering nearby. They were silent. Waiting.

Regan's shoulders began to shake. Was she having a seizure? He knew she wouldn't be crying.

"What's wrong?" he asked, leaning closer.

Her mouth opened and closed but no sound came. Finally her eyes opened. There *were* tears there. He stared at her, not sure what to do.

Finally she made a small sound, like a choking cough. It got louder and louder, and he realized she was laughing.

"Regan?"

She began to laugh in earnest. Tears poured from her eyes. "If you . . . could . . ." She paused to catch her breath. "The look . . . You were so shocked when I fell."

"It's not funny," he said, his tone angry. "You know better than to show off like that. You could have been killed."

She glanced at him, then at the men standing around protectively. "I know," she said, then erupted into giggles. No one smiled back. "I'm sorry." She cleared her throat. "I appreciate the concern. I'm fine. Really."

Jackson stood up and held out his hand. She took it and pulled herself to her feet. "Can you walk?" he asked.

"Of course." She walked around in a small circle, then held her arms out at her sides. "Sorry everyone. It was my fault." She giggled slightly, then covered her mouth to stifle the sound.

"You could have been killed," he said.

"You already told me that." She turned to Pete. "Let's start breaking the rest of the horses. I'll be in my office." She turned to leave.

"Wait," Pete called.

She looked at him. He pulled a gold coin out of his pocket. Regan grinned. "That's right, Jackson. I owe you five dollars. Come on, I pay my debts as soon as I can."

She started across the corral. Jackson walked after her. When he caught up with her, she darted a glance at him.

"You look like you want to strangle me," she said.

"I do. That was a dumb thing to do."

"Yeah, but until the horse threw me, it was a damn fine ride."

How had he been blind to Regan when he was last here? So she wasn't a beauty like her sister. There was more life in her than in any ten other women. He reached over and wrapped his arm around her neck. He pulled her close, then dropped a kiss on the top of her head.

"Yeah, it was a good ride," he admitted. "But I still want my five bucks."

Her office was off the tack room in the barn. He'd

been inside it several times before. She'd kept Sean's old desk and his chair, but the walls had been painted and a bright rug covered the worn wooden floor.

She sat down behind the desk, then unlocked the right bottom drawer. After lifting a strongbox, she unlocked it and pulled out a gold coin.

She flipped it to him and he caught it. "If you hadn't been showing off at the end, you would have won," he said, settling in the chair across from hers.

She grinned. "I was trying to impress you, Jackson. Besides, it was worth it. I didn't know you could run that fast."

Their eyes met. For a moment something warm and promising flickered in her gaze. He wondered what it meant. Had she really wanted to impress him? Did that mean she cared about him? He leaned back in the chair and studied her. He'd always been so wrapped up in his own thoughts about Regan that he never considered how she might feel about him. If she had any feelings.

He wanted to know. He opened his mouth to ask, then closed it. He only wanted to know if she cared about him. Better to wonder than be sure. She'd made it quite clear she thought he treated her sister badly. No doubt she saw him as a heartless bastard who preyed on innocent women. After all, a week ago he'd taken advantage of her.

She locked the strongbox and set it back in the drawer. "While I'm sure you enjoyed watching me fall off the horse, that wasn't why you came out in the first place. Is there a problem?"

"Maybe." He told her what he'd been thinking about. "Daniel is going to make a move soon. I can feel it. But he won't destroy what he wants."

"So the ranch is safe. I agree. I've always thought that, too."

"Which means some people are in danger."

She shook her head. "He wouldn't tangle with me."

"That leaves Amy."

He waited, wondering how she would take that. But Regan wasn't like other women. She didn't wince or start to cry. She paled slightly, then nodded. "Of course he'd want the one thing that's important to me. If he had Amy, he could make me do anything." She picked up a pencil and squeezed it. Her white knuckles were the only other visible sign of her concern.

"I thought about posting a guard," he said. "One of the cowboys, or even one of the hired guns. There are a couple I don't trust but—"

She cut him off. "Let's have it be one of the cowboys. They aren't as experienced, but Amy won't notice them around the house as much as she would a stranger. I'll talk to Pete and see who he suggests."

Jackson stared at her.

"What are you looking at?" she asked, raising her hand self-consciously to touch her short braid.

"You. You always surprise me. I tell you your daughter is in danger and you start making plans."

"Sitting here and worrying doesn't change the truth," she said. "If I want to protect her, I have to take action. It's only sensible."

He leaned forward. "You'd be surprised how many women aren't sensible. You see what needs doing, and then get it done. You don't care about how you look while you're doing it, or even failing."

She flushed and turned away. "Is this your way of saying I've got dirt on my face?"

"You know it isn't. I mean it, Regan. You're a hell of a woman."

She nodded. "I know what you meant. I'm sorry to be so contrary. I'm not used to compliments. Thank you."

She hovered in her chair as if not sure whether to stay or go. The uncharacteristic indecision reminded him of the last time he'd seen her ill at ease. It had been in her bedroom, in his arms.

Once again he wished he'd bedded her. Not to seduce her into marrying him, but because being close to her had felt damn fine. She might not dress like a lady, but she was soft in all the right places. She'd left him hard for days. Even thinking about that night made him swell up near to bursting.

He reached forward and placed his hand—palm up—on the table. She looked at him, confused.

He waited until she pressed her fingers against his. He captured her hand in his, then squeezed gently. "It wasn't about Elizabeth."

"I know," she whispered. With her other hand, she reached up and touched the end of her short braid.

"It'll grow back," he promised.

She looked doubtful. It wouldn't grow back fast enough to suit her. He didn't pretend to understand about being a woman, but even he knew how shocking it must be for her to look in the mirror every morning. She had so many ugly memories. He had a bad feeling the trouble with Daniel was only going to get worse. They'd been lucky, so far. Someone was going to get hurt. It was up to him to make sure that person wasn't Amy or Regan.

But he didn't want to think about that now. The day was too nice to waste inside thinking about trouble.

There would be enough time to think about it when the trouble found them.

He stood up, keeping Regan's hand in his. "Come on," he said.

"Where are we going?"

"For a walk." He tugged her to her feet.

"I don't have time for your foolishness, Jackson. It's springtime here on the ranch. I need to—"

He bent down and pressed his lips against hers. She was silent instantly. "That works good," he said, and grinned. "I'm going to have to remember it the next time I want to shut you up."

She tossed her head. "You keep doing it, and it's going to lose its effectiveness."

"Funny, I'm not one bit worried about that." He drew her hand through the crook of his arm. "Come on, darlin'. You and me are going to take a stroll."

"Why?" She eyed him suspiciously.

"Because I have a mind to spend some of this beautiful day with a pretty lady at my side." She opened her mouth to speak. He gave her a warning glance. "You're going to walk with me, Regan. You can come quietly, or I can drag you."

She stared at him, then laughed. "How can I refuse such a gracious invitation?"

"That's better."

He led her outside. They circled around the barn, moving away from the large corral where the cowboys worked at breaking the horses for the roundup. The air was clean and sweet. Most of the wildflowers had disappeared, but the land that stretched as far as the eye could see was still lush green. All the trees had budded.

"You've got a nice place here," he said.

"Papa chose well." She inhaled deeply. "Spring was always my favorite time. It's busy, but that makes it exciting." She looked up at him. "Is there a reason we're walking so slowly?"

He'd adjusted his stride to accommodate her smaller size. Figures she wouldn't expect him to. "No reason," he said, walking faster. She kept up easily.

"It's been a good season for us," she said. "Mild weather, plenty of rain. Our cattle should bring in a fair price when we sell them."

"You've worked hard for it."

She shrugged, dismissing the compliment. "Everyone has. It's going to take more though. I want to make it bigger. Add more blooded stock. Start buying up land."

"Why? It's free."

"You sound like Pete." She looked around at the cattle grazing nearby. "It's free now, but for how long? More and more people are coming through to settle. Once I own it, I can fence it. Then no one can take it away from me. Using government land means we don't know what's going to happen. Even a lease is no guarantee." She waved her hand toward the west. "If I owned enough, I wouldn't be having as many problems with Daniel. I could keep him away, then have him and his men arrested for trespassing if they came too close. It's been an expensive lesson."

"I don't know that a fence would be much protection against your cousin." Jackson figured Daniel would just go through it. "Have you started buying land?"

She shook her head. "Not yet. I don't have the capital. My father and I talked about it. We need cheap fencing. Wood is going to cost too much to buy and maintain. But I have a plan. Someday, when the time is right, I'll be ready. Until then, I keep Pete and Hank riding potential fence lines. They hate it, but they do it for me."

"They respect you."

She glanced up at him. "I hope so. I've worked hard to do the right thing. Papa trained me well." Her mouth curved down at the corners. "Sometimes I wish it was enough."

"Isn't it?"

"Cowboys don't like taking orders from a woman. Even one they know does a good job. I swear, I'll never understand men."

"That's fair. We'll never understand women."

Her slow smile hit him low in the belly. Lord give him strength, because he had the sudden urge to take her in his arms and kiss her until she couldn't even remember her name.

Instead, he focused on her concerns. He had enough money to buy her the land she needed. He could even afford to fence it. He could offer it to her. She wouldn't take it. Maybe a loan—

He shook his head. What the hell was he thinking? He wasn't staying here. As soon as the trouble with Daniel was over, he would be moving on.

"Did you always expect to run the ranch?" he asked.

"I suppose. When I was younger I thought about getting married and having a family. But even so, I pictured my husband living here, rather than me moving to his place."

"You have anyone in mind?" he asked.

"No." The single word sounded sad. "No one specific. Just a young girl's dream."

"You could still marry."

"I don't think so. Even if I met someone willing to overlook my reputation, I'm not sure I would be a good wife. I wouldn't stop running the ranch. There's barely enough time left for Amy. I can't think of a man who would be willing to put up with that."

He wondered what she would think of a man who wanted to help her run the ranch. Not someone to take control away from her, but someone willing to share the responsibility.

She paused beside a large budding pecan tree and kicked at a fallen branch. "The way things are going with Daniel, I'm not sure I ever want anything to do with a man again."

"Leave Daniel to me," he said. "I've promised to keep you and Amy safe and I aim to keep that promise."

She sat down on the thick branch and wrapped her arms around her raised knees. "I believe you, Jackson. Sometimes that's all that keeps me going."

As she stared off into the distance, he saw the lines of exhaustion around her mouth. The shadows under her eyes were darker. If this kept up much longer, Daniel would win by default.

Jackson hated the thought of Regan defeated. She was too strong, too proud. He leaned against the pecan tree and folded his arms across his chest. Less than a month ago she'd shot him, and he'd sworn to have his revenge. Now he was annoyed that she wouldn't agree to marry him, which made keeping her safe more difficult. Worse, his nights were spent wishing she shared his bed.

Apparently when he fell and hit his head, he jarred something loose.

He settled next to her on the branch. He could feel her heat and smell the sweet scent of her body. He'd never known a woman like her. She didn't need a man to provide for her, although he suspected she needed one to chase away the loneliness at night.

In the distance a cow moved to a fresh section of grass. Her wobbly calf trailed after her. He liked the ranch. He'd planned to start one himself, so it made sense that he was comfortable. Maybe he *could* stick around for a while, not just to help Regan but to be around Amy. He'd come to care for the bright-eyed little girl. She was quick and smart. She was still trying to wheedle her mother into letting her ride. He put his money on Amy.

Could he do it? Could he walk away from his old life and settle here? Would Regan let him? Did he want her to? Had he changed that much or was this all an elaborate game to justify getting Regan into his bed.

He wouldn't put it past himself.

"It's very peaceful here," she said. "I'm glad you made me come out with you. I'll remember this when I'm hip deep in calves and only halfway through the branding."

"Spring is busy on a farm, too," he said. "I remember my pa being gone until an hour past sundown. Once we were old enough, we joined him in the field. There was always planting to be done. Then weeding. Vegetables were the worst. Seemed like six weeds came with every seed."

She grinned at him. "I can't see you as a farmer."

"I couldn't either. My family were sharecroppers."

"How many children?"

"Six." He grimaced remembering how much trouble it was for his mother to keep them all in clothes.

At least in the summer shoes weren't necessary. "I was the fourth one. We were probably the poorest family in the county, but our neighbors weren't doing much better, so we didn't notice. Not until the war."

"You must have been too young to fight."

"I was fifteen. I could have gone, but I was left behind to look after the family." He hadn't thought about it in a long time. "My pa went and my two older brothers. My oldest sister had married and moved away. That left my mother and me in charge. The crop that first year was the biggest we'd ever had. We worked long hours bringing it in, then took it over to be weighed."

He pulled his hat low over his forehead. "The overseer refused to pay. Did the same with all the women. I guess he figured with no menfolk around, there wasn't anyone to stand up to him. He sold off the crop and kept the money for himself."

"How awful."

Regan placed her hand on his arm. He knew she could feel his tense muscles, but he couldn't seem to relax. Perhaps it was because the past was too close and far too real. As if it had just happened.

He didn't want to tell her. He desperately wanted her to know. She might turn away from him if she knew the truth, but he was willing to risk it. Regan was probably the only woman alive who could stand to hear the truth.

"Without the money, there was no way to buy new seed for the next year or the supplies we needed to survive the winter. There were twenty families in our little valley. None of them would have made it."

"How did you—"

"I shot him," he said, cutting her off. "I took the

gun my pa had left and shot him. It wasn't as hard as I thought it would be."

"Were you arrested?"

He shook his head. "Several of the neighbors helped me escape. I wrote my mother from time to time. She said when it was safe to come back, but by then I'd already started making my way. My pa didn't return from the war, but my brothers did, and they were taking care of her. There didn't seem to be anything to go home for."

Besides, he'd already started wondering if his family would understand the kind of man he'd become.

"I didn't have anywhere to go when I left, so I sort of wandered around. I found a couple of people in trouble, and helped 'em out. Pretty soon I figured out I was good with a gun, and I didn't scare easily. I started getting some work and here I am."

"You said you were thinking of giving it up."

"Yeah. Maybe." If he could.

"Why a ranch instead of a farm?" she asked.

He grinned. "Farming's too much hard work."

She turned toward him and laughed. "And ranching is easy? I'll be sure to tell Pete you said that."

He liked her to smile at him. He wished he could tell her and have her believe him. Not to convince her to bed him but because he wanted her to believe he thought she was pretty.

"I could give you the money I've saved," he said without thinking. "You could use it to buy up the land and put up fences." He paused and stared at her. "Why is your face all scrunched up like that?"

She shook her head. "I can't decide if I should be flattered or punch you. That's your money, Jackson.

For your future. You'll need it to start your ranch, or whatever you decide to do."

"It's not that easy to walk away," he said, not looking at her. The hand on his arm tightened. "I've come to see that."

She sighed softly. "You're a good man. You'll find your way."

They sat in silence. His body ached for her, but it was enough to be close, like they were. It was enough that she trusted him. He was ten kinds of fool, but it didn't matter a damn. A man only got to be a fool once over a woman. He'd rather be a fool over Regan than anyone else.

"Jackson, was Elizabeth really free with her favors?"

He jerked away from her. "What kind of question is that?"

"One I would like answered." Her eyes were dark and troubled. "I need to know. Please be honest with me. Did my sister come to you that night in the barn? Did she want you to . . . do those things with her?"

He didn't know what to say. If he lied, he would look like a heartless bastard. If he told the truth, he would destroy her memories of her sister. It should have been an easy decision but nothing with Regan was easy.

"Elizabeth was a virgin when I took her," he said, staring at his hands clasped loosely in front of him. "I seduced her, then I lied about it."

Silence.

He waited for her to yell at him for his sins. Finally he glanced at her. The last thing he expected was tears. They glistened in her eyes.

"That's the first time you've lied to me," she said.

"Regan."

"No. It doesn't matter what Elizabeth did. She's still my sister, and I still love her. It's just if I'd known she lied to me, I might have been able to break my promise to her."

"I don't understand. What promise?"

She sniffed and rubbed a knuckle by the corner of her eye. "I promised not to tell my father the truth about Amy. I knew he would be disappointed. I kept waiting for him to figure it out. He never did. He died thinking I'd disappointed him."

"I'm sorry," he murmured, pulling her close. She went easily into his arms. Her hat tumbled to the ground. Her face nestled against his chest, one hand clutched at his shoulder. He rubbed her back. "I would change everything if I could."

"I wouldn't. I love Amy. I would do anything for her. I just wish I'd been able to tell Papa the truth."

She shivered in his embrace but didn't cry anymore. The starkness of her pain left him feeling as if he'd witnessed her most private thoughts. She lay vulnerable before him. He wanted to protect her always. He wanted to make it right.

He could never take Amy from her, but how could he leave his child when he'd just found her?

"I would change one thing," he said against her silky hair. "I would change that night. If I had it to do over again, I'd take you in my arms and kiss you until you begged me to stop. And then I'd kiss you again."

She raised her head and glared at him. "Your pretty words are wasted on me. You're just trying to make me feel better and it's not going to work."

"Good," he said, bending toward her. "I love a challenge."

18

Jackson had always been dangerous. From the first time he rode into her life, until this moment in his arms. She'd known he would break her heart and he had. She'd been afraid she might not be able to forget him, and she'd found out her fears were well founded. So now, as his mouth searched hers, as his arms held her close and his warmth enveloped her in a cloak of safety, it made sense that she wouldn't have the power to resist him.

Jackson had always been her greatest weakness.

His touch was as sweet as she remembered. In the week since they went into town, she'd had time to relive that single night. His lips parted and his tongue swept into her mouth. She clutched at him, wondering why her memory paled in the presence of what was happening. She'd imagined his sweet taste, the heat of him, the tingling that invaded her arms and legs, leaving her weak and trembling, yet it was a feeble imitation of his embrace.

She told herself to hold back. It was madness. She was drunk on the delight of Jackson. Yet she wouldn't release him. And when his tongue circled hers, she countered his action with a thrust of her own. When he teased her into mindlessness, then retreated, she followed, repeating what he had done, reveling in the ripple she felt in his hard muscles.

He reached behind her and tugged at the ribbon on the end of her braid. His fingers freed her curls. She felt them spring around her face. He buried his hand in her hair and breathed her name.

"I want you," he murmured against her mouth, before kissing her cheek, then her eyelids, then her nose. His warm lips trailed fire over her jaw and down her neck. She leaned her head back against his shoulder. His arm supported her.

Her heart pounded in her chest, her fingers curled toward her palms. She was powerless in the face of his passion. The thought of refusing him made her want to weep. It was wrong, perhaps even something she might regret later. Nothing had changed. She was still just Regan O'Neil and he would still ride out of her life leaving her heartbroken.

She remembered how she felt when he left so long ago. She'd ached for him, been furious and betrayed. She'd sworn revenge for the way he'd turned her away. Her pain had been about things undone, not things experienced.

They'd changed, as had their circumstances. Yet one truth remained. She loved him.

When his hand settled on her breast, she did not push him away. When his thumb swept across her taut nipple and turned her blood to fire, she sighed his name. His gaze questioned her intentions, she could not refuse him. While she was with Jackson she knew she lived and breathed—and loved. It would be enough to last her a lifetime.

If that made her a whore, she would accept her punishment.

He cupped her face, then traced her mouth with his thumb. His smile was a little shaky at the corners. "You're a powerful temptation, Regan O'Neil." He frowned. "Is that your whole name?"

She shook her head. "Regan Catherine O'Neil. Regan comes from my grandfather on my mother's side."

"Why didn't you go by Catherine?"

"I like Regan. Besides, it's my name."

"You never take the easy road, do you?"

"I don't understand."

"I know." His smile turned tender. "You probably won't believe me, but that's one of the things I like best about you." He sobered. "I want you, but I won't compromise you. I haven't done a lot of decent things in my life, but I intend to make this one of them." He took her hand and placed it against his crotch. Her fingers cupped the hardness there. He caught his breath. "But I want you to know I'd sell my soul to bed you right now. Do you believe me?"

He was so earnest. It made her love him more. She leaned forward until their faces were close. "A soul is one thing. Would you sell your horse?"

"What?"

She giggled. "Would you sell your horse to bed me?"

"Regan."

The single word was a growl. His hardness jumped against her hand and she felt the thrill of power. Perhaps he did find her the tiniest bit attractive. She rubbed her palm up and down. He groaned.

"You haven't answered the question," she teased.

"Yes," he ground out, grabbing her wrist and pulling her hand away. "Dammit, woman, do you think I'm some gelded creature unmoved by what you're doing?"

"I hope not, Jackson. If you are, I might have to shoot you again."

With that she reached for the buttons on her blouse. When she undid the first one, his mouth opened slightly. When she opened the second one, his gaze met hers. She read questions, but they were quickly burned away by the fire flaring. His irises darkened to the color of moss, his mouth straightened, and his hands reached for hers.

"Enough," he said as he slipped off the log. He stretched out on the ground, then drew her next to him.

"Don't you want to . . ." She motioned to herself, not sure what to say. He couldn't be turning her away. Not again. She would die of shame.

"Of course I want to be with you," he murmured, leaning close to her and nibbling on her neck. "But undressing you is half the fun."

"Half?" She frowned. "Are you sure? I'd hoped that, ah, the bedding part would be more exciting than that."

He drew his pistol out of its holster and set it on the log beside them. Then he reached for the buttons on her blouse. "You tell me when we're done," he said.

"All right."

She was still a little disappointed. After all the things Elizabeth had told her . . . She sighed. Being with Jackson was enough, she reminded herself. If their joining wasn't all she'd hoped for, she would still have these memories.

As his fingers worked down the row of buttons, his knuckles bumped against her breasts. Her nipples hardened under her chemise. The delicate lawn seemed almost scratchy against her skin. She wiggled to get away from it, but that only brought her legs in contact with Jackson's. He pressed his knee against her thigh, pinning her. She wasn't afraid. Not of him. Not even of what they were about to do. She'd seen animals breeding. She'd seen men naked. There was nothing to worry about.

So as he drew her into a sitting position, she slipped off her blouse. When he would have let her lie down again, she shook her head.

"Are we taking all our clothes off?" she asked.

He sat up and looked at her. "Well, that is the usual preferred method, yes."

"All right." She unbuttoned her skirt. "I don't mean to deprive you of all the pleasure, but I have to step out of this skirt."

"By all means."

He reclined on one elbow and watched. She stood up and let the skirt fall to the ground. She was dressed in pantaloons and chemise, socks and boots.

"Shall I take the boots off, too?"

"Please." He smiled.

She sat on the log, next to his gun, then removed her boots. Her socks followed. She looked at him. He had the oddest expression on his face.

"Are you sure we're doing this right?" she asked. "It doesn't feel very romantic."

"It gets better," he promised.

She hoped so. If disrobing was half the fun, she wasn't expecting a very good time. She disrobed every night and it had never been exciting. Although a man watching her did add an element of excitement that she didn't feel when alone in her room.

"Should I take off anything else?" she asked.

"No, I'll take care of the rest." He patted the ground next to him. "Come lie down here. There's a good girl."

"Don't talk to me like I'm a horse."

He grinned. "Any other instructions?"

"No." She slid next to him and stared up at his handsome face. "You're supposed to be the expert. This is my first time."

"I'll remember that."

She had the feeling he was teasing her, but she wasn't sure how. Or what he was thinking. The fire still raged in his eyes, but his words and tone were caring.

"Do you really want to do this?" she asked.

"More than you can imagine."

When she would have spoken again, he pressed his mouth to hers. She had lots more questions and would have protested except at the same time he rested his hand on her left breast. She arched toward him, suddenly needing more. Her eyes fluttered shut and her questions were forgotten under his sensual assault.

The grass was prickly and cool against her bare calves and arms. The ground smelled sweet from the recent rains. Jackson teased her mouth apart, then dipped his tongue inside. He touched hers, tip to tip, then retreated. He circled around her mouth, dampening her lips, stroking the sensitive inner skin.

Her hands clenched at her sides, her fingers curled into the grass. Her breathing increased.

His fingers on her breast moved slowly around and around as if searching for her nipple. She wanted to scream out loud for him to find it and ease the quivering ache inside. She wanted to place her hand on his and show him exactly where to touch her. Instead she arched again and grabbed his shirt.

"Yes," he breathed against her mouth. "Touch me, Regan. Touch me everywhere."

She'd never thought a man might want to be touched. The idea was a little shocking, but she liked it. She reached up and began to unbutton his shirt. His skin was as warm as she remembered, the crinkly hair tickled her palms. She traced his ribs and the muscles clenching and releasing. His fingers still had not found her engorged nipples, so she searched for his, sliding her fingers along his skin until she felt the flat circles. She pinched them gently between her thumb and forefinger, then squeezed again.

Jackson groaned. "You could have just told me," he said, then closed his fingers over her nipples.

She gasped in pleasure. It was too sweet. Tendrils of pleasure coiled through her breasts to her belly, then lower to her most secret place. She pressed her thighs together, as if to hold in the sensations.

He drew his hands away. She murmured a protest. He laughed. "Patience, darlin'. It gets better."

He untied the ribbon at the front of her chemise. Before she knew what he was doing, he'd opened it and bared her breasts. The afternoon air was warm against her exposed skin. She'd never felt so wicked before. It was lovely.

A puff of hot air was her only warning. Her eyes flew open as his mouth settled on her breast. She clutched at him, determined to pull him away. Then his tongue touched her nipple and she relaxed against the ground. If his fingers had been magic, then the damp heat of his mouth was paradise. He suckled her like a babe, drawing more of her inside. She felt the pull clear to the bottom of her feet. Her knees raised. She reached up to hold him closer. Her fingers tangled with his blond hair. So soft, like the finest silk. She traced the shape of his head, his ears, his neck. Even as her body began to swell and change, even as her blood raced faster and her breathing came in pants, she was overwhelmed by tenderness.

At last she held him. At last she touched him. No matter what happened, she would always have this moment.

"Thank you," she whispered.

He raised his head to look at her. His mouth was damp, his eyes unfocused. "I haven't done anything yet."

"Yes, you've done everything. It's perfect."

He grinned. "Darlin', you haven't even seen my best."

She returned his smile but knew he was exaggerating. She couldn't imagine anything more wonderful than lying here like this with him.

"I can see you don't believe me," he said. "That's another challenge. I'm going to have to prove myself."

She didn't want to hurt his feelings so she indulged him when he pulled off her chemise. A flicker of alarm swept through her as he untied her pantaloons and took them off as well, but she reminded herself this was Jackson.

When she reclined against her clothing, he knelt over her, staring. "You're beautiful, Regan Catherine O'Neil."

She blushed.

He grinned, then glanced down at her arm. His grin faded as he picked up her hand and turned her wrist so he could see a bruise by the inside of her elbow. He kissed it gently. Next he found several scratches on her shoulder from when she'd been silly enough to pick up one of the barn cats. There was a cut by her right ankle, another bruise on her thigh. He kissed them all, murmuring how they made her more precious to him. The kiss on her thigh made her jump.

He pressed a hand against the inside of her knee, urging her legs apart. When she complied, he moved between them, then bent over and kissed her belly. Her muscles quivered. He cupped her breasts in both hands and kissed her nipples. He went back and forth, sending her into mindlessness.

When she thought her heart might jump from her chest, he stopped, then moved lower, kissing her ribs, her belly, then lower still. Her mind froze, her eyes widened. He couldn't mean to kiss her *there*.

He did. She sat upright. "Jackson?"

He looked up and sighed. "It was just a kiss."

"It was most certainly not."

His grin was very satisfied. "All right. I won't do that anymore."

She didn't trust him. "You're sure?"

"I promise."

She lay back down.

"Can I have just one more kiss?" he asked.

"No."

"A quick one. You won't even notice."

It was only then she realized his hands were resting on the tops of her thighs with his thumbs sweeping back and forth, close to her most feminine place. He wasn't touching anything, exactly. But there was a heat that hadn't been there before. And she felt as if her skin was prickly. Her breasts swelled even more. Was it pressure or something else?

Back and forth, back and forth.

"A kiss will make you feel better," he said.

"Just one," she said, hoping it made her feel better and fast. Something was very wrong. It was as if every part of her needed more.

He swept his thumbs down her auburn-colored curls, then he gently drew her skin back, exposing heaven knew what. She'd never looked there. She was about to protest his indecency, when he touched his tongue to her.

It wasn't a kiss at all. It was liquid pleasure, hot and slippery. It sent fire to her fingers and toes, it made her knees draw back and her eyelids flutter closed. A single kiss that went on forever. He stroked against her, slowly, so very slowly, she thought she might drown. A foolish idea, but she couldn't escape the image of falling, falling somewhere wonderful.

It had to be wrong, but she didn't care. Nothing mattered but the slow steady pressure, then gentle flickering. Around and back, up and back, over and back. So slowly.

She could think of nothing but his touch. She wanted

nothing but for him to continue. It was better, as he had promised. Much better. Later, when she could think and breathe and speak, she would tell him so.

Then he moved faster and she could think of nothing but the building pressure. The need. It overwhelmed her. She wanted to die. She never wanted him to stop. She wanted this to go on forever. The scents—the grass, the trees, her body and his, all blended into a heady perfume. She called out his name, because only he could understand. Her body shook as her muscles tightened. It was unbearable. It was heaven.

Then he stopped. She died inside. She'd waited a lifetime. He touched her once, gently. Then a small flicker of his tongue. Then he moved quickly, carrying her forward. She was caught up in something she didn't understand. Faster and faster until she could sense the end. It would be brilliant. Bright and perfect. It would be like Jackson himself.

And it was. She was held for a moment, immobilized, then her body surrendered to the ecstacy. Her skin rippled, as did her muscles. It was as if a thousand tiny points of pleasure sang for her alone.

When the sky ceased to spin above her and her breathing returned to normal, she opened her eyes. He stared down at her. She thought she might be embarrassed, but his face held such a look of tenderness she forgot to blush. Without thinking, she touched his cheek. He captured her hand and pressed his lips to her palm.

"Thank you," he said softly. "It was better than I'd imagined."

Why was he thanking her? "I—"

"Hush."

He bent over and kissed her neck, then her breasts. Every bit of her had been sensitized. She didn't ever want to have to move again. She wanted to go on lying here, having him touch her, touching him in return.

She placed her hands on his chest. He sat up and shrugged out of his shirt, then returned to let her fingers stroke him. She liked the way his muscles tensed and released against her palm. She drew his head down and kissed his mouth, then sucked on his lower lip, all the while tracing patterns on his chest and back. His breathing grew rapid. She remembered her own anticipation from a few moments before. Could he be feeling the same thing? Did he want her to touch him more boldly?

Was he aroused? In her reclining position, she couldn't see. Slowly, hoping he wouldn't even notice, she slipped her hand down his belly to the waistband of his trousers. She wanted him to feel the magic she had. She wanted him to know that incredible sensation of building then release. As her mouth taunted his, she moved her fingers lower, over his trousers to the hard ridge straining against the buttons.

She laid her hand against him and he jumped. She started to pull away, but he grabbed her wrist and held her close.

He sucked in a breath and swore softly. "If you knew what you were doing to me," he muttered.

"Tell me."

He raised his head and looked at her. The flames in his eyes glowed with an incandescent brilliance. Instead of answering, he popped his trouser buttons free, then pushed his pants down to his knees. Still holding her gaze with his own, he took her hand and placed it on his maleness.

He was hard. As her fingers closed around him, she wondered how he could be so hard and yet feel so smooth. She moved her hand, not sure what would pleasure him. He placed his fingers over hers, showing her the motion. Back and forth, up and down, until his eyelids fluttered closed and she was free to study him.

She looked first at his broad, bare chest, at the pattern of hair, at his tanned skin. His muscles flexed in time with her ministrations. Her gaze dropped lower, to his waist, then to the site of his pleasure.

As always, Jackson was beautiful. His maleness thrust forward, surging into her touch. The curls at the base were only a shade or two darker than his chest hair. She moved a little faster, then smiled when he groaned. She liked the feeling of power.

Then he drew her hand away and moved back between her thighs. She knew instinctively this moment would change her forever. He would take her innocence and leave her a woman.

She'd thought she might be afraid. She wasn't. Not of him. He stared at her. "I care enough to ask if you're sure," he said. "But it'll kill me to stop."

She smiled. "I'm sure." This was Jackson. She'd been sure since she was eighteen years old.

He bent down and kissed her breasts. As he teased the puckered tips, he slipped a hand between her thighs and touched her most sensitive place. She'd never thought she could feel that kind of excitement again and was shocked when her body responded and her blood began to quicken.

He taunted her until she couldn't catch her breath and her skin was on fire. Only then did he move his hips forward, pressing against her. She braced herself for the pain she'd heard about, but before she could tense completely, he returned his fingers to her. Instantly she could think of nothing but the feelings he evoked. Some part of her felt him sliding inside. As her body stretched to accommodate him, she wiggled slightly. Her eyes opened and she saw his face tightening.

His fingers moved faster. He pressed in deeper. She waited for the pain, but there wasn't any. Just a sensation of fullness. Then he began to move in her. The steady thrusts provided a counterpoint to his fingers' magic. She became lost in what he was doing. She clutched at his shoulders; her hips flexed in an instinctive rhythm. He growled her name. It was happening again.

She lost all ability to breathe, then it didn't matter. She felt him convulse inside of her. Seconds later, her own body began its rippling release. She pulled him close and heard their two hearts thundering in unison.

Naked legs tangled together. His large hands brushed her hair from her face. She opened her eyes and smiled at him.

"What's so funny?" he asked.

"You lied to me. Getting undressed wasn't half the fun at all."

"Yeah, well, it can be. I'll show you sometime."

She studied his eyes, the expression of contentment, the relaxed grin that tilted up the corners of his mouth.

"You look happy," she said.

"I am."

19

They lay there together until the weight of him grew heavy and he reluctantly pushed off her. He rose to his feet, then held out his hand to assist her. Regan glanced down at her naked body and was surprised she didn't feel embarrassed. She couldn't be. Not after what she and Jackson had shared. Maybe later she would have regrets, but not now.

He bent down and grabbed her undergarments, then tossed them to her. She slipped into her pantaloons, but before she could fasten them at her waist, he grabbed her and pulled her close.

"What are you doing?" she asked.

"Nothing," he said, his voice innocent. But his hands roved over her back before slipping inside her pantaloons and squeezing her bottom.

"Jackson!" She swatted him away.

"I'm not doing anything," he protested, then winked.

"Sure you're not. Leave me alone to get dressed. And put some clothes on yourself. What if someone comes riding by?"

"Then they'll get an eyeful of something mighty impressive."

"Oh, please." She shook her finger at him but couldn't stop the laughter from bubbling out. She thought there could have been awkward pauses as they dressed, but Jackson made sure that didn't happen.

When she went to lower her camisole over her head, he pulled it away from her and held it just out of reach before relinquishing it. He demanded a forfeit of three kisses before giving her her skirt. Her stockings cost her five minutes of rubbing his back. She paid them all gladly and wished she had more clothes he could hold hostage.

But at last they were dressed and her hair was once more pulled into a braid. He turned toward the ranch house. "It's getting late. People are going to wonder where we've gone off to."

She nodded. "I wish—" She wished they could stay out here forever.

Jackson looked at her. "I know." He held out his hand. She ran to his side and burrowed against him. He squeezed her close.

It was enough, she told herself. She'd had this magical morning and it had been more than she ever dared to dream about. She had touched him and tasted him. She'd been able to show with her body that which she dared not say. As Jackson placed her hat on her head, he touched her nose.

"Sweet Regan."

She gathered her courage. "You must be used to this kind of thing," she said quickly. "But I thought it was very special. Thank you."

He cupped her face, forcing her to look at him. "Regan Catherine O'Neil, for a smart woman, sometimes you act like a fool. There's bedding a woman and then there's something more. This was definitely more. There's a fire between us people don't find very often. I don't want you thinking otherwise." He hesitated. "There was only two of us lying on that bit of grass. You hear me?"

She knew what he meant. He wanted her to know he hadn't thought of anyone else. That she'd been enough. "I know," she said.

"Good."

They started back toward the house. Regan wanted to call out her joy. She wanted to tell him what this had meant. She wanted to say that she loved him. Instead she held the feelings inside, holding them close, knowing they would be with her always.

"I never did this with Elizabeth," he said, reaching for her hand.

She stopped and stared up at him. He'd pulled his hat low over his forehead, making it hard for her to see his eyes. "But you had to. You had a child together."

He brought her hand to his mouth and kissed the backs of her fingers. "It wasn't the same," he said. "I know you don't want to know this, but I didn't care for her."

The way I care for you. He didn't say it, but she heard it in the silence. "I understand."

They talked of other things. She had to force herself to walk slowly when she wanted to run and skip and dance. He teased her and pulled at her braid. She swiped his hat and made him chase her across an open field. When they were in sight of the outlying ranch buildings, Jackson pulled her to a stop.

"You're going to be sore tonight," he said, placing his hand on her shoulder. "You should take a bath."

Sore? Oh, from falling off the horse. "Don't worry," she said. "The ground was soft where I fell. I had the wind knocked out of me, but that's all."

"That's not what I meant. You're going to be sore from the loving."

The loving. The sweet words tore at her heart.

"You'll want to take a bath so you can sleep," he said, then lowered his voice to a whisper. "About nine o'clock would be best."

"Why does it matter when?"

"So Amy will be good and asleep."

"I don't think taking a bath will wake her," she said.

Jackson shook his head. "It might when I slip in the room and wash your back."

Her mouth parted. Visions of him with her— She didn't know exactly what would happen then, but she was willing to wait and see when he got there. Very willing.

He looked at her. "That is, if you want me to visit."

Why would he bother asking? Then she realized he was as unsure as she was. Love filled her. Jackson cared. Nothing could ever hurt her again.

She took his arm and leaned against him. She didn't know how long they would have together, so she was determined to make it last. "I would love for you to visit me."

"Good."

Jackson stared down at her. He'd expected to enjoy being with Regan. He hadn't expected her to leave him shaken and needing more. He glanced over his shoulder to make sure no one was around, then hauled her close and kissed her. It was a fleeting, hard kiss, full of passion and promise. It would have to last them until tonight.

Despite his recent release, the tingling in his groin told him he could take her again. He let her go. "We've got to get back."

"I know." She stepped away from him and started walking toward the barn.

He followed, trying not to smile. He had a bad feeling he looked as stupid as he felt. But damn, it had been good between them. Loving her wasn't like anything he'd done before. He'd meant that. He wanted Regan to know that she was special. He sobered. Maybe too special. He didn't want to start to care about her more than he did. It would make his decisions harder.

Or maybe it would make them simpler. He looked at the ranch spread out in front of them. There was enough work for two, if she would be willing to share her responsibilities. With his money they could buy up the land she wanted.

He shook his head. What the hell was he thinking about? He couldn't mean to stay here. That would be impossible.

So why had he proposed to her last week? Had he planned to marry her then ride off? He rubbed his temple and realized none of his plans had been thought through. Right now all that mattered was keeping Regan and Amy safe from Daniel and counting the hours until he could join Regan in her bath that night.

But the thought of staying wouldn't leave him alone. He wondered if his desire to find somewhere to belong had to do with getting older or with Regan herself. Was he reacting to his child? Could he—

A sound caught his attention. A sharp cry from the main barn. He glanced at Regan. She was staring straight ahead.

"You hear that?" he asked.

"Yes. It sounded like Amy."

That's all he had to know. Jackson took off running. His long strides and faster speed sent him ahead of Regan. He entered the barn and stopped suddenly. In the dim cavernous main room he saw Quincy, one of the hired guns, holding a small kitten over the open storage cellar door in the floor. Amy stood across from him, her hands twisting together, tears streaming down her face.

"Such a pretty kitty," Quincy said, his voice low and mean. "What a shame if she fell."

"Don't hurt her," Amy pleaded. "Please, mister. Don't hurt my kitten."

Quincy laughed. "You're a pretty thing yourself. Maybe you'd like to join your kitty." He dropped his arm slightly, as if he'd let go. Amy screamed. The calico kitten squirmed and mewed in protest.

"I suggest you give the girl her cat," Jackson said.

Quincy glanced toward him. As he straightened, his expression went blank. "I wasn't doing anything. Me and the kid were just playing, weren't we?"

Amy was crying too hard to answer.

Jackson had never worked with Quincy, but he knew the older man's reputation. He was mean and hard, and he sold his services to the highest bidder, even if that meant switching sides in the middle of a fight.

"Give Amy her cat," Jackson said, then heard Regan run into the barn.

"Mama." Amy flew toward her.

Regan bent down and picked her up. "Hush, Amy. It's okay. I'm here."

"He's got my kitty. He was going to drop him."

Regan walked over to Quincy and took the kitten from him. Amy hugged the animal close. The hired gun glanced around the barn as if looking for a way out.

"You're not that lucky," Jackson said. "Regan, take Amy outside. I want a few minutes alone with this man."

"Hey, Tyler, I don't work for you."

"I'm in charge, so yeah, you do."

Quincy straightened. He was an inch or so shy of six feet, so Jackson was taller, but the older man outweighed him by about forty pounds.

"Look, I was just playin' with the kid." Even as he tried to talk his way out of trouble, Quincy began circling Jackson, as if looking for a place to get in a blow.

Jackson drew his pistol.

Quincy held up his arms. "I'm not armed."

"I know." Regan was still standing inside the barn. Even Amy had grown quiet as she watched the two men. He handed Regan his gun. "Get her out of here," he said, then gave Amy a reassuring smile. "I'll take care of him."

Amy snuggled closer to her mother. Regan stared at him, then nodded. She held the pistol in her hand as she left. Jackson turned back to Quincy.

Dark beady eyes glared at him. "You think you're

something better than the rest of us," Quincy snarled. "Tell me, boss man. Do you push her petticoat over her head so you don't have to look at her face when you fuck her?"

Jackson didn't react to the taunt because he'd already shut down inside. It was the ability to close it all off that made him survive in a business where the foolhardy and desperate died young. He bent down and pulled a sharp lethal-looking knife from its sheath in his boots.

"You're a dead man," he said, starting to circle Quincy. "Fast or slow. It's up to you."

"I ain't scared of the likes of you," Quincy said, but sweat popped out on his forehead and upper lip. He used his sleeve to wipe it away, then pulled his knife out.

The two men bent forward slightly, never taking their eyes from each other. The barn was silent, only the snuffling of a lame horse provided relief from the steady sound of their quiet steps. The open cellar door was between them.

Jackson lunged forward. Quincy ducked back. Jackson used the time to kick the cellar door closed. The last thing he wanted was to trip and break his leg. Or worse. He wouldn't be any use to Regan if he was dead.

"What kind of a man tortures little girls?" he asked. "You'll give gunfighters a bad name."

Quincy sneered. "I'm better than you, Tyler. Always have been."

Jackson smiled. "Prove it."

As he'd expected, Quincy lunged forward. Jackson sidestepped, then snaked out his hand, slicing the other man's arm from shoulder to elbow. Quincy yelped in pain. The wound wasn't very deep, and it was on his left arm, so it wouldn't affect his fighting, but it would be a distraction.

"You're making this too easy," Jackson said.

"Bastard."

"I've seen my parents' marriage certificate, Quincy. You're going to have to do better than that."

Jackson continued to circle the other man. He kept his knife raised, his stance relaxed. He was balanced on the balls of his feet so that he could turn or lunge in any direction. Fighting with a knife was his weapon of choice. There was an elegance in the combat, a quickness. It was as much about thinking and reacting as power and speed. Quincy was already breathing hard. He was a back shooter, not used to fighting a man face to face. His kind of filth never lasted long in a fair fight.

Quincy came at him again. Jackson waited until he could hear the whisper of the knife at his side, then he moved an inch to the right. Quincy stumbled as his weapon didn't connect, his forward momentum making him awkward. Jackson spun neatly and pressed his knife into the other man's thigh. Blood spurted out.

When they circled again, Jackson saw defeat in his opponent's eyes. He could smell death. From the corner of his eye he caught a movement. He didn't turn toward it, trusting his gut. His senses told him there was no danger, so he didn't react. After a few moments, he knew Regan had returned to watch the fight.

Jackson closed his mind to her. Quincy was losing strength with every beat of his heart. Blood dripped from his arm and leg. He tripped on a bit of straw and almost went down. A foolish man would have taken advantage of his opponent's weakness. Jackson stayed well clear. As he suspected, the stumble had been a ploy. Quincy turned, lunging forward, only to find empty air in front of him.

Jackson moved in behind him, quickly, silently. He grabbed the other man's hair, forcing his head back, then placed his blade against the soft exposed skin on his neck.

"Drop your knife," Jackson said.

Quincy let it fall to the ground. Only then did Jackson look up at Regan.

"You hired him," he said. "You want me to kill him?"

She looked from him to the defeated man. As she made her decision, he found himself hoping she would choose death. A part of him wanted to kill Quincy. He would take pleasure in hearing the man breathe his last.

"Let him go," Regan said. "Mr. Quincy, you're fired. Get your things and get off my land. Mr. McLane will escort you to the property line. Don't ever show your face around here again. My men will have orders to shoot you on sight."

Jackson released Quincy, then stepped back so he could watch the man in case he tried something. The gunfighter staggered slightly. Blood still trickled from his arm and leg.

"Bitch," he said, glaring at Regan. "Fucking whore."

Jackson took a step forward. Regan stopped him with a shake of her head. "No more," she said. "Get out, Quincy. If you're not gone in three minutes, I'm going to let Mr. Tyler finish what he started."

Gage stepped into the barn. "I've brought your horse, Quincy," he said.

Jackson watched his friend lead the other man out. When they were both gone, he squatted down and cleaned his knife on the straw, then slipped it back into his boot.

"Are you all right?" Regan asked. "Did he hurt you?"

"No." He walked to the front of the barn and watched Gage mount his own horse. The two men circled the house and headed east. "I wish you'd let me kill him, though."

"I know. I wanted to do it myself. When I think about what he did to Amy." She drew in a deep breath. "Thank you." She moved close to him, but he stepped away.

She didn't understand. How could she? "You ever kill anyone?" he asked, even as he knew the answer.

"No. What does that have to do with anything?"

"You remember how you felt when you shot me?"

She flushed. "Of course. It was awful. But this is different. He threatened my child."

"It's not that different. It takes a certain strength inside. An ability not to feel. You feel too much, Regan. You'd best leave the killing to others. To someone who knows what it's about."

"Someone like you, you mean."

"Yeah. Exactly like me."

He couldn't see Gage and Quincy anymore, but the coldness still filled him. He would have done it. If Regan had agreed, he would have slit the other man's throat and not had a moment's trouble sleeping that night.

"I'm glad you fought him," she said, moving close and placing her hand on his arm. "I appreciate your willingness to protect Amy."

"Most people manage to hold on to what's theirs without murder."

"Some people deserve killing."

He stared at the two-story house, at the well-kept outbuildings, at the garden just starting to break through the carefully tended ground. "Gage was right. Once it gets in the blood, there's no way for a man to put it behind himself." There was no way for him to fit into this world. Quincy had shown him that. The killing was too easy.

"I don't understand." There was a note of panic in her voice. He thought about trying to reassure her, but his words wouldn't make her feel better.

He stared down at her, at the wide blue eyes that had darkened with passion just an hour before. He wondered if he would survive losing her, then knew it didn't matter. He was going to find out as soon as the trouble with Daniel was over. He pointed up along the slight ridge where a few of the hired guns sat in front of a campfire.

"They'll never be anything else," he said. "They'll die in some man's fight that was never their own. They'll be lucky to get a marked grave."

"They could change if they wanted to. You can." She squeezed his arm.

He stepped away from her, away from the touch that burned clear down to the bone. "No. They can't and I can't."

"Jackson?"

"You were right from the beginning. What was I

thinking about? I can't take a child with me to my next job."

"I thought you wanted to get away from it," she said. "I thought you weren't going to do this anymore."

"I don't think I get a choice. But it'll be fine for you. When the trouble is over with Daniel and I move on, I'll be leaving Amy with you. I don't have anything to offer her."

She stepped in front of him, forcing him to look at her. He didn't want to see the hurt on her face, so he closed himself to it, refusing to feel anything at all.

"You can't mean that. You can't just walk away from all of this." *From me.* But she didn't have the courage to say that.

"I have to. I'm not the kind of man you need. In the end, I'll only make things worse. I'm sorry."

"Sorry? You're sorry?"

She turned away and walked toward the house. He knew if he gave in, he would never find his way back. Better to feel nothing. Better to have her hate him. At least then she would be able to let the memories go. Even though he knew it was going to take *him* a lifetime to forget.

The clock in the hallway struck midnight. Regan sat huddled in her bed and listened to the steady sounds. When the house was silent again, she returned her gaze to the tub resting in front of the fire.

He hadn't come to her. She'd known he wouldn't. She told herself she was a fool to dream, even as she filled bucket after bucket with water. She hoped his leaving hadn't changed at least one thing between them. She'd been wrong. About that and so many other things.

Elizabeth had lied. Not only about Jackson's seduction but about her own innocence. Regan had lied, if only to herself about her ability to avoid regrets. Jackson had lied. He'd made her believe there was a chance. He'd never told her he would always have the soul of a killer and that blackness would keep him from her.

Elizabeth had told the truth. Jackson had never promised marriage. Regan had told the truth. She'd spoken it with her touch, her hands, and her mouth. She'd sworn love and she would carry that promise with her to her death. Jackson had told the truth. He'd said loving and bedding weren't the same thing. He hadn't promised her more than he'd been able to give. The fault was hers for dreaming.

She prayed for the words to help him change his mind, then knew they didn't exist. She could beg, but that would only make him despise her. She could speak of love, but that would only make him pity her. When this was over and he had won, he would leave her with nothing but memories of what could have been.

20

Jackson leaned against the barn and stared at the house. It was well past midnight. He told himself he should try and get some sleep, but he wasn't tired. He couldn't think about anything except Regan and the light that still burned in her bedroom window.

Did she wait for him? Had she given up hope? Did she hate him yet, or would that take longer?

He'd promised to go to her tonight. He'd whispered what he would do when he joined her in her room. He'd made her blush and giggle with delight. He'd made her want him almost as much as he wanted her.

All for nothing. His brief fight with Quincy had shown him the truth. He was trapped, with no way out. Staying away from her was better for both of them. He knew that. He just wished it wasn't so damned hard. If only he could stop thinking about what they'd shared that afternoon. If only he could forget. But he couldn't. Regan O'Neil was a hell of a woman. Memories of her were branded into him. He would die with her name on his lips.

So he stood alone, watching her window, wishing she would turn out the light and go to bed. He hated knowing she waited for him, almost as much as he hated not going to her.

"You want to tell me about it?"

Jackson didn't bother turning toward Gage. He'd heard his friend walk up a few minutes ago. He'd wondered if he would simply go away. Jackson had been torn between hoping he would and needing to talk.

"About what?"

"About why you look like a dog that's just had its last meal. I've seen happier expressions on men about to be hanged."

"You always did have a way with words," Jackson said.

"Trouble with the lady?"

Jackson turned on his friend. "What the hell does that mean?"

"Nothing." Gage raised his hands as if to show he wasn't armed. As always, he was dressed in black. His face was in shadow; his hat shaded his eyes. "Just askin'."

Jackson drew in a deep breath. "Sorry. I'm—" He shook his head. He didn't know what he was. "I can't quit. Gunslinging is in my blood," he blurted out. "I can't forget what I already know or what I've done."

"Do you want to?"

"Of course. I want to walk away from it. Make a fresh start."

Gage leaned against the barn and reached for a slim gold case. He offered a cigar, but Jackson refused. Gage pulled one out for himself and lit it. When the tip glowed red, he glanced up. "Don't be a jackass. If you don't like the line of work, then get out of it."

"How? How do I change the fact that life is cheap and killing way too easy? How can I turn my back on what I've become?"

"If you've got a chance to walk away, you're a fool if you don't grab it."

"But you said—"

"Hell, I was probably drunk."

Jackson knew he hadn't been. Gage didn't drink when he was working. Neither of them did. It helped keep them alive.

"Try it," Gage said. "What's the worst that will happen?"

"I could hurt Amy and Regan."

Gage tilted his hat back. It was as close to asking what Jackson was talking about as he would get.

"Amy's my daughter."

Gage gave a slow whistle. "I didn't know you knew Regan that well."

Jackson was about to say he didn't, then realized it didn't matter about Elizabeth anymore. In every way that mattered, Regan was Amy's mother. Elizabeth had given up any claim to the title the day she walked away from her baby.

"I was here a few years ago," Jackson said by way of an explanation.

"And now you're back."

"I wish I knew what to do about it. I figure the best thing for Amy is to let it be. She's got family here. People who care about her."

"What about you?"

"I can still make a living doing what we're doing now."

"They're getting younger and faster," Gage reminded him. "If you've got a way out, take it while you still can. If you don't, you'll always wish you had. One day the wishing'll get so strong, you won't draw in time. Hell of a way to die."

"Do you ever think about getting out?"

"No. I've got nothing else."

"What have we got to show for all this?" Jackson asked. "I can't think of one thing."

Gage looked at him for a long time. "Seems to me you've got a daughter and a lady who looks at you as if you're responsible for making the sun come up in the morning."

Regan? Jackson shook his head. Even if she had cared about him, after tonight she would never be able to forgive him. She would be strong enough to handle a straight fight, but he hadn't given her the pleasure of a confrontation. He'd simply not shown up. She would try to tell herself it was because of what happened with Quincy in the barn, but in her heart she would wonder if she wasn't enough. In the end, the doubts would win. She'd wind up hating him.

Gage was right about how the wishing might get a man killed. He only hoped one day Regan figured out he was doing this all for her.

*   *   *

Two mornings later, when Jackson climbed out of his bedroll, he felt as if he'd polished off a bottle of whiskey all by himself. His head ached, his eyes were gritty, and his body didn't want to stand upright. Still he forced himself to his feet, wincing at the pain in his knees. He was too damn old to be sleeping on the ground. Gage was right. The ones comin' up behind them were younger and faster.

"Let 'em have at it," Jackson muttered.

"You reduced to talking to yourself?" Gage asked.

Jackson turned toward the sound. His friend sat by the fire, nursing a cup of coffee.

"Better than talking to you," Jackson said.

Gage held out a steaming mug. "You look like horseshit."

"Thanks." Jackson took a sip, then sighed. He might live. If the lack of sleep didn't do him in. He hadn't closed his eyes in two nights. As soon as he lay on his bedroll, he couldn't stop thinking about Regan. She'd been avoiding him, not that he blamed her. The only sleep he got was from sunup until someone around the gunfighters' camp woke him. If this kept up much longer he wasn't going to be any use to her.

He was no closer to knowing what was right. His head told him to walk away and forget it. His heart . . . He took another sip of coffee. He didn't want to think about what his heart told him.

"Pete was by a few minutes ago," Gage said.

"What'd he want?"

"You and me to come to the barn. There's going to be a meeting."

Jackson had a bad feeling about this. Unexpected

meetings were never good news. "Let me wash up and we'll go over."

It took longer than it should have to splash water on his face and shave. He pulled a clean shirt out of his saddlebag and stared at the wrinkles. He missed Fayre's washing and cleaning up after him, not to mention her cooking. But after the incident with Quincy, Jackson had moved out of the house. He felt it would be safer for everyone that way.

When he was as cleaned up as he was going to get, he slid his pistol into its holster, then grabbed his hat and started for the barn. Gage fell into step beside him.

"You know what this is about?" Jackson asked.

"Pete didn't say."

Figures. The cowboy had never trusted him. Not from the first moment he'd found out Regan knew who he, Jackson, was. Hell of a mess. He just wanted out. The sooner he rode away, the quicker everyone could get on with what they had been doing before this whole thing started.

They entered the barn, then made their way into Regan's office. Pete and Hank were already there, but Jackson ignored them. He stared at Regan.

It had only been two days, but he felt as if it had been a lifetime since he saw her. She sat on the corner of her desk, studying a piece of paper. Her hat rested beside her. Light from the window illuminated the bright color of her hair.

She didn't have to look up for him to know exactly how many freckles she had on each cheek. He knew the pattern they made across her nose and her chest. He knew her taste and scent. He knew how passionately she could hold on to a man, and the sound of her breathing when she sighed his name. He wanted her. Not just in his bed but in his arms. He wanted her to trust him, to love him with the same vulnerable, chin-first, consequences-be-damned sort of love she gave to her child. He wanted her to forgive him, to understand. Even to beg him to stay. Because he was weak enough to think she might be able to convince him.

She put the paper down. He waited, ready to smile at her. She raised her head and looked right through him. He'd never seen her eyes so cold.

"Thank you for coming, gentlemen," she said and nodded at Gage. "This won't take long." She brushed a stray curl off her face and tucked it behind her ear. "I'm tired of waiting. I want this trouble with Daniel over right away."

"Are you talking about starting a range war?" Gage asked.

She stared at him. "If that's what it takes, yes. I won't live this way anymore. I want things back to normal."

I want you out of here. She didn't say it; she didn't have to. Jackson heard it clearly without the words. If not for the trouble, she wouldn't have to keep him here. Because he'd told her he wouldn't take Amy away from her home, Regan didn't have to worry about him anymore.

The sharp pain surprised him as much as the first cut had surprised Quincy. Like the gunfighter, he felt his strength start to drain away.

"A range war will cost you," Gage said, when Jackson remained quiet.

"I've spoken to my men," she said. "They agree with me."

Pete nodded. "It's gone on too long. Roundup is in a couple of weeks. We can't move that many cattle through and still watch our backs. Better to get it over quickly."

"How fast?" Jackson asked, speaking for the first time since he'd entered Regan's office.

She stared at a point beside his right shoulder. "How fast can you do it?"

How fast can you be gone? "A week. Ten days at the most. We'll need more supplies from town. Maybe reinforcements."

"Fine. Make up a list of what you need, then in the morning, go into town and buy it. Hire the men. Whatever."

They spent a few more minutes discussing the arrangements, then agreed to meet once more in the morning before Jackson left for town.

"Then it's settled," Regan said. "I'll talk to you later." She picked up the paper again, dismissing them all.

Jackson stayed after the other men had left. He waited. Regan didn't look up at him. "Why are you doing this?" he asked.

"I told you. I'm tired of waiting and being afraid of a bully. I want it over."

"People could die, Regan. Have you thought about that?"

She glared at him, for the first time meeting his gaze. "I might be merely a woman, but I'm not stupid. Daniel's always had surprise on his side. We've just reacted. If we want to win, we're going to have to try something else."

She was right. He'd known that from the beginning.

The surprising part wasn't that she'd figured it out, but that she was willing to act on that information.

"I'll do my best to keep you and Amy safe."

She blinked and looked out the window. "I'm sure you will."

"Regan, I'm—"

"Sorry," she said, cutting him off. She spun back to face him. Color stained her cheeks. "I'm sure you're very sorry. What is it this time? That you took my innocence? Or that you didn't bother showing up that night? Whatever it is, I don't care anymore. I don't have time for you, Jackson. I have a daughter and a ranch to take care of. Finish your business here and move on."

"As easy as that?"

"Yes."

He hadn't realized how much he'd hurt her until this moment. The Regan he knew didn't give up on her dreams. Her sweetness was as much a part of her as her strength. But he'd taught her that sweetness had a high price of pain. He shouldn't be surprised that she'd turned away from him.

"It doesn't have to be like this," he said.

She stood up and walked toward the door. When she reached it, she turned back and stared at him. There was nothing in her eyes. Not anger or hurt, or any sign of affection. He'd destroyed it all.

"It has to be exactly like this," she said. "This is all we have left."

Regan woke an hour before dawn. She lay in her bed telling herself not to think about it, but it was no use. Every waking moment was filled with thoughts of Jackson and the war she was about to start. Who would give their lives in payment for her bruised pride? How many men would die because she wanted Jackson off her ranch as quickly as possible? Would she look back, years from now, and regret what she'd begun?

She rose and gathered her clothes for the day. But instead of dressing she walked to the window and stared out into the darkness.

Today it would begin. Today Jackson, Hank, and Pete would make their final plans and Jackson would go to town to buy the needed supplies. Tomorrow they would attack Daniel and his men. In a few days or weeks it would be over. She wondered what the cost would be.

If only . . . If only he hadn't promised her that night. If only Quincy hadn't been tormenting Amy. If only Jackson hadn't given her hope. If only she didn't love him. For those few hours in his arms, and the time after, she'd allowed herself to believe there might be a way to make it all work out. She'd thought he might come to care for her, not just as someone he respected, but as a woman he could love.

The hardest part was that she understood what he was thinking. He believed he was a killer, that he couldn't change. He abandoned her to protect his daughter. A father's love for his child. She understood that.

"What must you think of this, Papa," she whispered. "I know I disappointed you. I never meant to. I wanted to tell you the truth." She leaned her forehead against the cool glass and closed her eyes. It had seemed so sensible when Elizabeth suggested Regan claim Amy as her own.

"I wanted her, Papa," she murmured. "I wanted a child. I was afraid I would never marry. I didn't want to be alone. But it didn't work out the way I thought it would."

Perhaps Elizabeth never forgave herself. Jackson's lie, his claim that her sister was an innocent, had changed everything. Regan hadn't wanted to accept the truth, but she had to. So many half-heard conversations now made sense. So many stifled giggles in the barn, all the avoided glances. Her sister had been giving herself to the cowboys for years and Regan had never known. She didn't want to think Elizabeth had been selfish, but there seemed no other explanation. Why else would she have her virgin sister claim her bastard child?

"I forgive you," Regan said, because Elizabeth was her only sister, and because in the end, she'd paid a high price.

From the time he was old enough to covet Sean's ranch, Daniel had wanted to marry one of the sisters, thereby linking her father's and her uncle's ranches. Sean had always claimed the girls could marry whomever they wanted, but both she and Elizabeth had wondered if the old man might give into Daniel's pressure tactics. Perhaps it was guilt that drove Elizabeth to accept Daniel's proposal. Perhaps she truly believed his charming facade.

"Papa, I hope you understand this now. I hope you forgive me and love me. I hope I can do as good a job as you did."

Regan didn't remember her mother. Her father had never spoken of her. If Regan thought about her at all, she always assumed he hadn't loved her very much and didn't miss her. Now, looking back with the eyes of an adult, she saw things differently. Sean's quiet moments had been pensive. What had he remembered as he watched his daughters grow? How he must have missed his wife at his side, yet he'd gone on. As she would. Because the alternative was giving up and she would never do that. She was an O'Neil.

Slowly Regan turned from the window. She dressed quickly, then grabbed her brush and tidied her wayward hair. She would survive this day and the next and the next, until Jackson was gone. Then she would close her mind to the memories and go on as before. Once the trouble with Daniel was over, she would be free to concentrate on the ranch and on her daughter. They had a good life here.

She reached back and quickly wove her hair into a braid, then secured the end with a ribbon. Perhaps she would go to another town and make friends. It would be farther away than Hampton, but Amy needed to get out from time to time. Perhaps she could even talk to Pete about getting the girl a docile horse to ride. Jackson was right; Regan couldn't protect the girl from everything. Maybe it was time to let Amy grow up.

Regan stood up and walked toward the door. A faint glow caught her attention. She glanced toward the window. What was that? It couldn't be the sunrise. Her room didn't face east.

She crossed the floor in three long strides, then drew in a sharp breath. Outlined against the black night sky, yellow-orange flames licked toward the heavens. The barn was on fire.

She raced downstairs and out the back. Hanging

from a rafter in the porch was a large bell. She pulled down hard on the rope. The sharp sound cut through the silence. She jerked the rope over and over again, then started for the barn.

Cowboys poured out of the bunkhouse, most of them dressed only in trousers and boots. They saw the blaze in the barn. As she got closer, Regan could smell the burning wood and taste the smoke.

Fayre came running up to her. Her long gray hair hung loosely around her shoulders. "Where's Amy?" she asked.

"In the house."

"I'll stay with her," Fayre said, turning in that direction. "Do you have your rifle?"

Regan shook her head.

"I'll bring it out first thing," Fayre said. "Daniel and his men might still be around."

Regan hadn't thought of that. Damn. One more thing to worry about. Sparks and ash danced through the air, landing all around her. She watched anxiously, but the green grass didn't burn easily and the dew snuffed out the surviving embers.

The men had already started a line from the creek to the building. The fire had been set on the northeast corner, where the food and supplies were stored. Smoke poured from the open double doors. Before she could duck inside and check on the horses, Pete came out leading one with each hand.

"How many more?" she called loudly to be heard over the roar of the flames.

"Four."

She started to go inside.

"Don't," he said. "I've got two men in there

already. We can't risk any more lives." He lead the horses toward the far corral.

Fayre returned with her rifle. "Amy's awake," she said, "but I'm keeping her inside with me."

"Thanks."

Regan glanced at the barn and saw the recent rains had left the roof damp. The fire spread slowly. The men were steadily gaining on it. She might not even lose her office. The smoke was thick, making it hard to breathe. She thought she saw a familiar dark shape moving through the shadows.

"Mr. McLane?" she called.

The man turned toward her. "Get the hell back, Regan," Gage said, grabbing her arm and forcefully pulling her away from the barn. "You'll be trampled if the horses come out wild."

She nodded. "Where's Jackson?"

"On the other side," he said, jerking his head toward the far end of the barn. "He's bitchin' about having his first good night's sleep disturbed, but other than that, he's fine. We've set up a second group of men with buckets. Good thing you keep a large supply."

Her eyes burned and her chest felt tight. She coughed. Smoke was everywhere. "My father believed in being prepared."

"So do you." He pointed to her gun.

"I'm concerned Daniel and his men might still be around. In the confusion it would be easy for them to sneak in and start another fire. Or God knows what."

"We've already thought this might be a diversion. Guards are being posted."

"Thanks."

He turned and walked around the flaming barn. Behind her, the sky lightened as the new day began. In the corrals, the horses neighed in terror as a gust of wind sent fire up into the sky. But the smoke was more gray than black, and the men with the buckets seemed to be winning.

She prayed for their safety. The barn could be replaced. She moved close to where Pete was working. He was covered with black soot.

"Everything all right?" she called.

"Yeah." He wiped his forearm across his face, leaving behind a black streak. "You must have seen it about as soon as it started. If the fire had had another two or three minutes head start, we would have lost the whole barn. As it is, we can salvage most of the building."

"Good."

Before she could say anything else, a man appeared on her left. "You hurt?" Jackson asked, his gaze searching her for signs of injury.

"I'm fine," she said, trying to ignore the way her heart started beating faster. He'd managed to pull a shirt on, but he hadn't buttoned it. The open garment reminded her of their time together. Her barn was on fire, Daniel's men were probably waiting to attack a second time, they were surrounded by cowboys and flying sparks, and all she should think about was how much she needed him to take her in his arms.

"We've posted guards," he said. "They should keep the men safe."

"Good. I guess the fire will be out shortly. Then we—"

"I'll have it all, Regan," a voice called. It was faint, muffled by the hissing of water on the fire and the men talking to each other.

Regan turned slowly, trying to see who had spoken to her. A movement on the far side of the corral caught her attention. Four men on horseback broke out of a grove of trees. They rode by the house, where they were joined by another man. One of them stopped and looked at her.

"This is just the beginning," Daniel said, his voice carrying to her on the morning breeze. "You could have made it easy on yourself. Now I'll see you in hell."

Jackson swore under his breath. He pulled out his pistol, then shoved it back in its holster and reached for her rifle.

"No," she said, stepping away from him. "I'll do it." She raised the stock to her shoulder and took aim.

Behind her Jackson stomped away. "Does anybody have a goddamn rifle? You'll never hit him, Regan."

"He's not that far away."

She closed her left eye and concentrated. Despite the moving horses and uneven terrain, she had no trouble getting Daniel in her sights. One more moment. She shifted slightly. There.

She rested her finger on the trigger.

"You can only ever count on family."

Her father's words filled her head. She hesitated. Her father had considered Daniel family, she remembered, fighting indecision. But he wasn't really. He was dangerous. He had to be stopped.

She concentrated again and drew in a deep breath to steady herself. Her finger pulled steady, slowly. Almost, almost.

The horse and its rider disappeared over a rise. Daniel was gone. She caught her breath, shocked at her own inability to act. It had been the perfect opportunity and she'd let it get away. Now they would have to hunt Daniel down.

Jackson jerked the rifle away from her. "I knew it. I knew you couldn't shoot him. But you didn't want to listen. You have to do everything yourself, just to prove you can. You let the same son of a bitch who wants to see you and your daughter dead ride away, but you can shoot me for no good reason." He glared down at her. "I swear, as long as I live I'll never understand women."

"I'm sorry," she whispered.

"It's too late now. I can't believe this." He bent toward her, and stuck his finger in her face. "He burned your barn, poisoned your cattle, murdered one of your men and your sister, and you let him ride away."

"I couldn't shoot him."

"So you should have let me do it."

"Stop yelling at me," she said loudly. "I made a mistake. So what? We'll get him again. Besides, the sheriff is going to have to pay attention to us now. We all saw Daniel and his men here, and the barn is burned. Even he won't be able to ignore that."

Jackson turned away, obviously disgusted. Her shoulders slumped. This wasn't starting out to be a great day. She looked up at the building, now illuminated by the first rays of the sun. Half the structure had burned away, but most of the support beams were still standing. Her office was untouched and all the animals had gotten out. None of her men were hurt. It could have been a lot worse.

The back door opened. "Regan!" Fayre called.

Regan watched wide-eyed as her friend stumbled down the stairs. A cold, ugly feeling started in the pit of her stomach and began working up toward her chest. "Fayre? What's wrong?" She ran toward the older woman.

As she got closer she could see blood pouring down Fayre's head, as if she'd been hit on the temple.

"No," Regan said softly, running faster. "No, not that. Anything but that."

She reached Fayre and grabbed her just as the older woman sank to her knees. "He's got her," Fayre screamed, between sobs. "Regan, I tried to protect her, but one of them hit the man guarding us, then me. I fell. He's got her. He's got her."

"Who?" Jackson demanded, appearing at her side.

But Regan already knew. Hank rushed up and took his wife in his arms. Regan stepped back. She looked up at Jackson.

"Daniel has Amy."

21

"It's a trap," Jackson said.

"I know." Regan lifted her saddle onto her horse's back. "He's taken the one person I care about. Now he's going to use Amy to get what he wants."

"You can't just ride onto his place."

She tightened the cinch, then looked up at him. Worry drew his eyebrows together. She knew exactly how he felt. "Amy is only five years old. She's my daughter. If I have to choose, I don't care about the ranch."

Pete pushed off the corral railings. "I'm coming with you."

"Yeah, me, too," Hank said. Several of the men agreed.

Regan looked at them, at the concern in their faces. They were all willing to go up against Daniel and his hired guns for her and her child. "Thank you," she said. "But I have to do this alone. If it's just me, Daniel might be willing to listen to reason. I want Amy. He knows that. If he gets the ranch, he'll probably just let us go."

"And if he doesn't?" Pete asked.

She didn't have an answer for that.

"I'm not going to let you ride in there by yourself," he said. Hazel eyes glared at her. Pete could be as stubborn as a hungry cow, if he set his mind to it.

"She's not going in alone. I'm going with her." Jackson ducked into the corral and grabbed his horse.

Pete looked at her, waiting for her to decide. Regan adjusted her hat and stared out the way Daniel had ridden away. Jackson had the experience in dealing with these kind of problems. He was also Amy's father.

"Hurry up," Regan said. She started to step up into the stirrup.

Pete grabbed her arm, stopping her. "Regan, is that the way things are?"

He'd been her friend for so long, she hadn't yet gotten used to keeping secrets from him. She felt herself flush. "I'm sorry," she said, then raised herself up on her tiptoes and kissed his cheek.

He nodded. "Bring her back safely." He laced his fingers together and bent over. She stepped into his hand and swung her leg over the saddle, then glanced impatiently at Jackson.

"I'm leaving," she said.

"Fine." He'd almost finished with his horse. Before mounting, he motioned for Gage to move closer. The two men had a whispered consultation.

Regan didn't bother waiting. She kicked her horse

and headed out toward Daniel's ranch. Behind her she heard Jackson cursing.

When he caught up with her, she was halfway across the valley where they'd found the dead cattle.

"You could have waited," he grumbled, coming up beside her. His voice came in uneven bits, some of the sounds pulled away by the wind.

"No, I couldn't," she called loudly over the thundering of their horses' hooves. "He's got Amy."

"You think I don't know that? If you'd let me shoot him. . . ."

"I didn't," she said. "I was wrong." Her eyes burned. She told herself it was just the nip in the air. "You think I won't tell myself that every day for the rest of my life?"

"Hell. Don't get all upset. That won't help things, any."

"I'm not upset."

They both knew she lied. Regan clenched her jaw tight. The fear in her belly made it hard to think. Amy. Please, Lord, let her daughter be safe. That was all that mattered. Just Amy.

They rode in silence, until they reached the grove of trees close to Daniel's house. The leaves had filled in since they were here last. The grass was thicker, the birds louder. Regan reined in first and stared down the path. Daniel was waiting for her there. He'd promised to make it hard on her. She didn't doubt his word.

"You have a plan?" she asked.

Jackson grimaced. "No. He's probably got lookouts. We might have been spotted, but I don't think so. Still this isn't a surprise. He's expecting you."

"I'm riding in alone," she said. "You figure something out, and come in after me." She swallowed hard, then looked at him. "If there's a choice, you get Amy out."

"Regan."

"Swear to me," she said, leaning toward him. "Swear, Jackson. I'm not leaving here until you do."

He moved his horse closer to hers, then reached out and touched her cheek. The familiar feel of his hand on her face gave her strength. She turned and pressed her lips against his palm.

"I swear," he said.

Their gazes locked. She read his concern and anger, the frustration and steely determination. The latter made her grateful he was on her side. "I trust you," she said. And I love you. But those words went unspoken. She thought them, hoped he saw them in her eyes, but she didn't say them. Not now. If they both survived, there would be time to discuss their feelings. Or hers, at least. She still wasn't sure about Jackson.

She kneed her horse. The bay gelding started forward. She reined him in. "Tell Amy I love her," she said, then rode off.

The last few yards through the trees were quiet, except for the call of the birds. She felt as if she was walking to her death. She'd never been so afraid before. It wasn't just for herself, although her imagination kept coming up with all kinds of tortures for Daniel to inflict, but for her child. Amy was so young. She wouldn't understand why her uncle was being mean to her. She would be terrified and confused. She would call out for her mother, and that's what Daniel would punish her for.

Regan came out of the shade and into the sunlight. This time there were no men around the house, but she could feel them watching her. She glanced at the porch, then toward the barn. Nothing. Now what?

She dismounted and tied her horse to the porch railing.

"Over here, cousin," Daniel said.

She turned toward the sound. He was in the barn. The door stood open. She could see the darkness beyond. Slowly she walked in that direction. She wasn't armed. She'd left her rifle tied to her saddle and her pistol back at the house. She tried to console herself with the thought that Daniel wouldn't shoot an unarmed woman, but it didn't help. He'd killed her sister, and Elizabeth's only crime had been to marry him.

Her boots sounded loud on the wooden floor as she entered the barn. The darkness engulfed her. As her eyes adjusted, she heard rustling and muffled conversation. She couldn't make out the words or figure out how many people were in the barn.

She blinked several times, straining to see. At last she was able to make out the stalls, and the tack room off to one side. Daniel stood in the middle. He was alone.

His hands hung at his sides. He looked calm, but there was an odd expression on his face. Her stomach lurched. Had he slipped into madness? If he had, there would be no chance of escape.

"Where's Amy?" she asked quietly, making sure her voice was pleasant.

Daniel smiled, a cold, eerie smile that sent chills

slipping down her spine. "You're so predictable, Regan. It's one of your best qualities. The bastard brat is fine." He chuckled. "Your concern is sweet, especially considering the fact that Amy's going to be an orphan soon."

"I'll give you the ranch," Regan said. "I'll sign it over to you and walk away."

"Not good enough." Daniel took a step closer. "You had your chance. You should have surrendered to me before."

He reached out and placed his hand on her shoulder. She forced herself to stand still, enduring his hateful touch. She wished she'd brought a knife. She could have plunged it into his belly and watched him bleed to death.

He leaned toward her. His breath fanned her face. She looked away, searching for a weapon. A pitchfork, a piece of wood, anything. She had to stay ready, in case there was a chance to escape. She had to escape. She and Amy only had each other.

"This will be better," he said, still smiling. "You'll die knowing your precious daughter is going to be with me. I've already told her to call me Daddy."

She lunged without thinking. She raised her hands to his face and raked her nails against his skin. He yelped in pain and jumped back. Before he was out of reach, she hit him as hard as she could, her fists pounded into his chest and stomach. She brought her knee up toward his groin, but he ducked away.

"Get her! Get her!"

She heard footsteps behind her. She tried to run, but strong arms grabbed hers. "I'll kill you, Daniel," she growled, still kicking out with her feet. "I swear, I'll kill you."

"I think she means it, boss," one of the men holding her drawled.

"Shut up," Daniel ordered. He held his hand over his left cheek and cursed. "The bitch clawed me." He drew his hand back and stared at the blood on his fingers.

More oozed out of three deep scratches on his face. Regan felt a small amount of satisfaction. She tried to jerk free, but she was held fast. A quick glance told her both of the men holding her were a good head taller and they outweighed her by about fifty pounds each.

"You had your chance," he said, glaring at her. His eyes glowed with an unholy rage. For the first time she acknowledged her fear. "You should have agreed. I would have married you."

"And killed me, just like you killed my sister."

"I might have kept you around longer. Just because you had the potential to be more entertaining."

"I would rather die."

He grabbed her chin and squeezed hard. "You're going to get your wish. In the end, I'll still get what's mine. The ranch, Regan. I'll own your ranch."

She knew she should be trying to figure out a way to escape, but she couldn't think. She could only react. He was going to kill her anyway. "You'll destroy it the same way you destroyed your own property. You thought marrying Elizabeth would make my father leave you the ranch, but he didn't. In his heart he knew you weren't worth it. You're nothing but a failure, Daniel. Some kid my family took pity on. I still pity you. You're nothing but a worthless—"

She saw the blow coming, but with the two men holding her arms, there was no way to duck. His hand connected with her face. Her head jerked to one side as pain exploded in her temple, cheek, and mouth. The room spun suddenly, then disappeared to a tiny bright speck circling through darkness. She could taste blood.

Voices came from far away. Angry accusations. They didn't make any sense. Then her vision cleared and she was back in the barn. The throbbing in her head got worse.

"Pity me all you want," Daniel said, then encircled her neck with his hand. "I'll still have everything in the end. The town thinks you're crazy."

"Only because you've been telling them lies."

"People don't care about the truth." His smile was sickening. "They want to hear something shocking. Everyone has been so curious about why your cowboys are especially loyal to a woman like you. Can you guess what I've told them?"

She didn't understand at first. Then she realized what he was saying. "No!" she cried, trying to get away from him. "Damn you, Daniel." She forced herself to calm down. "All right. You've won. You've got me and you're going to get the land. Let Amy go. She's never done anything to you."

"She's your daughter. That's enough." He motioned someone to step out of the shadows.

Regan bit back a moan when one of Daniel's hired guns moved into the light. The dark-haired man had his hand on her daughter's shoulder. The child had been tied up, with her hands bound in front of her and a gag in her mouth. There weren't any visible marks, but Regan could see her child's terror in her wide-eyed stare.

She tried to pray, tried to think of something, anything. But all she could see was Amy.

Amy stared at her. Questions filled her daughter's eyes. Questions and trust. Regan gathered her strength and forced herself to think.

"Are you all right?" she asked.

Amy nodded.

"We're going to get out of this. Do you understand?"

Amy nodded again.

Regan had never been prouder of her little girl. "I love you, honey. When we get home I'm going to give you the prettiest horse you've ever seen."

Amy's eyes crinkled at the corner, as if she was smiling behind her gag.

"How touching," Daniel said. "Who's here with you?"

Regan turned to look at him. "What are you talking about?"

"I'm not stupid, Regan. I know you didn't come here alone. Is it Pete? One of the other cowboys?" He leaned his head to one side and brushed his dark hair off his forehead. "No, not them." He jerked his thumb toward the door. "Take the girl outside."

The hired gun dragged Amy out into the light. Regan twisted around until she was able to see what was happening. Daniel followed more slowly. He pulled a knife from its sheath at his belt and walked over to the child. He pressed the point to her pale neck.

"Come on out, Jackson, or the brat dies."

Jackson lay on the dirt, hidden by a clump of bushes. In the time he'd been listening to Daniel tormenting Regan, he'd worked himself to within fifteen feet of the barn. He'd only needed another couple of minutes. Hell, nothing had gone right since he set foot in Texas. Why would he think his luck was going to change now?

He thought about not moving. Daniel would have to come looking for him. Then he looked at Amy. She was shaking with fear. He couldn't do that to his kid.

He stood up, then raised his rifle in one hand and his pistol in the other.

Daniel motioned for him to come forward. "Slowly, my friend. Very slowly."

Jackson kept waiting for some plan to form, some idea as to how to get them out of this. But he knew from hard experience the good guys rarely won because they were supposed to. The victor often had the money and the power, not to mention the weapons. As he handed over his pistol and rifle, he acknowledged he was severely outgunned.

Two men grabbed him and pulled him into the barn. He glanced over his shoulder, but Amy was being led away. He thought about protesting, then didn't. Better for her not to see whatever was going to happen.

Once in the barn, the hired men stepped back, releasing Regan and forming a circle. There were six of them altogether. A seventh was taking Amy to the house. That meant all of Daniel's gunslingers were right here. If only the part of the plan he'd worked out came through.

His eyes adjusted to the dim light inside the barn. He moved nearer to Regan, then saw the imprint of a hand on her face. He reached up and gently brushed the back of his fingers against her skin. "You're going to have a black eye in a couple of hours."

"Imagine how it will look with my hair." Her voice was shaking, but she didn't look as if she was going to panic. Good. *Stay ready,* he told her silently, holding her gaze. She nodded slightly.

"Now I have the two of you together," Daniel said. "I've waited for this for quite a while. For you, especially, Jackson. I owe you."

"Sure you do," Jackson said, folding his arms over his chest. "Do those guns make you a man?" The gunfighters snickered but didn't move. They wouldn't be any help. They were paid to make sure Daniel won.

Daniel's eyes narrowed. "Go ahead, Jackson. It doesn't matter what you say, because you're going to die in the end."

"It takes a lot of courage to shoot an unarmed man. Must make you feel pretty tough."

"Dead is dead."

Daniel had a point. Jackson moved slowly to his right, angling his body between Daniel and Regan. If the bullets started flying, he wanted to protect her.

Daniel raised the pistol Jackson had relinquished. "Stop trying to shield her. While I appreciate the drama of your sacrifice, I don't have time. You see this is all part of my plan. Jackson"—he waved the gun at him—"a notorious gunfighter, went on a shooting spree and killed his poor misguided female employer. Fortunately my men were around to see justice served. It's very tidy. The sheriff has been so understanding, listening as I poured out my concerns about my sweet cousin. The last time I saw him, I mentioned I thought you, Jackson, were dangerous. The sheriff agreed. It seems you've been imagining dead cattle." He shook his head.

Jackson tried to ignore the crawling feeling at the back of his neck, but it wouldn't go away. He'd been in bad spots before, but nothing like this. He reached out and captured Regan's hand. He didn't look at her; he didn't have to. Her fingers squeezing his told him what he needed to know. Hell of a thing to have come this far only to lose her and his kid before he even had the chance to do the right thing and leave them. He'd wanted to ride off at sunset, the noble father and lover, sacrificing his own happiness for what was right. Now he was going to get shot by some crazy fool who couldn't fight his way out of a girls' school.

"Before you go, Jackson, I want you to know the pleasure I'll take in raising your daughter."

Jackson took a step forward. Daniel cocked the pistol aimed at Regan. Jackson backed up slightly.

"I see by the look on your face you're surprised I figured it out. Who else but you would be the 'handsome drifter' who sired Regan's bastard? No one else guessed, but I did."

Regan gave a strangled sound that was as much a moan as a laugh. He turned to her. She looked as shocked as he felt. The secret was safe.

Daniel looked at Regan. "Good-bye, cousin."

Jackson was still holding her hand. He jerked hard on her arm. She stumbled toward him.

Daniel laughed. "It doesn't matter to me who dies first." He shifted the pistol toward Jackson.

Damn, he needed a much better plan. This is *not* how he wanted to die.

"I love you," Regan said from behind him.

"What?" He turned toward her.

"Enough!" Daniel yelled. "Time to die, Jackson."

He watched as Daniel cocked the hammer back another notch. Shit, he needed a plan and fast.

"This is Sheriff Barnes," a loud voice called from outside the barn. "Everybody drop your guns to the ground and come out with your hands up."

Daniel spun toward the sound.

"You, too, Daniel," the sheriff continued. "I know you're holding a gun on Miss Regan. You'd better put it down, son."

Jackson sent a quick prayer of thanks that Gage had come through. Regan stumbled toward him. He caught her. He wanted to get her out of here and fast, but he didn't dare move until Daniel dropped his gun.

"You all right in there, Regan?" Pete called.

"So far."

"We're waiting," the sheriff said.

There were a few seconds of silence. "It looks like we're going to have to prove ourselves, boys," the sheriff said. His voice was followed by the sound of a dozen pistols being cocked.

"I'm not out here alone," the sheriff called. "I've got Regan's men with me. We can all fire on the barn if we have to, but I think everybody is smarter than that."

One by one the hired guns set their weapons on the floor. Daniel lowered his arm to his side. He looked stunned, as if a trusted horse had suddenly thrown him. Jackson started backing away from the door. Regan hesitated, but he pulled her along with him.

Daniel hadn't dropped his gun yet.

"Everybody come out slow. Keep your hands up where I can see 'em."

The hired guns started filing out. Jackson felt Regan move. Something inside called out a warning. He looked down for the closest pistol. It was lying right by his foot.

Everything happened slowly. Daniel began to turn, bringing his arm up at the same time. Jackson shoved Regan away as hard as he could, then dropped to the ground. He grabbed the pistol, rolled on his shoulder, across his back, and onto his feet again. He heard the sharp, loud explosion of a bullet being fired. It hit the wall, right where he'd been standing.

He glanced up, took aim, cocked the pistol, then pulled the trigger. The bullet impacted in the middle of Daniel's chest. His mouth opened with surprise. He stood there for a second, then fell forward and landed in a heap on the ground.

Only then did Jackson look for Regan. She was crouched where he'd pushed her. Before he could go to her, several men ran into the barn, followed by a small brown-haired blur of blue calico dress and wide hazel eyes.

"Mama, Mama!" Amy ran up to her mother. Regan opened her arms and pulled her close.

22

"What are you going to do now?" Jackson asked the next day as he sat on the porch steps and leaned against the railing.

Regan used her foot to push off the floor, setting the swing in motion. Hank had hung it early that afternoon. Fayre hadn't made new cushions yet, but Regan didn't care. The swing was always a symbol of spring on the ranch. She hadn't had time to worry about it before, but now, with Daniel gone, everything could go back to the way it was supposed to be.

"We'll start the roundup next week," she said. "It's going to take even longer with Daniel's herd to deal with. We're going to have to cull the bad stock, find out what's worth keeping, take a look at his bulls."

"You'll be busy."

"Yes." She supposed the polite response would be

to ask what his plans were, but she didn't want to know. Actually she did know, but she didn't want her fears confirmed.

"Sheriff Barnes was real apologetic," Jackson said, then grinned at her. "I wish I could have seen the look on his face when Gage held a gun on him and forced him to ride out to Daniel's place. The old man sure got an earful of Daniel's threats. Gage always had great timing." He pushed his hat back slightly. "Word will spread all over town about what kind of man Daniel was and what really happened to Elizabeth. Without him spreading his lies, I expect you'll have a friendlier reception the next time you go in for supplies."

"Probably." Funny how at one time the thought of being accepted by the town would have been enough to make her happy. She would wait until after the roundup to ride into Hampton, but if all went well, she might even take Amy later in the summer. The little girl would enjoy picking out fabric for her dresses and maybe a toy or two from the general store. If she was truly accepted, perhaps Amy could go to school while the weather was good. Fayre was an excellent teacher, but the housekeeper couldn't be as exciting as a roomful of children Amy's age.

She turned her head and glanced at the small corral by the house. Amy sat on top of a dainty gray mare. Her daughter listened raptly to everything Pete said. As he led her around the ring, she clutched the saddle horn and smiled broadly. Regan hoped the excitement of riding would chase away the horrible memories of what had happened yesterday. At least Amy hadn't been in the barn when her uncle was shot.

She glanced at her hands, at the scars and scabs, at the calluses. Then she rubbed at a smudge of dirt.

"You didn't ask," she said quietly. "But I want you to know all the same. I'm not sorry he's dead. He would have killed us if he'd had the chance. I'm glad you did it. I'm glad he's gone."

Jackson looked at her. His gray-green eyes held her own. She couldn't read his expression, but there was a certain comfort in that. She didn't want to know what he was thinking.

"Thanks for saying that," he said. He'd drawn one knee up to his chest and stretched his other leg out along the top step. "At that moment, I didn't have a choice. But with him being kin and all, I wasn't sure what you'd feel."

"He was no kin. He was evil. Better that he's gone." She glanced up at the green pecan trees surrounding the house. "I hope wherever he is, he knows that I'm going to inherit his ranch. I hope that haunts him until his soul turns to dust."

"What did Sheriff Barnes have to say about that?"

She smiled. The victory had come late, but that didn't make it any less sweet. "He told me I was doing a fine job with my ranch, so I might as well work Daniel's too, until it's all official and legal. But there aren't any other relatives and he didn't leave a will. So I'll inherit. I'm thinking of sending Pete to work it. He can buy it from me slowly."

"And you'll use the money to purchase more land."

"Exactly." He remembered her plans. It shouldn't mean anything, she told herself, but that didn't stop her from being happy about it. "If the talk I've been hearing about someone inventing a cheap wire fence is true, I'll be able to mark off what's mine and never have this problem again."

"So everything is all set," he said.

It wasn't, of course, but she couldn't say that. She couldn't say what she really thought about any of it. She didn't want to know, but the feeling in her chest wouldn't go away. The steady, throbbing pain, the sensation of something precious slowly being ripped away warned her he was leaving. She would have given anything to keep him. She understood why he had to go, yet that didn't help her. She had never been a part of his world; he chose not to be a part of hers.

Loving him wasn't enough.

The soft clink of spurs caught her attention. She saw Gage McLane walking toward the house. Jackson stood up and shook his friend's hand. They spoke quietly for several minutes. Regan stayed on the swing, not listening. All the gunslingers had been paid off. Most of them had already ridden away. Gage was the last to go.

She studied the hired gun. He was dressed in black. His hat hid his eyes, but she knew they would be cold and dark. She wondered about this man. What had happened to him to make him so willing to live alone? He existed in the shadows of life. At least Jackson had always been willing to come inside for a while, even if in the end he was forced to move on.

"Ma'am?" Gage tipped his hat. "I'm going to be riding out."

Regan stood up and walked to the edge of the porch. She stepped down two stairs, so that she was eye level with Gage. He held out his hand.

"Thank you Mr. McLane. For everything."

"My pleasure, ma'am. You ever need anything, you let me know." For once his dark eyes didn't seem so cold. She thought she might have seen a flicker of life, then it was snuffed out and she was staring at the forbidding expression of a killer.

She placed her palm next to his, but instead of shaking, she leaned forward and kissed his cheek.

"Keep Jackson safe for me," she whispered, and straightened.

Gage squeezed her fingers before releasing them. His mouth curved into a slight smile. "You have my word."

Her throat tightened and she couldn't speak, so she nodded and stepped back. Jackson called out his good-byes as his friend walked toward his horse, mounted, and rode off toward town.

From the corral Amy squealed with excitement. "Mama, I'm riding," she called.

"I can see that." Regan waved at her, then turned away. She couldn't do this anymore. She couldn't pretend to be happy. Daniel was dead and would never bother her. The hired guns were gone, her child was laughing, the ranch peaceful. Yet little of that mattered. She knew what he would say. Still, she had to ask.

She walked to the door and grabbed the handle. Instead of turning it, she held on for strength. "Are you leaving now or in the morning?"

Her breath caught in her throat. Silent half-formed prayers filled her mind. Let him dispute her words. Let him want to stay. Let him offer to marry her again. This time she would say yes. If he stayed because he wanted to, she wouldn't mind if he didn't love her. Caring would be plenty. She would make it last. Her high ideals of marrying for love faded in the cold light of losing him forever.

"I don't want to leave you, Regan."

But . . . She heard it in the pause, in the pain lacing his voice. She felt it as her heart crumpled, as her legs grew weak and her throat tightened with unshed tears.

"But I don't belong here. I can't be what you need me to be."

"I need you exactly as you are," she said.

"You need something better."

Of course. He was doing it for her. He was being kind. The ultimate sacrifice of a caring man. He would do what was best, when all she wanted was what was right.

She heard his footsteps on the porch as he walked up behind her. He placed his hands on her shoulders.

"Regan?"

"Amy will want to say good-bye," she said. "She's having supper with Fayre and Hank tonight. I thought staying up late with them might help her forget what happened. You should make sure she sees you before you go."

"That's not what I'm asking."

"I know."

He wanted to know if he could have one last night with her. A part of her was pleased that it mattered at all. In her heart, she knew she couldn't refuse him. She needed one last night as well. She needed to have memories to protect her from the storms of life sure to follow. She would need them to keep her warm through the winter, and to make her smile fondly when she was old. The practical side of her thought if they were together again, she might even get pregnant. She would love to have Jackson's child, but she didn't think she would be that lucky.

She opened the door and stepped inside. Jackson grabbed her hand and followed. At the bottom of the stairs, she hesitated, then turned and walked down the hallway to the room Jackson had occupied. In the last week, he'd moved out to stay with the hired guns. There was nothing of his in the room, no saddlebags, no clothing. But his scent lingered. She inhaled it as she folded back the coverlet, then drew the sheets down. She felt his presence behind her as she pulled the window shade low and lit the lantern.

Her fingers trembled as she blew out the match. At last there was no reason not to turn and face him. She forced herself to meet his gaze. He'd removed his hat. His eyes glowed with a familiar fire. She felt an answering spark in her belly. It flared higher, sending heat to her thighs and her breasts.

He smiled, causing the lines by his eyes to crinkle. How many times had she stared at his handsome face? She would never forget him. Never.

"Why are you so serious?" he asked.

"Because I've lost Elizabeth and my father. Now I'm going to lose you."

His smile faded. He stepped in front of her and pressed his knuckle to her chin. She didn't know she was crying until he reached up and wiped away a tear. "Don't cry, sweet Regan. I'm not worth it."

"You are to me. I meant what I said, Jackson. I love you. I've loved you for a long time. I know it doesn't mean anything to you—"

"Don't say that," he said fiercely. "It means every-thing. You mean everything."

She chose to believe him because the alternative could not be borne. When he reached for her, she stepped into his embrace. His hands moved over her body, touching her gently, stroking her into mindless passions. But even as he unbuttoned her blouse and drew it down her arms, even as he loosened her skirt and pulled off her boots, she felt the sadness. It made the shadows darker, the passion not quite as bright, the sweetness taste faintly bitter.

He slipped her camisole over her head, then low-ered her pantaloons to the floor. While she stood naked before him, he removed his clothing. His broad chest, the gold hair that narrowed at his waist before flaring out to crown his maleness, the strength of his legs, all made her long for him. She needed him to hold her, be in her, to chase the sadness away.

He looked at her, studying her as if he'd never seen the female form. She turned her mind from his leav-ing, focusing only on the pleasure they would share together. She held out her arms and he closed the dis-tance between them. He bent down and slipped his arms behind her back and knees, then gathered her in his arms.

She clung to him, burying her face in his neck. She could feel the rapid beating of his heart against her lips. Around and around, he circled, holding her tightly against him. He murmured her name as if it was a prayer. Tears escaped from her tightly closed eyes and fell to his bare skin. She willed herself to think of nothing but him.

When he stopped turning and placed her on the

bed, she raised herself into a sitting position and pulled him close. Her mouth sought his, her tongue plunged forward. They kissed wildly, a dance of heat and need. Her fingers traced the muscles of his back and sides. Slowly he lowered her to the sheets.

Their legs tangled together, her breasts brushed against his chest. Delicious sensation shot through her nipples and down to her feminine place. She arched against him, feeling his hardness. They were both ready.

When he lowered his mouth to her breasts, she sucked in her breath in anticipation. Her skin was on fire, her mind mercifully empty. There was only this moment and the man. She touched him everywhere she could reach. She buried her fingers in his soft gold hair, loving the way it felt against her skin. She traced his ears, his neck, his spine. She pressed her hips up toward him, inviting him to take her.

He raised his head. Sexual need drew his face taut. "You tempt me."

"Good. Give in." She smiled. "Be wicked."

She wanted to know she drove him to the edge of madness. They could be mad together. He slipped his hand down, between her legs. His fingers searched through her damp curls to the wetness inside. He groaned as she tightened her muscles around him. She raised her hips again and drew back her knees. His jaw tightened as he fought for self-control, then he swore softly and pulled his hand free. With one quick thrust of his hips, he filled her.

Instantly her body began to hum. It was as if she'd been ready for this moment her entire life. He supported himself on his hands, his eyes locked with hers.

It felt too wonderful, she was drawn too tightly. She would surely explode. Her body arched up to meet his. He slipped in and out, moving faster, driving deeper until she knew she'd been designed to be taken by this man and no other. Their harmony was exquisite. She felt his muscles tensing, and her own did the same. Her breathing quickened, as did his. She wanted to look away from the intensity of his gaze, but she couldn't. He held her captive. She felt herself reaching for her final release. She drew her legs back. Her hands reached for his hips, urging him on. She could see him, but he was slipping out of focus. There was only the heated power between them.

The first tendril of paradise began to curl through her body. She sobbed out a breath. He bent close, his mouth hovering over hers.

"Look at me," he demanded, his voice harsh with pleasure. "Look at me."

She blinked, trying to see him through the haze. He reached his hand between them and touched her, moving rapidly against her sweetest place. Instantly her body rippled with pleasure.

"I will love you forever," he promised, as the moment claimed her.

The startling ecstasy and his words became one, filling her to her soul, healing her, carrying her to a safe place.

Only when she had calmed enough to catch her breath did he follow her, thrusting deep inside, keeping his eyes open as she had, exposing the rawness of his soul, his passion and his need. The fire of his love burned hot against her skin. He shuddered in her arms, expelling his seed. She prayed it would find a waiting haven that would, with time, become a child. A strange peace settled over her, as if the angels had listened.

They lay together under the sheets, her head on his shoulder, his arms wrapped around her.

"Why do you leave me?" she asked.

"It's best for everyone, Regan."

"No," she said, raising herself up on one elbow and staring down at him. "Tell me the truth. Why are you going?"

His gray-green eyes darkened to the color of a coming storm. He wouldn't look at her. "I'm afraid," he said grimly. He started to sit up, but she pressed against his chest until he quieted.

"Of what?"

"Hell, everything." He stared at the ceiling. The hand on her back began to move up and down. "I don't want to make a mistake. What if I do? I could react without thinking. You saw me with Quincy. I wanted to kill that bastard. I would have, too, if you'd said one word. What if I frighten Amy? Or worse. I could destroy all of you."

"Leaving is its own kind of destruction."

His smile was sad when he looked at her. He touched her cheek, then tucked his hand behind his head. "You'll be fine. You're stronger than all of us."

"I go on because I have to. I have responsibilities. You do, too. What about your daughter? What about you? Will you survive? If you really love me, how can you leave me?"

He slipped his hand up her back to her head. He ran his fingers through her hair, allowing the curls to settle against his palm. "Regan Catherine O'Neil, doubt the rest of the world, but don't doubt that I love you."

His pain convinced her. If he'd been glib and teasing, she might have wondered, but the harsh lines of his face, the icy gray of his eyes told her he was telling the truth.

She lowered her head back to his shoulder and sighed. She wanted to demand that he stay. She wanted to find the right words, the right set of promises. She wanted to use guilt about Amy and maybe even about herself to convince him it would be good for him here.

She did none of those things. All her life she'd fought against what was ordinary. She ran a ranch; she didn't sew or cook. She wasn't like other women. She made her own way. Sometimes it was hard, sometimes she had second thoughts, but in her heart she knew what was right. She knew this was where she belonged. She could deny Jackson no less than what she demanded for herself. He had to be free to choose.

She pushed the sheet down to his waist and studied his broad chest. She rested her hand against the hair, feeling the crinkly curls tickling her palm. His skin was warm and smooth, his heartbeat strong. Somehow she had to find the strength to let him go.

"Marry me," she said.

"What?"

She smiled and rested her chin on his shoulder. "I'm not asking you to stay. I just want you to marry me. You offered once. Didn't you mean it?"

"Sure, but that was to give you the protection of my name. You don't need that anymore."

"I need it more, now."

He drew his eyebrows together. "I don't understand."

"You know me, Jackson. If we're married, I'll be true to our vows. I'll be your wife. This ranch will be yours, as well as mine. I'll be here for you to come back to, when you're ready."

He scrambled away as if she'd put a snake in the bed. "This is crazy," he said, standing by the foot of the bed. "You want me to marry you, and then ride off leaving you alone?"

"Yes. I want you to know that I'm yours. No matter what happens."

"No. What if you meet someone? What if you want a real marriage? I wouldn't tie you down like that."

She pulled the sheet up to her shoulders and leaned against the headboard. "You would marry me to protect me, but not because you love me?"

"You're twisting my meaning."

"I want you to believe this is right. One day you'll get it. You'll figure out we belong together. I'm strong enough for you, Jackson. I don't claim to understand about the killing and what you've done, but I don't fear it. I don't want this just for Amy, although she would love to have a father. I want it for you and for myself. We need each other. I can help you not be afraid. You can remind me being female isn't so bad. Together we can make it work."

Her words had no effect. She saw it in the stubborn set of his jaw and the rigid stance of his body. He stood naked before her, so beautiful she thought she might perish from seeing him. His pain stabbed at her.

"I'm sorry," she whispered, holding out her hand. "I wouldn't have said anything if I'd known it would make things worse."

He moved around the bed and took her in his arms. "Damn you, Regan. Why couldn't you have been more like Elizabeth?"

For the first time in her life, the comparison didn't upset her. She brushed the hair from his forehead. "I'm glad I'm not like my sister. You won't be able to ride away and forget me."

"I'll never forget you."

She caught the sob before it escaped. When he bent his head over her body, she welcomed him. Tears slipped from the corners of her eyes, down her temples, and through her hair to the pillow. Even as his mouth worked magic against her skin, even as he began to love her again, she cried silently. He would never forget her, but he would ride away.

Jackson lifted his saddle onto his horse's back, then fastened the cinch. It was barely dawn. Behind him, the half-burned barn stood out in stark relief against the sky. It was silent. No one was around to see him leave. He checked his saddlebags one last time. Everything had been packed away. There was nothing to keep him here anymore.

He looked around at the grassland and the cattle, at the trees, the garden, the outbuildings. Regan and Amy would do well here. He was glad he'd been able to help them both. He was glad he'd had last night with Regan.

She'd left him a few minutes before Amy returned from her supper with Fayre and Hank. A couple of hours later, Regan had returned to his bed. She'd crept in silently, as if afraid he was asleep and might be disturbed. A slow smile pulled at his lips. He'd made sure she knew he'd been disturbed in the most delightful of ways. He'd loved her until they were both too weak to do more than cling to each other. This morning, he'd left her sleeping.

Everything inside of him screamed in protest. He didn't want to go. Leaving her was the hardest thing he'd ever done. But it was right. He knew it in his heart. If he stayed, he put her at risk. What if he couldn't control the darkness inside of him? What if he hurt her or Amy? He wouldn't be able to live with himself. Living without her was going to be its own form of torture, but he would survive knowing they went on without him. He trusted Regan's strength.

The back door slammed as it hit the porch wall. Amy came running toward him. She was dressed in a nightgown that trailed to the ground, stirring up little puffs of dust. Her hair was pulled back into a single braid. In her hands, she clutched a rag doll.

When she was a couple of feet away, she stopped and stared up at him. Her hazel eyes, so like his youngest sister's, were wide and questioning. Her usually mobile mouth was still.

"You're up early," he said.

She nodded solemnly. "Mama says you're leaving."

Regan must have told her last night. "It's time, Amy."

"But I don't want you to go. I like having you here. You tell good stories."

He touched her bangs. They needed trimming. "Thank you," he said. "That's a fine compliment coming from an expert like you."

She moved a little closer and tilted her head way

back so she could see his face. He bent at the knees, crouching so they were almost eye to eye.

Amy drew in a deep breath. She glanced back toward the house, then at him. She released the breath and drew another. "Mama said you're my daddy. She told me last night. I'm not 'posed to ask you to stay, 'cause you have to leave, only I don't know why." She sucked in another breath. "So I thought I'd come and tell you good-bye. So are you?"

He felt as if something cold and hard was coiling around his heart and squeezing. He touched her face, then placed his hand on her shoulder. She was adorable. She was going to be the death of him. "Yes, Amy, I'm your father."

Tears sprang to her eyes. Her mouth trembled. "Then why do you got to go?"

"I—" Hell, what was he supposed to tell a five-year-old. The truth would terrify her. "I wouldn't be a very good father. I don't know how to live on a ranch."

"Mama could teach you to be a cowboy."

In spite of his pain, he smiled. "I know she could, Amy. But it's not that simple. I don't want to be a bad man and hurt anybody. That's why I have to go away."

She thought about that for a moment. "You're not a bad man. You smell good, like Grandpa did. And you look nice when you smile." She tugged on her doll's braided hair and kicked at the dirt. "I know you have to leave. It's like Auntie Elizabeth and Grandpa, only not 'xactly. Mama said you won't be dead."

"Amy, I'm sorry." He pulled her close. His large hands spanned the length of her slender spine. She didn't seem big enough to survive. How could he go away from her?

She began to cry in earnest. Her sobs tore at his guts, leaving him bleeding and defeated. He searched deep down for the strength to put her away from him, then wiped her face.

"I'm not 'posed to cry," she said, and sniffed. "Mama said to just say good-bye." She flung herself at him again and clung to his shoulders. "When I'm bigger, I'll bring Mama and come find you. By then you'll know how to be a good daddy and we can all live together."

He shut his eyes tightly, hoping to hold in the pain. A single tear snuck out of the corner. He brushed the back of his hand against his face and blinked the rest away.

"I hope so," he said, and stood up.

Amy tilted her head back. " 'Bye, Daddy." Then she turned and trotted back to the house.

He couldn't stand to watch her go, but he had to look one last time. He told himself he was doing the right thing. There'd been too much killing; his soul was too black to risk the light again.

He watched her approach the porch. Sometime while he'd been talking with Amy, Regan had come outside. She'd pulled on a night shift and her robe. Her shoulder-length hair blew in the morning breeze. Her feet were bare. She looked like some stunning beautiful wild creature, only partially tamed. Pride made her raise her chin up as he grabbed his horse's reins and moved toward her.

When he was three feet from the porch, he stopped. Amy climbed the stairs and stood in front of her mother. Regan placed her hands protectively on her child's shoulders.

"You're leaving," Regan said.

"Yes."

She studied him. He prayed for a miracle. He needed her to make it easier.

It was not to be. With the sun turning her hair to the color of fire and her blue eyes darker than the Texas sky, she glared at him. "I know what you're thinking and don't imagine for a moment that I'm going to help you leave. If you want to be a fool, then go. But ride away from here knowing you'll regret this for the rest of your life."

"Probably."

"The regrets are going to get mighty old, mighty fast. If you plan on coming back, you're going to have to crawl on your belly. Don't expect me to forgive this."

"You're a hell of a woman."

"And you're a coward." She stared at his face, searching, as if memorizing his features, as if this moment would have to last her a lifetime. Anger fought with love. He read it in her face. She looked away. "Get the hell off my land, you bastard."

"I'll always love you."

The anger faded as her shoulders slumped. "I know," she whispered and went into the house.

He touched Amy's head, then turned away and got on his horse. He headed north, knowing he had to get as far from here as possible.

" 'Bye, Daddy," Amy called.

He didn't look back. He couldn't. He was doing the right thing. He had to be. Leaving was the purest form of hell. He would love Amy forever. He would love Regan twice that long.

He reached the far corral. Ahead of him was nothing but open territory. He could ride for days without encountering another person. Good. He wasn't going to be fit company for a long time. Gage had mentioned a job in Colorado. Jackson was welcome to join him there. Maybe later. Maybe when it didn't hurt so damn much.

He crossed the land, past the herds of cattle, past the cowboys who waved their farewells. When he came to the edge of the stream where he'd been caught by her men, he drew his horse to a halt and dismounted.

The water was just as deep as it had been before, but it didn't flow as quickly. He bent down. It was warmer, too.

With a sigh, he glanced up at the sky, then around at the trees. He loved this country. He didn't have to look any farther to find exactly what he wanted. He could have been happy here, if he'd been someone else. For once he could have belonged. If Regan was here, he would tell her that. If there was one person in the entire world who understood about the pain of not fitting in, of being different and solitary, it was Regan.

The thought startled him so much, he stood up and swore. Of course Regan knew what he was feeling. She'd felt it, too. She was always on the outside looking in. She was tough and vulnerable, capable and lonely. Nobility and all the right reasons didn't mean a damn in the face of what he was losing. Regan was strong enough to risk it, why wasn't he? What was he so afraid of? Loving her? She brought out the best parts of him. She was his road out of the blackness. She was everything he'd ever wanted.

She was his perfect match and he'd been fool enough to leave her.

If you want to come back, you're going to have to crawl on your belly.

He tugged at the neck of his shirt, then swallowed hard. He'd just made the biggest mistake of his life. Hell, he'd had nothing but bad luck since he got to Texas, why would he expect it to change now? He could have figured this out an hour ago, or even while he was still saddling his horse. But he'd had to go and be late for the most important moment of his life.

So be it, he thought, walking toward his horse. He'd crawl if that was what she wanted. Because for Regan he was willing to do anything.

A soft breeze whispered against him. He took hold of the saddle, then glanced back at the stream. The water gurgled invitingly. If he was going to crawl, he might as well crawl clean. After glancing around to make sure he was alone, he grabbed his rifle and returned to the stream's bank.

Ten minutes later he was knee deep in the water and singing loudly as he splashed. This had been a fine idea, he thought, feeling the morning sun warm his body. He would collect his thoughts, plan what he was going to say to convince her to let him come back, then—

He froze in the stream, the last note of his song hovering in the air. He waited, then bit back a curse when the hairs on the back of his neck rose. He could feel it. Someone watching him. The loud *click* of a rifle lever being cocked filled the morning.

Not again, he thought grimly. Not naked. Not one more goddamn time. He deserved better than this. He deserved—

The breeze stirred slightly, bringing with it the faint scent of something familiar. Something wonderful and feminine. He grinned.

"Turn around and put your hands up," Regan ordered from behind him.

"Where the hell am I supposed to be hiding a gun?" he asked, slowly moving until he faced her.

She stood on the bank of the stream. Her hat was pulled low on her forehead so he couldn't see her eyes, but that didn't matter. Her plain tan blouse and rust-colored split skirt were the same. He recognized her dusty boots, her callused hands, her well-shaped mouth.

"What are you doing here?" he asked.

"Why are you taking another bath? Hasn't this stream gotten you in enough trouble?"

"You'd think I'd learn, wouldn't you?" He took a step closer to her.

"Hold it right there," she said, still pointing the rifle at him.

"You didn't answer my question."

"If you thought I was going to let you ride out of my life, you don't know me at all, Jackson Tyler. I love you and you love me. We belong together."

He took another step and moved up the bank. The rifle in her arms wavered slightly, then she lowered it to her side. He stopped in front of her, took her rifle, and placed it on the ground, then pulled off her hat. Her blue eyes stared up at him. He could see clear down to her soul, to the longing there, and the love. He read her questions and hopes and fears.

"I don't deserve you, Regan, but you're stuck with me. I was about to come back. Crawling on my belly."

"So I could have saved myself a trip?"

"Yeah, but I'm glad you didn't." He touched her face with his fingertips, then bent over and picked her up.

She clung to him. "What do you think you're doing?"

"Inviting you into my bath." He walked down the slippery bank and into the stream.

"Put me down!" she ordered, then gasped when he did so. The water sloshed around her boots and the hem of her skirt.

"I love you, Regan," he said, reaching for the buttons on her shirt.

"And I love you." She pressed her palms against his back.

Before he kissed her, he stared into her face. "I would have crawled for you," he said seriously. "You deserve that and more."

"You can spend the rest of your life making it up to me." She drew him close and pressed her lips on his.

As the birds watched, as the sun warmed them and the water provided the music, they held each other. Their bodies spoke the words, their souls received the vows. A breath of promise, a whisper of love. They were together as they were destined to be. For always. Secure in the fire that blazed hot enough to last forever.

101 $\mathcal{D}$AYS OF $\mathcal{R}$OMANCE
BUY 3 BOOKS, GET 1 FREE!

CHOOSE A FREE BOOK FROM THIS OUTSTANDING
LIST OF AUTHORS AND TITLES:

HARPERMONOGRAM

____LORD OF THE NIGHT Susan Wiggs 0-06-108052-7
____ORCHIDS IN MOONLIGHT Patricia Hagan 0-06-108038-1
____TEARS OF JADE Leigh Riker 0-06-108047-0
____DIAMOND IN THE ROUGH Millie Criswell 0-06-108093-4
____HIGHLAND LOVE SONG Constance O'Banyon 0-06-108121-3
____CHEYENNE AMBER Catherine Anderson 0-06-108061-6
____OUTRAGEOUS Christina Dodd 0-06-108151-5
____THE COURT OF THREE SISTERS Marianne Willman 0-06-108053-5
____DIAMOND Sharon Sala 0-06-108196-5
____MOMENTS Georgia Bockoven 0-06-108164-7

HARPERPAPERBACKS

____THE SECRET SISTERS Ann Maxwell 0-06-104236-6
____EVERYWHERE THAT MARY WENT Lisa Scottoline 0-06-104293-5
____NOTHING PERSONAL Eileen Dreyer 0-06-104275-7
____OTHER LOVERS Erin Pizzey 0-06-109032-8
____MAGIC HOUR Susan Isaacs 0-06-109948-1
____A WOMAN BETRAYED Barbara Delinsky 0-06-104034-7
____OUTER BANKS Anne Rivers Siddons 0-06-109973-2
____KEEPER OF THE LIGHT Diane Chamberlain 0-06-109040-9
____ALMONDS AND RAISINS Maisie Mosco 0-06-100142-2
____HERE I STAY Barbara Michaels 0-06-100726-9

$\mathcal{T}$o receive your free book, simply send in this coupon **and** your store
receipt with the purchase prices circled. You may take part in this exclusive
offer as many times as you wish, but all qualifying purchases must be made
by September 4, 1995, and all requests must be postmarked by October 4,
1995. Please allow 6-8 weeks for delivery.

MAIL TO: HarperPaperbacks, Dept. FC-101
10 East 53rd Street, New York, N.Y. 10022-5299

Name_____

Address_____

City_____State_____Zip_____

Offer is subject to availability. HarperPaperbacks may make substitutions for
requested titles.   H09511